Beyond the Fields of Fire

A Civil War Novel Sequel

By

Jessica Elam and Alexandra Haliti

TELEMACHUS PRESS

Cover designed by Telemachus Press, LLC

Cover art:
Copyright © iStock/1255804588/setory
Copyright © iStock/1050010226.jpg/Zeferli
Copyright © iStock/1441096459/Zastavkin
Copyright © iStock/1556260297/kim Willems

Interior images:
Copyright © iStock/171101595/NSA Digital Archive
Copyright © iStock/935824926/benoitb
Copyright © iStock/1274178415/pictore
Copyright © iStock/1295295923/ilbusca
Copyright © iStock/1389559162/duncan1890
Copyright © iStock/ 1578973095/Christine_Kohler
Copyright © iStock/ 1602116905/Christine_Kohler
Copyright © iStock/ 2204209990/Ken Wiedemann
Copyright © AdobeStock_606184409
Copyright © AdobeStock_332668930

Song Credits:
"Amazing Grace" (John Newton, 1772)
"Fairest Lord Jesus" (It is unclear who wrote this hymn, but it is said to have first appeared in a German manuscript in 1662, with the first English translation being in 1850)
"Siúil a Rún" (An Irish Love Song) It is unclear on the original writer of this song or of the date. It is believed to have been written in the 1800s.

Credits:
"At Gettysburg" or "What a Girl Saw and Heard During the Battle" by Tillie Pierce Alleman
"Joshua L. Chamberlain" by Thomas A. Desjardin
"Bayonet! Forward: My Civil War Reminiscences" by Joshua Lawrence Chamberlain
"Gray Ghost: The Life of Col. John Singleton Mosby" by James A. Ramage
"Behind Enemy Lines: Civil War Spies, Raiders, and Guerillas" by Wilmer L. Jones
"The Memoirs of Colonel John S. Mosby" by John S. Mosby
"They Fought Like Demons" by DeAnne Blanton
Visiting the Gettysburg National Military Park and Museum and learning the history there
Researching various websites and first-hand accounts of the battle and aftermath

Publishing Services by Telemachus Press, LLC
7652 Sawmill Road, Suite 304
Dublin, Ohio 43016
http://www.telemachuspress.com

ISBN: 978-1-965121-22-1 (eBook)
ISBN: 978-1-965121-23-8 (Paperback)

Library of Congress Control Number: 2026900205

Version 2026.01.05

Introduction

Dear Readers,

We are so excited to bring you the sequel to our first novel, "Beyond the Bleeding Heart." We pick up right where we left off in September of 1862. Jessica is writing Elizabeth's story and Alexandra is writing Amy's chapters.

In the last book we covered topics like the prisoner of war camps, nurses in the war, women who disguised themselves as soldiers, and men who fought like phantoms in the night. All these are based on true events.

Women aiding the army in any way were sometimes taken as prisoners of war along with the men. They were even kept in the same prisons with the men in some cases, as was portrayed in the first novel. There were many organized escapes made from these camps. In this second novel we will dive a little more into the prison camp situation and what it may have been like to be part of these escapes. I (Jessica) used true stories of escapes as my foundation and adjusted them to fit the timetable, while of course adding in my own characters and speculation of how they may have done it. All the prison camps I mention in this novel were real: Libby Prison, Castle Thunder, Belle Isle, Camp Sorghum, and Camp Asylum. I researched these prison camps to bring you an accurate description when describing them in this novel.

As for nurses in the army, women like Clara Barton and Elizabeth Thorn aided the cause by nursing the wounded after battles. Other women moved with the army, usually following their husband's unit and helped in whatever ways they could as cooks and seamstresses.

The battle and aftermath of Gettysburg was particularly thoroughly researched for this novel. Much of my (Jessica's) research came from a book written by a fifteen-year-old eyewitness of the events in 1863. The book is called "At Gettysburg" or "What a Girl Saw and Heard During the Battle" by Tillie Pierce Alleman.

While Amy's character and those in her life are fictional, I (Alexandra) loosely based their stories off of true persons in history that have intrigued and inspired me. I commemorate this part of the novel in honor of the hundreds of women known and unknown who fought and gave their lives in the American Civil War. Not only to those women, but also to the many valiant heroes whose names have never been written in history books or found on gravestones.

The Phantom Regiment's colonel and soldiers are based off of the infamous "Gray Ghost", Colonel John Singleton Mosby, and Mosby's Raiders, whose mysterious lives and brilliant secret operations have captivated me. While writing these novels, I (Alexandra) dipped into several books and memoirs. I took great pleasure in reading many exciting true tales of Mosby from the book "The Gray Ghost" as well as "Behind Enemy Lines" and "Mosby's Memoirs."

I read many online articles and also the book "They Fought Like Demons", to familiarize myself with the lives of disguised women soldiers. It is in the memory of these soldiers that I (Alexandra) am honored to write a historical fiction novel, based on the untold stories of their lives and ultimate sacrifices on the battlefields of America.

Please look for more books written by us in the future, however, we will be writing separately from now on. So, be on the lookout for books written by both of us individually!

It is our hope that this novel will instill in you a desire to learn more about the history that made our country a great nation, and that it will inspire you to take action to keep our freedom and rights alive for future generations to come.

Pleasant Reading,

Jessica and Alexandra

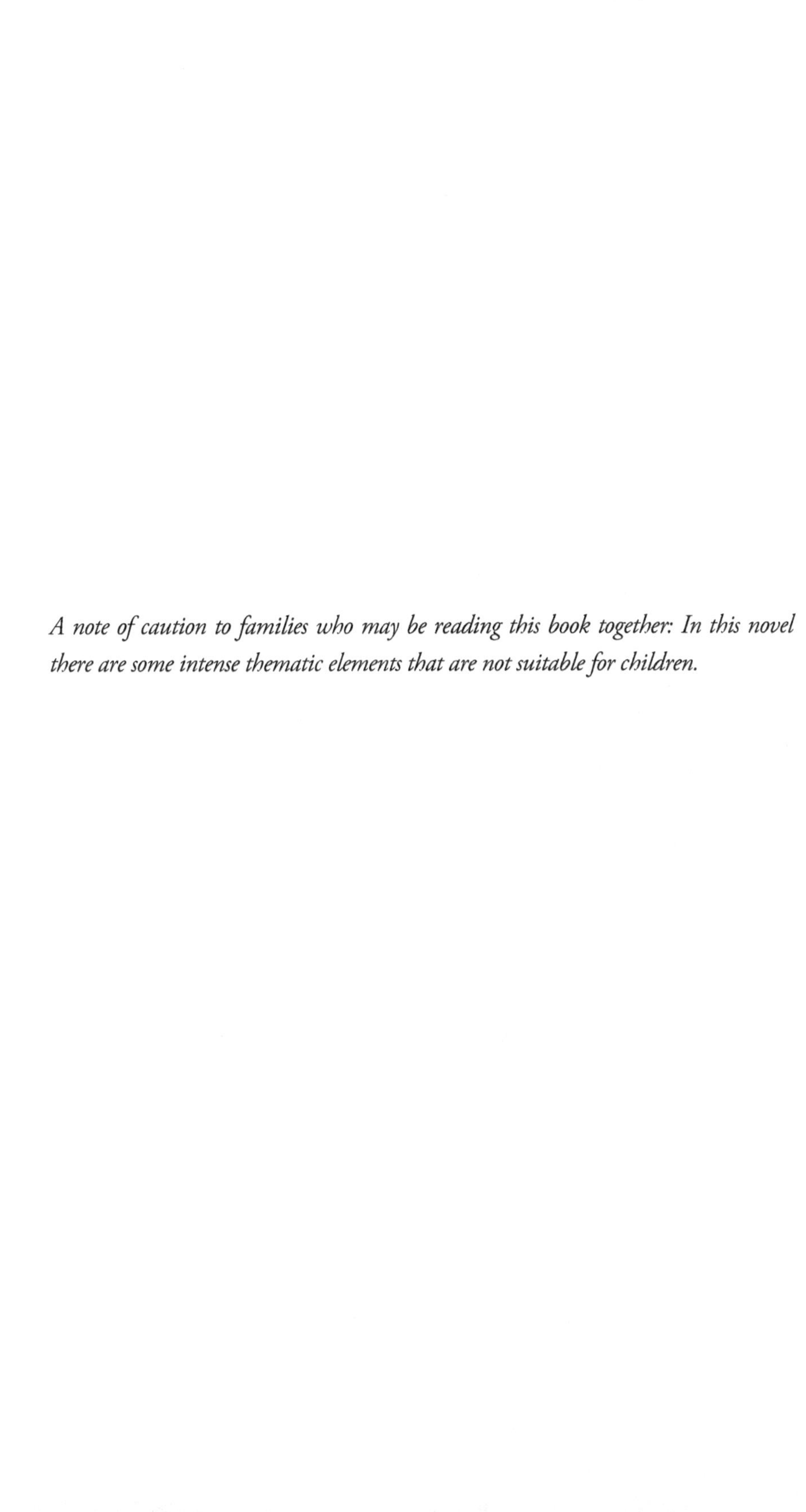

A note of caution to families who may be reading this book together: In this novel there are some intense thematic elements that are not suitable for children.

Photo Gallery

The town of Gettysburg, Pennsylvania

THE CIVIL WAR IN AMERICA: SKETCHES FROM RICHMOND, VIRGINIA, THE CAPITAL OF THE CONFEDERATE STATES OF AMERICA.

RICHMOND, FROM HOLLYWOOD.

The City of Richmond, Virginia

JOHN S. MOSBY.

Colonel John Singleton Mosby – "The Gray Ghost"

JOHN L. BURNS, "THE OLD HERO OF GETTYSBURG."

John Burns of Gettysburg, Pennsylvania
(Our character, John Barnes, is based on John Burns)

Many women acted as nurses in the Civil War

An example of Prisoner of War camps in the Civil War

Gettysburg

Gettysburg
N
W
E
S
The Denny's House
The Matthew's House
The Blacksmith's Shack
Kennisburg Road
The McCarthy's House

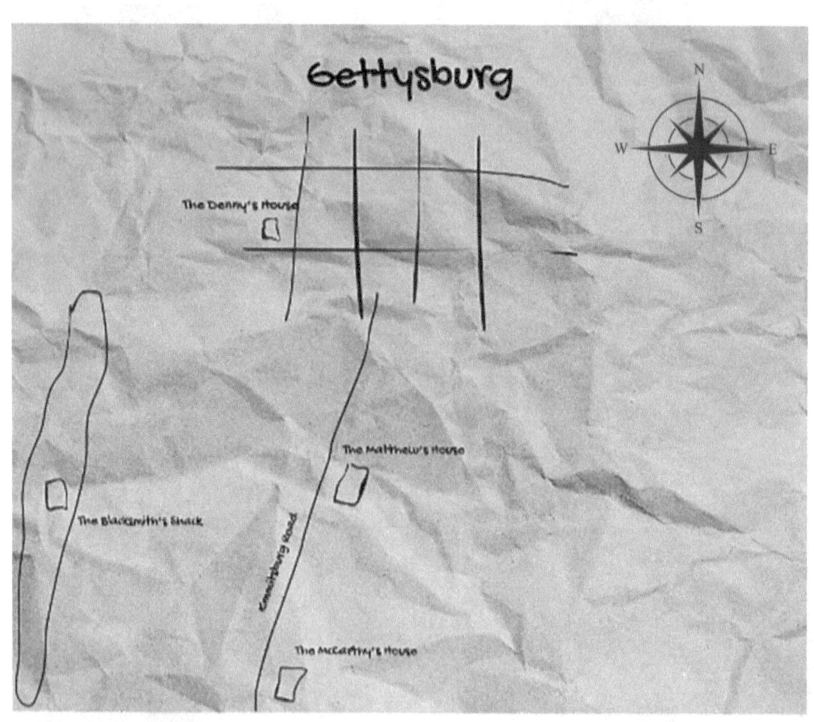

Acknowledgements

To our Lord and Savior, Jesus Christ: We thank you for entrusting these talents to us. May we always use them for Your glory and to impact the lives around us.

To our parents, Kurt and Anna Elam: Thank you for giving us the opportunity to be homeschooled and instilling in us a love for our country and its history. Thank you for believing in us and encouraging us to accomplish our dreams, we love you.

To Steve Himes, our publisher, and the team at Telemachus Press: Thank you for your assistance and encouragement. It was a privilege to work with you again on this second book. We look forward to bringing you many more novels in the future.

To Chuck Hollabaugh, the Bookstore Director at the Gettysburg Visitor Center: Thank you so much for advocating for our first novel to have a place on your shelves at the Gettysburg Bookstore. This has been a dream of ours for many years and you helped to make it a reality. We are so grateful.

To my (Alexandra's) husband, Lirim Haliti: My own soldier, you inspire me with your selfless dedication to justice and compassion. Thank you for your unwavering love, support and pride in me while I follow my dreams as an author.

To my (Jessica's) friend, Gregg Farrier: I had a lot of fun brainstorming ideas with you. Thank you for your input and suggestions for my novel. I look forward to seeing your stories published too one day.

To my (Jessica's) boss, Bryan Wilhelm: Thank you for working with me to give me the time and opportunities I need to accomplish my dreams of being an author. I am so grateful for your understanding and support. You're the best!

To our friend, Kristin Smith: Thank you for being our "secret agent" and re-reading the first novel for us and proofreading the sequel before publication. Your lifelong friendship is so appreciated!

To our wonderful friends, family and coworkers: Without you these books would not have been possible. You encouraged us, gave us what we needed to be able to write, and helped us fulfill our dreams. You are our inspiration!

Dedication

In loving memory of our grandpa, Gustavo Zapata: You were a prince and a great man (2 Samuel 3:38). The world didn't deserve you, but God took you home, because He knew that you were an angel. We only wish we would have told you that more. We love you and miss you deeply, but we know we will see you again someday.

This is for you, Grandpa...

Table of Contents

Beyond the Fields of Fire

A Civil War Novel Sequel

The Mansion Prison
Chapter 1

Amy

September 1862

THROUGH DARKNESS AND fog we traveled by the light of the moon, sometimes crossing rivers, wide expanses of valleys and rugged mountainous terrain. When daylight came, we hid from its rays, like creatures of the night, afraid of its exposing light. Days passed in slumber, long nights in weary travel. The scorching summer sun burned bright above the thick canopy of green foliage as we lay in the shade of many trees sleeping deeply, worn out with fatigue. My captured Union comrades lay in a circle and were not allowed to rise unless given permission or otherwise suffer the consequences of a bullet through the heart. So Major Morgan threatened and not a soul was willing to test that ominous threat.

I had noted by the insignia on his uniform that Kelsey's once friend, the Lieutenant I first met in Gettysburg, had now been promoted to a Major. How such a detestable man had obtained this high rank I could not understand, but my imagination told me that it was not through honorable deeds. Memories of our last exchange, along with my own worst fears, haunted me. At last he had me in his control, a prisoner…a woman and perhaps *a valuable piece* in his game, as he had stated on that terrifying night we'd met.

If only I had died in that midnight attack. There is nothing in life worth living for anymore. I've lost my sister, my fiancé and my best friend, even Major Sanders…he had always looked out for me with an encouraging smile, a warm blanket, a reassuring hand on my shoulder. How could God allow this?

Anger filled my heart, a burning smoldering feeling deep in my soul. *He doesn't care anymore…perhaps He never did… He's given up on me…and so, I will give up on Him.*

* * *

I awoke, trembling in a cold sweat, startled by the sound of distant thunder. The Major, who never seemed to rest, turned toward the noise and listened intently.

"Cannon fire," he declared indifferently and instantly returned his attention back to a small leather-bound pad in his hand, in which he was constantly scribbling.

The loud thunder from the big guns shook the earth I lay upon and leaves fell quivering to the ground. Listening, I imagined the horrible battle that was taking place miles away. *Is Kelsey out there somewhere, perhaps entangled in the raging battle at this very moment? Or has he truly run from the duty to his country, like a coward?* Sorrow and shame filled my heart. My gaze rested on the form of Major Morgan, still standing beneath a large oak tree. After his peculiar, yet strangely coincidental visits to Gettysburg, I couldn't help but wonder if, perhaps, *he* held the key to Kelsey's disappearance. Or maybe, at least, he knew what had become of him.

Overwhelmed, I turned my face away, lying on a rough horse blanket, unable to bear the scene of my disheartened comrades, once so gallant, now lying in the dirt. They had been humiliated with their hands bound behind them while guarded by this black clad enemy. The enemies' faces were smeared with a dark substance, making them barely distinguishable, rendering them less than human. Any time I tried to catch a glimpse of their features they would quickly turn away.

As the days passed, my injury, though the bullet had been removed, became infected and a fever once again took control of my weak body. All night I drifted in and out of feverish nightmares. The days began to melt together, and I saw vague images of a surgeon leaning over me.

"Will she make it?" A familiar voice inquired one night in the thick of the pain. Fear was winning the battle over me. It occurred to me that I could die from this wound, in the middle of a God forsaken land with no family or friends to comfort me or hold me during my last moments.

Delirious, I reached out a hand into the darkness. "Father, please take my hand. I'm so weak."

A strong hand took mine and I fell into a dreadful sleep, clinging to it every second, afraid to let go.

* * *

There it stood, the capital of the Confederacy: Richmond. The sweat dripped from my brow as I stared at the beautiful, white brick buildings glistening in the sunlight.

"Richmond at last, boys," Major Morgan announced as the regiment halted at the peak of a hill overlooking the historic city.

Slowly we descended into the main street as all of Richmond came forth to meet us. They stared, they studied us with hatred in their eyes…we were the enemy, coming into the South to destroy their dreams of a new nation. I saw some women gathering into a group to whisper. As they locked their eyes on me, there was no doubt as to the subject of their conversation. Since my identity had been found out, I had now no reason to hide my feminine features. A gasp broke loose and the whispering continued more frantically as we drew nearer to the gossipy group. Catching the Major's eye upon me, I kept a stiff indifferent expression. *No Major, you shall not see me turn away embarrassed.*

As the pressure of the moment increased, my vision clouded and sweat poured from my brow stinging my eyes. The din of the city and the clopping of hooves on cobblestone became an overpowering roar. Grimacing, I squeezed my eyes shut trying to quiet my mind and groaned between gritted teeth, but the pain caused me to crumple forward. The Major suddenly pulled my horse away down a quiet dirt street. As the din of the city faded, a large white mansion could be vaguely seen near the end of the narrow street. Weeping willows waved their sorrowful branches almost blocking the entire house from view. Flower gardens surrounded all that arose within the white picket fenced yard. Exhausted, my eyelids began to flutter shut. I felt myself lowered down to waiting arms and carried through the fog of my demented mind down a brick path guarded by large white rose bushes. *This must be paradise…the fragrant smells, the gentle chirping of songbirds…*

"Oh, she looks nearly unconscious. Hurry and get her inside. We'll put her in Mary's old room," said the kindly voice of an elderly woman doing her best to keep my weak form upright.

"Post a guard, Captain Hamilton," I heard the Major order as he quickly lifted me off my feet.

"Yes, Sir!" The voices of strangers surrounded me as I was carried up the winding staircase.

It seemed like weeks that the fever raged inside my body. I had no sense of the passing days and long nights. Occasionally someone would awaken me and lift my head gently to press a cold glass of water to my dry lips. After finishing, I collapsed onto the fluffy pillow again. A restless sleep controlled my nights and vivid dreams haunted me.

Thunder shook the house one terrible night and I was aware of several figures standing around my bed. I tried to cry out for help and thrashed about to get their hands off me.

"Hold still, hold still, young lady," an elderly man's voice beckoned.

Not for the words, but from pure fatigue, I gave up. The pain was more than I could endure as the wound was cleaned and covered again. I heard my own voice as if from outside myself screaming in pain as others tried to soothe me. Someone put a cloth to my mouth to bite on.

Later, I awoke alone while flashes of lightning, breaking through the darkness, lit my room. Feverishly I stared at the doorway, which was usually closed, now standing ajar. A strange anxiety came over me. *Someone's there, I know they are…. They're going to kill me!*

Crash! Another lightning bolt sprinted through the sky. Terrified, I was convinced there was a tall cloaked figure standing in the doorway.

"Who's there?" I cried, doing my best to pull myself up and prepare for a fight. "Answer me!"

"Miss Matthews?" A distant voice came from below. A murmur, and then footsteps came quickly down the hall, led by a dim candle.

"It's all right Miss, it's only the storm raging outside." I was laid back and tucked into the heavy consuming quilts by a slave woman with soft black eyes and a round face.

"There was someone there. I saw him." My voice was but a whisper.

"It's all right, Miss Matthews, we'll takes care of ya." A rustling of skirts and the candlelight disappeared again.

* * *

Bright sunlight streamed in through the lace curtains of an opened window. A warm breeze blew in, filling the room. It was the most wonderful fragrance I had ever experienced. The fever had left my body at last, I concluded, as I wiped a pale thin hand across my wet brow.

Peering around the large room, still feeling hazy, I noted my uniform neatly folded and my things placed carefully beside it on a large cushioned chair. A small fireplace with an ornate mantel and hearth stood on one side of the room opposite the bed. A large painting of an enchanting young Southern lady, not more than twenty, hung on the wall above the mantel. Luscious pink roses joyfully poked out of an elegant white vase on a delicately handcrafted round table. The bed posts that rose above me were overlaid with an embroidered canopy tied back by thick yet elegant gold ropes. Wincing, I fell back after attempting to rise.

"Where am I?" the words came in a raspy whisper. A wave of dizziness struck, and I grasped my head in both hands.

"Miss Matthews?" A gentle voice came from the doorway where a petite, beautiful young woman stood gazing at me from under a furrowed brow. Her black ringlets fell onto the cool blue gown that matched her eyes.

"Who are you?" I demanded, pushing my back up against the headboard. She smiled courteously and placed a tray down on the small table nearby.

"I'm Jane, the Major's sister," she stated in a thick Southern accent as she began lifting the lids off the delicious dishes on the tray. "I don't know if you remember, but you've been brought to Major Morgan's home. Well, my late father's home."

The smell of cinnamon and sausage quickly filled the room and relaxed my tense nerves. My stomach ached from hunger.

"After you're finished, Mother ordered a warm bath for you…if you're up for it," she motioned toward my wounded side. "The Doctor said it would be all right."

I stared up at her confused and yet suspicious at the hospitality shown me by my captors. Too exhausted to ascertain their strange behavior at the moment, I resigned myself to gratitude that I had been left unharmed…thus far.

* * *

I rose from the warm soapy water, wrapped in a soft towel, marveling at how good it felt to be clean. Puzzled, I stared at the dark green simple day dress laid out on the bed. I had fully expected to be wearing the garments I had arrived in. One of the Morgan's house slaves attended me, and I was grateful for the help, though I wasn't ready to hold a conversation with anyone at the moment. The woman remained quiet, but I caught her curiously studying me every so often and I recognized her kind smooth round face with dark eyes peering out from under thick lashes. Sliding into the several layers of skirts, it felt strange to me after all the time I'd spent as a soldier. A hand over my bandaged side, I braced myself to finally look once again at Miss Amy Matthews.

Holding my breath, I stepped before a full-length mirror and stared. A thousand emotions ran through my mind as I gazed at the girl before me. The girl I had left behind in Gettysburg so many months back. How frail, how drawn that face, how dimmed those eyes from the darkness they had seen and been through… They had long since lost that spark of excitement and vigor for life.

Struggling to do something with the blonde hair that was quickly growing to shoulder length, I gave up after a few frustrating moments of pulling it back, only to have it fall out of the ribbon again. Then I felt the slave woman gently take control of the struggle. After a few gentle movements my hair was styled in a simple, yet feminine way.

"Thank you," I whispered, feeling embarrassed. She smiled tenderly and retreated from the room. Stiffening, I set my face and prepared to descend into the heart of this Confederate mansion, but as the quiet conversation grew closer, I suddenly felt a tightening in my throat. *I need air. Perhaps I will take Miss Morgan's offer to stroll in the back garden.*

It was a slow and sore journey down the stairs, but worth the pain when I entered the magical garden. The elegant bushes and vines of glorious flowers that encompassed me seemed to stretch on for miles without any sign of a city. I lost myself in the rich green beauty and the strange sensation of aloneness that surrounded me. For the first time in ages, I felt peace. Gently, I let my hands caress the many beautiful flowers as I slowly passed and then fell onto the soft green grass, forgetting about the war, my sorrow, my worry of Elizabeth, the Rebels, and Kelsey. I didn't want to think of anything. In the warm summer sun, surrounded by this beauty, I fell into a deep and almost dreamless sleep. For moments I felt myself floating in an abyss of gentle naturalistic sounds, soft breezes and fragrant aromas.

"Lassie?" A gentle hand stroked my forehead, "Don't forget me, Amy." Startled by the strange feeling of someone watching me, I suddenly sat up frightened, heart pounding. Only the sound of chirping, from happy little birds, accompanied me.

"Kelsey?" I whispered half believing he would answer me. Laying back with a heavy sigh, I stared up into the trees. *Why would they allow a prisoner back here without a guard? Even as crippled and slow moving as I was, the major knew that I had discovered the so-called journalist Peter Kingston was their informant. He knew I had a little inside information about them. Wasn't he worried about leaving me alone?* Puzzled, I went further into this paradise. Then I saw it, a large iron fence with a gate and a lock. Even my little paradise was a prison. Here I was, locked inside this Confederate mansion with two women for my guards and only my memories for company…those memories that haunted me like a wearisome companion. I was not free…I never would be…

New Beginnings
Chapter 2

Elizabeth

October 1862

"SHOULD WE GO back home…to the house on Emmitsburg Road?" I asked, hesitating a little. We stood on the dirt road just outside of town. The autumn sun was casting its last rays across the fields, setting the tops of the distant trees on fire with radiant hues. It was a cloudless sky. A cool and crisp breeze chased the fallen leaves across the road and tossed them around our ankles. Nathan reached down and clasped my hand in his strong one, a slight smile played on his lips. Bending his head until his forehead touched mine, he whispered,

"Unless you'd rather I go over to Seminary Ridge and tidy up my blacksmith shack?"

A gentle laugh escaped me, and my heart raced as I dared to meet those blue eyes staring so closely into mine. Pulling away shyly, I tugged on his hand and moved toward our old home. As soon as I was able to catch my breath, I replied.

"I think I would much prefer my house, Mr. Tyler." I teased and glanced back, tugging a little harder on the warm hand encompassing mine.

After Nathan had asked me to marry him, the day he returned to Gettysburg from the prison camps, we knew we had to clear the air with the townspeople. After all that had transpired with Adam Carter, and all the false accusations against Nathan, the truth had to be told to remove any uneasy feelings still lingering in the town. We had called together some of the leaders of the town and asked their advice on how to proceed with the idea.

At the conclusion of the next Sunday service, Nathan and John Barnes moved to the front to speak. I had sat pensively tugging and twisting my gloves until they matched the tight knot in my stomach, as I waited to determine the reaction of the congregation. In his low, usual calm voice, Nathan told his story from the beginning of how and why he came to Gettysburg and what had happened with Adam Carter. John Barnes confirmed his words and added his own to clear Nathan's name and any suspicions anyone might still harbor against him. The knot in my stomach gave way to a sudden swell of pride as I realized how much Nathan had grown. He used to be so cynical and cold toward people. I watched his handsome face as he continued speaking. I couldn't believe how far we had come even in just one year.

Suddenly, interrupting my daydreaming, Nathan approached and reached a hand toward me. The whole congregation turned its eyes on me. I swallowed nervously, the knot returning, then rose and moved to Nathan's side. He took my hand and gazed into my eyes as he announced our engagement. I could feel the crowd's shock thick in the air as no one spoke a word. There were a few gasps and Mrs. Denny's jaw nearly fell into her lap. Finally, after what felt like an eternity, Dr. Phillips stood and began clapping with a genuine smile on his face. Others soon found their manners and followed suite. I smiled in relief as I gazed out over our friends and neighbors. I only wish Amy could have been there. As I looked over the crowd, some faces still held doubt, but I had to reconcile myself to the fact that we could not please them all. I turned back and looked up at the strong, patient face above me for reassurance. Soon I felt I could face anything as long as he stood there beside me.

The wedding had been perfect, just as I had always imagined as a young girl. The townsfolk had gathered in our little church, which was beautifully decorated with large sunflowers from a neighboring field. I hadn't even noticed who attended the ceremony, as I walked down the aisle, gripping John Barnes' arm tightly. Their faces were all a blur as my vision focused solely on the impressive figure before me. Nathan's ever serious face held no fear, no distrust, no suspicion as it used to. He stood calm and confident in his officer's blue uniform. He looked away for a moment, out the stained-glass windows, and I saw a tear fall on his tanned cheek. How strange life is. Only two years before I had been so filled with irrational anger and judgement toward this man. Now, here I was promising to love and respect him until death. I didn't know exactly when it had changed. All I knew was that this was the man I wanted to stand beside forever.

* * *

I kneaded more flour into the dough and wiped the dust onto my apron. Taking a cloth, I dipped it into the bucket of water and began wiping the sticky dough from between my fingers. Walking over to the nearest window, I gazed out and smiled contentedly, leaning my head on the glass. Nathan was out chopping wood for the fire. It had taken some time, but he had recovered his strength and normal frame after the grueling months in the prison camp. My smile faded as I remembered all that he had recounted to me upon his arrival to Gettysburg. He had been very short with his story, telling me that he had led some more escapes, had been caught and sentenced to be hung, and was then unexpectedly rescued and taken to a Union regiment. Eventually, he was given a promotion and a leave of absence.

He had paused, "That's when I knew I had to come back here. I guessed that this is where you would be." His story had left me shaky. All the terrors from the prison camp were still so vivid before my eyes.

My mind snapped back to the present as I watched Nathan wipe the sweat from his brow and move toward the house. I quickly cleaned my face and hands again with the damp cloth and untied the filthy apron from around my neck and waist. The door creaked loudly behind Nathan as he hung his hat on the peg near the entryway. Carrying an armload of firewood, he moved through the hallway into the parlor and set the stack down beside the fireplace. Wiping his face again with the sleeve on his forearm, he then ran his hand through his thick black hair.

"That should be enough for a couple evenings," he said. I watched him as he walked into the kitchen and over to the oven where I had the first loaf baking. "Smells good." Still receiving no reply from me, he suddenly straightened up, "What's wrong?" he asked hesitantly, eyebrows furrowed.

I tried, but I couldn't speak, even I didn't understand it. A warm wave of emotion overtook me. My mind was filled with so many memories with this man, some terrible and some wonderful. There was something about going through a common suffering and coming out on the other side of it…together… that overwhelmed me. After a moment, I moved quickly toward him and wrapping my arms tightly around his waist, I laid my head on his chest.

"I don't know," I smiled softly, "I'm just…so happy…I guess." A small laugh suddenly escaped me. A slight chuckle came from deep within him as he gently returned the embrace.

* * *

I moved my finger along the covers and titles of the books which had grown dusty in Father's small sitting room. Curiously, I pulled one off the shelf and blew the dust off the leather binding. The writings were about plants and the different uses for them. I thumbed through the rough pages, seeking answers. I had seen so many men die. Surely there was more we could do to save lives, to heal wounds and even just to nourish bodies. If the soldiers had the right foods, surely, they would be more effective. But how could they find nourishing foods? They were constantly on the move, and even if they did, it would never be enough to feed armies. So, if we couldn't nourish the healthy ones, surely, we could at least find a way to heal the wounded and sick more effectively. There must be so much we still don't understand, even with our advances in medicine.

I hadn't asked Nathan about it yet, but when he arrived, he had said he was on leave, which meant he was going back. I wanted to believe we could stay in Gettysburg and shut out the world with all its chaos and suffering. I didn't want to go back into that horrible reality, but…again I felt that same old pull to help and have a purpose in this delicate time of our country's existence. Moreover, Nathan was going back, and I had to go with him. And…since I was going to be there, I wanted to learn everything possible so that I could help more efficiently.

I tied my bonnet on determinedly and stepped out the big creaking door. Glancing at the barn, I smiled as Shadow arched his neck and perked his ears on seeing me.

"Not this time, boy. I think I need the walk into town," I called to him softly and approached the gelding. It had been so wonderful to ride Shadow again after being away so long. The other horses I had ridden in Virginia and in the West just did not have the same gliding gait that my dear companion had. I rubbed the velvety muzzle and patted his sleek neck. The gentle eyes gazed into mine fondly.

Soon the sound of hoofbeats approached. I turned to see Nathan riding up on a black mare. The sight took me back to our meeting years ago in this very place when Kelsey and Amy had been with me. I had been so filled with fear toward Nathan. He looked just the same now, with his shirt and arms covered in soot and his dark hair ruffled by the breeze.

"Going someplace?" he asked calmly.

I smiled up at him, shading my eyes from the sun, "Into town. I want to visit Doctor Phillips."

His brow furrowed, "Are you all right?"

I laughed, "Oh yes, I just want to see if he has any books I can borrow."

Nathan tilted his head and raised an eyebrow. Realizing I wouldn't get away without a more detailed explanation, I continued.

"I feel that I need to know more about how to help people who are ill…and wounded." My voice trailed off.

He sat quietly for a few moments, then dismounted and approached me. "I *am* going back to the army Elizabeth, but you can't come this time. It's not safe. It wasn't safe before, but this time…it's just going to be different."

I wondered what he meant by that. Searching the ground with my eyes, I said softly, "But Nathan…I need to help." There was a long pause. "I learned so much from the doctors I helped, and I know I can learn more. I want to make a difference, even if it's a small one." I raised my eyes. Nathan was staring hard into mine, but his face barely carried an expression. He said nothing, so I continued. "I can't stay here, not if you leave. I can't lose you again. Please…," I reached down and took his hands in mine. Nathan looked away, staring off toward the tree line of Seminary Ridge.

"I need to finish up a job. I'll be back before dusk," he turned to move away. I held onto one of his hands. He turned back to face me; his tanned face was smudged with soot from his blacksmith shop. I reached up and slid my hand down his strong jaw.

"Please Nathan. Think about what I said." He slowly nodded, and I felt him squeeze my hand before walking away. I sighed and turned in the opposite direction toward town.

As I made my way through the streets of our beloved town, I sighed contentedly and smiled up at the sun, high in the clear sky. Suddenly a plump hand caught hold of my arm.

"Miss Matthews! Oh, dear…I mean Mrs. Tyler!" Mrs. Denny slapped a chubby hand over her round mouth, "A thousand apologies, my dear girl! I do tend to forget that you are now a married woman. Many of us thought you would never marry, seeing as how you were getting older and still no man in sight. You must be so joyous!" The old irritation rose up within my chest at her words. She laughed and linked her arm in mine as we walked down the dusty streets. The trees along the road were shedding their colorful leaves upon us and lining the streets with their beauty. Mrs. Denny continued, though I had not yet said a word. "You know, I am still a bit shocked at your choice of husband though. To think you married that blacksmith…the one we all believed to be a murderer!" She hissed, "I don't think I would have been able to do so." She leaned closer and whispered intensely, "Don't you still feel a little unsure as to his true character, my dear?"

That was enough. I was getting tired of this. I stopped in my tracks and turned toward her. "Excuse me, Mrs. Denny. I don't appreciate you speaking of my husband that way. He is the best man I have ever known, and I would be obliged if you would leave your dramatic speculations out of our lives." I pulled my arm away and resumed my journey to Dr. Phillips, leaving the meddlesome woman to find her next victim.

Turning quickly, I bumped directly into Gustav, the kind German shoemaker. The older gentleman laughed awkwardly in his endearing way.

"Oh, excuse me, excuse me. I'm sorry Mrs. Tyler!" He apologized again and again.

"Gustav, oh think nothing of it. It was my fault entirely," I laid a hand on his shoulder to steady him. Then helped him pick up some items we had both dropped. Glancing around I whispered, "Although, that Mrs. Denny…she does get on my last nerve at times."

The sweet man smiled and nodded, then after a moment whispered, "Perhaps we can say it is her fault then?"

I smiled back, "Quite so, it's settled then. It is all Mrs. Denny's fault!"

Gustav chuckled and waved to me as we began moving on our separate ways. "God bless you!" he called in his thick German accent.

"Same to you!" I answered waving. *What a dear man he is, almost like a grandfather to Amy and me.*

The doctor's facility was connected to the Phillips' home. It consisted of a small waiting room, an examination room and his office. The kind doctor sat me down in a comfortable leather armchair. The large brown desk was covered in papers, and books lined the wall behind him. I stared eagerly at them. *How much knowledge they must contain.*

"How may I help you today Miss, uh…Mrs. Tyler," he smiled as he corrected himself.

"So good of you to see me, Dr. Phillips, I know you are a busy man." I glanced over at the books once more. "As you know I was a nurse in the army for the past year. I learned so much, but the need is much greater. I…," I hesitated, wondering if he might think it strange for a woman to be so interested in expanding her knowledge in the medical field. "I was wondering if you would be so kind as to lend me some of your books?" Doctor Phillips raised his eyebrows in surprise. I continued, "Nathan will be going back to the army soon. I want to go with him and help with the wounded. But I need to know more. So many men suffered and died needlessly, I want to know how to help them…how to heal them." I leaned forward, my mind re-living visions of the past. "Please help me to help them."

Over the next few weeks, I visited Doctor Phillips' office in the early hours of the morning, and he imparted more of his knowledge, mostly in the field of infection, wounds and disease. I would carry home a new book every so often and pour over it as I leaned over the fireplace cooking or by candlelight after Nathan had drifted off to sleep.

Tonight, the chill kept me huddled close to the fire as I flipped the pages of the big weathered medical book. I tucked the woolen blanket around my legs and snuggled closer into the armchair. The fire popped and crackled in the hearth. The autumn nights were growing increasingly cooler and the wind whistled around the house. I paused from my reading and looked over toward the big oak framed bed that used to be Mother and Father's. Nathan slept calmly tonight. I was glad for that. The firelight flickered on his face as he slept soundly. He had been agitated by nightmares lately. I tried to ask him about them, but he would just brush off my questions saying, "It's just the prison camps." It pained me as I saw the torment in his eyes and recollected my own night terrors from all I had seen. He seemed preoccupied lately and restless. I knew it wouldn't be long before he returned to his duties in the army. I had to go with him, but how to convince him of that I wasn't sure. I was learning so much to be able to help the suffering soldiers that I could not stay here and hide all this knowledge away while men died on the field of battle. So, whether he liked it or not, I *was* going with him.

The Lady Captive
Chapter 3

Amy

October 1862

IT WAS PITCH black when I sat up amongst the heavy quilt and pillows. A horse's scream had pierced through my deep slumber. *Is it another nightmare?* Pulling the blanket back, I treaded over to the window, my hand outstretched. This night was darker than most nights as there was no moon above to shed its pale light over the gardens below.

A murmuring sound in the rooms above caught my attention and I went to crack open the door. Two figures were descending the stairs. It was the major who I'd not seen since I first arrived. At the sight of that all too familiar stone-like countenance, with a black patch across one eye, my heart quickened to a frightening pace. Jane Morgan was carrying a candle accompanying him and speaking in a hushed, rather nervous, tone. I pulled the door closer as they neared but left a slight crack to hear through.

"He's waiting outside. I don't think anyone has seen him come through town. Do be careful, Seth."

"Don't worry, sister. I'll go down to him. Go back to your room." The major's voice was uncharacteristically gentle as he spoke to his sister.

As the light disappeared, I carefully closed the door and, just as I did so, one of the tall double wooden mansion doors creaked open downstairs. I paced back to the window, hearing a murmur outside and tried to adjust my eyes to the darkness. The faint image of the major standing on the terrace appeared outlined by the dim yellow glow from inside. For a moment the scene gave the impression that he was speaking to no one. Then a glint of light shone on a horse's black muscular neck. The rest was obscured in the bleakness of the night. The major turned and as he opened the big doors, light revealed the dark figure spinning his horse around, his black cape enveloping him as they took off at a gallop, the night instantly swallowed them up. A chill ran down my spine at this mysterious encounter as I returned to my bed.

* * *

Gently I ran my hand along the ebony woodwork of the elegant bookshelves in the rather large, but cozy, library. After living a month in this mansion, I had finally gathered the courage, and strength, to explore a little on the first floor while the family was busy outside. Peering through the lace covered window, I checked the small party in the garden to be sure Mrs. Morgan and her daughter were still preoccupied with setting the table for the guests they were expecting. Then glancing through several books, I quickly chose one, eager to be removed from this Southern mansion and taken to another world between the pages. Time soon ticked by at a rapid speed and I became so deeply engrossed in my reading that I hardly noticed an intruder.

"That's one of my favorites," said a voice.

My heart leapt into my throat at having been discovered here without permission and I slammed the book shut. Jane stood in the doorway; hands clasped in front of her elegant yellow dress. For a moment I waited to be scolded that I had been so brazen as to forget my place as a prisoner here and had taken liberties to explore the house.

"I didn't think…anyone would mind if…," I paused awkwardly.

Glancing up to where she stood quietly, a strange sense of familiarity and then foreboding overcame me once more. Her delicate perfectly shaped face haunted me from the first moment I'd met her. As did that strange and irritating sense of familiarity that I could not excuse.

"Miss Matthews," she approached timidly, "I know this is a rather awkward situation for you…but since you have no other place to go it may be in your best interest, and for your own comfort, if you accept our invitations to join us for meals and walks,…if only for the change of scenery and mental stimulation. You've been locked up inside your room for weeks and it cannot be healthy for you." She paused for a good minute while I occupied myself by gently fingering the pages of the book in my lap.

"And of course, you're always welcome to the library." There was a pause and I kept my eyes glued to the book. Then in a very gentle tone Jane added, "Whatever you may think, we don't hate you, Miss Matthews." Another minute passed and when I peered up, she was gone. *Hate me? How could they not? I hate them…every one of them!* Rising from the chair, I was led more by boredom than curiosity through the open door. Glancing up to where the constant guard stood at the gate entrance, I turned to walk around to the back of the house. The sound of laughter reached my ears. A sound I had not heard in many months.

The stone path led around the house and separated at the back of the house in two different directions. The garden scene was surprisingly charming and peaceful. Some white outdoor furniture was placed in the center of the surrounding pink roses and the fragrance of an array of flowers mingled with the scents of herbal teas and biscuits. Mrs. Morgan's slight figure was bent over the lace clad tea table as she poured the steaming liquid from an elegant pot. Jane offered cakes to several guests whom I had never seen. Young Confederate officers. I choked. *Perfect! Why had I let Miss Morgan talk me into joining them? Why had she even asked me? To be their entertainment? Something for her guests to gawk at? To no doubt impress her young suitors. It would be bad enough to have tea with Southerners, but soldiers no less!*

"Miss Matthews!" Mrs. Morgan exclaimed with a pleased, yet surprised, tone as her eyes lighted on me. Too late to turn back, I clenched the thick green skirts anxiously. All eyes turned upon me and, much to my surprise, the gentlemen rose from their chairs. "Please come and sit beside Jane and have some tea."

The major's gaze was upon me with that cold uninviting air, the complete opposite of his mother's warm welcome. *If I had known he was here, I most definitely would not have come.*

Swallowing hard, I approached the offered seat and glanced quickly at the other two gentlemen, also in elegantly decorated gray Southern uniforms. The major had seated himself and indifferently begun to light a cigar while the others waited and watched my every move with anticipation.

Awkwardly, I looked down at the exquisitely decorated and charming tea table and then up at the two officers who remained unseated with their intrigued gazes still fixated upon me.

"The lady captive," one stated with a devious smile. "Well, I'll say she's rather enchanting when she's not pointing a gun at us." I leaned back stunned by the young man's rather callous comment.

"Mark," scolded a horrified Mrs. Morgan.

"I'm sorry, Ma'am, you must excuse my rather impertinent remarks." The young man said to me, "It's just that we don't often capture a woman in arms." The young officer gave a little bow with a terribly charming smile and I couldn't decide if he was being sincere or mocking me. "You have my highest regard for your bravery."

"Mark Hamilton, sit!" Hissed Mrs. Morgan, following with a little nervous laugh, her eyes darting to each of her guests. "Miss Matthews," she turned to me looking a little embarrassed, "You must excuse Captain Hamilton. He never finished etiquette school," she gave the young man a sharp look. "He says whatever comes into his mind without a thought of how it will appear to others," she added, chastising the captain.

The young man sat back with a dejected look on his handsome face.

"Why Mrs. Morgan! It's not 'foolish nonsense' to inform this lady of my sincere admiration. Why, most girls I know won't even pour a cup of cold water for a tired dirty soldier because they may soil their hands. While this young woman has even taken up arms for her country."

"I wouldn't doubt it, considering the kind of girls you know," muttered Major Morgan as he tapped the cigar.

Captain Hamilton gave him a smirk and turned back to me, "I'm sorry Miss Matthews. Allow me to properly introduce myself. Captain Mark Hamilton at your service." Motioning to the captain beside him he stated, "and my dashing, yet silent comrade, Captain Joseph Rogers." Captain Rogers gave a quick nod of his head, looking rather uncomfortable by the situation he now found himself in.

"And in what part of Pennsylvania did you live, Miss Amy Matthews? It is Amy, isn't it?" asked Captain Rogers

"You fool! Everyone in the regiment knows her name except for you!" scolded Captain Hamilton.

Rogers' face flushed and I studied the pair of them. Here I was sitting in a beautiful garden having an odd, but civil, conversation with the men who, just a short time ago, were my worst feared nightmare, who were thrashing us down with blackened swords from their galloping steeds in the dead of night. I felt as if my mind were in a constant state of denial since I had arrived at this impeccable prison mansion. The profoundness of it made my head spin and after a few moments I realized I had been staring straight through them.

"Gettysburg," my voice sounded strange to my own ears and the word had a hollow solemn ring to it, "I'm from Gettysburg, Pennsylvania." The major glanced up at me and we locked eyes for a long moment. He laid down his cigar and blew the smoke into the gentle breeze.

"Gettysburg, you say. Don't believe I've heard of that city," stated Captain Hamilton, breaking the silence.

"It's a quiet place," Major Morgan piped up. "Small population. More of a country hamlet."

"You've been there, Seth?" Mrs. Morgan, confused, looked from me to her son sitting opposite us. He glanced up calmly and then back at the cigar.

"Yes, ma'am. Almost two years ago now"

"Really? On an assignment?"

"Of sorts," he answered, gazing into the garden.

"More tea, anyone?" Jane interrupted her mother, looking suddenly nervous and added to Captain Rogers' already nearly full cup. A little splashed over the side beside his hand.

"Oh dear, excuse me, Captain," she began nervously dabbing the tablecloth.

"No worries, Miss Jane." As she leaned over closer to me cleaning the spill, her fragrant perfume instantly caught my attention and a horrible, nostalgic feeling overwhelmed me. As I gazed intently up at the girl whose features were now so obvious to me, I wondered how I could have overlooked the similarities. Chest tightening, I rose from the table, unable to endure the sudden sensation.

"Miss Matthews, are you going so soon?" Mrs. Morgan's voice faded as I followed the stone path back toward the house. Into the large foyer, up the grand staircase, down the hall and into the quiet room, I retreated to my solitude. For ten minutes I paced the room, unable to compose my thoughts. *It is her. It must be her! She's the reason. All the secrecy, all the betrayal…Of course, it all makes sense now. Only a rich family could afford such expensive perfume. And her brother must have been the connection.* In my mind I recounted the moment I had first laid eyes on the perfumed letters and that locket going over and over every detail following.

Staring out the window down upon the little party, my heart burst with this new horrible emotion. All the memories of my discoveries in the McCarthy's home came flooding back. The guilty look on Kelsey's face when I confronted him. I had tried to tell myself it was all some odd misunderstanding. After his strange disappearance, I had tried to deceive myself into believing his dishonesty had not been about another woman. But now, seeing her face, a picture that had now come to life…no, it was true…and she was the one that had taken him from me, from the life we meant to build together. She had lured away my dearest friend. This nightmare, this suspicion, was all true. *How on earth, how will I live every day in the same house with that…*

"Miss Matthews," A voice pierced through my fog of anger and despair.

I turned to see Major Morgan standing inside the room several feet away.

"Major," I stated indifferently before continuing my pacing, laying the cool back of my hand against a flushed cheek trying to calm my nerves. For a moment the Major said nothing but only stood studying me in my agitated mood. In irritation at his silence I snapped.

"Don't tell me this is part of my punishment as a prisoner here…to endure the social gatherings and friendly interrogation of my captors."

"Interrogation?" He walked across the room to the small mantel before glancing up to the painting above. There was a long silence and I felt the frustration and fury rising in me like a trapped animal.

"Why am I here?" I demanded angrily, unable to hold back the question any longer. "So you can try to squeeze whatever information out of me that you can get before you kill me like you have other innocent women and children?" Slowly he turned and faced me, folding his arms across his chest. I waited for some terrible repercussions for the words I felt were risky, but necessary to speak.

A look of disbelief and anger covered his face, "Are you really so blind that you continue to fail at seeing the truth," he stated with a scoff.

"I *know* the truth, Major," I shot back, shaking with rage, "I've seen the path of destruction your regiment leaves in its wake. The innocent dead… You have no concept of the suffering you cause, no idea, until the same has touched the lives of those you hold dear. Then I wonder how self-righteous and arrogant you will be. And yet I doubt your privileged, wealthy family has or ever will experience *any* kind of hardship. Though they inflict suffering on others they deem lesser than themselves."

"Let me explain something to you!" Suddenly stepping directly in front of me, I could see a terrifying anger rising in his face, "You may *choose* to remain completely ignorant of the truth about who the guilty party is in the atrocities you've seen, but understand this, if it weren't for the kindness of my family taking you in, God only *knows* what would have become of you! So be careful when you speak so arrogantly against them! You know *nothing* about my family!"

"Seth! Major!" a voice shouted down the hall seconds before Captain Hamilton came breathlessly, stumbling into the room.

"What is it, Captain?" The Major turned, his voice instantly calm and aloof again. The young captain was wide-eyed, almost terrified and gasping for air.

"He's back! He's back, Major! We must depart at this very minute!"

The Major placed a hand on his sword, "Go spread the word to the other officers and rally your men, Captain. You know where to meet me."

"Yes, Sir!" The young Captain was gone as fast as he had come. Major Morgan's lips were suddenly inches from my ear as he paused before passing.

"If I hear of any harm that befalls my family because of you…you'll be wishing you had been left in a prison camp to rot. Clear, *Corporal.*" He threatened in a menacing whisper, just before abandoning the room. With my heart still pounding from the intense confrontation, I went to the top of the staircase hearing the chaotic commotion below.

"Is everything prepared?" the major questioned his mother as she handed him a pile of folded black cloth.

"Yes." She said solemnly, "Only go my son for the sake of our country."

No sooner had the words left her lips then her gaze lifted to where I stood at the top of the cascading staircase and I caught sight of the brief glint of fear in her eyes. Major Morgan followed her gaze to me and then leaned in to whisper something in his mother's ear before kissing her lightly on the cheek and disappearing out the large open doorway.

As they left the foyer, I descended, curious at what was taking place. Only Jane and Mrs. Morgan stood on the front terrace now. The sky seemed blood red as the sun set over the glistening city of Richmond. The enchanting scene drew me out to lean against one of the big white pillars. Instinctively, I clutched my side feeling the throbbing return. Jane grasped her mother's arm and muffled a sob.

"Strength, my daughter."

Suddenly three blackened riders on pitch black horses burst from the stables in a full gallop. One of the horses shrieked and tossed its head up angrily and I saw the major with face now covered in that strange black war paint, glance back at his family from high on the agitated steed before they all disappeared around the bend.

Mrs. Morgan and Jane stood, still staring in the direction the men had disappeared.

Minutes passed as the sun sank down and I was just about to retreat to the house when a thunderous ground-shaking noise disturbed us. Louder and louder it grew until I found myself drawn to the edge of the road where the guard stopped me. Many others had gathered in anticipation. Suddenly a mob of black horses and riders appeared at full speed; they galloped, not marching through the town in an orderly fashion. *Black, everything completely black. Not a single button, buckle or spur glistened in the fading sunlight.* Every horse was tar black from their ear to their hoof. It seemed as if the gates of hell had been opened. I felt myself quivering uncontrollably, wanting to run and cover my ears. Then the horrific deafening din of that destructive legion thundering upon the ground was accompanied by the outbreak of the Rebel cry.

I was trapped in my own fear, wishing to run, but frozen to the spot where I stood. Just as the last rider galloped past, I began to regain some control over my senses…until my eyes caught sight of him.

There standing just opposite of me, a mere twenty paces away a lone horseman held his protesting mount in check. The excited animal lunged, snorted and kicked under the tightly gripped reins. Foam at his mouth, sweat dripping from his glistening coat as if he'd been ridden hard for hours. Yet the muscles surged under his dark coat and he fought to be released. The dim light did not reveal the rider's dark face, but I could feel his eyes on me. Then kicking his heels into the horse's flanks, the big animal rose up on his back legs, the dark rider's black cape flaring as the horse plunged forward into a full gallop. And as suddenly as he had appeared there, he vanished.

Jane, who had also witnessed this frightening yet powerful scene, turned to me with a strange expression on her face before retiring to the mansion. Glancing back down the road, I watched as the last of the black riders faded into the darkness. I then turned away, wanting to believe this nightmare of phantom riders and the secrets that seemed to surround them was past, but in me rose a haunting fear…it had only just begun.

Concealing Truth
Chapter 4

Elizabeth

November 1862

OVER THE WEEKS I had not ceased to search for Amy. After discovering which of the surrounding towns had been recruiting for the army last year, I would ride out to each of the towns occasionally and make inquiries as to when and where the army units may have gone. People began to be suspicious of me and I tried to explain that I was only worried for my younger brother who ran off and joined a unit. But the trail grew cold and I felt desperate. I rode back toward Gettysburg after yet another attempt at finding information on the whereabouts of my sister. *How am I ever to find her?* It would be impossible amidst the thousands of soldiers who went off to war. All I could do was trust that God would keep her in His hands. My heart ached to see my sister again. I almost forgot how it felt to laugh with her…and cry with her. Sometimes it felt as though I had lost a part of myself. When I was in the West, it was easier; I was so distracted by all that was happening there. But now, being home…walking the streets without her, wandering through our old home, not seeing her smiling face in the kitchen, no more talking late into the night, laughing until we couldn't breathe, telling each other our deepest secrets, sitting with each other as we cried.

I don't know what I would have done without Nathan. He was such a comfort as I missed my sister. Though he was as dear to me now as life itself, I still felt a hole in my heart where Amy used to be. When I had realized she was gone, it felt like part of my heart had been ripped out ruthlessly. She had taken a part of me with her and I felt desperate to get it back. I tried to keep busy, and to focus on finding a purpose, which only added to my desire to help the Union cause with Nathan. I needed to have something to work toward. I needed to pour into people, not focus on my own miseries. *If I stay in Gettysburg, without Nathan…without Amy…I can't even think of living like that.* Amy and I had never spent more than a few days apart, until I had left to help with the army in the West. Now it had been over a year since I had seen her. *My dearest friend…when will I see you again?* The tears fell relentlessly down my cheeks and I kicked Shadow into a canter down the dirt road. My bonnet had fallen and hung from my neck, my hair blowing unashamedly about my face. *I have to find her.* As I neared Gettysburg, I heard a familiar hammering coming from the livery. Slowing Shadow, I dismounted and tied him to the nearest hitching post. I entered the stables, greeted by the strong scent of hay and manure. Nathan was alone, fitting shoes onto one of the horses. I stopped in the doorway. After dropping the horse's leg and patting his sleek coat, Nathan turned.

"Elizabeth. What are you doing here?"

I tried to speak, but my throat was so tight. Nathan wiped his hands on a soot-covered rag and approached me.

I finally choked out, "I…I can't find her, Nathan. She's gone." Tears streamed down my face, as I wiped at them, frustrated. "I'll never find her. I know that now." My voice broke suddenly, "Nathan…I just miss her so much." Covering my face in my hands, Nathan's strong arms encircled me.

"Amy made her own decision," he whispered into my hair. "You can't keep her and protect her from everything, Elizabeth."

"But how could she do this to me? How could she leave and not tell me?" I cried as the sorrow intensified. "Why did she have to go away? I need her to come back. Nothing is the same anymore and I can't stand it." I choked in between sobs.

"Let her go, Elizabeth," Nathan said softly after a few moments. "It doesn't mean you have to give up on finding her, but you cannot control her life. You have to live too, remember?" He pulled me back and reached up to brush the tears off my cheek.

I sighed, trying to calm myself. My heart felt like it was held down with heavy chains as I brushed the last tears from my eyes.

Nathan gently moved me forward, "Come on. Let's go home." Grabbing his tool caddy, he put his arm around my shoulders and turned me around to walk out of the barn.

Walking down Main Street on foot, we led our horses by the reins, passing through the busy street. Coming toward us, I noticed the constable, John Barnes. He stopped as he reached us and tipped his hat.

"Mrs. Tyler," he smiled at me, then shook hands with Nathan. The men talked for a while about their work and the town. I tried to listen politely as I watched the townspeople going in and out of the shops lining the roadway.

As their conversation began to die down, I offered, "Mr. Barnes, would you join us for dinner tonight? We haven't seen you much since I arrived back in town." I looked to Nathan for confirmation.

Mr. Barnes nodded, "Well, that is right nice of you, Ma'am. I would like to see how you are getting along with all that's changed since you left."

Nathan reached out and shook his hand once again, "Come by any time, John."

That evening, I ladled warm soup into the bowls set in front of the men as they sat discussing the war at the big wooden table. Bringing a warm loaf of bread, I sat down to share the meal with them. After a prayer, John Barnes turned to me.

"Elizabeth, seeing your stone hearth there reminded me of the intruder you had last year before you left to the West. During your absence I tried to keep a sharp watch over the house. I never did see anything suspicious happen. Still doesn't make any sense to me."

I dropped my eyes to the napkin in my lap as my mind flashed to my father's plantation and the realization that I had a mulatto half-brother. Surely the intruder *was* him. With everything that had happened on arriving back to

Gettysburg, I had pushed these thoughts to the back of my mind. I had not even told Nathan about it. Father's box with his journaling and the papers about his son I had hidden away in the old chest upstairs. *Could it really have been my half-brother who had broken into our house in search of something? How would he have found us? Was I ready to reveal this information?*

"No…I don't know why someone would have done that either…," I cringed guiltily, and noticed Nathan suddenly stop eating and stare at me. He was always so perceptive. I tried to avoid his gaze and added more confidently, "It was very strange indeed…does anyone want more soup?" I asked, quickly pushing back my chair and taking the bowls from the men. Nathan leaned back in his chair and watched me as I hurriedly ladled more soup from the pot into the bowls I held.

Later that night I sat combing out my long brown hair in front of the mirror in our room. My eyebrows were drawn together pensively as I journeyed through the memories of being at Grandfather's plantation and finding the information about my half-brother. Suddenly Nathan appeared in the mirror before me.

"What was that all about?" he asked in his usual low tone.

"What?" I asked innocently, braiding my locks slowly.

"Something has been bothering you ever since John brought up the intruder that broke in last year." He paused and waited for my answer. Seeing I had nothing to say, he looked away, sighing softly. After a few moments he asked, "You want to tell me what is going on?"

Getting to my feet I flipped the long braid behind me and brushed past him.

"It's personal," I answered a little too coolly. I wasn't sure I was ready to dive into all that this conversation could reveal…my grandfather's inheritance, my parents, my father's past, my mulatto half-brother, and possibly even… Captain Preston and my stay in the Southern town. Nathan stood, arms crossed watching me as I scurried about the room trying to look busy folding and refolding laundry. I felt the exact same way I used to; constantly trying to hide from that penetrating gaze. I continued my folding until I heard Nathan walk toward the doorway.

He turned in the entrance, put his hand on the frame and locked eyes with me, "One day I hope you will trust me enough to tell me about it." With that, he left the room.

I fingered the lace along the hem of a dress. *He's right. I need to tell him everything.* Guilt spread through my veins. I knew how much trusting each other meant to him, after all we had been through together. *Soon…I will tell him soon.*

My Precious Dove
Chapter 5

Amy

November 1862

FINGERING THE DELICATE lace curtain, I shifted on my feet and leaned against the windowsill. Outside in an open area of the garden in back, Mrs. Morgan was squawking orders to two slave women on how to properly hang the thick ornate carpets for cleaning. Amazed at how anyone could be so comfortable allowing others to do all their work for them, I scoffed as the women continued to struggle under the heavy weight, with their master all the while judging their every move.

Then there was Miss Jane sitting ideally on a bench nearby, a shawl wrapped around her shoulders to protect from the autumn chill, her dark ringlets hanging around that delicate face, her brow furrowed, engrossed in a letter that had just been delivered…perhaps a letter from Kelsey….

My heart sank and I turned away leaning my head back against the wall to stare up at the ceiling. *How can I be so jealous over someone I hate so much? I thought I had let him go. But how could I hate my best friend from childhood…the person I loved as dearly as my sister. Oh Kelsey….*

"Miss," I turned to find a young negro slave girl carrying a bouquet of wildflowers into my room.

"Yes, what is it?" I asked, obviously not in the mood for any visitor.

"These is for you, Miss. I just found 'em in the kitchen with a note that had your name on it." She smiled and placed the small, yet beautiful, bouquet of wildflowers in a little vase.

Blinking, I stared in confusion, my mouth hung open, "Umm, I…you can… excuse me, who?" Stuttering, I tried to imagine who on earth would send *me* flowers and more importantly, why?

"Oh, I just found 'em, Ma'am. They was sittin' there on the kitchen table. I can't tell ya how they got there." She smiled sweetly, chuckling while adjusting the flowers. "They jus' appeared. Same as the last two bouquets that I set up here a few weeks ago. They had your name on 'em too."

Baffled, I stared at the young girl, "You put flowers up here before…that someone had left…for me?"

The girl straightened, a worried look came over her face and she wiped her hands down the white apron, "Yes Ma'am. Oh, I 'spects I should've told ya they was sent, but then ya been out walkin' in the garden, readin' or sleepin', and I didn't want to disturb ya. I's awful sorry for not tellin' ya, Ma'am."

"No, no, it's not your fault. I'm just…confused." The girl smiled again and curtsied before leaving the room. Staring oddly at the flowers across from me as if they were some intruder sitting on my nightstand, I searched my mind. *Who on earth would have the nerve to send flowers to me…a prisoner?* Bewildered, I gave up after ten minutes of trying to figure out such a mystery and decided to wander downstairs, since there was no chance of happening upon the Morgans while they were busy outside.

Finding myself on the big empty front porch, I paced over to a comfortable white rocking chair and sat down. Staring around at the four large white columns and ferns that hung so elegantly around the large porch, I wondered how anyone could justify living in such a ridiculously expensive and elaborate mansion, especially when it required bought human slaves to keep it tidy. I hadn't even seen the entire house, but the ground floor alone, I had noted, was an incredibly marvelous area. The most delicately made lace hung on every window, thick enormous rugs on every floor, exquisite fireplaces, the eloquently detailed furniture…the equal of which I had never beheld. One room alone with all its furnishings must cost more than our home in Gettysburg. What sort of people were these to imagine they deserved such an outrageous lifestyle?

"Mother, please, I must go. I'll be back soon." Suddenly I heard Jane's voice on the path leading around from the back to the front of the house.

"My dear girl, there is a war on! You can't go up north! I won't allow it! Your brother would die if he found out. And why all this secrecy?" The anxious voice of her mother seemed to soften the girl's heart.

Gently she explained, "I can't say, Mother. Please just trust me. I will be very careful." I strained to hear the cause of this confrontation.

"Jane, this is about him, isn't it?" There was a long pause.

"He hasn't returned in months...and the letter said," Jane choked a heartbroken sob. "I have to go. Please don't stop me."

"He will return, I know he will, my dear girl. He loves you so... Don't be afraid. But I know I can't stop you." There was a little sob as I could see the two embracing through the tall bushes that obstructed my view. As quietly as I could, I rose and crossed the porch to slip inside, gently closing the door behind me. Climbing the steep staircase, Mrs. Morgan's words still rang in my ears, *He loves you so…* Panting lightly, I fell back against the heavy door staring up at my bedroom ceiling. Then Jane's words came back to me.

"He hasn't returned in months…and the letter said," *The letter…all of Kelsey's letters, they must be here in this house somewhere.* A sudden longing to see them, to read exactly what he had written, to know the truth of his heart that had caused the destruction of our engagement. *I must find them. But can I endure such an undoubtedly painful revelation of the contents hidden in those letters?*

A heavy sigh escaped from within me and a determination rose in my chest. *No, I must know the truth, I must see with my own eyes what Kelsey had written to Jane Morgan. And perhaps even be able to find the last of his letters. I will wait until everyone is asleep.*

* * *

The house was deathly silent as I turned the handle of the closed bedroom door. Jane had long since departed, and all the slaves had retired, as well as Mrs.

Morgan, who routinely went to bed at eight o'clock. Darting into Jane's room, I held my breath surveying the lavishly furnished room, cushioned chairs, a bed, and a chest with elegantly carved decorations. The large oak writing desk that sat near the window seemed promising and I gently slid a drawer open but found only writing supplies. I searched through all other cabinets and drawers to no avail and to my surprise found nothing incriminating. Frustrated, I turned to the chest at the foot of the bed and quickly lifted it open. Sinking my hands down into the bottom, I felt around. Then, in the last corner, wrapped in some thick blankets, my hands touched a package. Careful, I slid it up and out. Staring satisfied at the bundle of envelopes, I stopped to listen again. The main door downstairs creaked open and I stuffed the papers into my bosom and made for my room. Just as I closed my door, I heard someone reach the top step. Pressing myself hard against the door, I held my mouth in an attempt to quiet my panting. One of the Morgan's slaves must be making a final check of the house. They moved on to the next flight of stairs and I hurriedly locked my door and pulled the envelopes from their hiding place. A dark red ribbon was tied around the many letters and the same inscription was on the front of each one.

Gently I slipped one envelope free without disturbing the tied ribbon and opened it. Staring down at the message, I noted how rather untidy and smeared it was in places. As if it had been written in a hurry and even from the back of a horse. Confused by the message, I opened several more letters. They were all written in the style of poems or riddles and the only thing that was inscribed on the front was: *My Precious Dove.*

However untidy they were, there was no denying that the handwriting was indeed Kelsey's. Yet none of them was dated more than a year earlier. Reopening this painful chapter of my life was more difficult than I had imagined. But for some inexplicable reason, I felt it was necessary. With each letter the knife was driven ever deeper into my wounded heart and I sank onto the bed, still gripping the pages.

As I continued studying the messages. I noticed an odd pattern to each one. Nothing was written in them…*except* for the riddles and poems. And they were all signed: *The Devoted Servant.* Opening the last one at the bottom of the stack I read:

> *Dove, how gently you must fly*
> *overhead the darkened sky.*
> *To rest your wings at home*
> *and yet speak not of the unknown.*
>
> *Your message must not speak*
> *or danger you may meet.*
> *But rest and wait another day and*
> *I'll send the raven home to stay.*

I stared down at the strange scribblings in my hand. *My Precious Dove… Dove…* An idea grew in my mind, yet I could not understand what this message could mean. It wasn't a love message like the others had seemed to be but carried a more foreboding ring. Something of a warning. I fell back onto my pillow, still holding the letter. *My Precious Dove….*

The words of the love poems had reawakened the dormant deep sorrow that always slept within my heart. *When had he made the decision that I wasn't enough for him? That all our years together…our friendship, all our love, meant nothing?*

The Devoted Servant… I glanced down at the signature, pondering the words. Deep into the night my mind searched the past, anxiously trying to discover what could have caused this painful ending. Finally, I drifted off to sleep.

"I love ya, Lassie. Don't let anything ever make you forget that."

"Never," I whispered.

* * *

Sitting on the tall bed, I did my best to mend the gaping tear in my uniform. There was a slight creaking of floorboards and my head shot up to see one of the Morgan's slaves watching me quietly with a pile of folded laundry held gently in her hands. I recognized the kind round face as that of the woman who had tended me during my feverish nights.

"If you pardon my sayin' so Miss, I don't think you'll be needin' that anytime soon."

Glancing back down to the worn, yet beloved uniform that had seen me through so much, I nodded defeatedly and set aside the needle. "I suppose you're right. It's more a matter of respect,"

Her dark eyes seemed to smile from her ebony face, "Ya's very different from the Morgans, ain't ya? Pardon me, I'm Millie, Millie Hodges." She paused before continuing, "I've seen a lot of solemn faces since this war started, but ya have a deeper sadness about ya. Like there ain't one good thing in this world and nothin' to be thankful for. I ain't never seen even a glint of happiness or peace in your face since ya been here. Yet ya've been treated well and should be thankin the good Lord ya was saved by such good folks."

Irritated, I glanced up at the middle-aged woman once more, "Is that what they tell you?" She smiled gently, undeterred at my sarcastic tone and came into the room to lay the laundry on the bed next to me.

"Na, miss," she stated gently. "They don't tells me what to say or whats to believe. They's good people, the Morgans."

Shocked, I stared up at her in disbelief. "You can say that? *You*, a slave and their property?" To my surprise the woman sat down on the bed beside me, straightening her pristine white apron. She shook her head and sighed.

"I been watching ya closely. Ya's so angry, Miss Amy," she stated, as if to herself, and then looked me directly in the eyes for a long moment and those deep black eyes seemed to be looking directly into my soul. I turned away uncomfortably, unwilling to reveal to anyone the darkness I felt there.

"When I's just twelve years old I's bought by a Southern plantation owner in South Carolina. He bought me not to cook or clean…but for another purpose. I was a pretty little thing." She smiled for a moment, but then a tear slid down her dark cheek. "But beauty is a curse to any slave girl." My eyes met hers and I saw pain deep inside, but also a strength rooted even more powerfully. She straightened and shifted before continuing.

"Three years had passed since I had learned what my purpose on that plantation was and what my existence would be. I gave up all hope. I made plans," she paused, and her voice became rigid. "Plans to makes myself free, in the only way I knows how. One day I stole my master's pistol and hid it in my mattress. That night I planned to take my life. Nothin's worse than the hell I was livin'. But that day was the day my freedom came...only not in the way I expected. A man came to my master's home. I don't know how much he offered or what threats he made to my master, but somehow, he bought me and saved my life. He freed me and offered me a job in his home with good wages the same as white servants make. Not even up north would I be so well taken care of or protected. Not only financially but physically. I was safe and I was free." She seemed to come out of a dream-like state and turned to smile at me, "That man was Mrs. Morgan's late husband."

Feeling embarrassed at my assumptions, I shifted, then felt the bed lean as she arose from the mattress.

"No, there ain't no slaves in this house, Miss Amy." She paused for a moment, "I know all ya have is hate in yar heart for the Morgans and folks like them, but truth is, ya don't know nothin' 'bout them. I know ya was fightin' for the Union and thinkin' yar precious president is making all the right decisions trying to destroy the South, to stamp out this rebellion. I ain't no politician, Miss. I don't know all the ins and outs about who started this war and why. I can tell ya, it didn't start to free us slaves. Cause there's just as many people up north as there's down south that wouldn't lift a finger to help folks like me the way the Morgans have."

"Frankly I don't believe there is ever one side that's all right or all wrong in war. There's bad folks of every size, shape and color. And some of them Yankee soldiers have just as much evil in their hearts as my old master did." She paused for a long time staring down at her boots. Then in a voice more gentle and calm than any I had heard, continued, "All I knows is, I ain't met no people more close to God than the Morgans, and I know they ain't done nothing to deserve this war or what it's doin' to their lives. All they want is to be left in peace and protect the home they love." Crossing over to the open doorway she turned back to me, her eyes narrowing thoughtfully. "I means no disrespect, but before ya judge others, Miss Amy, perhaps you should learn what it's like to live in their shoes."

A Special Assignment
Chapter 6

Elizabeth

November 1862

I STARED DOWN at the dainty teacup in my hand and listened to the
chattering of the women around me. I would much rather be out in the late
autumn sun studying one of Dr. Phillips' medical books than cooped up in this
house listening to the ladies' usual gossip. However, Mrs. Denny had invited me,
and I felt obliged to come at least for a little while. I scarcely listened as they spoke
about the ladies who had not come today and how they "should" be living. I
knew that they would have been saying the exact same things about me if I had
not come. My choices never seemed to please everyone. When I was younger, it
was about my education as a lady. Later they were constantly concerned for my
lack of a husband, and now that I had one, apparently, he wasn't who *they*
thought I should have married. What was the next standard they would raise for
me? I had quickly learned that I could not live to meet people's expectations,
because they were always changing from one person to the next. In each stage of
life, someone would take it upon themselves to inform me of what they thought
I should be doing or how I should be living.

"And then…what do you think I said next, my dears?" Mrs. Denny's loud
voice snapped me out of my thoughts. She was leaning forward over her plate of

cookies, wide-eyed. The other ladies in the circle listened with no less intensity. "I said to him, listen closely my dears, I said, 'you have not seen the last of me, Mr. Craig, I shall return…with vengeance!'" Mrs. Johansson's mouth dropped open and the other ladies cheered and affirmed Mrs. Denny's latest tale. I rolled my eyes subtly and gazed out the nearest window. My mind soon drifted to the news of a battle which took place a couple months ago near Antietam Creek in Sharpsburg, Maryland. It was reported that it had been an extremely bloody fight with high casualties. The need for supplies was great and the doctors were overwhelmed. *Is Nathan really waiting for orders for his next move? Or is he hiding something from me? I know he doesn't want me to go with him, but I certainly can't stay here living like this, especially if he is in the war.* When the teapot was finally empty and all the spare muffins had been devoured, mostly by Mrs. Denny, I took my leave and stepped out into the streets of our little town. I breathed a sigh of relief.

My next stop was the market to gather some extra supplies for dinner this evening. I walked slowly down the lane, enjoying the fall breeze and the hue of the autumn leaves. Two figures on horseback came toward me. As they drew nearer, I recognized Nathan on his black mare. The other man looked familiar, but I couldn't place him. They soon stopped their horses before me. I halted my steps on seeing the man closer. He wore a Union officer's uniform and a saber at his side. Swinging down off his tall horse, he removed his hat. I couldn't contain the smile that spread over my face.

"Colonel Brandt! I'm so pleased to see you!" He took my hand and bowed slightly. "How did you find us? What has brought you to Gettysburg? I did not think I would ever see you again! It seems like so long ago! Did you travel far? You must be so tired from your journey. How long have you been in town?" I suddenly put a hand to my mouth, embarrassed at the unending fountain of words and questions. "Excuse me, I'm just…very glad to see you, Sir," I laughed softly and curtsied.

From the time I had served under Colonel Brandt and interacted with him and observed his leadership, he had taught me many things. It seemed as if God had used Colonel Brandt, and other soldiers I had worked with in the army, to fill gaps in my life and to teach me things that I lacked after my parents passed away.

Colonel Brandt's dark brown eyes twinkled amusedly as he listened to my stream of questions. When there was finally a pause in my words, he spoke, "It's all right. I came to Gettysburg to speak to Captain Tyler, uh, your husband…as I understand." He chuckled, raising a thick eyebrow, then added more seriously as he looked over at Nathan. "I have an opportunity for him."

"Colonel Brandt was promoted to staff officer for one of our top generals, Elizabeth." Nathan reported to me, a gentle smile on his face as he turned to the colonel. He seemed proud of his superior. I knew he had always respected him.

"Oh! Congratulations, Sir." I added, "I know it is well deserved."

"Thank you," he nodded to me. Then he turned to Nathan, "Captain, do you think it would be all right if we go back to your house and discuss business there?"

Nathan agreed, "Yes, Sir. Elizabeth, would you be able to prepare some food for Colonel Brandt?"

I nodded, "Of course. I am on my way to the market now. I will be there shortly." The men mounted their horses, tipped their hats to me and rode off down the road toward Emmitsburg Lane. Excitement and nervousness swirled inside me. *What news had the colonel brought? Why was he of all people sent here?*

I was soon hurrying down Emmitsburg Lane with a basket full of food. Stepping into the warm brick house, I could hear the low voices of the men talking in the parlor. A fire crackled in the hearth. Once the soup was started, I ventured to the parlor, pausing in the entryway. Both men stood up upon my appearance.

"Elizabeth," Nathan motioned for me to sit down next to him.

"Oh, I don't want to impose…," I said questioning and looked to the colonel for confirmation.

"No, Mrs. Tyler, I think you need to be part of this conversation." Colonel Brandt nodded toward the chair as well. I suddenly felt very nervous as I sat down next to Nathan. *What is this about?*

Colonel Brandt started the conversation, "I'm sure you are wondering why I am here, and even how I came to be here instead of out West. At the Battle of

Shiloh, I was taken captive as well. Since I was an officer, I was placed in a separate area of the prison. I had no idea if any of my men were still alive or what had become of them. Then one day, I was told we were going to escape. I had heard of a soldier who had led multiple escapes and was now going to make the most difficult attempt yet: breaking out the officers. When the night arrived, we were led out by a brave young man." He looked at Nathan and a small smile came over his face, "I recognized that young man as one of my own soldiers." He continued, "After that successful escape I got word that the man who had led all the escapes was found out and was going to be hung by the Confederates the next day. I could not let that happen if I could help it. So, I gathered a group of the men who had escaped with me and we went back to secure his rescue. It was successful and we all rode north together and found a regiment who took us in. Of course, that's when Nathan was given his promotion and leave of absence. But I'm sure Nathan has told you most of this already."

I glanced over at him, "He did some, but never mentioned that you had been there, Sir."

Nathan looked at me, "Elizabeth, I knew Colonel Brandt would be coming with my orders after my leave of absence was complete. I just wasn't ready to share all the details of everything that happened in the prison camp."

I nodded, then said softly, "I understand." I stood up suddenly, "I need to see to the meal, if you'll excuse me please." I walked into the kitchen. After a few moments of listening to the low voices continue in the parlor, footsteps approached. Nathan placed his hands on my shoulders and turned me toward him.

"Colonel Brandt wants to explain my orders. Can you come back into the parlor?" His eyes were calm but determined. After receiving no reply, he continued, "Are you angry with me for not telling you the details of the prison escapes like Colonel Brandt did?" I looked away, through the window into the fields, my mind filling with the memories of that awful place. "Elizabeth, before you feel hurt, remember…you haven't told me your whole story either." He waited a few more moments, then touched my cheek gently with the back of his hand. "Come on." Leading me back into the parlor, we sat down. *It wasn't anger.*

I wanted him to be able to tell me everything, all the details. I wanted to be there for him. He was right though. I wasn't ready to tell him the details of my story.

Colonel Brandt began, "This assignment is not an ordinary one. This is a special mission, Captain Tyler. Due to your exceptional work at the prison camp in Virginia, the commanding generals have requested that you be stationed in the Southern capital of Richmond. There you will work undercover. Your main objective will be to go into the nearby prisoner of war camps and help prisoners escape. Your focus will be prisoners who are high commanding officers. We can't afford to lose good leaders. But, of course, if we can get other men out, we want that as well."

Colonel Brandt pulled out a map and laid it on the table between us. "Here is the town of Richmond. There were three main prison camps formed this year. This is Belle Isle, a prisoner of war camp on an island located on the James River." Colonel Brandt ran his finger along the map as he pointed out each section. "Libby Prison, which is used almost exclusively for officers. And lastly, Castle Thunder, which is a tobacco warehouse now used to house mostly civilian prisoners." He looked up at me, "If you would have stayed a prisoner longer, Mrs. Tyler, they probably would have transferred you there once it was opened as there are some women being held there. But it may seem God had a reason for you to be where you were," he smiled somberly. He returned his gaze to Nathan. "I'm presuming that you will be focusing mostly on Libby Prison since this is where the officers are being held. However, there may be need for you to breakout some of our spies at Castle Thunder or other prisoners from Belle Isle for whatever reason." The colonel paused, sighed, then continued. His deep voice had hardened, "This is not an assignment to be taken lightly. It will not be without grave danger. If you are caught it means certain death." His eyes shot up to meet Nathan's. After a few moments of eerie silence, the colonel leaned back in his chair, dark eyes scanning the map.

Nathan had sat intently listening to the colonel's every word. His face never changed its demeanor. I, on the other hand, had been trying to control my emotions, sure that they would hear my heart as it thudded uncontrollably. I twisted and untwisted the lace trimming my wrists, then inhaled deeply, letting my breath release slowly. I turned cautiously to look up at Nathan's face. That same familiar look of determination rested on every feature. *He has made up his mind, he will take the assignment. And I'm going with him.*

"If this is where I can serve most effectively, Sir, it would be an honor to accept the assignment." Nathan stared at the map, "Can you give me any details about where I will be stationed, Sir?"

Colonel Brandt leaned forward again, his boots scraping on the hardwood floor, "Most likely a decent home right on the edge of the city of Richmond. Do you have a profession, Nathan? The reason I ask is it may be a good coverup for you."

"Yes, Sir. I'm a blacksmith."

"Very good," the colonel thought a moment and rubbed the stubble on his chin. "I'll see if we can get you a forge where you can set up shop in town. You will have to learn to live among the townsfolk just as if you are one of the civilians. No one can suspect anything. You must appear to be sympathetic to the Southern Cause of course and learn how to converse in their terms."

I had been completely quiet up to this point, but I could not contain myself any longer. "Colonel Brandt, Sir, might it be advantageous if I were to go along? It might be less suspicious if a man arrives in town with his wife…rather than alone." I offered, hoping that would make sense and be a good case for my going along.

Colonel Brandt shot Nathan a glance before answering. "I see your point," he said slowly, "but…I will have to leave this discussion up to you and your husband. As I said, it is a very dangerous assignment. If he were to be caught, they would surely find you out and would include you in the sentence, since you would be a part of the mission. Richmond is not the most pleasant place to live right now. It is overcrowded lately. There have been food shortages and crime rates have risen. Please, take some time to think this over and discuss it amongst yourselves. I will be staying in town until you have decided on the matter. It will take some time to make all the arrangements, but I would like you to be there before winter sets in." The colonel stood to leave. Nathan and I followed his example.

He reached out his hand to Nathan and stepped closer, clasping the younger man's shoulder with his free hand. "I have complete faith in you, Captain. You are the perfect man for this assignment. You have shown yourself to be trustworthy and dedicated to the cause." He firmly shook Nathan's hand, then turned to me and smiled, "Mrs. Tyler, I am very glad to see you safe. You serve your country well. We are very lucky to have you."

I curtsied, "Thank you so much Colonel Brandt, it is our pleasure to have you in our home." Nathan and the colonel exchanged a few more words and we saw him to the door.

* * *

Nathan and I walked down the dirt lane my arm linked in his. We were both quiet, lost in our own thoughts since leaving the house. We had decided to go for a walk in the cool of the evening for the purpose of discussing all that Colonel Brandt had brought to our attention. I gazed out over the fields to the rocky hills and the dark mountains beyond. *Can I really leave all this again?* I was torn between the comfort and protection of staying in Gettysburg and the call to be something more and help in Richmond. *Life is so short…if I can do something to help a greater cause…I have to do it.* Colonel Brandt's warning rang in my ears, "if you are caught, it means certain death." My throat tightened and I glanced up quickly at Nathan. He stared straight ahead; eyes fixed on the road ahead of him.

"Nathan…," I ventured quietly after some time, "Please, hear me out." He slowed to a stop and looked down at the dirt road between us. I reached for both his hands and held them, also looking at the dust around my boots. "All my life, I've wanted to live with a purpose. And as much as I want to stay in the safety of this beautiful town…I can't just live an idle life here knowing that you are in Richmond risking your life every day. You have to let me go with you. I can help. I know I can. I've been learning so much about how to help people…maybe there is something I can do in Richmond. Please, Nathan."

He raised his head to look me in the eyes. I could see the tension and struggle in them. "Elizabeth, if I get caught…they *will* kill me. How am I supposed to let you enter into that kind of danger with me?" His voice trailed off as he looked down again, "I'm supposed to protect you."

I paused, then whispered quietly, "We can't control everything, Nathan. The times and epochs are in God's hands. Our days are already numbered. We won't die one moment earlier than we are supposed to. So," I lifted his chin in my hand, "let us live every day fully…with a purpose."

After a few minutes, he turned, and we continued down the lane. After some time of walking in complete silence, we stopped near the dying wheat field begging to be harvested. Nathan looked into my eyes. Those cold blue eyes had softened and taken on a look of acceptance. He wrapped his arms around me and whispered, "All right. We'll go together."

The Return
Chapter 7

Amy

December 1862

"MISS AMY?" A timid voice came from my doorway and I glanced up to see Mrs. Morgan peeking in. Her eyes were dim and her face gaunt since the departure of both her children.

"Yes?" I asked gently, feeling a little compassion for this fragile looking old, lonely Southern woman.

"I'm going into town and I," she hesitated, "thought, perhaps you might …well I think it would be best if you were to come and…"

I could tell she was having an awkward time trying to relay her feelings about having a prisoner of war roaming her house when the family was absent. My heart began to beat faster at the prospect of leaving this mansion that had been the place I had been confined to for the past months. I glanced up at her as I rose from the bed without waiting for any further explanation from Mrs. Morgan. Grabbing some warmer garments from the armoire I saw the relief on her face as I turned to follow her downstairs.

Treading along the path that led away from the mansion and toward the city, I felt a strange sensation come over me. This was the first time since I had entered that I had ever passed back through that gate. Suddenly anxious, I looked over at the young soldier that instantly abandoned his post to follow behind us. Every neighbor that we passed stopped to stare with shocked looks on their faces as I walked beside Millie, who followed close behind Mrs. Morgan. The demure woman mustered as much grace as she could, smiling and greeting neighbors with simple "Good afternoons," as if nothing were out of the ordinary. People began to whisper and gather in clusters behind us and I heard a few gasps from disgusted neighbors.

The city was a bustle despite the cool temperatures. Everyone was hurrying about. A layer of snow covered the streets, roofs and anything that had sat still for more than an hour. I stopped abruptly to let an older man, hunched over and hobbling on crutches, pass. As he did so, he glanced up at me and to my surprise, the face, though weather beaten, could not be that of a man more than forty-five years of age. By the two stripes on his worn and tattered sleeve I realized that he was in fact a Confederate soldier, though his garments were home spun. The man looked more a farmer than a soldier. As he gradually made his way further down the street, I watched the empty pant leg dragging in the snow behind him. As Mrs. Morgan and Millie climbed the stairs onto a small terrace of a mercantile shop, I stopped at the bottom, my stomach turning.

"If you don't mind, Ma'am, I would prefer to stay outside."

Mrs. Morgan seemed to understand exactly why I didn't wish to enter the shop full of gawking stares from intrigued citizens. She nodded gently to me and then to the young soldier who instantly stepped off to the side.

As the two ladies entered, I placed myself on a small bench just off to the side of the stairs and began "people watching" as I liked to call it. *How wonderful it is to see something other than the inside of my room and that mansion.*

Many months ago, the Confederacy had moved its capital to the glorious and historic city of Richmond, Virginia. I observed that the once agricultural center was fast becoming a booming industrial city. Also, with the change of capital cities came all the officials from the various Confederate states to set up government in Richmond. The capital was overflowing with the new arrivals and their families, and soldiers seemed to constantly stalk the streets in droves.

Breathing in deeply, I watched as groups of women followed by their negro companions passed tittering and gossiping. A lone soldier plodded past on some solitary mission or home on furlough. Elegant horse drawn sleighs with bells jingling and tall prancing trotters skidded by with riders, their fur coats blowing in the wind and laughing as if there wasn't a care in the world. A young, handsome soldier standing near his warmly, yet daintily, wrapped female companion caught my eye. The young girl shyly tilted her head and smiled that flirtatious, yet innocent, smile so well mastered by the Southern belles of Richmond. The soldier, no more than a schoolboy, confidently kept one hand on his shiny saber sheathed at his side while gesturing with his other hand. They were lost in a world that was still only an exciting dream. My heart sank. *What kind of a life awaited such a beautiful young couple when it seems the whole world will soon be engulfed in war?* As I continued watching the two, I found myself lost in the charm of the scene as a light flurry gently fell around them. *It seems more like a painting than real life.* Suddenly I heard a clattering of shoes on the terrace as a group of women burst out of the shop. Standing on the top step, in loud whispers they clucked and gossiped excitedly.

"What an odd family the Morgans are," one woman stated in a loud whisper not truly seeming to care who heard her. "Strange eccentric family, taking in a female Yankee soldier like that. I don't believe the Morgans ever think about how their actions will affect their family's reputation or status."

"Indeed!" Another woman spouted to fuel her companion's wagging tongue.

"And the way they sold all their property to fund the cause. It is noble to donate to the cause, but one has to think of where your family will be after the war. Land is everything!"

"Yes, but it's not as if they have any slaves to work the land." There was a sudden burst of laughter,

"Oh, how right you are! What an odd man the late Mr. Morgan, God rest his soul, the way he coddled those slaves they 'rescued' as they put it." In a hushed tone the main and most knowledgeable speaker continued, "You know he freed them all and now his poor family has to pay them like hired hands."

"Imagine paying negro people like that!"

"But all that is nothing to their latest escapade, takin' in that Yankee woman! Why Mary is probably rolling over in her grave with shame. She was the only proper woman in that family. But she was married into the family and not blood, so that explains it."

"God rest her soul she was the most beautiful bride." There was a sigh before the gossip continued, "What a shame. She would have kept that family in proper order. Now with a Yankee moved in, they've nearly lost all respectability! Seth Morgan should be ashamed!"

"Ashamed?" One woman blurted before very abruptly lowering her voice so that I could scarcely hear the next words, "I wouldn't be surprised if it was his idea. Did I tell you about…" Suddenly the jingle of the mercantile bell sounded, and my head shot up to where Mrs. Morgan stood in the entrance way, all eyes now on her small yet commanding frame. Head held high, she passed confidently through the group of gossipers, no doubt, she was well aware of the topic of their conversation.

Reaching the bottom step, she turned toward me and very loudly declared, "Come along, Miss Matthews," and with a smile she nodded a goodbye to the now mortified group of hens on the terrace.

Following as quickly as I could behind her, I stifled a smile imagining what Mrs. Denny would have done if her gossip group had been so interrupted by its latest prey and apparent formidable adversary.

A few paces ahead of me, I could hear Mrs. Morgan spouting off angrily to her companion. The ever-cheerful Millie peeked back at me and I saw a large grin spreading across her face as she too was relishing in the thought of how embarrassed and yet horrified those gossiping hens had been by Mrs. Morgan's interruption. I held back a smile, glancing backward at the mercantile that now stood blocks away, when suddenly a small group of tattered soldiers standing to one side of the street caught my eye. A large, stocky sergeant at the center of them chewing a round of tobacco stared directly at me, a menacing smirk on his face. An unexpected chill ran down my spine at the ill intended stare and something in my instinct told me to stick close to Mrs. Morgan and my armed guard who suddenly seemed more like a protector. For a moment I couldn't tear my eyes away from this daunting scene, and I nearly froze in my tracks as the man continued to deliver an unwavering foreboding grin, while his companions whispered and snickered behind him. Suddenly I felt the guard grip my elbow,

"Miss," he motioned me to move forward with Mrs. Morgan and Millie who were now disappearing into the crowd. With one last glance, I quickly turned away and almost ran to catch up.

* * *

The dull ache that was my constant companion grew overwhelming as I stared out at the northern rolling hills that were shrouded in a misty haze. It was never as strong as it had been on this day. I could almost feel the warmth of the sun on my face, the rough Pennsylvania farm soil under my feet, as I pictured in my mind that peaceful path, I had so many days trod homeward on. The smell, the emotion, the relaxing feeling that came over my body at the end of a long day of teaching when I saw that beautiful familiar scene rise into view: the two story brick house with blue shutters, Elizabeth working busily in the garden, and the fields of wheat in the distance that stretched to the wooded hills.

I'll be home soon, Elizabeth, I promise. I could hear the words in my head. The words I'd whispered into my sister's ear as she lay unconscious… possibly, on her deathbed.

"Home…where is home…?" I whispered. Raising my head, I held back the tears and swallowed hard, breathing in the fresh cool winter air. The pain was almost more than I could bear. How I longed for home. Not the home I had left that fateful day, but the home I had grown up in and shared with my sister. One where the world felt safe and peaceful and with a heart full of young hope and joy, the home in which I had embraced life…and love. That place now seemed, not a physical place but only…a memory.

Suddenly there was a loud snorting and clopping of hooves on the cobble stone path leading up to the mansion. Jolted out of my solemn, dream-like state, I glanced nervously down to see the little band of black horses and officers plodding wearily up the path. *So, they've returned.* Slowly the officers dismounted, not a word was spoken between them. It had been almost two months since the regiment had vanished from the city before our very eyes. Observing their tattered and dirty uniforms, and faces smeared with blackened pitch mixed with blood, I knew instantly they had endured horrible conflicts, and no doubt caused even more death and fear amongst innocent Yankee civilians.

Major Morgan, still seated on his war horse, stared up at me unmoving, and I felt the instant tension rising within me. Then the officers, handing over their horses to the young stable hands, paraded onto the porch and I heard the large mansion door open to welcome them inside. I pulled the shawl tightly around me, now determined to stay as long as possible on the terrace to avoid the downstairs "welcome home" scene and the tales of their "heroic deeds."

A few flurries began to fall softly around me as memories of last winter invaded my mind: sleeping outside on the frozen ground, listening to the wind howling in the forest trees, breaking holes in the iced-covered rivers to fill my canteen, treading through the pine forests, glancing over my shoulder whenever I heard an unexpected noise deep in the woods, the sudden sound of a sniper bullet thudding into the man beside me, a horse's shrill shriek as a bullet perforated through its skull, the blood draining from my face as the first Rebel cry pierced the air in the dead of night, and the sudden thunder of hooves resounding through the night air, announcing the invisible ghost of an enemy. The faces of slaughtered civilian women and children lying cold in the snow, eyes trapped in an unearthly stare, gazing up into the cloudy sky. A black bayonet still jutting out from a frozen body encircled by black hoof prints all around it: the mark of the enemy.

"Miss Matthews?" I whipped around, my heart pounding as sudden beads of sweat collected on my forehead despite the chilly air. Major Morgan stood a few yards away eyeing me, a slightly puzzled look on his face. "Are you well?"

"I…uh…yes." I nodded, grasping my twisting stomach. When I looked up again the Major was still staring at me, clearly not convinced of my answer. He raised a hand motioning for me to go inside. Entering the library, I tried to force my body to stop trembling as I reminded myself that during my two months here I had never once been harmed by anyone. The terrace door closed and locked behind me. Keeping the shawl still tightly around my shoulders, I felt my heart beating at a furious pace as I tried to wipe away those haunting visions that had intruded into my days, as well as my nights.

Major Morgan crossed the small sitting area and struck a match, lighting a cigar. Motioning to a chair near the hearth, he sat down opposite and crossed his legs letting out a long stream of smoky air. Keeping my eyes on the fire burning bright, I lowered myself to sit.

"I must say I'm surprised to see you here." The comment caught me off guard and I glanced up at him quickly. His young, yet continually stoic, face was still partially covered in that black, sooty substance. And he had clearly not shaved in quite a few days. His clothes carried the stains of battle and a part of one sleeve had been slashed open with, most likely, a long saber. That black patch he always wore, the strap cutting a vertical line through his shining black hair, created an even more dark and sinister look.

I ignored his dreadful state and casually answered, "Why would I not be here? It's not as if I can't see the armed guard that keeps watch over the house day and night, or how I'm constantly watched by your family." In a softer, almost whisper, I heard the words slip, "Or that I have anything left to go back to…"

The leather chair creaked as he shifted in his seat. There was a long silence in which I could feel him studying me. "Most prisoners would have made at least one escape attempt in this situation…but you…" His gaze narrowed as he held my attention for a long moment. "You've never once tried. And I have to wonder, why?" Pausing, he watched as I squirmed in my chair nervously, not knowing how to answer. "You're too intelligent to make an attempt, I believe. *Too* intelligent, and that's what makes me a little anxious, Miss Matthews. You've put me in an uncomfortable position. You discovered my spy in Anderson's regiment, you've seen a little of our operation…you know things about us. Day by day you become a greater risk for me," he paused. The menacing underlying insinuations in the major's tone sent a chill down my spine, as I knew all too well what this man was capable of.

But to my surprise the major broke the tense moment and in a less intimidating tone, changed the subject, asking, "How well do you know Jason Anderson?"

"Not very well."

"Why did you choose his outfit then?"

Glancing up to where the Major still sat very relaxed in his chair, I answered, "It was mostly by chance, they happen to be coming through town. I saw an opportunity and quickly caught up to them." Hesitating, I added, "If you're looking for inside information, Major, I'm not the source."

"I'm not so sure of that," his gaze intensified. "From my observation of you over the past months, I have a hard time believing you're as innocent as you say you are."

"Innocent?" I scoffed, "Major, I wonder how a man such as you can speak of innocence." Standing up quickly, I began moving toward the door.

"And do you think your Colonel Anderson is innocent?" Something in his voice caused me to turn around in curiosity. Major Morgan seemed to have a smug look on his face,

"I don't know what you're talking about," I shot back.

"Really?" There was a glimmer in Major Morgan's eye as he seemed to be debating the truth of my response.

"Can you truly say you've never been part of his midnight rendezvous?"

"What do you mean?" I demanded to know, feeling more confused and frustrated with this topic. Rising from the chair, he stepped in closer to me with an intense stare.

"The Irish woman, you still have no idea what truly happened?" Scoffing, he seemed to suddenly burn with anger. "He has no honor, no compassion, no respect for life. How could you not realize how truly wicked that man is when you were with him every day! Do not tell me all his schemes just completely escaped your notice." Suddenly feeling extremely pressured to give an answer, I opened my mouth, but no words would come. The major leaned back, a frustrated look on his face as he turned away and began moving toward the fireplace, staring down into the flames. "But then I suppose that isn't surprising when one reflects on your lack of judgment. Considering that you abandoned a truly good man the moment his honor came into question."

The words cut through my heart like a knife, and anger came flooding over me. Never once, since the moment I had entered this mansion, had Kelsey ever been mentioned, though the obvious unspoken thoughts seemed to create a deep tension between us.

"How dare you! You have no right to judge my actions!" Unable to control my emotions, I shouted, "You have no idea what I went through or what happened between us!" In a fury I rushed to the door, my hand on the knob ready to fling it open.

"Amy, stop!" A commanding shout came from behind me, but I threw open the door and suddenly ran into the figure standing right behind it. Flustered, I stepped back, wiping my hand angrily at the tears now pouring down my cheeks in unchecked emotion.

"Corporal Michael Jones! Well! I do say we seem to have a habit of always *running* into each other in different places."

I stumbled backwards in shock my eyes wide. "Peter Kingston?" My voice cracked in disbelief.

"In the flesh, my lady, and if I do say…it is quite a delight to see you in your proper role. You really do look quite lovely." He smiled that terribly charming smile under the perfectly kept mustache. Regaining my composure, I pushed through the doorway, knocking Peter Kingston back against the frame.

"Miss Matthews!" I heard him gently call after me, seeing my distress.

I darted down the hall, blindly pushing aside anyone who happened to be in the way and flew down the stairs not knowing what I was doing. The house was full of young officers who had recently returned, all very worn and tattered, being given drinks of cold water. The Morgan's servants attended them, some bandaging wounds with torn white cloths. It was as if the mansion had suddenly become a clinic full of wounded warriors.

Unable to compose myself enough to face anyone, I burst out the front door where more soldiers were now arriving and even more critically wounded were being brought and laid on the porch. Snow was now beginning to fall heavily as I ran past the scenes of bloody and bandaged soldiers now reaching hands up to anyone who passed them, begging for help or a drink of water. Screams for mercy came from further up the road as the river of wounded continued pouring into the city. Suddenly overwhelmed by the terrible carnage before my eyes, I couldn't even stop to question what had happened to these men. The line extended to the horizon of wagons full of badly injured and dead, the wounded hobbling beside them. Hordes of citizens were turning out into the street, some to stare in shock, others rushing to help, tears in the eyes of many. Turning away, I ran to the back of the mansion and deep into the lonely garden unable to comprehend the scene of suffering.

Panting, I fell onto a snow dusted bench and, for the first time since my capture, began sobbing uncontrollably. Everywhere there seemed to be only death and despair. Life no longer seemed to carry anything other than a dark ominous future.

Suddenly something soft yet heavy enveloped my shoulders.

"You'll catch your death out here like that." Peter's gentle voice sounded above me, and I heard him move around to seat himself on the bench beside me.

"I can only wish," I answered, wiping my face with a trembling hand.

"Now, what a waste that would be." There was a long pause then in a soft tone he continued, "You're not alone, Miss Amy. Every one of us has fallen into that pit of despair during this terrible war at some time or another. It seems overwhelming but you can overcome it."

My head shook, "No, I don't think I can. I don't understand anything anymore. I've lost…everything." A heavy sigh escaped, "And I've lost trust in everyone."

"Well now, I know I wasn't exactly who you thought I was, but I'd like to think we are still friends. We endured many hardships and some good times. Isn't that true, tentmate?" He stated in a gentle jest, trying to lighten the situation as he always had done before.

"Friends," I almost smiled, "I don't even know what you're doing here."

"Oh, come now, I know you're not all that surprised. You're a smart lass. I know you haven't forgotten that last night we were in the same room. Tell me you haven't put all the pieces together. After all, you are the reason I couldn't go back to Colonel Anderson again. You're a rather good spy yourself."

Feeling a prick at the mention of that frightening night, I stiffened. "You mean that night when you let Major Morgan interrogate and threaten me."

Our eyes met and Peter gave a sheepish grin, "I knew Seth wouldn't hurt you. Believe me, he's not nearly as frightening as he makes out to be."

"No, just cruel."

Peter glanced down at his boots and scratched his chin. "I don't know how to convince you otherwise and I'm not even sure it matters, but he's truly a good man, whatever you may think. There's always a reason he says and does the things that he says and does." Under his breath he added, "In fact he's probably the only person who truly understands how you're feeling."

Feeling ever more confused and exhausted, I scoffed slightly, shaking my head while wiping my face again. Peter glanced around and then back toward the front of the house where the sounds of the wounded were becoming more and more audible.

"Miss Amy, I know you probably have a considerable amount of questions and feel very confused and hurt about the past, and even perhaps about how our last meeting went. I would truly love to shed some light on the truth about my people and our cause, but at this moment I must go and help with the wounded."

I glanced up at him as he rose and smiled kindly at me. A warm feeling melted over me. Although he was in fact my enemy, there had always been something about the charming gentlemanly "journalist" that had always made the world seem, as ironic as it sounded, a calmer and safer place when he was near. I took comfort in the feeling that I was no longer alone in this strange world of Southerners.

"What happened? What battle were they in?" I asked before Peter could turn to walk away.

He sighed and I could see a dark look come over his face, "A very terrible fight. A beautiful city now in ruins…thousands of Union dead. They call it a great victory for the South in Virginia, but in such a war how can you ever feel proud by the death of so many. I'm glad you were not there to see it," He smiled fondly at me, almost in a fatherly way. "But it did cause General Burnside to retreat. Yet so many civilians were driven from their homes by the fighting and now some are left without a home to return to. A victory, but a terrible battle to behold all within and around the city of Fredericksburg."

The Confederate Capital
Chapter 8

Elizabeth

December 1862

I LOOKED AT the old house once more, leaving it for a second time. A few of our close friends stood on the road watching as Nathan helped me into the wagon. They didn't know the details of our assignment, only that we were going back to the war. I had only told Sarah Phillips that we were headed to Virginia. Many of our belongings lay strapped by thick ropes in the wagon bed. *I wonder if I can discover anything about Amy while we are closer to the fighting.*

Colonel Brandt had told us of a townhouse in the city of Richmond with a little forge near it for Nathan to set up his blacksmith shop. He said the house was only furnished with the necessities and could use some additional items to lend it a more home-like atmosphere. Dr. Phillips had been so kind as to send a couple of his books with me, since I was still studying them.

My sense of adventure was rekindled after some months of rest in our quiet town. Yet, there was a sick anticipation of traveling back toward all the horrors I had experienced in the prison camp. After we had made the decision to accept the assignment, Colonel Brandt discussed more details with us and then left town. He would keep in close contact with us in the months to come. We waved goodbye to our friends, our home, our safety and stability, and turned our faces south toward Richmond and whatever may lie ahead.

* * *

My body was weary from travel; the jolt and the rumble of the wagon beneath me. I stepped down from the uncomfortable seat that I had been attached to for so long. We had taken a longer route than originally planned. We had heard from Colonel Brandt that the Confederate and Union armies were encamped directly across the Rappahannock River from each other at the town of Fredericksburg, Virginia. If the Union was victorious, surely, they would move further south in an attempt to capture the Confederate capital of Richmond… directly where we were headed. Colonel Brandt had sent word of an alternate route to avoid passing near this inevitable battle.

Gathering a couple of bags in my hand, I stood staring up at the tall townhouse before me. This was to be our new home. It was so different than the beautiful old house situated on the rolling farmlands of Gettysburg. It felt cluttered here. All the houses clung closely together for lack of space. The winter sky was overcast, creating an even more dismal appearance. A couple steps with an iron handrail led up to the door. To the left was another house very similar to this one. The houses were so near each other that perhaps only two people could walk side by side between the two buildings. To the right of me was the blacksmith shop. There was no house directly on the other side of the forge: which afforded us a little space away from other neighbors. Nathan left the wagon and walked around the back of the house. I followed.

A very narrow plot of land stretched back, surrounded by a white picket fence. This was closely set beside the neighbor's backyard as well. *There is a small area where a garden could grow,* I thought hopefully, trying to look on the bright side. In the distance was a field and then woods, as we were on the edge of the city. A large cellar was attached to the back of the house and a privy was not far off. After a brief look around the yard, Nathan moved toward the blacksmith forge. It was spacious and equipped with several tools, though Nathan had brought all of his own. At least we had some space to move around with this area so near to the house. Nathan walked around, inspecting all the details of the forge with an expert glance.

After a few minutes, he moved back toward the horses and wagon. "I'm going to take the horses down to the livery. I noticed one as we drove in. There's no room for them here with us." He climbed up into the wagon and gathered the reins. "Do you want to come?"

"I think I would like to stay here and explore the house," I answered, gazing back at the tall, cold building curiously.

There was a pause. "All right," Nathan hesitated a bit, then said, "I'll be back soon."

I smiled assuredly back at him and turned to go into the house. He was very protective, especially now that we had moved into unknown territory. The team and wagon rattled off as I moved up the stone steps and reached for the brass handle. I entered into a dusty, dim entrance hall. Straight ahead were stairs leading to the upstairs bedrooms, one on each side. To the left I entered into a dining room and kitchen combined. It was small and not like the warm, lovely kitchen back home. I approached the back door that exited into the yard and granted access to the cellar. Moving back through the kitchen and across the hall, I entered the rooms on the opposite side of the staircase. A parlor with sheet-covered furniture greeted me. The hearth sat lonely and cold. Further in was an empty room, save a desk and chair. *Maybe an office?* I moved back out and ventured up the stairs. The bigger bedroom on the right consisted only of a bed and dresser. Across from it was a smaller bedroom.

I walked back out of the rooms and sat down at the top of the staircase. Placing my head in my hands, I hoped and prayed we were doing the right thing accepting this assignment. The weight and gravity of the mission suddenly rested heavily on me in the cold, stony silence of the abandoned house. We could tell no one of what we were doing here. We must keep up a façade, an appearance of normal civilian life…and all the while Nathan would be risking his life, helping officers and soldiers escape under the cover of darkness. *How will it all work out? What are we to say and do in our normal day to day lives? With neighbors so close by, how will we hide it all? What if they find out…what if they report us for even just acting suspicious?* The anxiety of everything that lay ahead suddenly crashed heavily onto my heart.

One day at a time. All we have to think about is today, I reminded myself. I laid a hand over my heart, calming its quickening beat. Sighing, I leaned back and looked up at the cobwebs on the ceiling. There would be plenty to keep me occupied in the first few days at least. I sat for nearly a quarter of an hour before daylight suddenly poured into the entrance as the door creaked open. Nathan stepped over the threshold, eyes adjusting to the bleak lighting inside. The sharp blue gaze soon fell upon me. I smiled, standing up and making my way down the stairs to meet him. He took off his hat and reached a hand toward me.

"It isn't much," he said rather apologetically.

"It will do just fine." I reached my arms around his waist and tilted my chin to look up at him, pushing my own anxieties away in my attempt to assure him. *I wonder what he is feeling. The knowledge and the fear of going back into the prison camps must be clawing at him.* I hesitated as I ventured, "Nathan…are you all right…with all this? Surely, it must be very hard for you to think of…going back there." I recalled the nightmares that had tormented him for so long in Gettysburg. His brow was tense, and I could almost see the memories flashing through his mind. He turned and stared out the open doorway, a deep sigh followed.

"I have to do the right thing, Elizabeth. I know what it is to live in those prison camps. If I can help someone escape that kind of death, I will do whatever it takes." My heart filled with fear for him as much as with pride in the man that he had become. I held his arm gently with both my hands. He turned and shut the door, then laid an arm around my shoulder and led me into the parlor.

I sat down on the sofa, then decided to say what else I had been pondering as I had been awaiting Nathan's arrival.

"Nathan, do you think…perhaps I can somehow find out something about Amy while we are here? Maybe if I ask about the units that were recruited near Gettysburg, maybe someone might know something here, closer to the fighting."

"Elizabeth," Nathan turned to me, seriousness written in all his features. "No. You can't speak to anyone about that. It's too dangerous. We have been assigned to a mission and we can't take any chances." His features suddenly softened, "You understand that, don't you? You're going to have to trust that Amy is safe. You can't look for her…anymore."

My heart dropped within me. Give up. That is what I heard. Give up. I felt torn. I could have stayed in Gettysburg and had my own mission searching for Amy. But I had committed to this, and now that meant giving up my search for my sister. I felt my stomach sink at the realization. How could I let go that easily? But I had to. I had no choice. Our very lives were at stake. I had to trust God with Amy.

* * *

The next few days flew past as I busied myself making the dusty townhouse a home. I scrubbed floors, took down cobwebs, dusted…nearly everything and arranged our belongings to add a touch of home to the place. After several days of cleaning were over, I stepped back to gaze with satisfaction at what I had accomplished. What had started out as gray and dirty had now taken on a warm and charming atmosphere.

Nathan worked out in the blacksmith shop mostly, setting up his tools and all that he needed to make it a believable smithy to those around us. He would take in a fair amount of work, as we had found out that the nearest blacksmith was on the other side of town. I wondered how he would keep up when he started his true mission here.

I stepped out to gather the rugs which I had beat and hung on the fence rail behind the house. As I began to gather them in my arms, someone cleared his throat, making me jump a little. A short, middle-aged man stood across from me in his own backyard. *Ah, at last we meet the neighbor.*

"Good afternoon," I curtsied quickly, bringing to mind all Colonel Brandt had told us we must do to keep up a good appearance.

The man never smiled but looked rather uncomfortable. Nevertheless, he greeted me politely, giving a short bow, "Good afternoon, Ma'am."

I could see it would be up to me to strike up some conversation. I smiled, "We just moved in a few days ago. My grandfather was William Matthews, you may have heard of him. He owned a plantation not too far from here," I added, waving my arm back and then clasping my hands together awkwardly. *Am I trying too hard to show that we fit in here?*

"I see," the man answered, his expressionless face still unaltered. "Your husband is a blacksmith?" I nodded my answer. He continued, "That's good, we need one around here. What brings you to Richmond during such an unsettled time?"

"Oh, my grandfather passed away last year, and I am just recently married. We've been looking for a place to settle and a friend recommended this area to us."

He didn't look thoroughly convinced, but he nodded and said nothing more of the subject. "Why is your husband not fighting in the army?"

The way the man was firing questions was starting to make me uncomfortable. "He was, but…he was injured. He's a very good blacksmith. He wants to be able to help the army in this way now. That's another reason we moved to this area, the Confederate Army needs somewhere they can easily access repairs and materials such as horseshoes and other supplies." I forced myself to sound confident. Then fired back, "And why are you not fighting?"

The man suddenly chuckled dismally at my presumptuousness. "A bad back injury."

I smiled and nodded. "Well, it was a pleasure to make your acquaintance, Sir. I'm sure we will speak again soon. And your name is?"

"Josiah Amerson," he gave another bow.

I curtsied again and gave my name as well as Nathan's. *Is it all right to give our real names?* I quickly lifted the rugs and carried them back inside. Underneath that reserved exterior, he seemed that he might make a pleasant enough neighbor.

Judge Not by Words
Chapter 9

Amy

December 1862

OVER THE WEEK, I solely devoted myself to helping Millie by making bandages and taking up kitchen duties, while she cared for the wounded soldiers who continued to pour into the capital from Fredericksburg. The house had transformed into a sort of hospital after the battle, and many soldiers had found their way here once the real hospitals had become too full and conditions had turned extremely grotesque.

My heart softened ever so slightly, feeling compassion on these wounded and dying Confederate soldiers. As I watched them suffer and listened to their cries in the night, I could see them not only as enemy soldiers, but as men each with their own unique life: they were fathers, husbands, brothers and sons. They had the same fear in their eyes I had once felt when faced with the possibility of death far from their loved ones. Seeing everyone in the home, even Mrs. Morgan taking on such humble duties stirred something in me. Yet, I also was glad to have a reason to avoid any interaction with Major Morgan.

"If ya not gonna lend a hand and ya just come to gawk at Miss Amy then get yo' lazy butt out of this kitchen!" Millie scolded one afternoon, waving her wooden spoon high at Captain Hamilton and one of his comrades who were suspiciously always appearing in the kitchen while I was working.

Captain Hamilton's undeterred smiling continued as he guarded himself from Millie's weapon. He seemed to take equal delight in vexing Millie as he did in haunting the kitchen. Millie, it seemed, was loved by several of the younger officers under Major Morgan's command. They were very fond of her and seemed to have known her since their childhood. She appeared to be a motherly figure to them and did not hold back in her scolding of them, but she also seemed to take delight in making them special treats.

Carefully cutting strips of white cloth, I rolled them into neat bandages to await any new arrivals that should happen to find their way to the Morgan's Mansion. Out of the corner of my eye, I saw Millie waving her spoon again as she hissed something under her breath at the captain and his companion.

"Awe Millie, we're not bothering anyone," the Captain smirked and then gave Millie a terribly dramatic, yet adorable, pout. "You wouldn't raise a hand against one of the most gallant captains who's been off serving his country to keep all you women folk safe, would you?"

"If ya two don't beat it and find somethin' useful to do, I'm gonna tell Major Morgan how yar underfoot an' keepin us from our work! Or better yet I'll take this spoon to yar hide the way I did when ya was just in diapers!"

Delighted at the reaction, the young Captain leaned in, "I always knew I was your favorite, Millie."

"Get!" Millie's spoon made a whooshing sound and the Captain quickly ducked. There was a snicker from the two soldiers as they sheepishly left the kitchen, satisfied with their playful bantering.

"Seems I just missed a very entertaining duel?" Peter Kingston stepped inside the kitchen, glancing back at where the two young men had disappeared.

Millie looked up briefly from her work, "Just missed a possible whoopin' is what ya missed," she muttered under her breath.

"That boy is something," Peter chuckled, dipping a finger in Millie's latest pudding for a lick. Glancing over to me he added, "Hard to believe he's one of the best."

Millie shook her head and I could see a proud smile on her face, yet she still wasn't ready to let go of her playful feud with the Captain. "From all the lessons I taught him as a child," she muttered.

"Miss Amy, I haven't seen much of you these past couple of days," Peter directed his attention to me.

"Just glad to keep busy, Sir," I stated, laying a towel over the neatly wrapped bandages.

"She's been a great help to me," Millie put a hand on my arm before beginning to ladle large portions of the hearty delicious smelling stew into bowls.

Peter smiled, "I need to go into town, for a few supplies…and a change of scenery, would you care for a break, Miss Amy? I could surely use the company."

I glanced back at Millie to be sure she didn't need any further help; I noted a strange look on her face as she cocked an eyebrow at Peter.

"If it's not going to be a problem," I hesitated, thinking of Major Morgan's displeasure if he found out his prisoner was out on an afternoon stroll.

"Not at all," the Englishman dramatically swiped a coat off the peg with a flourish. "I'll be a dutiful guard for you. Just don't make any attempts to escape." He winked and then made a playful bow to Millie.

As we plodded out into the snow, I adjusted the basket on my arm that would carry our supplies.

"Here, let me take that," Peter insisted and took the large basket in one hand. No one in this country had treated me so much like a lady as Peter Kingston, who was ever the proper gentleman. It seemed that because of my former role as an enemy soldier, most of the officers in the regiment found me interesting but seemed confused as to how to act around me. Which wasn't horrid compared to the downright hostility I received from the Major.

After a few moments of walking down the silent snowy path, I decided to take the opportunity to ask one of the many questions that had been rolling around in my mind since Peter had arrived in my life again. I decided to start with something simple and less invasive, since I wasn't sure he, being in a rather precarious situation as a spy, would even answer my questions.

"So, Mr. Kingston, how did you come to live in Richmond?" I asked, glancing up at the tall Englishman at my side. His neatly combed hair and mustache framed his handsome, thin face. He seemed amused at my initiative to strike up a conversation.

"Well, that was quite some years back when I was a very young man. Sixteen, I believe. I'd heard so much about America and the exciting new opportunities in this young country. It intrigued me. I've always been an adventurous fellow. So, I decided to try my fortune here in Virginia as a journalist." He winked, "Would you believe me if I told you I truly was a journalist before this war."

I couldn't help but smile, "Yes, but then I suppose I'd have no choice. And so, what made you stay here in Richmond?"

Peter smiled, a twinkle in his eye as his face brightened, "A lovely young woman. My wife now."

"You never said anything about being married?" I was surprised.

"Ah, Miss Amy, war's a dangerous place and the worst for spies." His face grew solemn, "One does not disclose such things."

We reached the main street of the town and were instantly sucked into the crowd that hurried to and fro. I kept close to Peter doing my best not to run into anyone.

"But you're telling me now?"

Peter glanced over at me with a warm look in his eyes, "Though I never take it lightly, I have my reasons when I do choose to trust someone."

Another nagging question came to my mind, "Why the Confederacy?"

Looking surprised, he glanced down at me, "Once you've lived among people, Miss Amy, you don't see the politics, you see their lives, you see their hearts. And now I see my brothers. They're truly some of the best men I've ever known. There really was never a question in my mind where I stood when this war began. It's not about North or South or free or slave states. It's about the basic rights of each individual. The right to have a voice and be heard by your government. That was the whole reason you Americans started your war for independence in 1776, wasn't it? The injustice of not being heard, being unfairly treated? Well, isn't it the same now?"

Confused, I stared down at my skirt, now caked with snow on the bottom. "But slavery is wrong! How can you support the supposed right for people to own other human beings? Isn't *their* freedom a basic right?"

Peter sighed heavily, "Yes, Miss Amy, it is wrong. But there are better ways to rid ourselves of that heinous institution than invading and destroying the homes of innocent people who have nothing to do with it. Two wrongs don't make a right. No one hates slavery more than I and more than the Morgans."

"But I've never heard Major Morgan say anything against it."

"Heard, heard," Peter shook his head, "If you think Seth Morgan is a man constantly overflowing with opinions and long speeches then you clearly don't know him. He's not one to openly go preaching on the street corners and lecturing his friends. But his father and he have spoken out and tried to advocate for changes on the Southern plantations for years now within the government. And they've caused some people to change their own beliefs. I believe they were making good progress before the start of the war. The Morgans are all well-known abolitionists. They've risked everything before this war, they risked their respectability in the community, their home, their family's safety. You don't know the danger of a Southerner speaking out against slavery and yet, so many do, and many risk everything to help slaves escape. You must not judge people only by what comes or doesn't come out of their mouth…but by their actions."

My mind was so baffled by the thought of a Confederate abolitionist, I almost didn't notice as Peter abruptly stopped before a small clinic.

"Ah, here. Let me see if the good doctor has some proper medicine inside."

Just before we could take the last few steps toward the stairs leading up to the clinic, a group of soldiers suddenly passed rudely in front of us.

"Hey, watch it!" A large rough sergeant bellowed as I ran into him.

"Excuse me, Sir," I stuttered nervously.

He suddenly grinned as he peered down at me, "Well, looky here, it's that lady soldier the Morgan's took in."

"Well, you looky there!" mimicked the half drunken soldier beside him.

"Miss Matthews," Peter stepped in between me and the sergeant, "is under our protection, gentlemen."

"No need to get your tail feathers ruffled, *chap*," spat the big burly sergeant, "We just wanted to have a chat with the corporal." He grinned and slapped his partner on the back. Turning his menacing gaze on me, I realized that he was the same sergeant who had been watching me leave with Mrs. Morgan that day we had gone to the mercantile.

Peter looked rather irritated, "I'm afraid we can't accommodate you. We're rather busy, Sergeant."

"Can't accommodate me, eh?" The sergeant scoffed in a fake British accent, "Well look here, King George, you can just move along, and we'll take care of the corporal lady. After all she's a prisoner of the Confederacy, not your house guest."

Smiling confidently, Peter placed a hand on his side where I instantly knew he had a concealed pistol. "Sorry, Gentlemen, I can't allow that. She is in our custody."

"Well your majesty, if you take a look around, you're a little outnumbered," the Sergeant said with a mocking bow. My heart began to pound louder in my ears as I realized we had slowly been encircled by this small band of tattered and half intoxicated soldiers.

"And you're outranked, Sergeant," came a voice from behind us. All eyes instantly turned to where Major Morgan sat on his tall black stallion. A nervous look came over the sergeant's face. The major nudged his black mount directly up to where the sergeant stood, until the horse's nostrils were even with the man's face. The magnificent beast snorted, irritated at the man in his path. Suddenly, realizing his easy prey was no longer under his control, the man quickly stepped to the side and motioned to his drunken friends.

"Come on, boys." He paused as he passed by me, "We'll be seeing you…corporal lady," he hissed as a chill ran down my spine.

"Move, Sergeant!" The major commanded, whipping his horse around. The men disappeared into the crowd before another word could be spoken. Major Morgan stayed mounted, watching where the group had disappeared to.

"Peter, finish your business. I'll take Miss Matthews home." With a lump in my throat, I opened my mouth to protest, when I noticed Peter, ever so slightly, shake his head.

Yet a look of empathy came over Peter's face, as he knew I had been evading Major Morgan since that confrontation that he had so innocently happened upon.

"I'll be back soon," Peter stated reassuringly. With a sinking feeling, I watched him glance back one more time before disappearing into the clinic.

With no alternative in sight I resigned myself to my awkward fate and stepped in beside the dismounted major as he led his big stallion through the main street. I tried to avoid the staring eyes and the gossiping whispers that seemed to have absolutely no effect on the major. Silently, he guided us through the busy streets until the sounds from the city quieted and we turned down the familiar road.

Pretending to study the large beautiful homes that lined the quiet street, I avoided any possible glance in the major's direction.

"I…," Major Morgan spoke hesitantly, then softening his usual commander-style tone, continued, "I want to apologize." Shocked by the words, I couldn't help but glance over at him. Was I imagining it? *Did he really just give what I think he gave, an apology? Impossible! Could such humble words truly come from this cold-hearted man who had been nothing but callous, and even offensive, toward me since I first laid eyes on him in Gettysburg?*

"I didn't mean to upset you the other day, I just…," he struggled to find the words. "It doesn't matter. I do want to apologize for my insensitive assumptions since I truly do not know everything, as you said." There was a long pause and I almost didn't know how to react to this uncharacteristic, gentleman-like behavior.

"Thank you." Awkwardly, I accepted the apology which somehow seemed to break down the wall of tension and animosity between us.

We reached the path leading up to the mansion, the guard still standing at the gate saluted as we passed. It was evident that over the last few days the house had become less busy. Recovered soldiers had made their way to camps and the more terminally ill and wounded were taken home by loved ones. The mansion was beginning to return to normal again. The enormous pillars stood like gentle guards overlooking the snow-covered lawn, with only a couple displaced wagons and randomly tied horses.

Mrs. Morgan appeared on the terrace, wrapped in a simple shawl. She looked incredibly tired, her frail shoulders slumped, her eyes dim and weary. As

I stared at the large mansion, now a place so many men had been tenderly ministered to, Peter's words came back to me. *Look at the actions…*

As I began to trudge through the snow up to the mansion terrace, I pondered the past few weeks and all I had witnessed. Not hearing the major following behind me, I turned back briefly to see him now seated on the stallion, silently watching me as I made my way to the house. After a moment, he touched his hat, turned the big stallion and cantered back through the gate, disappearing from view.

A Prisoner of War
Chapter 10

Elizabeth

January 1863

THE BATTLE IN the town of Fredericksburg, which we had avoided on our way to Richmond, had been a huge Confederate victory. The Union troops were slaughtered as they attempted to cross an open field toward higher ground held by the Rebel forces. Our most recent general, General Burnside, was immediately removed from his command after the disaster. The citizens in Richmond, however, had been buzzing with excitement as the news of their overwhelming victory spread through town, though many of their own wounded littered the town, being cared for in houses and churches.

The city of Richmond itself was not in the best of conditions. The war had caused food shortages, and crime had indeed risen as Colonel Brandt had warned us. In addition to that, Nathan had begun his special mission and had been gone several nights, planning and leading escape attempts from the prison camps nearby. There was much forethought and detail that went into all of this. Colonel Brandt was a regular visitor to our house as he met and planned out details with Nathan. This would surely be a cause of suspicion for the neighbors, so it was decided that if anyone should ask, he was my uncle who lived nearby and was helping Nathan with business matters in the forge. Due to all these possible dangers, I locked the door behind me every time I went inside. Both Nathan and Colonel Brandt had been very adamant about my safety precautions.

I was not used to this kind of life…living in this state of high alert. It wore on me, but I dared not weigh Nathan down with any more concerns. I tried to keep myself preoccupied with the house, but it was very small and did not need much attention after the first few renovations. It could use a fresh coat of paint perhaps, or maybe an entirely new interior design…but there was no money for that.

I would wander about the small backyard, wishing for spring so that I could at least plant a garden. At times I would catch Mr. Amerson and his wife watching me curiously from their window. I would smile, wave, and then try to awkwardly pretend I was doing something productive.

Very soon after we had arrived, I finished the books Dr. Phillips had lent me. If only there was a way I could help Nathan's mission. I had more medical knowledge now and I was itching to use it.

The nights that Nathan was gone were long and tense. Every creak and noise sent me sitting upright in the bed, listening intently. My imagination would get the better of me, and I would constantly find myself standing nervously at the threshold of the bedroom door, clutching the revolver Nathan had left with me. I would always shake my head at myself and retire back to the safety of my bed.

It was the dead of night when a noise sent me to the doorway once again. I sighed, ashamed of myself. *I cannot live in this constant state of fear.* I lowered the revolver and moved back to the heavily quilted bed. *There it is again.* A thud. Then another. A scraping across the back door. This time there was no denying it. Chills ran up my spine and my mouth went dry. I cocked the revolver in my hand and moved cautiously down the steps, being careful to avoid the spots that creaked.

On the nights that Nathan went out on a mission, he would sneak into the back of the forge and stay there until daylight so as not to cause suspicion entering the house in the dead of night. The back of the forge was rather hidden and easily accessible without much notice from the neighboring houses.

Now it was just a couple hours past midnight. I moved into the kitchen where the back door led to the yard. Movement and rustling up against the door panel sent me flying to the opposite room where I might be able to gain a better vantage point from a window. Peering out the glass from the old office room, my eyes adjusted to the darkness outside. Suddenly, I made out Nathan's frame, but he was carrying something…trying to lift it off the ground with much difficulty. *Wait…that is not something…but someone!* I rushed back to the kitchen door and pried it open as softly as possible. A body fell over the threshold with a cold thud as Nathan struggled to keep the big man upright. I gasped and stepped back. Then jumping to action, I helped Nathan move the figure inside the doorway and secured the door behind him. The man began to groan.

"Shhh, shhh…," Nathan knelt down and whispered in his ear, "you're safe now. But you must keep quiet."

"Nathan, let's take him into the parlor, on the sofa. Can I light a candle to exam him?" The man was so tall I couldn't imagine how Nathan had carried him here.

"No, Elizabeth, we can't take any chances. There's already been too much noise trying to get him in. Who knows who could have seen me bring him in." He heaved the man off the floor and dragged him carefully across the hallway and into the parlor, laying him on the couch. I knelt down next to Nathan as he situated the man.

After a moment, I glanced up at him, "What happened?"

Nathan leaned back, rubbing a hand over his face. "The escape didn't go as planned. We managed to make it out, but not without being seen, followed…and shot at. We were able to get away, but I didn't know where else to go with him wounded like this. I figured we could hide him until morning, then we could find a way to get him back to his brigade or a hospital. His name is General Trey."

I nodded, "Do you know where he is injured?" I strained my eyes trying to see in the darkness of the room.

"Somewhere near the shoulder, I think." The general seemed to have fallen into unconsciousness. "He was able to make it here, mostly on his own, until we neared the house." Both of us quickly began examining him for a wound. I moved my hand carefully along his arm, on coming to his shoulder my hand was met with a warm sticky liquid.

"It's his left shoulder." Standing, I turned and moved quickly up the stairs. Rummaging through the dresser I began tearing an old garment into strips. Back beside the general, Nathan and I dressed his wound as best we could.

"I can't tell for certain, but I think the bullet grazed his shoulder. Thank God, it is not lodged inside. I only hope he hasn't lost too much blood." Racking my brain to recall all I had learned to help heal wounds, it seemed that the stress of the moment had erased it from my mind. Nathan must have read the concern in my face, for he suddenly touched my shoulder.

"It's all right. I think he will be safe for the night. We will just need to keep watch for any signs of infection or excessive blood loss. I need to think of a way to get him back out. He can't stay here; it's too dangerous."

"Should we get him out tonight, while it's still dark?" I questioned.

Nathan began pacing the hardwood floor of the parlor, running his hand through his hair. Receiving no reply, I knew better than to ask further questions. Nathan didn't know what to do…at least not yet. If we tried to get the general out now, we would need a wagon and that would cause a commotion. If we waited until daylight, how could we avoid being seen? We couldn't pack the general in a crate to take him out in the wagon.

The rest of the night was long and stressful. The darkness slowly began to gray and soon the morning sun peaked through the window in the east, casting shadows along the far wall. Nathan and I had taken turns sitting up with the general. I tilted my head to each shoulder, trying to relieve the ache from the tension of the eventful night. Approaching the couch where the general lay, I examined the bandages and the wound. It seemed the bleeding had stopped, but I feared the general had still lost a large amount of blood. He had slept through the night mostly, whether from exhaustion or unconsciousness I wasn't sure, but he would awake occasionally groaning in pain. *I wish I had something that could help him. I wish I had been more prepared, but how could I have known?*

Later that morning, I set out to the market to find what nourishing foods I could to try to increase the general's strength. I also found a bottle of whiskey for the pain. Trying to ignore the glances I was receiving, I quickly tucked the bottle in my basket after paying for it and made my way back to the house. I'm sure it looked very unusual and improper for a lady to be buying whiskey…especially at this hour of the morning. I smiled grimly to myself.

As I walked along the streets of Richmond, my feet began to feel heavy and my body ached. What little sleep I did get last night was tormented with worries and new fears arising from having an escaped prisoner of war under our roof. The cold, crisp winter air swept through the streets and threatened snow. I shivered and tried to move quicker down the cold streets. Avoiding eye contact with the people who were around me, and weary from the night, I didn't notice the horse and rider coming up behind me. Finally, the familiar voice broke through my weary mind, causing me to jump.

"Elizabeth!" It was Colonel Brandt. I was not used to him using my first name.

I sighed with relief at meeting him, my legs nearly giving out under me. "Col-uh…Uncle!" I quickly corrected myself, remembering why we had to use these familiarities. "Thank God," I tried to control the anxiousness in my voice, "please, come to the house. We need you there." The colonel's brows drew together inquisitively, and he stared hard at me. He pulled his horse up alongside me as I continued my pace toward home. "Please ride on ahead, Sir. Nathan will be glad to see you."

The colonel didn't answer, but only nodded in a knowing way and urged his horse into a quicker pace. I tried to slow my steps, so as not to cause undue attention with both of us hurrying to the house.

When I finally reached the small townhouse, Nathan was outside working in the forge. A customer stood outside with his horse, likely being fitted for new shoes. I glanced around, my eyes resting on Colonel Brandt's horse tethered to the gate.

Nathan gazed up at me calmly as I approached, his eyes showing me to the door. I obeyed, entering and removing the heavy shawl that had blanketed me from the cold winter day. To my surprise, the general was sitting upright on the sofa, cradling his injured arm. He was an older gray-haired man, with kind eyes and a gentle tone of voice. Colonel Brandt had a chair pulled up next to him and straddled it backwards, resting his arms on the chair back. They were speaking in low tones. Both men looked my way as I entered, carrying the basket.

"Ah, the young lady to whom I owe so much. And to your husband. Such a brave young man. To risk his life in such a manner."

I glanced down at my basket, smiling sadly, "Sir, I'm very glad to see you awake. I've brought you some food and some whiskey for the pain." I set the basket on a small table and removed the brown bottle.

Colonel Brandt stood from the chair, "General Trey, this is Mrs. Elizabeth Tyler. She will take good care of you while we make plans to get you back to your unit." Colonel Brandt was very calm, never showing his deep emotions, but always keeping on the course of action. Yet, I could tell he was distressed by this situation. We were now in greater danger than before. As I took the basket into the kitchen to prepare some food for the general, Colonel Brandt paced the small house. By the time I had finished the meal, Nathan had come in and all three men were in the parlor discussing in low tones what was to be done.

The general was looking very weary. After setting the table, I approached him and exchanged the bandages for a set of clean ones. His shoulder was looking fine so far, no sign of infection and the bleeding had definitely stopped. I brought him a tray of food while Nathan and Colonel Brandt sat down at the table in the other room.

"Miss, I know I have brought great danger into your home, and I am very sorry for that. Very sorry. I hate to bring this kind of peril upon you."

I shook my head as I laid out his meal. "No, General, please do not trouble yourself. We are here for this purpose. We want to help the cause…and you."

The general was quiet for a long moment then, murmured, "The cause…will the cause be worth it in the end?" He sighed and after another long moment pondered, "What exactly are we fighting for? Will all this death be worth it?" He was not looking for me to answer. Besides, could one truly answer these troublesome thoughts?

Ghost from the Past
Chapter 11

Amy

January 1863

THE DEAFENING SCREAM of the Rebel cry filled the thick, foggy air around me. My hand, unable to hold onto the pistol, went limp, dropping the gun to the cold, pebble-covered ground. I stood helpless and frozen as the enemy came crashing through the mist, blackened sabers drawn. *Run, run!* My body would not obey what my mind was screaming for it to do. I heard cries for mercy and watched as my young, unarmed and unprepared comrades were ruthlessly cut down. Suddenly, the enemy was upon me. Then the line of charging cavalry split, going past me on both sides and I saw a lone horseman ten feet away. He jerked his mount to a halt, causing the large beast to rise up, lashing its front legs into the night air, sweat dripping from his muscular neck and foam at his mouth. The black cloaked figure brought his saber down, sending the dark blade through my body as I screamed out in pain, and suddenly fell to the hard, wooden floor, waking myself into reality.

In a death grip, I crumpled into a heap on the rug, still clutching the quilt that now hung half over the side of the bed. Footsteps, coming quickly, echoed down the hall. There was a rapping at the door.

"Miss Matthews," Major Morgan's voice spoke muffled on the other side of the door. Then another pair of footsteps followed and paused outside the door. I heard a quick murmuring and then my door creaked open.

"Miss Amy?" Millie entered cautiously, glancing around the room before her gaze rested on me. Then a look of shock came over her face, "Oh, Miss Amy!" Hurrying over to my side, she laid a hand across my forehead and grabbed a cloth off of the nightstand, dabbing my forehead gently. Her dark eyes filled with compassion, she stated in a motherly tone, "Yous just had a terrible dream, Miss." Trembling and unable to speak, I stared wide-eyed into the darkness.

"It's all right now. Yas safe here." The woman lifted me by the arms as I weakly collapsed back into the bed, "Try to sleep." Feeling her rearranging the quilt gently around me, I closed my eyes. Quietly her footsteps retreated across the room. There was a long pause as she seemed to be waiting to be certain I had fallen back asleep, then stepping outside she gently pulled the door behind her. "She's all right, Sir, jus' a nightmare. She's been havin' 'em regularly. She was shaken up, but I think she's sleepin' now."

Turning over in bed, I opened my eyes again, afraid to fall back asleep. Millie's footsteps headed back down the hall to the right and a few seconds later, I heard the major's footsteps disappear in the opposite direction. An hour passed as I tossed and turned in bed, until I decided to go down to the kitchen for a drink of water. The floor was cold and stiff under my bare feet. Sneaking out the cracked door, I glanced both ways before heading silently down the long cascading staircase. I made my way through the large rooms and long hallways until I reached the kitchen door. The moment I stepped in the doorway, I instantly drew back and pasted my body up against the wall. Unable to comprehend the scene I had just briefly beheld, I decided to take another glance into the kitchen to confirm. There in the center of the room were Peter Kingston and a woman, wrapped in warm clothing and riding boots, engrossed in a passionate kiss. Holding my breath, I leaned back against the wall.

"My Jane," Peter's voice was not more than a whisper, "You nearly killed me with worry, why did you go, my love? Why didn't you wait for me here?"

"I…I couldn't. I was so afraid when you didn't come in time. I couldn't stay here idle, worrying about you."

"You could've been killed, my darling."

"Please don't chastise me, Peter. We are both safe now. That's all that matters."

"I know, let's get you to sleep now. You look exhausted,"

My mind was in a whirl at what I had just witnessed. As quickly and silently as I could, I hurried back up to my room, glancing backward to be sure I hadn't been seen. I almost didn't want to believe it, but there was no denying it, the secret lover of my once fiancé was in fact Mrs. Peter Kingston!

* * *

The morning was still dim as the sun had not yet risen over the mountains. Sliding on my boots, I gently cracked open the back door and slipped out into the icy, snow-covered world. My mind had been too preoccupied to fall back asleep and, after hours of trying to distract myself with a book or some meaningless task in my room, I had decided to seek some reprieve from my wild and distressed thoughts in the large barn. *"Animals are sometimes our best comfort,"* I remembered Kelsey saying when we were children. I smiled at the thought, but the remembrance of Kelsey brought a sad feeling over me once again. *How does Peter not know? His wife is keeping a secret lover. We've both been betrayed.* Five horses' heads popped up nervously at my entrance, with mouths full of hay.

"Hello there," I spoke softly to them, keeping the big war horses calm. Reaching over to the brush lying beside a few black saddle pads, I carefully approached the gentle looking gelding whose ears perked up at me. Still munching on hay, he plodded over to me sniffing at the brush in my hand. Observing the beautiful animals, I realized how tall and lean they were, more like elegant saddle bred or racehorses, very different from the hardy quarter horses assigned to the Union cavalry. Suddenly, the door opened, and a gust of wind entered. *Major Morgan. How does he always know where I am? No doubt he's worried I'm trying to escape.*

Sighing, I muttered, "Major, I-,"

"Sorry girl, it's not the major." An evil snicker came from behind me and I spun around quickly. Horrified to find the infantry sergeant from town and two others had somehow come onto the Morgan's property unnoticed. My mind flashed to the big iron gates and the guard standing out front. *How had they gotten inside?*

The sergeant grinned, "Told you we'd meet another day. Now *corporal*, I think it's time you come with us instead of playing house guest to Major Morgan and his mama." My heart leapt into my throat. I knew any cries for help I made would not be heard.

Gathering my courage, I stated as calmly and authoritatively as I possibly could, "I'm the major's prisoner, sergeant. It's none of your concern where they place me…and nothing you can do about it."

"Well, aren't we high and mighty? Looks like we need to break that proud Yankee spirit of yours, woman." Suddenly, a strong hand clamped down on my wrist and I struggled, twisting it to get free. The gelding reared back, upset by the sudden tussling outside his stall and he lunged at the door kicking it open, just as one of the men grabbed hold of his halter.

"Let me go you beast!" I shouted and jammed an elbow into the sergeant's face, the blow knocking him backward. The private with him instantly stepped up, ripping my hands roughly behind my back in a tight twist, shooting pain into both my shoulders as I gasped.

The sergeant wiped the blood from his nose and spat.

"Why you dirty," he suddenly tossed me onto a pile of hay, then grinned down at me. "See how proud you're feeling after-," the sergeant choked abruptly as a black blade pressed up against his throat.

"I wouldn't reach for that pistol if I were you," a voice came from the shadows. The wide-eyed sergeant grunted, trying to shake his sudden look of fear.

"Look Mister, whoever you are, this is none of your business. So, move along, because you're far outnumbered.

"I'll take my chances," came the calm answer.

"Hey Serg', let's get out of here." One of the other men stuttered nervously and shoved the other soldier toward the barn door with a sudden look of terror in their eyes.

"I never run from a fight and-,"

"Serg, let's go!" The man stated more adamantly. "Don't you realize…?" His eyes grew wide with emphasis and he whispered hoarsely, "It's *him*… Let's go." The sergeant glanced over into the shadows from where the saber had been drawn.

There was a defiant look in his eyes, but he finally snorted, "All right…let's get out of here boys." He glanced down upon me and spat into the dirt next to me, "Filthy Yankee." The three soldiers retreated from the barn, and the door was swiftly shut behind them.

Shakily, I glanced over to the single lantern that lit the big barn and then toward the dark shadows where my mysterious companion, for all I knew, was still abiding. Realizing there was a pitchfork near my arm, I slowly inched a trembling hand toward it and tightly gripped the wooden handle.

"I think you're a little confused, Miss Matthews." The voice echoed from the dark corner.

"Who are you?" I demanded, trying my best to sound unafraid. "Why don't you step into the light if you're not my enemy?"

There was a pause. "But to you I am an enemy…," the words were spoken in a regrettable tone, "though I would never harm you."

As the voice softened, I suddenly heard a strange hint of familiarity in the tone, though it was muffled by a cloth of some sort. I rose to my feet swiftly, the hay falling from my skirts as I did so. There was a long pause and I felt the eyes on me. A chill ran down my back with a sudden revelation.

It's him! The frightened soldier's words haunted me.

"You're their leader." The illuminating words were almost a whisper. "The leader of the phantom regiment." With a million memories flooding into my mind, I felt my legs grow weak.

"I am." The voice spoke again, and I saw movement in the corner. Frozen to the spot, I waited, captured in this terrible moment. Waited for the long months of mystery and wondering who this unseen enemy was to come to an end. He stepped closer and I could see the dark cloaked figure, black boots caked with mud, black spurs, like every other part of him, a tall black plum draped over the hat with a colonel's insignia. All time seemed to stand still, and then I saw an arm reach up and lower a black scarf.

"Amy." The word was spoken gently.

"How do you know my name?" I gasped fearfully.

"How could I forget it?" the words I could tell were said with a smile. Then more softly, "*Lassie.*"

A hand flew to my lips with a gasp that shook my body, at that moment the black-caped soldier stepped into the dim, yet revealing, light.

"*Kelsey!*"

** * **

A look of shock came over every face as we entered the large parlor room where everyone was gathered to celebrate the safe return of Jane Kingston. Major Morgan, Peter, Captain Hamilton and two other officers instantly rose upon seeing their commander. A look of shame and disappointment shrouded Major Morgan's face when he saw I had uncovered the identity of their mysterious leader. He stepped forward into the middle of the room, lowering his head apologetically,

"Colonel, forgive me. I didn't know Miss Matthews was-,"

"You have intruders on the property, Major." Kelsey stated calmly, pulling the hat and gloves off and handing them to a rather dumbfounded Millie, who had appeared behind us. "Sergeant Smith and two frightened privates." For a moment no one moved from their spots, then Major Morgan sprang into action.

"I'll take care of it immediately, Sir," he quickly disappeared into the hall. After the footsteps faded and the front door slammed shut, Peter stepped forward and, to my surprise, he and Kelsey embraced.

"Glad you're safe, old boy," Peter stepped back, smiling like a man relieved at the return of a brother.

"Colonel," Mrs. Morgan came forward, smiling warmly. "Would you care for something hot to drink?"

"Thank you, Mrs. Morgan." Kelsey accepted graciously, then turning toward me with an unsure look in his eyes, he asked apprehensively, "Miss Amy, would ya join me in the Library? Privately?" Unable to speak, I saw Jane intently eyeing me from across the room.

Suddenly, unable to bear the weight of all the emotions of this monumental discovery, I stuttered breathlessly, "I…a sudden headache… please excuse me." Without waiting for a reply, I darted for the hallway that led toward the stairs, heart pounding, gasping in shallow breaths as my fingertips traced the wall to steady myself. There was a low murmur behind me as I began climbing the winding staircase. The sound of spurred boots quickly approached behind me, then stopped at the bottom of the stairs.

"Amy, please," I turned to the young colonel who had followed me. A pleading look in his eyes as he begged, "Please let me explain …everything."

For a moment I hesitated, as much as I longed to be near him, I couldn't endure the pain I felt when I stared into that familiar face. *He has betrayed me, he abandoned me without explanation and now he wants a second chance?*

"I'm sorry…I can't." I gulped down the heartbroken sob that constricted my throat. He nodded understandingly and I quickly made my way up the remainder of the stairs, with doubt in my mind that I would ever be ready to face him.

* * *

"How many supply wagons are following?" Major Morgan's voice met my ears and I froze just outside the doorway.

"Fifty, I counted," Kelsey answered, "packed full of food, blankets, some clothes and ammunition." There was a pause and I breathed softly, glancing around the dark hall. Clutching the book to my chest and staying in the shadows, I peered around into the dim library, lit only by the fading evening sun and a small fire in the hearth. Kelsey was leaning against the mantel poking aimlessly at the embers, the light playing on his handsome young face. Major Morgan was studying a large map rolled out on the small round table between several chairs, one in which Peter Kingston lounged contentedly, a cup of steaming tea in his hand.

"Word has been spreading about how low supplies are, what with the blockades. Many farmers have abandoned their farms to join the war and the ones left behind can't keep up with such a demand for food. The civilians are always willing to give even more than they can spare."

"I know, Seth…, let's just pray it's only a problem this winter." Kelsey interrupted, laying a hand on the major's shoulder as he approached to peer at the map. "If the army eats up all the supplies the South can give, where will the Confederacy be in a year? Or in a few months? Things are tight as it is."

"As long as we can get our hands on Union supply trains we should be in pretty good shape. But with the 22nd Cavalry trailing us, it's becoming more and more difficult to have free reign over the territory." The major sighed, "Nothing but a constant thorn in our side."

"A thorn," Peter scoffed, "They are a serious threat. You chaps had best get rid of them before Colonel Anderson fits *our* regiment with a spy," he stated, glancing up at Kelsey who smirked.

"Hardly a chance of that now," he confidently nudged Seth Morgan, who smiled and shook his head.

Peter shrugged, not sharing his comrade's confidence, "I wouldn't put anything past that man. He caught onto the plan the two of you concocted when you were yet two pupils of his at West Point Academy. Created a whole regiment just to counteract and, I'm betting, to destroy it."

"Yes, but that was too easy for him to do with his father being a personal friend of the President. He can get anything he wants…and that's what he's always been used to…," Major Morgan's voice faded, a distant burning look in his eyes.

"I just wonder why he never revealed your names to the press when he made the discovery. Or at least yours, Seth," Peter stated, setting down his cup on a saucer. "He may not be completely certain who is leading this operation. But I'll bet he has a pretty accurate guess."

Kelsey watched him for a moment, "Doesn't matter now. He's kept the secret for his own reasons and so we keep taking precautions as long as possible. Even if our names did get out, we can continue to move in the shadows, evading his cavalry or any others out to hinder us."

There was a pause and then Peter continued, "You know Kels, I'm mighty fond of Miss Amy…she's a smart one and to keep so well concealed for so long as the colonel's aide. I have to hand it to her. She had Anderson fooled. But she's been very infiltrated with the idea of why the South is fighting this war, and she seems to be struggling with the horrific scenes she witnessed during her time as a soldier. The evidence against us, as you know, is pretty damning when it comes to those massacres. I don't think she'd ever believe us after seeing that. Kelsey, if you can't reach her, I wouldn't put it past your girl to find some way to get back to her regiment. And with as much as she has witnessed and discovered since she got here, her information could be a fatal blow for us."

"She doesn't understand…," there was brokenness in Kelsey's voice. "I have to hope, one day, maybe she'll see why I did what I did…why I kept it from her. I should have told her. Especially after all she's witnessed through the lies Anderson created." He paused defeatedly, "I should have trusted her with everything. Maybe she wouldn't be so set against our cause and against me… if she only understood." Peter and Major Morgan exchanged a concerned look.

"You know there were only a handful of people who were involved in the beginning…and at the risk of our own lives. It was dangerous." Major Morgan tried to console his friend, "Not even my own mother knew, and I still share as little as possible with her…it's too risky."

"Yes, but I think I've lost her forever now, Seth." Kelsey's head hung as he paced back over to the fire. "She doesn't trust me, and I don't blame her. It was too much for her." The struggle and frustration in his voice now more apparent than ever.

"My friend, even if she knew everything, I'm not sure you could change the mind of someone willing to die for their cause. And your Amy seems to be rather bull-headed I've observed."

A smile bloomed on Kelsey's face as he chuckled, "Amy's always been a bit of a strong willed, lass… short temper too, but that's one of the things I love about her."

Peter shook his head and laughed, "I'd say be careful with that kind of a woman, Colonel. But that seems to be something every Irishman looks for in a wife."

Kelsey grinned sheepishly back at Peter, "Amy's a good lass, Pete. She's just got a little fire in her and has had since childhood. There's no changing a lass like that…but she's solid. She has a good heart and she's very determined when she is fighting for justice. I just don't think she's had a chance to see the full picture of what's truly going on here."

"I'm afraid you'll find her different now than what you remember, Kelsey." The major's words seemed to hold some ominous secret, "War changes people…the struggles, heartbreak…the deep fear that she seems to be holding onto. She's having trouble trusting anyone it seems. Peter's the only one she has been able to open up to even a little. She's struggling, even as I observed her behavior in Anderson's regiment-,"

"What?" Kelsey suddenly turned, confused, toward Major Morgan who met his gaze, his green eyes flashing with a look of revelation in them. There was a sudden tension and Peter slowly rose out of his chair uneasily. Kelsey's eyes narrowed as he studied the major's face. "You knew Amy was in Anderson's regiment? All that time we were hunting down that regiment and you knew she was in it?" The look of shock and pain on Kelsey's face told me he had never known what apparently the major and Peter deemed a secret worth keeping from him. Kelsey stepped in closer to the major, who now, realizing he had slipped up in his secret, straightened and prepared to take responsibility.

"Yes," he stated in that familiar, unfeeling tone, "I knew it. But Peter was with her almost every moment and I knew that-,"

"*That what?*" Kelsey cut him off, disdain in his voice. "That he could keep her from being injured…or killed?" The words escaped in a hoarse whisper, "You're mad, Seth." He glanced from one of his companions to the other. "You knew, Peter? And even *you* kept it from me?" The young colonel's voice broke. Peter turned his gaze down, too ashamed to meet the look of betrayal in his leader's eyes.

"I ordered him to." Major Morgan side stepped to place himself as the sole target of Kelsey's indignation. "I knew if you found out, it would blow the whole operation and you couldn't possibly follow through with it."

"The hell with it, no, Seth! How could I?" Kelsey's anger had risen almost explosively as his wrath rained down on the major. I pressed myself into the corner, my heart now beating harder as the voices had risen.

"You could've killed her! *I could've killed her*, Seth! And you *knew* it!" There was a deep sense of hurt in his tone, that of a betrayed friend. The chastised major stood in silence a moment before attempting to defend himself yet again.

"Nothing could've been done, Kelsey. She made her choice and she knew the risks." He stated factually, ever true to his reasoning character. "You cannot control her life!"

Kelsey's hand smashed down on the table, causing it to shudder under the weight of his fist, "She's my fiancée!"

"Yes, she is! And much more!" Seth shouted back, "She's headstrong, determined and she's got guts! Nothing you would have said could have stopped her! She believed in *her* cause the same as any of us believe in ours. She's a soldier, Kelsey!" For a long moment the two friends stood facing each other, mere inches apart.

"If I didn't love you like a brother, Seth…," Kelsey's words faded before he could finish. Slowly, he stepped back and his countenance seemed to soften.

"We can't always keep the ones we love from danger. Especially when we are doing this kind of work…sometimes it's just as dangerous for them to be in their own homes as it is on a battlefield."

Kelsey stared long and hard at Seth Morgan before retreating, "You should've told me…" Turning swiftly he snatched his cloak and hat from the nearby hook and disappeared. There was a deafening silence until the sound of hooves galloping down the side path and into the night faded.

Peter and Seth stood in silence until the major calmly said, "Give him time. He'll calm down." Peter raised his eyes to the major's figure standing opposite him, and gently shook his head in sorrow at what had just transpired between the three friends.

"I knew it was wrong to keep it from him."

"Consider, Peter, if Anderson found out she was the fiancée of Colonel McCarthy, leader of the regiment he was hunting…He would have easily hunted her down in Gettysburg or anywhere else we could've hidden her. She was safer playing on his side, away from any suspicion. You can be sure Anderson would have used her against him to manipulate the whole situation."

A stunned look clouded Peter's face, "She's not Mary, Seth."

Major Morgan turned sharply to Peter, his face full of pain as he whispered, "Don't bring her into this." Quietly he retreated from the room.

The Secret Life
Chapter 12

Elizabeth

February 1863

NEWS HAD COME. Northern news came ever so slowly to the citizens of Richmond. President Lincoln had issued what was called "The Emancipation Proclamation." It had only been a threat back in September to the Southern states, saying that all their slaves were to be freed unless they gave up this rebellion. They had not given up, and so now the President had issued the proclamation. The slaves in the Union states, those who had not seceded, however, would still be held in slavery. Yet, the South would not listen to an order given by a Northern president to free their slaves, would they?

This news brought thoughts of my half-brother swirling back into my mind. *Is he a slave somewhere? What had become of him after he had left our home that day?* My mind wandered back to Grandfather's plantation and how I had visited...with Captain Preston. I recalled Father's box with his notes and writings. I suddenly longed to learn even more about my Father and his history. *What had become of the plantation after the auction?* Perhaps I could visit soon. We were not a great distance from it now. However, everything was so tense at the moment with General Trey hidden under our roof.

The blacksmith business was picking up as word spread of Nathan's good work. Even some Confederate soldiers were seen in the shop from time to time. I wondered how Nathan would keep up…with all the work during the day, plus the occasional mission work at night. He was young and strong, but the work was both physically and mentally strenuous. I worried about him. If only Colonel Brandt would allow another person to be part of the mission, it would take some of the load off of Nathan. But Colonel Brandt was very adamant that we could be the only ones to know about the mission. The more people involved, the greater the risk.

I had kept busy nursing the general back to health the last few weeks. Not only did his wound need healing, but he was malnourished from being a prisoner of war for so long. Colonel Brandt had decided it was better to keep the general in our home until he was well enough to walk out on his own. I began reading what few books I had to the general in order to pass the time and give him some diversion. I enjoyed the times I spent with him, as we discussed what we read. He was such a kind older gentleman and the time lifted even my spirits. And so, we spent those wintery days reading, talking, and hoping spring would come soon.

* * *

One wintery morning, much to my surprise, our neighbors, Mr. Amerson and his wife, stopped by with a small pie for us. The knock at the door sent me flying about the house trying to hide any hint that we were harboring someone. Thankfully, the general was upstairs at the moment in the spare bedroom when the neighbors had come calling. I felt so rude, but instead of welcoming them in, I stood frozen in the doorway and carried on a brief exchange of words with them there. I could see the inquisitive look on Mr. Amerson's face as he subtly peered around me into the house.

"I'm sorry, the house is a disaster. Maybe I can invite you in for tea another time?" I tried to remain cheerful and calm, all the while wondering how on earth we would keep up this charade with neighbors so close.

"Indeed," he said rather stoically. His wife gave me an understanding smile. She seemed very elegant, yet kind and understanding.

In the following weeks, I began having some more encounters with these neighbors. Mrs. Amerson invited me for tea, and so it became a sort of tradition of ours; to meet for tea once a week in her house. It was very nice, but the conversation was sometimes hard for me as I wanted to open up to this kind woman as we discussed our lives and histories. I didn't realize how much I missed female companionship. This kind lady was older than me, and she gave me a sense of what it may have been like had my mother still been alive. I felt guilty when I had to fabricate some storyline in order to protect the mission. *Perhaps I should not visit too often, yet it is so good to have a friend in this lonely town.*

Even Mr. Amerson was coming around. It seemed that he only tried to keep up an appearance of gruffness, but deep down he was a very amiable man. As the hope of spring drew nearer, I began planning my garden and Mr. Amerson decided to help…without my request. We stood at two separate corners of my yard.

"I think we should place tomatoes here. And your lettuce will do very well in this area." Mr. Amerson moved about the yard planning *my* garden. "Oh dear, this spot is most inconvenient for your peppers. You had better do it over here." I was beginning to feel that he was rearranging my entire plan.

"Mr. Amerson, wouldn't you like to go over and plan *your own* garden?"

His head shot up, "What? Well, of course. But I have no time, because you obviously need my help here." He surveyed the area, "It is apparent to me that you have no idea what you're about." My jaw dropped. *How presumptuous!* He said this without any sign of it being only a joke. I cocked an eyebrow and sighed at him. *Was there a crooked smile that threatened to overcome his face or was I only imagining it?* Mr. Amerson quickly moved to continue about the yard. I shook my head.

As time went on, I began to treasure this new-found friendship with this Southern couple. When the time came to till and plant, Mr. Amerson was out in our yard preparing the soil with me. I found he also loved to read, so we spent time talking about our favorite quotes and ideas in the common books we had read. We always had these conversations as we were planting and tending the gardens. Sometimes Nathan would walk over from the forge for a break and join in on our conversations. Yet, we always had to remind ourselves not to let our guard down. They must never know the truth about why we were here or what we were doing.

* * *

April 1863

The day soon came when it was time for General Trey to go back to his unit. Nathan entered through the front door one early afternoon, a sweet-scented spring breeze following after him through the door. In the parlor, I folded the last few items of clothing and placed them in a basket on the sofa.

"I was able to get some extra supplies to send with General Trey," he said setting a knapsack on the old sofa next to me. "I think it will be fine for him to leave tonight." It seemed simple enough. He would walk out the front door at dusk in civilian clothing and make his way out of Richmond. Surely no one would notice that he hadn't come in that day, would they? Did the neighbors pay that much attention to the comings and goings at our house? I shuddered thinking of what would happen if he were caught.

Nathan watched me, reading my thoughts. He said nothing, then began organizing the supplies he had brought in. After a few moments he said, "Elizabeth, be careful when you go out in the streets. There seems to be more and more crime as the war continues. The people of Richmond aren't able to obtain as much food as they were before. I've heard there's been an increase in theft lately. Even stealing from people's gardens." He paused, then he added, "Don't go out after dusk."

I nodded silently. This town…these cold streets and buildings… sometimes it seemed they were more like a prison every day. I tried to keep a positive attitude and remember why I was here and the cause for which we were sacrificing our peaceful lives in Gettysburg. Yet, there were times when I became so restless, I felt like a caged animal. Perhaps I should go somewhere…just for a bit. The thought of Grandfather's plantation reentered my mind. *Yes. I should go there now that it is spring.*

"Nathan," I started quietly, "What would you say to me going to visit my grandfather's plantation? It isn't too far from here. I could take a carriage. I wouldn't be gone more than a day."

Nathan's brows drew together inquisitively, and he sat down on the sofa, "Your grandfather's plantation?" My breath caught in my throat. The idea had been rolling around in my mind for so long that I just now realized I still hadn't even told Nathan about my visit to my Grandfather's land after escaping the prison camp. Time had moved so quickly, and I had left many things unsaid. In Gettysburg, when John Barnes had brought it up, I had not wanted to speak about it…I didn't feel ready to reveal all that it entailed. *But now…I had to tell him, about father's past…about my half-brother. But Captain Luke Preston? Surely, I could leave that part out for now. Yes, I will tell him about Preston another day.* I moved the laundry basket aside and sat down.

"Nathan, I…I never told you what happened after I escaped from the prison camp." He patiently watched my face. "I need to tell you about my father." And so, I began with father's history, how he had fallen in love with a slave girl and ran away with her…married her and had a child with her. The clock ticking on the mantel was the only other sound in the house as I explained about Marcus and how I believed it was he who had broken into our house twice in Gettysburg, in search of…something. After a long while, I ended with my desire to return to the plantation and learn more about my history and possibly discover more about my half-brother. Nathan said nothing during the entire story. He nodded slowly when I finished.

After a few moments, he walked over to the hearth. Leaning a hand on it, he stared pensively at the floor. I had grown accustomed to waiting a long while before receiving replies from Nathan. He never rushed into speaking but would always wait and think about things first.

After a while, he turned and exhaled, "That's a lot to take in, Elizabeth. I wish you would have told me sooner."

I looked down at my hands in my lap. "I know. I'm sorry. Time went on and, I don't know, maybe I didn't know how to bring it up…or didn't want to."

He nodded. "Do you want me to go with you? I don't like the idea of you going alone."

I smiled softly, "It's all right, Nathan. I've done a lot of traveling alone in the last couple years. It may not be proper, but I don't mind it. I think I need to figure this out. Besides, you don't need an extra duty…you have so much already."

"Only for a day?" He raised his eyebrows and approached where I was seated.

"Only a day, I promise," reaching up, I took hold of his rough hand.

* * *

It was growing dark. General Trey stood near the entrance, holding the knapsack and wearing fresh civilian clothing. He and Nathan talked over details. I had spent many hours with the general, caring for him as he recovered. I would miss his company. After the men had finished their discussion, General Trey looked over at me.

"Mrs. Tyler," he said in his gentle voice and reached out a hand. I moved forward and took it. "What can I say? You helped me regain my strength and were my constant companion during some very terrible times, particularly when I first arrived." His eyes glistened, and squeezing my hand he added, "I shall never forget you, dear girl."

My throat tightened, and I gave him a quick hug. "God go with you, General Trey."

The door opened and Nathan moved out into the darkness with the general…on his way through the dangerous streets of Richmond.

Exposed
Chapter 13

Amy

May 1863

AS I STARED distractedly down at the words that covered the pages of the thick book in my lap, I listened to the bustling below. The house seemed to be a flurry of activity this evening, making it impossible for me to slip silently into the gardens for an evening stroll. I winced at the sound of someone ascending the stairs. *They're coming for me, no doubt.*

"Miss Matthews?" A floorboard creaked and I lifted my gaze to where Major Morgan stood. There was an uneasiness in his demeanor.

"Yes?" I asked calmly, praying I had not been summoned to a meeting with Colonel McCarthy.

Since the regiment had arrived back in town, I'd done my best to evade any invitation to meet with the colonel…Kelsey. As the major stepped inside, I instantly noted the very elegantly decorated uniform. Exquisite hat, white gloves, the gold embroidered swirling pattern on each sleeve, polished boots, brass buttons shining, and a bright gold silk sash under the sword belt to finish the already extravagant outfit.

The major awkwardly removed his hat to reveal the neatly combed black hair.

"There is to be a ball tonight in the center of the city…in honor of Colonel McCarthy," he hesitated a moment, studying my face for a reaction, "and the regiment. All of us are expected to attend and, unfortunately I didn't have the foreknowledge to…and well, all the servants have the evening free."

Staring at him in disbelief, I stated flatly, "I must go?" The major's gaze lifted from the floor which he had been staring at and met mine.

"We'll try to make it as bearable as possible. One of us will always be with you of course as a guard, but not so obvious as to attract attention." Hesitantly he added, "Hardly anyone will know you're…a prisoner."

"You can't be serious, Major. Isn't there a corporal, a private, someone who could be posted as a guard here?" I begged, searching for a way out, panic rising in my chest.

"The Colonel has already given the entire regiment the evening, since the celebration *is* in their honor."

Resigning to my circumstance, I sighed.

"Jane can fit you with something to wear."

I shriveled at the idea of wearing one of Jane's own lavish ball gowns.

Clearly seeing my despair, the major stated softly, "I'm sorry…this isn't meant to humiliate you." Slowly he trod toward the door, hand resting on the sword hilt, then stopping, turned toward the painting of the young woman hanging over the fire hearth.

I followed his gaze as Major Morgan stood frozen for a moment staring, then turned toward me, a distant look in his eye like someone coming out of a deep dream, "My sister will be in shortly." The words were almost a whisper and he disappeared as I returned my gaze to the beautiful young girl in the painting.

Jane helped me with the finishing touches of the ball gown that was certainly the most enormous and, no doubt, most expensive dress I had ever worn.

"I hope this isn't too uncomfortable for you," she said, smoothing the skirts.

"Not any more than usual," I stated, irritated.

She glanced up at me, catching onto my harsh tone. "I'm sorry I didn't have anything simpler."

"I didn't expect someone like you to have anything simple," I said. With every word she uttered my annoyance grew.

Jane became quiet for a moment, then began sifting through the shoes she had brought up. Finally, she lifted a pair, "Why don't you-,"

"I can take it from here, thank you." Turning away, I continued straightening the skirts of my gown.

There was a pause, and Jane gilded silently over to the door. Then she said in a low tone, "Miss Amy, I've pretended not to notice but I can't help wondering why you're so particularly vexed with me. The past few months I've tried to be as kind and hospitable as possible to make your stay here bearable. I truly can't imagine what I've personally ever done to make you hate me so?"

"Can't you?" I shot over my shoulder.

Speechless, she turned before leaving the room, "I'll be downstairs."

Staring at the almost unrecognizable reflection in the mirror, I wiped a tear away and carefully touched the tight curls drawn into an elegant, yet soft, style that cascaded down onto my shoulder. The soft, rose-tinted dress was beautiful. *But how can I even enjoy wearing something that belongs to her and even enjoy being at a ball where I am an outcast and a prisoner? This will be unbearable.* Reluctantly pulling on the long satin white gloves, I breathed in deeply and prepared myself to descend the stairs. *I can do this. Just one night. It will all be over soon.*

Standing at the top of the stairs, I stared down at the little group preparing to go out into the cool night air. The ladies, in their finest apparel, now wrapping light silk shawls around them. The men, in elegantly decorated uniforms that proudly displayed each unique rank symbol, shining buttons and buckles, were a strong contrast from the usual black they wore. Everything seemed to sparkle in the light of the chandelier hanging above them. Major Morgan was helping Kelsey with his silk sash. As the young colonel placed a hand on his comrade's shoulder, the two of them exchanged a brotherly look of respect. Peter stood a few feet away with a pleased expression as he watched the two reconcile. I forced myself to take the first step, and when I had finally reached the middle of the staircase all eyes were instantly upon me. Kelsey, the first to turn toward me, stood frozen like a statue; the look of amazement on his face caused my heart to skip. When I had finally reached the floor, Peter stepped toward me holding out a hand, which I took shaking, feeling as if the tight corset had not even left room enough to breathe.

"You look very lovely, Miss Amy," he leaned in and in a softer voice added, "I promise I'll be right there for you." Feeling some relief, I was able to force a feeble smile at him.

Jane stepped up beside her husband, taking his arm, "We should leave now."

"Indeed!" stated Peter, "And whenever the gentlemen are able to regain their senses," he shot a knowing glance over his shoulder, "I believe they will follow." Mrs. Kingston leaned in and playfully slapped his arm.

Then I heard Peter whisper into his wife's ear, "Seems our lady captive has taken them *all* captive." My face flushed and I just knew Jane was looking at me. I dared not raise my eyes to meet Kelsey's as he came up beside me. Taking the gloved hand offered, I tried to swallow back the tightness in my throat as I allowed myself to be led from the house. Behind us I heard the footsteps of Major Morgan and several other officers, including the young Captain Hamilton, who had begun his usual excited chattering.

The lavish ball room was full of every officer, gentleman and lady in Richmond it seemed, and from the moment we entered almost every eye was upon us. The officers straightened and turned their full attention to the young colonel in the cape and plumed hat that had entered, with his equally handsome major at his side. Every young woman's fan began to beat more quickly; anxiously displaying her unmarried status. The room grew almost silent and all around I could hear admiring whispers from the men and excited clucking from the women.

"There he is, one of the most renowned heroes of the South."

"More handsome than his reputation has led us to believe, if that's possible," giggled some young girls beside us.

A richly dressed elderly man stepped forward, face beaming, arms opened wide. "Ah, our hero of the night! Colonel McCarthy!" He proclaimed before clasping Kelsey by the shoulders, "We are honored Colonel, and forever in your debt."

"Not at all, Sir, it is my honor to serve the cause." His Irish accent added a beautiful contrast with the Southern drawl of his companions.

"Well, tonight all of Richmond has turned out to pay respect to you!"

"My men deserve the only recognition," Kelsey smiled kindly down at the old man who now seemed so small beside the tall colonel.

Turning to Seth Morgan, the man smiled, a jolly twinkle in his eye, "Humble as always. Your young colonel has never strayed from the perfect depiction of the man you first portrayed to us, Major."

Major Morgan's face lighted with an extremely rare, but charming, smile that rendered his ever-strict countenance more the young handsome man, and not the harsh prison keeper I had come to regard him as. Taking Kelsey and Major Morgan by the arms the boisterous old man led them away through the crowd, which seemed to close in around them. I only caught a glimpse of Major Morgan looking back at us to be sure I had at least one guard by my side.

"Miss Amy, you're about to cut off my arm with that grip," Peter whispered into my ear.

"Oh, I'm sorry," I stuttered nervously. Peter straightened, happily glancing about the room, "Well now! I appear to be the luckiest man in the room! Two lovely ladies on either arm…of a rather handsome looking chap at that!" Jane laughed politely at her husband's joke.

Always so ready to play the part of the perfect little wife… I thought, as I saw the way she watched Kelsey so carefully.

Peter continued, "And since all the ladies have been rather distracted with that pair of handsome young officers, it seems I'm *finally* free to dance and enjoy an evening with my wife." He glanced backward at the few officers behind us who had accompanied us from the house, "Captain Hamilton!"

The young man's head popped up and he strolled up in a rather overly dramatic swagger, casting an alluring sideways glance to the ladies standing in clusters around us.

"Would you be so kind as to stay with Miss Matthews while I dance a waltz with my wife?" Peter leaned in toward the young man, "Perhaps you can persuade her to dance…would do her good." He smiled at me before escorting Jane onto the dance floor. Feeling abandoned, I peered nervously over to the young captain at my side, looking rather dashing in his formal uniform. For a split second I had a memory of my older students, which the captain reminded me so much of, and my heart sunk. *More than likely they have now joined the war as well.*

Captain Hamilton suddenly bowed, removed his hat and held out a hand, "Miss Amy, may I have the pleasure?"

Swallowing hard I glanced over to where Peter and Jane were dancing, and Peter nodded reassuringly toward me.

"I…uh, thank you, Captain." I took the young man's hand and was led out onto the dance floor.

The world was a swirl of bright colors and lights as I did my best to relax. I glanced around the room at the staring faces and caught sight of a few fans raised to conceal intrigued gossipers. Almost clinging to the captain's arm, I turned away, knowing even in spite of the clever disguise a few observant women from town had in fact recognized the outsider in their mists.

"Are you all right, Miss Amy?" The captain asked softly, noting my anxiety.

"Yes, I just…" Catching a glimpse of those hazel eyes watching me, I choked. Kelsey, surrounded by a crowd of mostly young ladies, stood watching us with a pleased look on his face. Major Morgan, ever by his side, noticed his friend's distractedness and leaned in to whisper something to the young colonel, slowly removing the hat from Kelsey's hand. The air caught in my throat, a faint feeling overtaking me as I was spun once more. Just as I was about to excuse myself from the dance floor, a tall figure stepped in our way and the captain stopped abruptly.

"Pardon, Captain Hamilton, if I may?" Kelsey stated, holding out his hand. My heart began to beat faster than it already had been.

Captain Hamilton smiled at his colonel and released me into his waiting arms. Staring up at that gentle gaze, I lost myself for a moment, unable to hear or see anything else around us. Then I quickly turned away, afraid of what those perceptive eyes might find if they looked too deep. As much as I wished to study the young handsome face that I had met in my hopeful dreams, now I was too afraid. *What could I say to him?*

"Amy," the soft tone melted me as it always had. "I've waited so long for the opportunity to speak with you. Please let me. I can't hold back any longer. I know you were hurt and upset at how everything ended in Gettysburg…but I had hoped, now realizing why I left, that you would at least understand."

"Kelsey, I can't…I can't understand anything until…," an overwhelming feeling of pain struck me, "I can't do this right now." Releasing my hand from his arm, I turned quickly, but felt my hand caught in his.

Pulling me gently off to a less populated area, he stopped and, taking both my hands in his, he looked intently into my eyes. "I didn't know that you were in the 22nd Cavalry all those months. If I'd have known, I never-,"

"No, it's not that," I said breathlessly, staring up at the colonel. "He's right… your Major Morgan…I made my choice, Kelsey, no matter the consequences. And it was my choice to make." Over Kelsey's shoulder I saw the major moving toward us with a concerned look on his face.

"What's happened to you, Lassie?" Kelsey asked, studying my face. Our eyes met and he hesitantly reached up, gently brushing the back of his hand against my cheek.

Reluctantly, I pulled his hand down, the pain too much to bear, "Please don't, Kelsey."

"Amy, you have to know now why I left like I did, why all the secrets. You have to know…I still love ya."

A gasp of pain caught in my throat and our eyes met, "How can you say that…after…"

Suddenly, Jane and Peter were drawing near us and, feeling overwhelmed, I turned and darted away to lose myself in the colorful crowd, pushing my way past anyone who was in my path.

"Ma'am, may I-," I heard voices around me.

"Well, I never!" A woman exclaimed as I bumped into her.

"It's that Yankee girl," came a hiss.

Bursting through the crowd, I stumbled through the open door, down a flight of stairs and into a small garden where I caught the sturdy wooden leg of a decorative archway. I clung to it unsteadily, a hand on my stomach, gasping in small breaths as tears began to stream down my face.

"Miss Matthews?" The major's voice came from behind me. Stifling a sob, I couldn't bring myself to face him. "Miss Amy," he hesitated, stepping closer. "I'm sorry…should I get the colonel?"

Shaking my head, I clasped a hand over my mouth. I couldn't bear the pain of reliving what I had lost now forever: of feeling close to him again and knowing it is a dream that could never come true. *How can I tell him…how can I relive the heartbreak…the betrayal? How can I tell him I know it all?* The major hadn't moved at all when I heard the terrace door open again and footsteps approach.

"Sir," Captain Hamilton's voice echoed in the silence of the evening. Neither officer spoke a word for a long moment, and I tried my best to compose myself. In silence, I stared straight ahead blankly, not truly seeing what physically lay before me.

"I believe Miss Matthews has had enough tonight, Captain." Major Morgan stated with a touch of compassion in his voice, "Would you-,"

"Yes, Sir, not a problem at all," the captain stated, anticipating his commander's request. I heard the sound of the major patting the captain's shoulder.

"Good man," a few seconds later the footsteps disappeared.

"Miss?" The captain's young boyish voice spoke behind me. I rose, finally turning toward him.

"I'm sorry, Captain," I stated, not even trying to hide the defeated tone in my voice.

"Not at all, Ma'am," he offered an arm, which I took gratefully.

Hours later I sat numb and alone in the dark room. A pile of envelopes and letters lay in my lap, along with a decision that must be made.

"Amy?" Jane's voice came from my doorway and I heard her footsteps enter uninvited. An aroma of spiced tea filled the room.

Ignoring her entrance, I sat on the opposite side of the bed still dressed in the uncomfortable and enormous ball gown. I stared out the window as my fingers clenched tighter to the stack of damning love letters. There was a long silence.

"Amy," Jane continued, "I can't pretend to know what you must be going through. But if I may speak plainly to you, as a woman…I know about you and

Kelsey. I'm not sure what all happened between you, but I can imagine it's difficult...his being here now, as the leader of the regiment you fought against but-,"

"No, Mrs. Kingston...I think you *do* know what happened between us." I snapped, rising from the bed to face her. I was done pretending, done playing the house guest, done acting the ignorant fool.

"I...," Jane stammered nervously, "I'm not sure what you can mean. I only know a little of-,"

"Oh, you suddenly don't remember all the letters that have passed between you and *my* fiancé?"

The young beautiful face grew pale as a ghost and her mouth hung open for a moment.

"Yes, I've seen quite a few of those letters. The perfumed envelopes and that gold locket." I stepped around the bed toward her, "When I first came here, I couldn't understand why the very sight of you irritated me, but then I realized. So, you can spare me your fake sympathy and your act of the innocent, kind hostess."

"Amy, I can explain-," Jane began in a trembling voice.

"Explain!" I exclaimed with fury, "Explain what? Explain how you seduced a man away from his intended wife, away from his duty to his country? Corrupted his heart? Explain how you've been entertaining a secret lover right under your husband's very nose? Explain how you twist men around your finger, deceiving them and using them like puppets for your own amusement? Peter deserves better than you! You're the most disgraceful woman I've ever laid eyes on, but I shouldn't be surprised I suppose. It's a perfectly fitting behavior I'd expect from a spoiled Southern brat who's had *everything* in life she's ever wanted!" Burning anger flooded over me as I shoved the letters into her hand. Looking as if she would faint, Jane stared down at them then looked back up at me. Suddenly, Peter appeared in the open doorway behind her, his face drawn and serious.

"Darling? What's going on?" The worried tone in his voice pained me. *Now he too must learn the truth the way I had.*

I waited for Jane to explain the pile of envelopes in her possession. Her hands shook as she turned to Peter, eyes wide.

"She's read them, Peter. I don't know if...," Peter entered and, very gently, took the envelopes from his wife's quivering hands.

"Don't assume anything just yet. They may still only be irrelevant messages to her." Their strange conversation and handling of the letters stunned me.

"How do we know that she didn't send any information before of-,"

"Jane, wait, Darling. I think we need to get Kelsey's opinion first." I stepped back in utter confusion as Peter turned his attention to me. "Amy," he said, calmly holding up the envelopes, "When did you happen upon these?"

The question was asked so calmly, but yet with such authority that I knew I must answer. "I found them the autumn before the war, before Kelsey left."

Studying my face, he tapped the letters in his opposite hand thoughtfully.

"Come downstairs to the sitting room, both of you, now," Peter commanded in his gentlest tone.

In a tunnel of confusion, I followed the couple down the stairs and into the small sitting room heated by a fire. The house was deathly silent, having been abandoned by nearly every servant and occupant. Peter sat down across from Jane while gazing down at the letters and shuffling through them. I waited in anticipation.

Finally, he spoke, "Amy, have you seen any more of the correspondence between Kelsey and Jane?"

"I discovered several envelopes in Gettysburg years ago, but didn't have the chance to examine them."

Peter nodded gently and fingered the envelopes, "And what do you know about them?"

Jane eyed me as she shifted in her chair, her hands folded in her lap. I glanced from one to the other.

"Secret love letters," I stated as quickly as I could, horrified that I had to speak the hideous truth aloud.

Peter smiled down at the envelopes and chuckled, as Jane sighed with relief.

"Not at all," Peter stated calmly and handed the envelopes back to Jane.

"What then?" I insisted, growing irritated with this interrogation game, "As Kelsey's former fiancée, I think I have a right to know!"

"Amy," Peter leaned forward and for a long moment studied my eyes, "Jane and I…we're in the same business. Those correspondences in the beginning were only to give information to Kelsey when the regiment was beginning to be formed, even before the war started. That much I can tell you without jeopardizing anyone's safety, since Jane is now relieved of her risky position. You must believe me that nothing was going on between them. As Jane's husband, and one of Kelsey's closest confidants, I can assure you beyond the shadow of a doubt," he stated, holding up the letters, "these were codes to avoid suspicion. All of it was for the glory of the Confederacy." Peter leaned back in his chair to study my complete state of bewilderment.

"And the locket?" my voice quivered.

Jane smiled, "For Kelsey to identify me as the correct person he should meet. If our letters had fallen into the wrong hands before the war, Kelsey and I, and anyone involved, would have been tried for treason under federal law. But those letters…the ones that you first saw in Gettysburg, are no longer of any use to anyone."

It was all for the Confederacy…all of it…never once had Kelsey ever betrayed me. And I had destroyed our engagement on the basis of those letters and that locket. Tears suddenly clouded my vision and my heart seemed to burst within me. A thousand thoughts flooded my mind, but only one mattered.

"Kelsey," I breathed.

The Plantation
Chapter 14

Elizabeth

May 1863

THINGS HAD SETTLED back into the normal routine after General Trey left us. I prepared for my journey to Grandfather's plantation. It was not too far, but just enough to be slightly uncomfortable. I stepped out of the carriage once again onto the path leading to the large plantation house that was once my grandfather's. Standing amidst the well-kept gardens, I stared at the large house in front of me, the cloud of dust from the carriage wheels still settling around me. I brushed my fingers along some tall wildflowers that rose up, lining the walkway toward the house. The sun shone relentlessly, casting shadowy patterns on my face as I walked beneath the vine arbors. Rounding a corner, I nearly ran into a tall, stately middle-aged woman.

I jumped in surprise, "Oh, I'm so sorry! I didn't know anyone was here." I quickly regained my composure and curtsied, "My name is Elizabeth Tyler...formerly Elizabeth Matthews. This was my grandfather's estate." I smiled, trying to relieve the awkwardness in the spring air.

The woman's face was cold and stone-like. She pulled out a fan and began waving the flies away from her face.

"I see. Matthews, you say? Indeed. Your father was James. My husband is your late father's cousin."

"Oh, certainly. I did not catch your name, Ma'am."

"Because I did not give it," she stated icily. Then added, "Catherine Matthews. My husband is Benjamin Matthews." She snapped her fan shut and turned to me, "We own this estate," then began walking toward the house. I stood frozen in her icy wake, not sure whether I should follow. The woman suddenly called over her shoulder, "Join us for dinner, Mrs. Tyler." I glanced around, not feeling I had much of a choice, then followed the woman toward the house.

Staring down at the large helpings of food, I wondered how they were able to afford such luxuries with all the food shortages that had fallen upon Richmond. I picked at the greens with my fork, my mind occupied on what to say to these stoic people and why they had asked me to stay, if they had very little to say to me.

"Mrs. Tyler, what brings you to our plantation?" Benjamin broke the awkward silence with his booming and stern voice. I nearly dropped my fork onto the lace tablecloth at his sudden question.

"Oh, I…uh…am living in Richmond and just wanted to visit again. It makes me feel close to my father to see where he lived." I looked up cautiously, hoping for some sympathy in the eyes that watched me, but found none.

Instead the man turned to his wife, "Funny, isn't it, Catherine, how when someone passes suddenly all the relatives show up." He spoke to his wife as though I had vanished, "Everyone seems to want something. I am glad Uncle William left the plantation to us and not to his direct line. James, of course, shamed the whole family with his behavior. Leaving us as the only reasonable options you see," he suddenly turned back to me as if I had reappeared. His eyes narrowed as he assessed me.

"Oh, my dear," Catherine suddenly laughed, "Remember the slave boy who we found shortly after we inherited the estate? He was sneaking about the grounds. Even he tried to claim he was of the family!"

Benjamin snorted, "Oh, yes of course, what fools he must have taken us for!"

I suddenly paused my fork picking and looked up.

"A slave boy?" I said a little too pointedly. The smiles faded from their faces.

"Yes. The knave claimed to be part of the family. Said his name was Marcus Matthews." Benjamin's face turned into a cold smirk. I felt my stomach drop…*that name.*

Catherine scoffed, "Well, my dear, he very well may have been family… who knows how many *slaves* James may have bred with that slave girl he called his wife or other slave women for that matter."

The heat rose in my cheeks and my stomach felt like a rock had just landed in it. Every muscle in my body tensed and before I knew what I was doing, I felt myself stand up, nearly knocking the glasses over on the table.

"How dare you," I said, shaking with anger, trying not to raise my voice. "How dare you speak about my father that way. His only mistake was to not care for that boy like he should have. Instead he was too concerned with pleasing horrible excuses for people like yourselves!" By this time my voice had raised higher than I had wanted it to. I threw the napkin down onto the table in disgust.

Benjamin had stood up as well and waved his hand, "Get out of this house, young lady, and never come back again. You and your disgraceful family are not welcomed here."

"I have no desire to be in company such as this ever again, Sir." I stated resolutely and turned to leave.

Just then, Catherine called in an irritatingly gentle voice, "Mrs. Tyler, in case you want to find your *family*…you may want to search the neighboring plantations. I have good reason to believe your half-siblings may be there picking cotton and such." She picked a grape with a smile and placed it in her mouth. I clenched my jaw and bit my tongue so hard it must have bled. The nerve of that woman. Oh, the things I wanted to say to her and her insufferable husband, but I knew it would not do any good. The dishes clattered as I shoved my chair back in. Then turning, I walked quietly out the door and down the staircase to the entrance. The growing warmth of spring outside matched the growing heat within me as a slave girl helped me gather my belongings. Walking out the door, I suddenly turned back and stopped the door from closing.

"Excuse me," I spoke to the young negro girl. "I know you heard that whole conversation." She looked down, but I stepped closer and continued softly, "They mentioned finding a slave boy here a while ago…Marcus Matthews. Do you know what happened to him after they found him?" The girl looked nervous and a little suspicious of me. I reached out and laid a hand on her shoulder, "It's all right. I just want to help."

After a long moment, she spoke, not raising her eyes, "They sold 'im to the Johnson's plantation. The next plantation over. I remember Mista Johnson happen' to be here tha' same day and he bought 'im on the spot."

"How long ago was this, do you know?"

She thought for a few moments, "'Bout a year or so, I reckon."

"Thank you," I said quickly and turned to go.

The girl called to me, "But you can't go there, Missus! Mista Johnson a hard man! It be mighty dangerous!"

I forced a smile to her and waved, trying to calm her anxious expression as I turned down the dirt path to the road, the fire still burning in my stomach.

* * *

I informed the carriage waiting at the gate that I would not require their services at the moment, but to please come to the plantation down the road in about an hour. I stalked down the dirt road, shaded on both sides by large, old white oaks. I needed the walk to remove some of the tension, and I needed a little time to figure out what exactly I was going to do. I could feel the beads of sweat on my back, soaking through my burgundy dress. The only sounds penetrating the air were a few bird calls and the sound of my boots against the dirt road. I shrugged my shoulders trying to relieve the tightness that came from the recent conversation. Breathing in deeply, I attempted to calm the boiling inferno within me. I would not allow their miserable attitudes to overwhelm me and pull me down to their level.

Soon the road surrounded by trees opened up to a broad sprawling plantation. My walking slowed as I drew nearer to the fields. Many negroes worked in the fields. Under the sun, their dark skin shone from the sweat covering their bare backs. Overseers stood, hands on hips surveying the land, some on horseback, some using whips to keep the slaves moving along. I shuddered. Along the road, near a fence rail, one of the overseers sat on a dark bay. As I approached, I placed my eyes on the road in front of me.

"Afternoon, Ma'am," he called with a Southern drawl.

"Afternoon," I answered quietly.

"Can I be of service to you?" The overseer swung out of the saddle and tipped his hat.

I hesitated, seeing an unnerving grin on his stubbled mouth. *This could be my only chance to find out where Marcus is...*

"Actually, yes, Sir. I am looking for the plantation of Mr. Johnson?"

The overseer laughed and spat tobacco on the ground. "Well, you found it, Ma'am." His eyes narrowed, "But what would a nice lady like yourself want to do with Mr. Johnson, huh?"

I stiffened up, determined to hold my ground and not let fear stand in the way of what needed to be done.

"I need to speak to him please."

The man stared at me, then another smile spread over his face.

"Sure Ma'am...whatever you say. I'll take you to him. Hope you know what you're getting into." He swung back up into the saddle and reached a hand toward me, "Wanna ride?" he asked, still with that irritating grin on his sweaty face.

"No. I will walk, thank you," I stated coldly.

"Suit yourself," he shrugged, then called out to another foreman, "Pete! I'm taking this fine lady to meet the master. Take over for me for a bit, eh?" He then turned back to me, "Follow me, Missus."

As we passed through the path in the fields, I watched the many slaves working the ground. The strain on their body was intense, and the realization that they did this from sun up to sun down, day after day, made my heart ache. Most dared not to look up to meet my eyes as I passed by, but if they did all I saw was a deep hollowness, a great emptiness, a hunger...not only for food, but for life...for freedom...for something more in this one life they had. I searched the faces of the many negroes as we walked along the dirt path through the fields.

They said he was here… I thought as I squinted, trying to recognize the mulatto man who I had seen in Gettysburg.

"You say somethin' again boy and I'll whip ya within an inch of yar worthless life!"

I spun around at the sudden harsh words just in time to see a taskmaster punch a slave in the face, knocking him to the ground which he worked. The young man lay still, then suddenly moved to get back up to his feet.

The foreman approached, "Get up boy, you get up right now!" He swung his leg back and kicked the slave in the stomach. My throat locked up and my heart dropped.

"Stop it!" I suddenly heard my own voice yell and found myself moving toward the field.

"Whoa, whoa, whoa, Missy! What do you think you're doing?" The overseer I had met earlier had realized what was happening and caught up to me, pulling me back. "What are you thinking, Lady?"

I twisted my arm free of him but stayed in place. *He was right. I couldn't do anything.* As the overseer turned me to follow him, I glanced back over my shoulder. The dark man's eyes looked up to meet mine as he got to his feet. *It's him! The mulatto from Gettysburg!* I recognized the face that had broken into our home, and the same one who I had met on the streets of our town selling peaches. We locked eyes for a few moments before the taskmaster shoved him back to his work. A sickening, apprehensive feeling overwhelmed my whole body. *Could it truly be that this was our half-brother? What was I doing here? How could I help him?*

Suddenly something made me stop in my tracks. *I just need to talk to him. Perhaps I don't need to see the plantation owner after all.* Something inside me told me it was better to avoid him, if at all possible. I ran up to the overseer who now walked, leading his horse in front of me.

"Sir," I touched his arm and he stopped. "If I could…somehow…I just would like to speak to that slave." The overseer watched me, eyebrows raised.

"And why would you need to do that? Ya know, Missus, you're being awfully suspicious," his Southern drawl deepening as he narrowed his eyes at me. "First you want to speak to the master and now you just want to talk to a slave?

What is going on here, really?" He crossed his arms and waited for an explanation.

"I…uh…," I searched around in my mind for a logical excuse. "I, uh…am with a journalism group and we have been having a debate about the plantations. To help settle the argument, we decided to go to some of the plantations nearby and ask a few questions. And uh," I smiled trying to cover up the awkwardness and added quickly, "And to make sure I am not being biased, I thought I should ask a slave as well… Oh! Oh, Sir, you would be perfect for my interview too! You seem to be a very good overseer and very knowledgeable. Perhaps I could speak with you as well?" I offered, shrinking inwardly as I waited to see how this flimsy excuse would fall on his waiting ears.

The overseer searched my face for a minute or two, then his usual grin spread over his face and he broke out in a laugh, slapping his knee. "Ah Missy, you are too much! A woman in journalism? Ha! Interviewing a slave and an overseer? What a ridiculous notion!" I grimaced, thinking it was surely all in vain now. "I'll do it!" He suddenly shouted.

"You will?" I asked, a bit shocked that he had fallen for my tale. Although… he did seem a bit dim witted at times, fortunately for me.

"Sure! You've convinced me. Sit down right here and we'll have a lil' talk." He motioned to a nearby bench. I walked over to it awkwardly, feeling this was too good to be true. After several minutes of the "interview" and listening to the overseer brag on all that he has accomplished in his life, we were finally done. I stood up, hoping to get to the real matter now. The overseer seemed to have forgotten, so I reminded him.

"You've been most helpful, Sir. Now, could I please interview that slave?" I motioned to the young mulatto man who was still hard at work in the fields.

"That one right there?" He pointed him out, "Well…I suppose. He's not much of a talker." He rubbed his stubbled chin and spat another wad of tobacco to the ground a little too near my shoe. "But come on!" He wandered toward the field. I followed quickly, in nervous anticipation. The taskmaster who had beaten the slave had moved on and so we approached him with no interruption. As we came closer, the young man slowly stopped his work and glanced up nervously. The overseer called to him.

"You there, come over here. This nice lady has some questions for you."

I turned to the overseer, "If you don't mind can I have just a moment to speak to him alone?" He stood there, hands on hips, looking a bit suspicious again. "It will be better if he's not afraid to speak to me…for our journalism group," I offered once more, forcing a sweet smile.

Finally, he consented, "Ah…why not. Can't hurt nothin'." He slowly moved several yards away.

I approached the dark young man cautiously. When I was close enough, I looked up. He was tall and strong from long hours of hard labor. Short black hair and a close beard surrounded a gentle, but mature face. His expression was worn and nervous. Blood still seeped from his lip where the taskmaster had punched him. He wiped at it and then stared at the ground.

"Who are you?" I asked gently. "I know we've met before…in Gettysburg. Do you remember?" The young mulatto man hesitated for several moments. "It's all right. I just want to help you," I offered.

He glanced up quickly as if to determine my honesty. After a few more moments, he stared at the ground and whispered, "You are the daughter of James Matthews, aren't you?"

I answered, "Yes, James was my father, but he passed away some time ago from illness."

He nodded, "I know, he…," the man hesitated again, then reached into the tattered folds of his minimal clothing and pulled out a piece of worn paper. He unfolded it slowly, handing it over to me. "I've carried this with me since the day it came. Just been trying to make sense of it."

Marcus   *July 1859*

I believe I may not be on this earth much longer and I need to be at peace with you. I should have done this long ago, forgive me. You should be a free man, and it is my fault that you are not.

Please, go to Gettysburg, Pennsylvania. Our home is the brick farmhouse with navy blue roof and shutters on Emmitsburg Road near town. Your manumission papers are hidden where my initials are carved into the house. I had planned to one day give them to you myself, but I didn't want my family to know. Then I just tried to forget my past. My daughters are living there now, I trust you to be discreet in your search of the papers. Go, claim your freedom.

James William Matthews

I stood silently, staring at Father's signature, trying to let all this new information sink in slowly. I cleared my throat, "So, you *are* my…brother?" The young man slowly looked up, not saying anything, then rested his eyes on the rows of dirt beneath his feet again. I continued, "The last time I saw you, you were trying to cut into the stone in the hearth with Father's initials on it. You think the papers are there?"

He nodded, still not making eye contact with me. Suddenly he spoke, "I don't know why he even wrote to me. He never cared."

I swallowed, not knowing what to say. It certainly seemed that way. I felt ashamed. But Father must have cared to some degree, deep down, or he would not have bothered with all of this. But his letter did seem like he was at war with himself over this matter. I handed the old paper back to Marcus, being sure that the overseer did not notice.

Marcus continued, "After I left Gettysburg, the day you found me in the house, I didn't know where to go. I wandered around for some months, did some odd jobs here and there. Then I decided to come back…Richmond is the only home I've ever known. I went back to the Matthews' plantation. I don't know why…I guess I thought maybe if I found something there it would help me figure out my story or maybe a different clue about my freedom papers again. That's when they caught me. I've been working this plantation for over a year now." He turned to look out across the fields. I grimaced as I noticed fresh whip marks across his muscular back and older scars beneath those.

"Why didn't you come to get your papers right after Father died?"

"I didn't know what to do. It was all so new and unknown. And my mother,…uh…the woman he left me with as a child, was old, and I had been caring for her. I always acted as her slave of course being in the South, but I was a son to her. When she passed on, nothing else was holding me here so that's when I left for Gettysburg. I wanted to know about my past." He was very well spoken, I noted. His "mother" must have educated him as she raised him.

I sighed, and after a long moment I decided, "Marcus, I'm going talk to my husband. I want to go back to Gettysburg and find the papers for you. It's only right. After the way Father…," I looked down at my gloves, "You could've been a free man for many years now." I continued, "President Lincoln freed the slaves in January this year, but it doesn't change anything for you…at least not immediately. I believe the only hope for the slaves in the South is to wait until Union troops come and free them…otherwise, you will still be treated as a slave no matter what the President has decreed. And who knows when or if the Union will be able to overtake Richmond. But if you have your manumission papers from Father, I believe you could be free right now." I paused contemplating, "I have to go back and find them."

Marcus looked up, his dark eyes, though still filled with pain, held a glimmer of hope in them.

To Risk All for Truth
Chapter 15

Amy

May 1863

THE DRIZZLING RAIN that had persisted throughout the day had finally come to a halt. As I stood on the terrace, staring out between the solemn weeping willows toward the entrance onto the Morgan's property, I felt the presence of someone behind me. Glancing quickly back, I saw Peter just a few feet away, a look of concern on his face as he watched me. Nodding a silent welcome to him, I turned back to gaze disheartened again at the vacant walkway.

"It's only been two weeks, Miss Amy." Peter stated, gently stepping up beside me to place his hands on the railing.

With a sinking feeling, I sighed, "I know."

"They'll return…in time. You've been very quiet these days." I noted the hint of concern in his voice, "No doubt you've had much on your mind. Are you all right?"

Solemnly, I contemplated the words I knew I must finally speak after so many months of wondering and waiting, "No. No I'm not." I admitted, turning to face him. I studied his ever serene, yet friendly, countenance. Peter possessed such an air of ease and openness that had always made, otherwise difficult, conversations feel simple and undaunting. Patiently, he waited in silence for me to elaborate.

"When you explained the correspondence between Jane and Kelsey, you made a declaration that's been on my mind…'this was all for the glory of the South.' And though I'm beyond relieved to discover my fiancé's loyalty and honor, in the respect that he has remained true to our engagement, I cannot shake this terrible nagging."

"About?"

The weight on my heart grew even more heavy as I tried to find the right words. Sighing again, I plunged into my troubled thoughts, "What other deeds have been concealed under the guise of 'the cause?'" Peter's brow furrowed as he tried to understand what I was alluding to. "So many secrets, so many mysteries, so many hidden deeds, dark shadows lurking in the woods, secret messages, the mysterious murders of innocent civilians." I continued frustratedly, "You know what I've witnessed Peter, as you were right there alongside me. Though you've explained your reasons for joining the Confederacy and even explained, as you see it, the 'cause of the South', in such an honorable way, *yet*, you've never once mentioned those horrific crimes, never once tried to deny them!" I exclaimed, astonished at the idea. Peter had slowly hung his head and I could read a rather painful discomfort on his face. "Now I ask you, how can I forget the horrific evil I have seen carried out against the innocent? How can I turn my back on murdered civilians and pretend I didn't see the black hoof prints in the snow, the black blades sunken deep into the chest of simple farmers, women and children alike? How can I forget the scenes of the tortured, mutilated and burned bodies?"

Choking on the tears now streaming down my face at the horrific nightmarish memories, I had to stop. Quickly averting my focus to the calm branches of the willow trees waving in the slight breeze, I composed myself. Overwhelmed, exhausted and defeated, the words came in a whisper, "How can I look into the face of the man I love and pretend I don't see the bloody stains on his hands and hear their cries for mercy ringing in my tortured mind? Would I have any integrity, any honor, if I were to simply forget the wrongs I have seen done?" Still unable to look him in the face I added gently, but painfully, "I've respected you, Peter, more than anyone in the Confederacy, you've shown me kindness, mercy, even the most unlikely friendship. Yet, how can I even trust you now if you were to deny such atrocities, when in my mind you have been linked with the perpetrators of such crimes? How am I to trust any of you, unless I see the evidence of your innocence? But then, how can you possibly be innocent? Even if I wish it so, I *do not* see how."

When I was finally able to look at him again, our eyes met. A deep sadness was in his eyes that I had never seen, yet no sign of repentance.

"I suppose that's something you must discover on your own. If you are to truly believe in our innocence. I don't blame you at all for your questioning or doubts. You have every right to them after all you've witnessed. How can you trust even a word out of our mouths after what you've seen and believed for so long? You've been betrayed and lied to in a sense that Kelsey was afraid to trust you with the truth from the beginning. Perhaps he was wrong to keep it from you, perhaps not. Nevertheless, trust has been broken. You've only seen us in the way Anderson wanted, the way he painted the narrative for so many. And now you must decide who the truly guilty party is, yet you cannot base that decision from merely our words…nor Anderson's. You must seek and find the truth for yourself. There's a lot at stake here Amy…the truth. And it must be seen and revealed."

In the dead of night, the darkness that enveloped me created a mood as forlorn as the bleakness of my mind. A dim red glow smoldered in the ashes before me as I sat, knees to my chest, curled on the floor, deep in a mental struggle. My mind would never be at peace until I had discovered the truth for myself. And I knew the only way to find the answers was to go back to where it all began.

* * *

June 1863

Heart pounding, I slid through the small crack in the barn door and silently approached the only occupied stall.

"Easy boy," stroking the sleek gelding's neck, I gently began slipping the black bridle over his head.

Hoisting myself up onto his tall back, I pulled tightly as he jerked forward excitedly. "Not yet," taking a deep breath, I let it out slowly to calm the fast pace of my heart. I closed my eyes, preparing myself. Leaning forward, I opened my eyes and whispered into the gelding's ear, "I need you to fly like the wind."

Then with one swift motion, I released the tension on the reins, kicking my boots into his flanks. The powerful animal surged forward flying from the barn and almost before I could realize it, we had reached the front gate. The guard posted there, now standing in the entrance, shouted, "Identify yourself!"

Undeterred by the obstacle in his path, the war horse charged forward and, at the last second, the guard leapt out of the way, the frantic shouts behind us fading quickly. Clinging as tight as I could to the long mane whipping wildly in my face, I tried to direct the gelding through the narrow street away from the town and toward the hills north of Richmond. Slowly the city faded behind us, and with one last look back I watched as the trees closed in around me and Richmond disappeared into the darkness.

Days passed as I traveled, relying only on my experience and the compass I'd snatched to guide me home. Too afraid to ask anyone for help I stayed clear of any towns and cities, where any stranger could be a spy. The world had become a strange place, neighbor distrusting neighbor...even when I did come upon a lone traveler on the road, I kept my head down and neither they nor I would speak a word as we passed. Camping out in the dark forest, I resisted the urge to light a fire and nervously clutched the knife to my chest at every unusual sound in the night.

As I moved among the shadowy pine trees, the wind whispering through their branches, I suddenly sensed someone watching me. Turning sharply, I glanced back, but saw nothing except the quiet forest. So, I continued. The hiss of the wind whipping through the pine needles was the only sound as we plodded cautiously forward. For nearly an hour I couldn't shake that strange but familiar sense that I was being watched. To my distress, I realized that it would soon be too dark to travel, and I would be forced to make camp. Exhausted, I fell asleep, but suddenly awoke in a fearful state. Quickly I scanned the darkened forest, with only the moon to illuminate the evergreens that surrounded me. Just then, a sudden movement caught my attention and there through the trees, I saw him. The outline of a dark rider. I dared not even breathe but squinting kept my eyes on him. Then, as if by magic, he vanished. Morning dawned and, as quickly as I could, I mounted the black gelding and resumed my course once more. By noon I heard the unexpected clattering and sounds of a military encampment. As I nudged the gelding forward cautiously, I saw through the trees a Union infantry camp that was quickly packing up to depart. I watched curiously, keeping within the shadows of the forest, as the camp was packed, and the regiment hastily began their march northward. Confused at their presence, I veered away from them. Hours later, I nearly stumbled upon an entire brigade of Union soldiers also heading in the same direction. I waited in the trees for an hour to be sure I wouldn't be seen. Passing through forest, I could see fires of military camps just outside a nearby town's limits.

What are they doing here? And headed up north? I thought the war was in Virginia... Weary, I pushed the thought aside, only longing to be home again and perhaps, just maybe, with Elizabeth. *Was she still alive? Had she made it back home?* A tear slid down my cheek at the thought of how I had seen her last. After several more hours of hard riding, I finally read the beautiful words on the distant sign: Gettysburg 1 mile.

North to Gettysburg
Chapter 16

Elizabeth

WHEN I ARRIVED back at the little townhouse in Richmond, Nathan was out in the blacksmith shop working on a customer's project. I nervously, yet determinedly, wrung my hands as I approached him. He was plunging the iron into the coals; it glowed red hot as the flames licked around the metal. Knowing he was focused on his present task, I sat down quietly so as not to disturb him. He wore a leather work apron, and his usual attire of soot-covered clothing. It was not my favorite thing to try to clean those smudges from his clothes. I smiled softly to myself and then watched the intensity on his tanned face. His strong jaw set fast, those eyes so cold and blue. He looked so much like he did those first days when I had encountered him in Gettysburg, full of determination and focus.

It was intriguing to watch him work. Watching the immovable iron suddenly become bendable and morph into something new. It was through the heat, fire and pressure that the iron was molded into what it was meant to be, a tool useful to its master. As I watched I noted the similarity in our lives. We did not want the fire, the heat, the pressure in our lives. But if we allowed ourselves to be molded by the Craftsman through the trials…we would come out of the fire a more…worthy vessel; useful to the Master, prepared for every good work.

My mind snapped back to the present moment and the news I needed to tell Nathan. He plunged the newly shaped iron into cold water, it sizzled loudly, steam rising quickly around it. After a little while, he set his tools down and straightened up the shop for the night, dousing the fire. I stood up, waiting patiently. He removed his leather apron and was wiping his hands on a rag nearby.

Without looking up, he said, "How long were you going to sit there without saying anything?"

I tilted my head and teased, "Oh, I don't know. I was quite enjoying myself just watching you."

Nathan chuckled, bashfully. "I just can't seem to get all this soot off my hands…," he approached me still working on them with the old rag. "Maybe if I just-," suddenly he reached up and swiped at my face with both filth-covered hands.

I squealed, "Ah! Nathan, no! Please! You're filthy!" Trying to escape him, I went from laughing uncontrollably to trying to maintain some dignity. "Nathan! The neighbors!" I hissed, looking wide-eyed toward the Amerson's house, half expecting to see them once again watching from their windows.

Nathan lifted his hands in surrender, laughing. "All right, all right," the smirk still full on his face. Putting his arm gingerly around me, he led me back toward the house.

"You know, *Sir*, there are some days you can be so aggravating!" I tried to sound stern, holding back my smile.

"Oh really?" Nathan raised his eyebrows, staring down at me as we continued toward the house.

"Yes! I liked you much better when you were distant and…*mysterious*." I furrowed my eyebrows at him. Nathan looked as though he wanted to reply but didn't know what to say. Then a smile broke over my face as I glanced up at him. Grinning back at me, he playfully swiped a little more soot on my nose. I slapped his shoulder, feigning frustration.

* * *

I hadn't forgotten the conversation I needed to have with Nathan. It was just so rare for him to have those moments of being carefree and playful, that I didn't want to quench his spirit. I waited until after we had some time to relax and eat dinner. As we sat in the parlor that night, watching the fire crackling in the hearth, I brought up the day and how I had met my half-brother on a plantation…working as a slave. Nathan's brow furrowed as I expressed my desire to go back to Gettysburg to find the manumission papers that would free Marcus.

"So, are you planning to just take the papers to his master and tell him to free your brother?"

I sighed, "No. Well, I don't know. I'm not sure how to go about it…legally. All I know is I can take one step at a time. The first step is to go to Gettysburg and find the papers."

Nathan scratched thoughtfully at the roughage that had begun growing on his chin lately. "I hear rumors of the Rebel Army beginning an invasion of the North. I don't like the idea of you going alone." He paused for a few more moments. "I'll speak to Colonel Brandt. Perhaps he can find someone to escort you. He may at least be able to find a safer route for you, away from any moving armies. More than likely they will head for the capital. You should be in no danger," he mused. I nodded quietly, leaning into his shoulder. It had been a very full and exhausting day. Though it had only been a few months, I felt excited to see my beautiful town again…the farmlands and my old home. The drastic difference between this city of Richmond and my country town had made the time seem longer since we had left.

* * *

June 1863

After a good night's rest, and a warm breakfast in a comfortable little inn, I joined another small group of people waiting for the next carriage to continue north. The road was long and dusty. Eager to arrive in my hometown as soon as possible, I traveled in several carriages, riding for a minimum of twelve hours each day. It was hard and my body was weary of the jolting and jerking of the coach. Yet, it was all worth it when I saw a small wooden sign on the third day stating: Gettysburg 10 miles. Smiling, I stared out the window and watched the road pass by. Oh, how good it would be to see everyone again and how peaceful to walk the beautiful gently rolling hills that enclosed our little world. As my mind wandered through the blissful childhood memories, I hardly noticed the time passing by so quickly. During a stop, I eagerly jumped out of the carriage, the warm breeze whipping around me.

"Sir, if you don't mind, I'd like to walk the rest of the way to Gettysburg," I announced.

The man wiped his brow with the back of his hand, "You sure, Miss? It's nearly night fall."

I nodded cheerfully, "It's but two miles." I always loved walking slowly to our home, taking it all in.

"Your choice," he clucked to the horses, and the carriage moved past me up the road toward Gettysburg. I knew I could have gotten there faster, but I just wanted to soak it all in. The sun slowly disappeared to the left of me as I walked toward home. After a while, I pulled my fan out of my bag and began waving it intensely. Even the night was hot. I continued up Taneytown Road. A voice suddenly rang out through the dusk.

"Who goes there? Speak now, or I'll shoot!"

My heart jumped, "Please! Don't shoot!" My throat went dry. *What is happening?* More voices muttered in the darkness. My eyes began adjusting. Vaguely, I saw soldiers lined against the fence rails. One of them approached.

"What are you doing out here, Miss?" he asked in astonishment.

I stuttered, "I'm on my way home…to Gettysburg."

A few chuckles ran through the line of men. The soldier in front of me motioned for me to walk toward the other soldiers.

"Miss, haven't you heard? Lee and the whole Reb army is up here!"

My breath caught in my throat, "What?" I cried in bewilderment, "Here?" I knew there were rumors of the armies moving north, but why come to this sleepy little town?

The soldier confirmed it. "They're camped near Chambersburg. I suggest you get into the middle of town and fast. Or better yet, leave town. This is no place to be." The urgency in his voice startled me. Quickly the soldier called for an escort and two men took me into town after I insisted on staying. Moving past the fields, I watched in wonder. Soldiers were everywhere.

The young soldier took me as far as Middle Street. Walking through, it seemed as though the town was deserted. *Did the people evacuate at the rumor of battle?* In the darkness, only a few houses showed signs of occupation. An apprehensive feeling suddenly overtook me, and I decided to stop at the Denny's, not knowing where else to go. Coming up to the townhouse, I knocked on the door.

Mrs. Denny's anxious face soon appeared. "Oh! My dear girl! Elizabeth! You're here! Oh, come in, my dear, come in!" The woman pulled me in and immediately sat me down on a chair in the parlor. "Oh! The Rebels are coming! The Rebels are coming! They even came into town earlier today and stole supplies. Oh, my dear, everything is turning out for the worst! I don't know what shall happen to us all!"

"Mrs. Denny, please, calm down," I said, feeling quite anxious myself. "Now, what happened?" I asked, laying a hand over hers as we sat face to face near a crackling fire.

Drawing in a deep breath, she began, "Well, I was walking about town, you know, just running my little errands, minding my own business, as I always do, when I saw the soldiers in gray in town. Oh, I was quite frightened as you can imagine, my dear. They went straight to the town square and…do you know what happened then, my dear? Well, they threw poor John Barnes in his very own prison, that's what happened!" She emphasized, slapping my leg and looking at me satisfactorily. "Now they have pulled out and are somewhere near Chambersburg, I hear. It's a good thing our men got up here as quickly as they did, for who knows what could have happened!" Nodding silently, I slowly took in the dramatic scene she had described. She seemed rather disappointed that I did not jump out of my chair and fly about the room in terror. So, she began her tale again in greater theatrical detail.

"It was a gloomy summer's eve…," Mrs. Denny leaned forward, "Mr. Denny and I were closing up the shop for the night. When a band of renegade Rebels came riding through the town, whooping and hollering fiercely! I, of course, rallied my courage and stood my ground. They began pillaging and plundering the town like the Vikings of old, I tell you! They took whatever they could get their hands on. Once they found our shop, they took all the food they could carry. I myself had to save Mr. Denny from being nearly carried off in the raucous!" Mr. Denny peered over his newspaper at his dramatic wife, with the ever-indifferent expression he wore on his thin face.

What a picture she painted. If it wasn't for the gravity of the situation, I might have burst into laughter. She continued, standing up and making dramatic demonstrations throughout her story, "I heard from a reliable source, that the men of our town did what they could. They rallied together a little band to oppose the invaders and tried to stop them, but to no avail. Why even I took up arms against the ruffians!"

With curiosity, I looked over at Mr. Denny again just in time to see him roll his eyes. Of course, Mrs. Denny would cast herself as the heroine of such a tale.

"I do believe the entire Rebel Army has found us. Indeed, I do, my dear! Why, they even stole our horses!" My eyes shot up in an instant. *Not Shadow...* If I could only get to our house and see if all was well. Perhaps tomorrow. Yes, perhaps tomorrow the Rebels would have moved on and all will be well.

"Well, then," she looked me up and down and sat back in her armchair. "Where have you been? What brings you back to Gettysburg."

I looked down at the floor, realizing with amusement the reaction that Mrs. Denny would have if I told her I had come to find the manumission papers for my mulatto half-brother. I knew I could not tell her the details, because I wanted to protect my family, so I would just give her a little something to keep her wondering. The reaction was just what I had hoped for. Mrs. Denny drew back, her eyes growing wide. Slowly standing up, she continued to stare at me, backing away toward the door.

Finally, when she had found her voice, she croaked, "Oh...I see...," she glanced around and began fidgeting, "Oh my...oh dear, dear, what shall become of this?" I watched in amusement as she began nervously pulling on a shawl and bonnet. "Stay here, my dear girl. You may have the guest room, for I know you shall not be wanting to walk about in the town at this time of night. It is not proper for a lady of good breeding. I shall return shortly. I have some business to attend to." She turned the knob on the door.

Suddenly a hand pulled her back. "Oh no you're not," Mr. Denny said firmly, suddenly rising out of his chair. "I've had enough of you sneaking about town whispering rumors to the neighbors."

"Oh, let me be, Hubert!" The woman demanded, yanking the back of her dress out of the man's hand. I pressed my lips together, trying not to laugh. Soon the matter was settled and Mrs. Denny shockingly, but obediently, went to bed. I gratefully sank into the guest room bed, wondering what would happen with the coming of dawn.

War on the Homefront
Chapter 17

Amy

July 1, 1863

THE SMELL OF gunpowder hung heavy in the air amid the distant shouts
and noises of military breastworks and entrenchments being constructed on
McPherson's ridge. Terrified, I gently nudged the gelding forward, constantly
glancing over my shoulders, squinting into the darkness for any movement,
knowing at any second I could be confronted by a scout or a picket. There was
no way of telling which army lay before or behind me. But the horrid question
lingered in my mind. *Why are they here?*

Every second was agonizing, trying to make it to the first farmhouse along
the Emmitsburg road. I longed for that sight which, after what felt like another
hour of carefully inching forward cautiously avoiding any sign of a military
station, I finally rested my eyes upon. As the gelding trotted closer to the familiar
stone farmhouse, a strange feeling rose in my gut and all the emotions of relief
and joy dissipated. *Something's wrong.* My heart beat faster as I noticed the
darkness through the lace covered windows, the unkept gardens and the vines
reaching claw-like arms up to the windows which cast a daunting abandoned
atmosphere. A barn door creaked on its rusty hinges hanging loosely ajar.

Slowly, I dismounted the tall gelding and tied his reins to the fence post. I raised a hand, hesitated, then knocked lightly on the big wooden door, not a sound from inside. Stepping up on a big stone, I peered into the deserted house. Everything was gone. As if no one had ever lived there. Not even the beautiful Irish tapestry hung on the wall. The fireplace was empty, without a trace of wood. The ghost-like desertedness of the house caused a chill down my spine. *Where would they have gone?* Defeatedly I turned away. *Thomas and Elga McCarthy would not be able to give me any answers.* With one last look back at the old farmhouse, I climbed quickly back onto my mount and, disheartened, trotted up the silent road that was quickly being engulfed in the thick shroud of night. Both the McCarthy's and my own home were deserted and no signs that anyone had been living there for at least a year. But perhaps someone in town would be able to tell me just what had become of the McCarthys…and Elizabeth.

* * *

Light shown from the back entrance to the Phillips' home and onto two figures, silhouetted on the terrace. At the sight of my old friend my heart seemed to break within me. Stepping in closer, I could see the young officer gently kiss the top of her forehead. Staring up into his eyes, Sarah laid a hand on his cheek. A few words were spoken and the lovers reluctantly parted ways. Sarah watched as the young man disappeared into the night and then, sighing, climbed the rickety stairs to her family's home. Seizing the moment, I darted across the empty space, skipped over the creaking stairs, and pulled myself up onto the small landing. Silently I pushed my way inside to the little kitchen where my unsuspecting friend stood with her back turned toward me, kneading dough with the white ribbon of an apron tied neatly behind her back.

The floor creaked under my boot and Sarah whipped around, gasping in fear at the sight of the strange soldier in her kitchen.

"Who are you? What are you doing here?" She demanded, gripping a knife. Raising a hand to calm her, I reached up and pulled the cap off my head. After a few moments of staring in the dim light, I wondered if she even recognized me.

"Amy?" She gasped, a look of amazement on her face. She rushed forward, wrapping her arms around me and sobbed. "Amy, I had given up hope that you were still alive. When I didn't hear anything for so long, I thought...,"

Our eyes met and I tried to force a smile. "Sarah, do you have any news...news about Elizabeth?"

"She returned last year in August, and then Mr. Tyler came back several weeks later. Nathan Tyler, the blacksmith that used to live here!" Her voice grew in excitement with every word.

"Nathan Tyler?" Confused, I stared at Sarah, waiting for an explanation.

"Yes...Amy," Sarah gripped my hand and almost laughed, "They're married."

Shocked, I took a step back, "Elizabeth...married to Mr. Tyler?"

Sarah nodded before erupting again in a string of information, "Yes. She's doing well. They were married here in Gettysburg! In the fall! She told me the whole story of how she had come to be assigned to the same regiment in which he served, then escaped a prison camp where they were both held! Such wild tales! You'd never believe it! But they're not here anymore, Amy. They went back to serve the Union army in Virginia."

My mouth went dry, "Down south?"

"I'm not sure of the particulars. Elizabeth wouldn't say much. But oh Amy, we must write and tell her you're finally home! Oh, but I don't know where to reach her. Perhaps if we send a letter to the army there in general...perhaps it will make its way to her." Sarah bubbled on excitedly, "Maybe she can come home on an extended visit! That is, if her situation allows it."

Sarah led me into the parlor where she served some warm biscuits and tea, and I entrusted her with the story of my service, capture and escape, carefully keeping Kelsey's involvement a secret from her.

"I'm so glad you're safe Amy. You escaped those Rebel demons and now you can leave the past behind and stay here with us. You're restored to us." She squeezed my hands with tears in her eyes.

"Sarah...I can't stay here," I stated, staring down at our hands. "I'm going back to Colonel Anderson."

A terrified look came over her face, "Amy, no! Before I said nothing. I understood. But now, you can't go back! Look what you've been through!"

Staring into the heartbroken face of my friend, I gave her hands a light squeeze. "I don't expect you to understand this, Sarah. But I have no choice. I can't explain it all now, but perhaps one day I will. After this horrible war."

We talked long into the night. Sarah recounted every detail of Elizabeth's wedding for me. My heart ached that I had missed my own sister's wedding. She told me of how Elizabeth searched for me, trying to learn something about my whereabouts…trying to find me. Sarah told me of the horrible battle that had taken place earlier this same day, drawing vivid images of the scenes I had passed by on the road to my mind. The smell of death and gunpowder still hung in the air as an ominous threat to our tomorrow. After recounting my tale of hiding behind trees and ducking down alleyways to avoid the Southern forces that now occupied the town, Sarah urged me to hide in their cellar until the Rebel troops withdrew. But I knew I had to press on to find Anderson before I missed my chance. No doubt Anderson had to be nearby, with such large forces amassed here and Union General John Buford's cavalry battle that had just taken place.

Wiping away tears, Sarah recounted the terrifying invasion of the Rebel troops upon our town and with trembling hands she pointed in the direction the armies had finally clashed.

"Dear God, may we never see the like again. But I'm afraid Amy…the armies don't seem to be pulling out. Neither one of them. It does not bode well." Lifting her eyes to peer around the room, she sobbed, "I only hope, if something does happen tomorrow, or the next day, that our little town can pull through. I pray that this war will not take everything and everyone from us, as it has for so many already. Oh, Amy!" Covering her face with her hands, she became overwhelmed again, "My own dear brother…John, he's gone, Amy."

Stunned and horrified at this news, I held my friend as we both heartbrokenly mourned the loss of her brother and the friend I had known for so long. The shock of death would never end it seemed, as this dreadful war continued on and on. When the smoke and the ashes settled, would there be any left to drink from the cup of victory and peace?

Finally, we strolled out onto the terrace. Sarah pressed a sack into my hand. "Some food for your journey." She swallowed hard, unable to meet my gaze for a moment, "Anderson is nearby. William…Lieutenant Sanders informed me. As foolish as you, he snuck into town with hardly a cause."

Watching my friend's downcast expression, I waited for a moment. "Lieutenant Sanders…was he the one I saw you with?"

Sarah's head popped up; her face flushed. The memory of the late Major Sanders' nephew came to my mind. Smiling, I nudged her, "I hope he deserves you."

Turning a shade red, she said, "Go now. You may be able to catch up to them if you hurry."

Staring for a long moment into the face of my old friend, I felt a bitter sadness growing in my soul. "How I long for the past, to be as we were before this wretched war. Yet now we are all forced into horrible situations, painful losses…and difficult decisions that must be made." The bleakness of the night engulfed me as I sunk into the shadows of the forest.

The Hero Professor
Chapter 18

Elizabeth

July 2, 1863

THE DAWN CAUTIOUSLY peaked over the horizon and into the bedroom window of the Denny's townhouse, as if it too was afraid to see the aftermath of what had occurred the day before. Feeling groggy from the fitful night's sleep, I slowly sat up and took in my surroundings, recalling all that had happened the day before. My heart started to thud in anticipation as I remembered the familiar sounds of cannon fire and muskets. But this was different. This time the noise rang through our little town. Never would I have imagined hearing the screams of the wounded or feeling the ground of our land quake with cannon fire. I unconsciously began rubbing my hands together as I paced up and down the little room, whispering prayers.

We had spent the day before hiding in the cellar from the sounds of war. Once night had fallen, the hours seemed to tick by quietly. I had moved back upstairs to try to get a little sleep. The Rebels had defeated our troops and sent them fleeing through the town. Shots had rung out in the streets and the Rebel yell echoed against the town buildings. Mrs. Denny was in hysterics. Mr. Denny continued to quietly, but firmly, tell her to stay calm. We had stayed in the cellar all day, knowing our neighbors were doing the same. Some were even leaving the town all together. Mrs. Denny, though she had seemed so nervous and cautious in the cellar, suddenly came alive and rushed out as soon as quiet had settled over the town and began her night's prowl. Coming back quickly with news of several families leaving, she begged and beseeched her husband to do the same. And so, they left in the middle of the night…asking me to go with them.

But I couldn't. I had come here for a reason, I reminded myself. I still needed to get back home and find Marcus' manumission papers. How to do that at this point would be more complicated. I knew I couldn't just hide away though. I had seen war before, and I knew I could help. With two large forces assembling around our town…I felt this day there would be no small battle. There would be wounded…many wounded, and they would need my help. The longer this war went on the more their groans and pain were a burden on my heart. I couldn't turn my back on them, no matter how much the anxiety and trepidation of another coming battle weighed on me. I paced back and forth a few more times in the bedroom. Then I changed my clothes and headed determinedly out the door, into the dangerous streets and fields beyond.

* * *

Gettysburg, my refuge from all struggle, my haven of peace, had suddenly become a war-torn land. I felt vulnerable, as if there was nowhere safe in this world. I found an officer just outside of town and spoke with him about helping with the wounded. He led me to a medical unit, who then directed me to the far end of the Union line, pointing out a line of blue soldiers who had just come up the Taneytown Road. They were moving quickly to be stationed along the little barren hill. He said they would probably be setting up a field hospital behind the lines. The officer assured me they would need help, as they were just arriving on the field and hadn't much time to get organized. I made my way along the back of the little rocky hill and sought to find the unit's surgeon to volunteer my service. As I neared the crest of the hill, I stopped short, seeing signal flags and a general moving in the same direction. The general stood on a large rock, glasses in hand, watching the troop movements in the distance. A soldier beside him waved a flag, signaling to our troops in the distance. Standing on the small hill overlooking the fields surrounding our town, I thought of how I used to come up here, only a couple years before, and sit on this same hill reading peacefully. Now…the roar of war echoed through the once serene meadows and hills. The sun scorched the earth and I eagerly took refuge in the shade of the trees. A soldier suddenly approached my position.

"Uh, Miss, I suggest you find a safer place to be. We have reason to believe the Confederates will attack this position very soon." He glanced around, confused, "What are you doing out here anyway?"

"I was hoping to volunteer to help with the wounded or anything else which is needed." I recounted how I had served in the Union Army out West for some time. The soldier nodded, then added, "Well, I suggest finding somewhere safer in any case. The Rebs look like they're planning to come right this way." Taking his advice, I moved back into the wooded area of the little hill.

* * *

Before long, cannon balls whizzed through the air with a shrieking sound and rifles cracked in every direction. I still had not found a doctor to speak with and had hidden myself away behind some boulders on the far side of the little rocky hill. Now I looked down the narrow passageway between this hill and the larger one beside it. In the distance I could distinguish gray uniforms beginning to move up the valley, in an attempt to attack the left flank. I hurried back into the woods, wondering how I could do anything and why I had thought I should come up here in the first place. If the Rebels can take the left flank, surely, they would sweep down and take the whole Union Army from the rear by surprise. Suddenly, I saw a new regiment moving into the very left position to defend against such an advancement of the Rebels. I watched the young colonel's face as his superior gave him his orders. Something in his face, the calmness and determination, drew me closer in to listen.

"I place you here! This is the left of the Union line. You understand? You are to hold this ground at all costs!" Leaving the young colonel, his superior moved away to continue his duties. *Perhaps I could help here…somehow.* Somewhat hesitantly, I moved toward the young colonel. His men filed into line facing the bigger hill, so as to repulse the Confederates who would soon be coming up the slope. His face seemed set and his eyes fixed on the task ahead.

My voice shook as I dared to interrupt his thoughts, "Sir?" The colonel turned and seemed a bit startled at seeing a young lady on the battle line. "Is there any way I could be of some assistance? Helping with the wounded perhaps, reloading rifles?" Again, I quickly explained how I had helped in the army out West and that Gettysburg was my home and how I wished to help defend it.

The colonel's eyes softened, and he answered, "Certainly, Miss. Move farther back into the woods. At some point the men will bring you those who are wounded if they can. You can help my brother, John, and the rest of our medical unit there." Thanking him, I began to move away, when he called back to me, "What is your name, Miss?"

"Elizabeth Tyler, Sir," I answered.

"I thank you, Mrs. Tyler," he nodded, touching his hat.

"And you, Sir?" I asked shyly.

He answered, "Joshua Lawrence Chamberlain."

* * *

Finding the medical unit, I was able to help begin preparations for the wounded away from the battlefield, behind the two hills. The Weikert's farmhouse stood close by, some of the family was coming out to watch the hills beyond in horror. More Union troops were in the area as well. As I cleaned the long knives in a bucket of water, rolled bandages and prepared the other tools, I prepared my own heart as well. It had been some time since I had seen the wounded after a battle, but there was nothing that could ever remove those images and sounds from my eyes and ears. Nothing could erase the scars they had left in my heart, and the nightmares that still came occasionally when I least expected them.

The crack of rifles resounded from the crest of the little rocky hill nearby. Cannon fire boomed. The ground shook and trembled under my feet. My eyes shot to the top of the hills, but I could not see what was going on beneath the shade of the trees. I envisioned the young colonel again…with his orders to remain in position…no matter the cost. What bravery these men had. To know you had to fight to the death, there was no escape, no way for you to leave. It was fight or die. Kill or be killed. I shuddered, returning my focus to the awful preparations at hand. The fighting continued. The Rebel yell kept coming. They kept charging up the slope toward the Union left flank. They would not give up. They would not relent. They were fighting for their beliefs too. I could not deny their bravery.

After doing all that we could to prepare the field hospital, I took off toward the wooded back end of the rocky hill. I had learned that tree moss was good for wounds. Bringing a basket, I maneuvered cautiously around the bottom of the hill and began collecting the green moss from the base of the trees. The smoke from the musket fire wafted down through the woods, the smell of it hanging thick in the air. On and on the Rebels kept charging in the distance. *Surely our men are running out of ammunition by now*, I thought as I listened to the discharge of many muskets. The screams of the wounded were already meeting my ears. What drove me onward, I do not know, but soon I was able to vaguely see the forms of the Union line guarding the flank.

After a lull, I heard a call coming from the Union line, "Bayonet!" The clang and clatter of steel echoed around the hills as the boys in blue fastened their bayonets onto their muskets. I could see in the distance our flag moving, leading the men. Suddenly the whole blue line swung down the slope, counter attacking the Confederate onslaught. Then they disappeared from my sight, but I could hear the deathly charge, the screams, the retreat, the chaos...

* * *

The wounded had arrived. We had taken over the Weikert farmhouse and the wounded lay inside the building and around the outside. The family offered their services to the surgeons and the other nurses who had come. They baked bread for the men and assisted in many ways. After my experience in the battles out West, and now with the knowledge I had gained from the countless hours of pouring through Dr. Philips' medical books, I felt confident in my work as I assisted the surgeons that evening. Yet, even though I had seen this before, my eyes still filled with tears at their groanings and my heart wrenched as I listened to their pleas to die.

"Miss, assist me with this man quickly," a surgeon hurried me over to the family's kitchen table. I quickly began going through the motions, assisting the surgeon as he began preparations to work on the young solider. "Administer the chloroform," the surgeon directed. The young soldier groaned loudly and began to resist the surgeon as he held him down. My stomach shrunk.

"Shhh, there now. It's all right. We're going to help you," I tried to control my shaking voice as I soothed him. The chloroform began to take effect as the soldier calmed down.

"Now, quickly." The surgeon began removing the man's arm. I shuddered and looked away. To my horror, the young man suddenly jumped upward and began screaming in pain. The surgeon yelled for me to help restrain him. Tears began streaming down my face as I held the young man as best I could. Even in his weakness, it took all my strength to hold him down. I felt myself rise above my own frailty, and though I felt I could faint if I allowed myself to, I kept calm…for his sake, and spoke words of comfort continuously in his ear as the surgeon performed his grievous task.

The young man jerked and screamed over and over again, "Why can't I die? Dear God, I want to die! Make me die! Please God! Please!" Finally, he became unconscious from the pain. As soon as his body went limp, the full force of the situation hit me. My stomach lurched and my legs collapsed beneath me. I grasped onto the table. The surgeon had just finished. I fought to keep my vision as I helped finish wrapping the soldier and stop the bleeding. I needed to leave. My throat was so tight I could barely breathe. I gasped and moved to a different room. I had to control myself. Who would help them if I couldn't even stay calm myself? *Do it for them. You have to do it for them.* Sinking to the ground, I gasped for breath and held my mouth as my stomach flipped continuously. But I couldn't pause for long, there were more, many more who needed my help. The surgeon called to me, as they moved the young soldier from the table and replaced him with another suffering soul. *I don't know if I can do it again. How much more can I handle?* I shook my head in desperation. *You have no choice. You have to do this.* I commanded my aching soul. All through the night we worked, we alternated taking small naps from pure exhaustion. I slept sitting on the floor, leaning against a door frame. Upon awakening in the middle of the night, I took a little bread. My stomach could not handle much. As I made my rounds by candlelight, checking on those recovering, I recognized the young man whose arm we had amputated. He was awakening and was groaning softly. I knelt down beside him and gave him some water.

Brushing back the sweaty hair from his forehead, I whispered, "It's all right now. You're on the mend." His eyes locked on my face and soon an expression of relief came over him. He relaxed and reached out a hand. I took it and held it in both of mine. After a little while of watching him to make sure he was indeed resting now, I began to pull away. He jumped and gripped me tighter.

"No! No, please don't leave me." He seemed to be in his right mind and for the most part he was calm, but afraid to be alone.

I smiled sadly and laid a hand on his blood-stained clothing. "You are not alone. I will keep checking on you. You're safe now." Seeing that he was drifting off, I began singing softly, trying to keep my voice from choking, until I determined he was fully asleep.

Amazing Grace, how sweet the sound
That saved a wretch like me
I once was lost, but now I'm found
Was blind, but now I see

The Lord hath promised good to me
His Word my hope secures
He will my shield and portion be
As long as life endures

When we've been there ten thousand years
Bright shining as the sun
We've no less days to sing God's praise
Than when we first begun

I arose quietly, straightened my dress and dirty apron, and moved forward to face the next assignment of that long, terrible night.

The Field of Fire
Chapter 19

Amy

July 3, 1863

"COLONEL, SIR," I saluted, trying to catch the attention of the officer who seemed too distracted to notice a lone corporal.

"What is it boy?" The officer, looking flushed and sweaty in the summer heat, gave me a disinterested glance.

"Sir, this is my hometown. I was on leave here-," the colonel rudely shouted something over his shoulder to a corporal who rushed away on an errand.

"Sir, please," I tried desperately to grab his attention, "I'm looking for Colonel Anderson of the 22nd Pennsylvanian Cavalry." Immediately he turned, his interest suddenly peeked,

"Anderson?" He huffed, "How should I know where a cavalry officer can be found? The man's off on his own mission. Cavalry are hardly ever around when the real fighting starts. It's up to the infantry to do the real work of driving the enemy back." Glancing back down at me, a look of pity briefly crossed his rough face, "Well…you should head three miles south of here. You'll find several cavalry units. Perhaps even Anderson, if he's man enough to soil his white gloves."

Wearily I turned, weaving between the many officers and soldiers that crowded this long stretch of open ground behind the low, roughly made stone wall. Turning, my eyes caught sight of the lonely brick building in the distance. It looked so out of place, so surreal amongst all this military presence. My heart sinking, I said goodbye to that beautiful yet painful sight once more.

Almost instantly as I turned, a thunderous roar exploded through the air as an unexpected cannon shell struck the ground several yards in front of me, sending earth and men flying up and backwards. Sudden blood curdling shouts and screams filled the air.

"*Get down!*" An officer shouted though nearly every soldier was already instinctively clinging to the earth as if it held their very soul.

Without even a second of warning, the ground began to shake with the roar of hundreds of cannons being fired in repetition, without reprieve.

Lying flat, covering my head with my arms, I tried to shut out the horrific thunder of the big guns. Another shell struck the ground unnervingly close and dirt rained down upon me. The air darkened with the smoke from the federal cannon as the artillery scrambled to return fire. The fumes of sulfur powder from the big guns only added to the thickening haze, making it nearly impossible to see the Confederate cannons bombarding us from across the mile-long stretch of farmland.

"I knew it was too quiet this morning," cursed a private nearby, as he quickly began loading his rifle. Our eyes met as I watched him anxiously ramming the bullet down the muzzle of his gun.

"Cavalry?" he stated more than questioned, as he observed the yellow stripe down my pants.

Nodding shakily, I jumped again covering myself as another shell burst overhead, raining burning shrapnel down.

"Boy you are in the wrong place at the wrong time," the private stated roughly as he finished loading and turned to lay flat in wait.

"Stay down boys! Stay down! Artillery will make 'em pay," shouted an officer moving around, hunched over, behind the line. No one could know exactly what would happen next, but this huge bombardment could only be the prelude to a more terrible calamity to come.

Trembling, I watched and waited, as flashes of fire burst through the thick smoke, followed instantly by a terrific thunder. Fearfully scanning the line of trees for a glimpse of the enemy, I wondered, *how could this be happening?* The beautiful open farmland and fields I had walked through so many times, the peaceful hills surrounding us that had been my sanctuary as a child, had become the scene of a terrible battle now, and there was nothing I could do but helplessly watch the destruction.

Then, amidst the chaos, the shouting, the screams of pain, through the thick of the sulfur and smoke came a most serene sight. Calmly a big war horse walked as if deaf to the noise of bursting shells and chaos of war around him. Steadily a corps general guided him, cutting a path through the rushing officers, the explosions, and the dirt raining down around us. His serene, yet unwavering, presence created a picture of true courage as he stared ahead into the terrifying barrage. His less than calm staff officers were surrounding him and trying to quiet their jumpy steeds.

A panicked officer ran up to the general, clearly fearing that the target of a mounted officer would be too easy to spot. Taking the bridal of the horse in his hand he pleaded, "General Hancock, please! We cannot spare you!"

The determination on the general's face was unwavering, undeterred by the man's fear he answered definitely,

"There are times when a corps commander's life does not count."

Stunned by the general's courageous answer, I stared in awe. How could such a high ranking general, so worthy of the protection he could easily seek, willingly put his life at risk to sit in the open attack of a heavy bombardment, amid his soldiers who lay cowering on the ground?

The storm of cannon fire, shells bursting, canisters shrieking their deadly warning through the air before bursting overhead, continued on and on for hours until there was suddenly an eerie, deathly…silence.

Then, the distant rattling of drums all inside the line of trees facing us echoed proud in defiance and then the Rebel cry, as the enemy formed in companies to cross the crater-filled smoking field between us.

"They're comin' boys!" A commander shouted.

With only a pistol on me, I rose, my hands hanging at my sides. My eyes searched the tree line until the first signs of gray appeared through the trees and slowly swelled into an exceeding army. Confederate artillery began to bombard our lines again, shooting high over the heads of the advancing Rebel lines. Lying in wait, the Union lines patiently watched as the Confederates, though coming under extreme heavy opposing artillery fire, pressed on.

With faces set like stone they marched, comrades falling to the left and right of them, cluttering the field with bodies upon bodies. Flags falling to the ground in the hands of their bearers, only to be raised again a second later. Given the command, the Union lines returned this display of determination with a volley of rapid musket fire from behind the stone wall, causing dozens more to fall to their knees as the bullets cut bloody holes into their faces and homespun uniforms.

The Union commander's shouts became distant to my ears as the Confederate lines continued to advance straight into the face of gun fire. Some coming face to face with the wide gaping hole of the cannon's black mouth. Written on the faces of the weather-beaten soldiers was a determination and courage I had never witnessed. Yet, a few younger ones quivered with fear, as they knew their short lives were drawing to a close. They were staring death in the face, knowing in their hearts these were their last moments, and still they marched on, ready to give their last breath for home and country.

As my eyes beheld the determined line of Rebel soldiers, I felt a strange softening in my heart and a great respect and admiration for these enemy soldiers. How could any man face such devastating odds, such paralyzing fear for anything but the greatest of convictions? Many of them were ragged, dirty farmers that had worked their own fields with their bare hands and the help of their sons, who now fought alongside them. They were fighting for something more…for an idea. *They're fighting for each other…*

A black hat rose up amid the chaos of the charging soldiers, they were exhausted, terrified, yet strong and undeterred. As the black hat rose on the end of a saber, I heard a distant shout "Come forward Virginians! Come on boys! We must give them the cold steel!" The soldiers seemed to rally, drawing strength from their heroic general's gesture. I strained but could not see the face of the valiant commander, yet his words echoed in my ears. A final shout resounded over the field, "Who will follow me?"

As volley after volley unmercifully poured into the bodies of the unyielding Confederate soldiers, I found myself standing, unshielded, in respect for the courage displayed in this unmatchable charge. The pistol I had unsheathed in fear, now hung from my hand before dropping to the ground. Hand to hand combat broke out, as the unrelenting soldiers reached the Union lines or were charged upon. Unable to move, I stood like a statue, watching in horror as brothers, neighbors…Americans…brutally slaughtered each other like animals before my unblinking eyes. The form of a big burly soldier came rushing, a bayonet leveled at my heart.

"Get down!" A scream pierced my ear as I was shoved to the floor. A gunshot sounded and the Rebel soldier fell on top of me, knocking the wind from my lungs. His eyes were wide, full of pain as he choked. Quickly pulling myself out from under the now lifeless form and gasping for air, I scrambled to my feet. The Confederates were overtaking our position and some Union soldiers began to flee. Rushing to the big guns the Rebels eagerly began to turn them upon us. But then I heard a rallying shout and the overrun Union soldiers charged forward, fighting back their brave enemy until the Confederate soldiers had no choice but to surrender, or…turn back in a frenzied retreat. Many were shot down as they ran or crawled back, or were captured on that blood covered field, strewn with bodies.

As the sound of gunfire began to quiet, Confederates raising their arms in surrender, some wounded, were being helped over the stone wall. The hills and forest opposite us lay in silence, commanders no doubt in stunned silence at the devastation left before them. Only a few out of the thousands that had so valiantly charged, struggled back to the Confederate lines. The heroic attempt had ended in disaster. The horrific battle had ended, with so many losing their lives on that field of smoke and fire.

The sun was beginning to set, though the dark clouds that hung heavily over this bloody field blocked out the light. Scanning over the bodies upon bodies of dead, wounded and debris, I fell to the ground overwhelmed, my back against the hard-stone wall. I dropped my head into my hands shaking, as silent tears flowed down my cheeks. All around the screams of wounded or dying filled the air. The shrieks of a mutilated horse pierced through the thick smoke and then a merciful gun shot was heard. I covered my ears, blocking out the sounds. There was a hand on my shoulder, someone shaking me.

"Get up soldier," a rough voice ordered, "Find your unit." The man was gone before I could look up. Wearily, I pulled myself up, adjusting the straps carrying my ammunition and supplies. Wiping away the tears, I turned my gaze south down the littered road strewn with bodies, parts of bodies, random muskets and personal belongings.

Out of the darkness rose the desolate ruins of the brick farmhouse. Slowly, I entered the debris cluttered room, bits of bricks crumbling and crunching under my boots. Beside a destroyed wall stood a chair perfectly untouched, the cushion dented in as if someone had just risen from it. A brush and sewing kit sat on a chest, creating the feeling that the house was still living in the past. Standing motionless in the midst of what once was my home, I felt the weight of all that had become of this place. *What has this war done to us?*

Carefully, I collected a few items for my survival then, unable to bear the scene any longer, I maneuvered my way back out of the house and to the barn still standing beside it. Finding a small pile of hay, I laid down weary to the bone, and closed my eyes and my mind to the horrors that I had beheld that day.

The Day the Sky Wept
Chapter 20

Elizabeth

July 4, 1863

THE TOWN WAS deathly still. Many people had moved out or were still hiding in their cramped cellars. I had managed to find my way back through the fields to Emmitsburg Road. The day before had seemed it was nothing but cannon fire. The heavens and earth shook from the continuous roar. All through the day we had continued to work on the wounded and help those we could. The Rebels had made one last valiant charge across the field…the field right in front of our home. But the Union line had held fast, and the Rebels had begun their retreat back into the heart of the South.

The sight that met my eyes when I finally made it out of the Weikert's farmhouse and through the open fields was sickening. Thousands of dead lay in the grass, on the hill sides and in the crevices of the rocks. Trees were splintered and riddled with bullets. Some houses were completely destroyed. Military equipment lay scattered about the land. A pile of amputated arms and legs reached above the fence near the farmhouse. It was difficult to walk about for the number of bodies strewn across the fields. Yet, even worse than the bodies of the dead were those that were still alive and in agony. Detachments of soldiers moved about, retrieving the wounded and taking them to churches and houses that had all been transformed into makeshift hospitals throughout the town and the outlying areas.

The rain poured down around me, helping clear the air from the smoke and the smells of death. As I finally approached our home, my pace slowed. Finally, I sank to my knees and knelt down in the midst of the brick house. The water poured through very large gaping holes in the roof. It soaked my cotton gown and ran through my tangled hair. All around me lay the ruins of the only home I had ever known. Most of the walls seemed to have held fast, but there was still much damage. I felt as if I were looking at an old friend who had just passed on. Throughout the war-torn land surrounding our home, bodies of both men and horses lay still and silenced or writhing in pain as they were lifted onto makeshift stretchers. Rain mixed the wet earth with the blood of soldiers. Near the ruins of our house, Emmitsburg Road had changed into a shallow stream and on it wagons lumbered past, loaded with wounded soldiers. Their groans and screams echoed hollowly through the downpour as if I were in a terrible dream. Getting to my feet, I wandered aimlessly around the outside foundations and old walls.

The pain of all that had just transpired on our beautiful land shook me to the core…it was as if our house, now laying in ruins, was an image of what had happened to our country. I laid a shaking hand on one of the walls and clasped the other over my mouth. I had seen war before…but this was so much blood and death all at once…it overwhelmed me. So much in only three days, on our very own farmlands…in our very own quiet little town. *Would it ever be beautiful again? Would life ever be peaceful and good again?* It seemed this horror would linger forever on this land. The death, the blood, the pain-filled cries, the sound of cannon fire and muskets clattering would never be fully removed. I could still hear it all…in my mind. The tears spilled down my cheeks. Wiping at them with equally wet sleeves, I swiped at the sopping wet hair and tried to think of what was next, but my mind would only relive over and over what I had just seen here. I would never get used to seeing and hearing death, it would always clench at my heart and tear it to pieces. I watched in pain at the view in front of my eyes. All across the fields, in every direction were bodies upon bodies. Chills covered my skin. I shook my head and covered my face with my hands. It was too much…too much.

Suddenly, I heard a woman's voice crying softly from behind our house, nearly echoing my own. Even with all the noise and screams, this voice somehow reached my ears. I moved cautiously around to the other side. Sitting near the rubble behind the house, was a young Union soldier with blonde hair. I stopped short at the corner of the wall. Something inside me called me to go further, but I hesitated. Laying a hand on the wall, I watched. The soldier stood up, removed his hat and turned to the side. *But wait…that is not a young man…it looks like…Amy! It couldn't be. How is she here? My mind is too overwhelmed. Perhaps it is only a vision.* I reached out a hand and tried to call out, but my voice wouldn't come. The girl, disguised in a man's uniform, began to walk away into the fields behind our home. My feet felt like lead and wouldn't move. My heart pounded inside my ears. *Amy…Amy!*

"Amy!" Suddenly my voice burst out in a cracked, weak and weary tone. I finally lifted my feet and rushed toward the disappearing figure. *No, please don't leave me again. Please…Amy. I can't go on.* After several steps, the mud underneath my feet suddenly gave way and I fell to the ground, mud seeping into my dress. I tried to scramble to my feet, determined not to let the figure disappear from my sight. Sobs suddenly shook my body and I heard my voice scream desperately, "Amy! Please! Don't leave!" Still trying to wipe at the tears, I only succeeded in wiping mud onto my face. My eyes burned with exhaustion and emotion. As I looked up, the figure stopped. Then, slowly turned. The breath caught in my throat. Fifty yards away my eyes locked on the one face I had prayed to see for so long. The face that I didn't think I would ever see again. Those dear familiar eyes…the girl I had played with as a child and laughed and cried with as an adult.

"Oh Amy," I choked, frozen in place, shoulders shaking with emotion. Surely, my heart would die if she was only a vision. "Please be real," I whispered softly. Suddenly, the girl ran toward me, arms open wide and then I felt the warmth and strength of her hug. The tears streamed down my face, "Amy. Oh, it *is* you. It's really you!" I cried, sobbing onto her shoulder.

"It's me, Elizabeth." She choked, "It's me. I'm here." She held me tight and stroked at my soaking hair, "Oh, God, thank you. You're alive! Thank you, God.

Thank you." I clung tightly to her, fearing that if I let go, she would disappear. Looking up toward heaven, as the rain spattered my mud-stained face, I thanked God for bringing my dearest friend back to me and prayed that He would never take her away again.

* * *

I stared into the flickering flames, hardly believing this moment was real. Amy and I sat close beside each other with an old blanket around us. We had found a dry spot under the shelter of our old roof. We were able to build a small fire on the stone floor in the ruins of our home and now sat huddled near it. The rain still pattered all around us, and a thunderstorm lit up the house occasionally. Yet we were finally dry and warm. In this moment we forgot all the death around us and reveled in each other's company and all the stories we had to share. There was so much…so much had happened since I had seen her…nearly two years ago.

She told me of how she had disguised herself as a man and fought in battles. I thanked God for His protection over her life and wondered at how she had found the courage to do such a thing. With much pain, she recounted the events between herself and Kelsey starting from before I had even left for the army. She then described how she had been wounded and captured by Southerners and taken to their mansion. I was surprised to hear that she had seen me after I had escaped from the prison camp. I could not remember much after I had escaped, due to the delirium of the fever. Except, when she told me of the regiment of men in black who had captured her, I suddenly had a vague recollection of men in black surrounding me in a darkened forest. I had always thought it was another nightmare. But they were real, she had met them, she knew them. I had many questions; some she couldn't tell me the answer to. She told me she had seen Kelsey and he was alive and well. Something had changed about her though. I could tell she had seen much war and suffering and it had impacted her greatly. She seemed hard and cold in a way…it hurt me to see the light gone out of her usually bright eyes. As she told me what she could of her story, she seemed to be searching for something. Then suddenly I knew…however much I wanted her to stay, there was a gnawing feeling in my gut that she would not be here long.

Hours later, I told her about the army in the West, the battles and the friends I had made. I then recalled the horrors of the prison camp, my body still shaking from the trauma of all that I had seen. I told her of the friends I had lost…and then, finally, I told her about Nathan. Amy reached for my hand and fingered the slender golden band on my finger.

"So, the mysterious blacksmith, is it?" She gave a small laugh, "Sarah told me." Then she leaned closer, head resting in hands, eyes eager and expectant, "Tell me more."

I smiled, it suddenly felt as though nothing had happened, and that we had always been together like this. We had both changed so much, and yet we hadn't. We were still the very best of friends…just as we had always been. So many things in life change, but some things stay constant. The unconditional love of a few people, and the never changing love of our great God. Those are the things we cling to and hold fast to as anchors for our souls in the midst of storms. For the first time in a long time, I felt like maybe…just maybe…one day life *could* be beautiful again.

I put my arm around Amy, "It's getting late. We've been out here for hours." Glancing out, I could see distant lanterns, groups of men burying the dead. "Shouldn't we go back to the Denny's for the night?"

Amy groaned, "But I want to hear about you and Nathan." She smiled sadly, then poked at me playfully, "Come on Elizabeth, please…" It seemed in all this pain and disaster around us, we had this one evening to try and forget, to rest our minds and forget…just for one night.

I rolled my eyes, "Oh, all right, little sister. You always did get your way with me." We huddled together and nearer the fire. Amy laid her head on my shoulder. I began, "I shall tell you a tale of a handsome knight who rescued a damsel in distress." I glanced down at her, "I really was in distress mind you." Amy laughed, though a tear slid down her cheek. I held back the many emotions surging through me as well and continued, "Once upon a time…in a far-away land, there was a girl who let her prejudice blind her to what a man truly was…" As I recounted the story, it felt as though a healing balm had come to my soul as we both processed through all that had transpired during the time we had been separated. I knew I couldn't tell her any of what we were doing in Richmond, but I told her mostly of being in the army in the West. Healing began in my heart as we sat in the ruins of our old home, near a crackling fire, surrounded by what surely seemed one of the bloodiest battles fought on American soil.

* * *

The cold, hard floor made my body ache, waking me from a slumber of utter exhaustion. Rubbing the sleep out of my eyes, I quickly glanced around. *Where am I?* Then, seeing the sleeping form of my sister close by on the stone floor, all the memories of the past days came flying back into mind. We had fallen asleep, telling each other stories of our recent pasts. Even in the midst of such death and horror, I smiled as I watched my little sister sleep, so thankful to have her back. Standing and stretching, I walked to one of the openings in the walls of our home. It was still raining and hard to determine the time of day. *Perhaps it was just dawn?* I suddenly looked away as the sight of thousands of dead bodies greeted my eyes once again. There were still groups of men, who must've worked all night, burying the dead where they lay. It was a wonder they never entered our home or saw our small fire last night. Or perhaps they did. But surely, there was so much work to be done over the surrounding lands that they had not made it this far yet. Was it only my imagination, or could I still hear the screams and groans of agony? It seemed that at least this section of the fields had been harvested of most of its wounded. My stomach turned as I looked over the deadly fields. *How are we ever to give so many a proper burial? Will our town and farmlands become a massive graveyard?* Waking Amy, we somberly emerged from our home and began moving toward the town up Emmitsburg Lane.

"I do hear it." I said suddenly, stopping in my tracks.

"The wounded," Amy agreed. "From the hospitals set up in town...and the outlying areas."

"I can help," I then quickened my pace, determined to find them.

The sound was coming from so many different directions. Try as I might to keep my eyes on the road, they were constantly pulled to see the disfigured bodies all around me. Some limbs lying alone, some headless bodies, so many faces…some with fear, some with a smile, some in agony. Some hidden in bushes, where they had crawled to die alone. Some holding clumps of dirt in their hands, telling of the pain they had gone through at their time of death. Broken rifles and other equipment lay all around the fields as well. Horses too, bloated and torn apart just like their owners. I clutched at my stomach and fought back the tears. I would never get used to seeing this…never. Amy suddenly grasped my arm. I knew she was feeling the same. The soldiers on burial detail were digging shallow ditches right where the fallen lay. Sometimes so shallow that hands and feet still stuck up from the ground when they had finished. *How can we do this? We can't just leave them there!* I shook my head, anger suddenly coming over me. Not knowing what to do or how I could do anything…there were too many…too many dead. Gazing back toward the fields behind our home and the little hills beyond, thousands of bodies speckled the wet earth as far as my eyes could reach. I looked at Amy and she met my gaze, tears wet both of our cheeks. There were no words for this kind of horror. What was there to say? How could one describe one's feelings when seeing such a display of grotesque death and atrocities on humanity? War is a nightmare…

A Special Invitation
Chapter 21

Amy

July 4, 1863

THE HEAVENS OPENED to weep yet another heavy rainfall upon the bloody battlefields now abandoned by the deserting armies. They had come, waged their war, slaughtered, destroyed, devastated our town and now left their wounded and dead strewn on the fields that had once fed them. As far as the eye could see lay the mutilated corpses of men, beasts, abandoned equipment littering the fields, abandoned rifles and cannons amid the turned-up mud mixed with the blood of those who'd sacrificed their lives there. The smell of death hung like a cloud above and around us, overwhelming every inhaled breath.

"Why, God?" Breathless, I took shaky steps forward, watching speechless as my sister knelt on the ground beside a Rebel soldier, who was gasping for his last breath, his body half sunk in a muddy crater. The homespun gray uniform was stained with the blood of his comrades who lay nearly on top of each other around him. His hand held tightly to a torn photograph, as the soldier forced a few words between clenched teeth, blood dripping from the corner of his mouth. Grasping his hand, Elizabeth muttered words that were in audible to me, but I suddenly saw the man's face relax as his eyes locked on hers. There was a deep, long sigh and Elizabeth bowed her head as his eyes became like that of a porcelain doll, with no life or soul in them.

Elizabeth sat defeatedly on the muddy ground, a soft sob escaped from her lips into the thick air. Kneeling down, I wrapped my arms tightly around my sister's trembling form. She was hurting. She was broken and I had to be strong for her…be strong to be able to say what I knew would only break her heart even more. This battle in our very home had been almost too much to bear, leaving me hardly able to think past the horrific scenes that lay all around me. But I knew I must act quickly, as with every passing minute my opportunity to find Anderson was slipping away with the army's retreat. The heaviness in my heart felt more oppressive than the suffocating humid heat.

"This war has been very cruel to us," I whispered, pressing her head to my shoulder, "but one of the most painful decisions I've had to make has been leaving you." In the painfulness of the moment I couldn't bring myself to continue.

A soft whispering answer came from Elizabeth, "I know…I know you have to go again, Amy. I don't know exactly why, but I know there's a heaviness in your heart, you're searching for something. Even if you don't say it, I can see it in your eyes. I don't know what answers you hope to find, but I pray it will give you peace, because there is darkness hanging over you like a cloud." Our eyes met and I knew there was no hiding the effects from the dark sorrows, memories and questions that filled my mind. She was my sister, no matter how many months of separation passed, she would always know me better than anyone.

"I will try to send word when the opportunity presents itself. However possible. I just know I can't live peacefully until I find the answers I seek." Lowering my voice, I forced the words, feeling my throat constrict with emotion, "Wherever this war takes me, whatever my fate, I'll always be with you."

Riding over the destroyed fields, roads and farmland, I set my gaze straight ahead. Clinging to the mane of the sleek gelding as he galloped away from Gettysburg, I moved forward to the one place I believed would hold the key to all the dark mysteries.

* * *

Determination rising in my chest, I stared across the small space between the tree line and the tents encamped in the open field. At last I had reached him, Colonel Anderson. The summer sun glared down upon the regiment of the 22nd cavalry camp, now missing a significant portion of their men from the losses at Gettysburg. The cavalry entanglements had been some of the most gruesome scenes that had occurred during those terrible engagements. Staring hard at the old familiar flag, I nudged the gelding forward. Holding my breath as we left the shelter of the forest, we moved into the clearing.

"Halt!" There was an instant shout and I instinctively pulled up on the reins, my hands shaking. Glaring from under a dust covered cap, with a gun drawn, the private walked up close, taking the bridle in his hand.

"Corporal Michael Jones," I stated, doing my best to sound as irritated at this interruption as possible. "I'm reporting to Colonel Anderson, as his former aide and an escaped prisoner of the Confederacy." The soldier's eyes narrowed, skeptical of my claim. *Obviously, a new recruit.*

"Never heard of a Corporal Jones," he wagged his head arrogantly.

"Well then clearly you're not a seasoned soldier of the 22nd Cavalry, Private!" I shot back, leaning down over him. For a moment I wasn't sure if the soldier would buy my claim allowing me into the camp. The arrogance of the young private was getting on my already strained nerves. I sat back in the saddle, trying to take a reasonable, less defensive, approach, "Look, Private, if you just take me to Colonel Anderson, everything will be sorted out. Just do your duty."

Annoyed, the private released the reins and motioned me to follow him deeper into the camp. Still mounted on the tall black gelding, I saw soldiers stopping to study the new corporal in their midst and some began forming a group, a few familiar faces among them. Reaching a larger tent where a few officers were gathered outside talking, the private saluted and said something to a major, who eyed me suspiciously. The officer stepped over to me and I saluted the middle-aged man with gray at his temples.

"Corporal?" He looked me up and down and then studied the horse I had arrived on. "You claim you escaped from a prison camp?"

"Not exactly, Sir, I was singled out and held in private quarters."

The major rubbed his hairy chin and glanced over at the private. Finally, he stepped toward the tent and ordered, "Dismount and I'll take you to the colonel." Sliding off the tall horse, I breathed deeply to calm myself and handed over the reins to the private who stood glaring at me. The tent was hot, but the shade created some reprieve from the blazing sun now rising high in the heavens. I instantly recognized Anderson who, standing with his back to us, was studying some papers, unaware of our presence.

"Colonel," the major saluted, waiting for Anderson to turn, "This corporal was brought in by one of the guards. Says he escaped as a Southern prisoner and belonged to this regiment." Anderson turned finally; his interest sparked. The moment he laid eyes on me a look of shock came over his face.

"Corporal Jones?" He croaked, stunned.

"Sir," saluting, I waited for the colonel to compose himself.

"Corporal Michael Jones!" He stated again and shook his head, "I thought you were dead." The colonel dismissed the major from the tent and looked me up and down with an entertained expression on his face.

"I sustained a rather serious injury during the surprise attack. Miraculously, as you see, I made a full recovery."

"Impeccable!" Anderson smiled, dropping down into a small chair, "And you were held in a prison camp?"

Hesitantly, I chose my words, watching his expression as Anderson listened intently. "No Sir, I was singled out and kept in a Southern mansion."

Anderson leaned forward clearly intrigued, "Singled out? Because you were a staff officer?" he prompted.

"I believe so."

"And in whose house were you kept, Jones?" Anderson's expression had changed, and I sensed he was asking a question that he somehow already knew the answer to. With growing anxiety, I realized I had to give an answer that may perhaps endanger Kelsey and anyone near him.

Before I could open my mouth, Anderson smiled delightedly and leaned forward, "Let me guess. In the home of Seth Morgan?"

Taken aback, I tried to keep my composure, "Yes, Sir. May I ask how you knew?

An arrogant grin spread on his face, "Just an educated guess. I've known about Seth Morgan's involvement in the Phantom Regiment for, well, shall we say, a long time." As Anderson puffed on a cigar, darkness suddenly clouded his gaze, "He's been a thorn in my side for more years than I care to reveal."

"Sir?" seizing the opportunity to pry, I took a step forward, which snapped Anderson out of the dark mood that had suddenly beset him. "Excuse my curiosity, do you know the major personally?"

Glancing up, he paused before answering, "Major? He was a Lieutenant last I'd heard. Yes, well *Major* Morgan and I have some past history, Corporal, yes. He was once a pupil of mine." Anderson tapped the cigar on a metal tray, "I was an instructor at West Point. As a top graduate myself, I was naturally the youngest teacher at the military academy. Even before then I knew much about the Morgan family, though I would never associate with such people." He scoffed, tapping the cigar and thoughtfully narrowed his eyes. "The leader of this 'phantom regiment' remains a mystery…but I have my suspicions. What of you, Jones, what did you see while in the Morgan's home? Anyone they referred to as their leader?" Anderson studied me, twirling the cigar in his fingers, the smoke rising between us.

"No, Sir, I'm sorry." Pretending to be ashamed, I lowered my gaze hoping to hide my anxiousness.

Anderson took a puff, "Shame. He's like a bloody ghost, off spying on his own, appearing and disappearing. Rumors and tales about him grow and spread like wildfire. I'm surprised you never saw him down there…especially being in Morgan's house and all."

"I was kept in seclusion, Sir. I didn't spend much time among the Southerners. It was torture enough to bare their company the few times I was forced to, almost worse than any physical torture."

Anderson laughed, "Well, that I can understand." Suddenly rising, he patted a hand on my shoulder, "You've done well, Jones, you not only survived the battle and injury, but you've managed to avoid the enemy's tactics to get information. And all while never giving up the determination to get back to your regiment. No doubt keeping your wits about you, despite Major Morgan's brainwashing attempt. Believe me, I know how that Southern brat has worked on pushing his and his father's agenda from a young age." Anderson's eyes narrowed again, "I can see that burning hatred for the enemy in your eyes…you've become a seasoned veteran of the horrors of war, not the innocent timid lad who first joined us. You may be ready…," his voice trailed off and a strange smirk played on his lips. "Well, Jones, you'll have to give me a detailed account of your capture and what you saw and heard while you were a prisoner, but for now, get some rest. I'll give you your old post back; the lad I have now is a terribly stupid fool and you seem to have grown in intelligence and stealth. I'd welcome a replacement."

Just as I opened my mouth to protest being the cause of any demotions that would create descension, Anderson shouted out, "Major Flint!"

The major instantly entered and Anderson directed him to see that I was fitted with proper gear by the quartermaster. As I left the tent to follow the major through the encampment of soldiers, I wanted to breathe a sigh of relief, but I knew this was only the beginning of my road to discoveries. Once again, keeping my identity hidden would be a constant challenge.

Lying in my tent staring at the canvas ceiling, I felt more awake than I had all day. *So, what Peter had said was true. There was a particular reason for Anderson's creation of this regiment. And though Kelsey had escaped his notice, Anderson had clearly known all along of Seth Morgan's involvement in the Phantom Regiment. He had known Seth Morgan.* My curiosity rose at the strange connection between these two men. There lay between them a dark abyss of a mysterious, yet incredibly ominous, past and a deep-rooted hatred.

Rolling over anxiously, I explored in my mind the possibility that Anderson indeed could be hiding much more than a frightening hatred for the enemy. A suffocating feeling crept over me and I pulled back the tent flap to try and flush out the stagnant air. Though there was no relief from the equally oppressive atmosphere outside, there was the familiar feeling of unrest that haunted the camp.

Whenever night grew near, a strange tension seemed to rest upon every creature, man or beast. Even the horses seemed aware of something lurking in the darkness and the idea that at any moment our peaceful night would become a sudden nightmare, filled with shrieks and ghost-like figures descending upon us from the trees. Uneasy, the horses shifted about with ears perked, only dropping their heads to grasp a bite of hay before popping back up to glance about. I laid back against the rough blanket, trying to rid myself of the fear that at any moment this quiet scene could be in uproar. Finally, weary from the day's excursions, sleep overcame my eyelids.

A rough hand shook me awake. Terrified, I whipped out the pistol from under my blanket and pointed it directly into the sergeant's face.

"Easy there, Corporal! The colonel just wants to see you."

Catching my breath, I gently placed the gun in its holster and, once the sergeant had left, quickly rubbed a hand over my burning eyes and prepared myself. The colonel's tent was dark and filled with smoke as there was no wind to vent the air.

Anderson greeted me in an informal manner, looking rather disheveled. His shirt collar was unbuttoned and open, and his hair as if he'd been running his hands through it. He motioned me to relax, and with a wave of his hand he dismissed the sergeant. Moving toward a wooden box, he opened it and pulled out a small yet exquisite bottle and poured a bit of its contents into a tin mug.

"You'll forgive me for waking you in the dead of night like this. I couldn't speak to you earlier, for security reasons." Tossing the whiskey into his mouth he swallowed hard, "seems there's a spy behind every tree nowadays," he scoffed. Shifting uneasily, I waited to discover the reason for this strange meeting. Finally, he turned his full attention to me.

"I have a special detail of men I use to conduct, let's say, my more intense operations. Men of intelligence, ones who can keep this mission a secret, and who don't squirm at a gruesome scene, but have been hardened by the horrors of this war." Squinting, he looked me up and down for a long moment then added, "I'd like you to join us, Jones."

"Sir, I'm honored," my heart beat rapidly. Anderson raised a limp hand to silence my appreciation. "May I ask, Sir, what is expected of me?"

"For the sake of destroying the enemy…this 'phantom regiment'," he sneered then narrowed his eyes intently, "you must be willing to make great and difficult decisions. Blood must be spilled to obtain victory. By whatever means necessary we will trap these devils in a snare so deep not one of them will be spared. Instant revenge, instant victory…instant death to each one of them. First the leaders…then all the rest. Not all have the intelligence to see the sheer brilliance of my plan, but if you're willing to open your mind, I believe you can catch a glimpse of the beautifully ruthless and infallible trap I have set in motion. Your complete and unwavering loyalty is key, Corporal. You must be ruthless in your desire to destroy our enemy. You will learn in time what is expected of you. What do you say, Jones? Will you join us?" Studying my eyes intently, he waited for my answer.

"Yes, Colonel, you can count on me, Sir, I won't let you down."

A wicked smile spread across his face and he slapped my arm, "Good man. Let's see what you're made of."

We Take Increased Devotion
Chapter 22

Elizabeth

FEAR HAD CREPT into my heart before seeing Amy off. She had come and gone so suddenly. We had only had one night…one night to talk with each other. *What if I was too weak to handle her leaving again?* But I realized quickly that the fear would not overwhelm me, because now I knew the truth. That precious night of talking together, helping each other acknowledge what we had learned from our experiences, had somehow healed my heart moment by moment. I knew I had changed. I had healed and grown. Now I felt strong enough and ready for her to go her own way again. I thanked God for giving me that short moment in time with her. We had always been so close…always together. But now, we had our own lives to live. This time, I knew we would never be truly separated. Seeing her here again, alive and well, gave me comfort to know that no matter where our paths took us in this world, we would see each other again. *She wasn't taking a part of my life with her. I wasn't losing her.* I knew deep in my heart…a relationship like ours could never die, no matter the distance.

* * *

August 1863

Would I ever sleep through a whole night again? I stared out the window at the full moon as it streamed beams of yellow light onto the bedroom floor. Dangling my feet off the tall bed, I unconsciously rubbed my hands on the soft blankets, smoothing and re-smoothing them. I stepped onto the wooden floor and began pacing about the small room. I had been living in the Denny's townhouse since the battle. I had helped every day with the wounded, and every night their screams and scenes from the battles I had seen played over and over in my mind. Pulling out a fountain pen and piece of parchment, I sat down at the rustic writing desk. Nathan had heard of the battle and was very concerned for my safety. Thankfully, we had been able to write a couple letters back and forth at this point. After writing a rather long letter, I suddenly crumpled it up and tossed it aside. Laying my head in my hands, I sighed. I had to be careful, I couldn't write many details. For whatever was said in my letter could potentially be used against our mission if it fell into the wrong hands. I began again, this time a shorter one.

Nathan,

I wish you could be here with me. I'm afraid my stay will be of some duration… perhaps months…as there are an overwhelming number of wounded soldiers. I know I can help, and that I am needed here. It is comforting to see so many people willing to help them. Please do not worry for my safety. I look forward to your next letter. Thank you for your continued prayers…

With all my love,
Elizabeth

Folding the paper up and sealing it, I climbed back into the bed, hoping… praying…to get at least a couple hours of sleep without nightmares.

* * *

The town was quiet. It was still dark as I tiptoed into the kitchen. The only useful part about not sleeping well was that I was able to accomplish many tasks very early in the mornings. Pulling the white apron off the hook, I tied it around my waist. Even though no one else was in the house with me, I felt I had to be quiet, so as not to disturb the stillness around me. Plunging my hands into the wash basin, I cleaned up before gathering my ingredients. I splashed the cool water on my face and sucked in my breath, startled at the temperature. Shoving open a window that looked out onto the street, I breathed in the fresh morning air. Then, I turned around and faced the ingredients laid out on the table and began mixing the flour, water, yeast, butter and salt. Mother had always been fond of baking bread and had taught us girls from a very young age. It made me feel close to her whenever I baked a fresh loaf. I peeled the sticky dough from between my fingers and laid it in rolls to rise in the heat. As I waited on the dough, I busied myself cleaning the house and preparing a basket to take over to the Gettysburg Presbyterian Church for the day. After a while, the whole house began to smell as the loaves baked in the oven. I closed my eyes and inhaled deeply, allowing the happy memories this aroma aroused to form in my mind. The sun had just barely risen, as I pulled out the loaves and let them cool on the counter. Tying on a fresh apron, a sudden knock startled me. Wondering who it could be at this hour, I straightened some straying hairs before pulling the door open. Before me stood an older woman with a young woman beside her.

"Good Morning," I said somewhat inquisitively.

"So sorry to disturb you, Miss," the lady laid a hand on the girl's shoulder. "My daughter and I just arrived in town. My son is among the wounded. We wanted to come and stay with him and help where we can. A man directed me to your home, he said you might be able to house us for the time we are here. He said there were many other families who had come and were staying in the town to be near their wounded loved ones. Can you spare the room?"

"Oh, yes, of course. It's only me. There isn't much room in the house, but I can make it comfortable for you."

"Don't concern yourself over that, I am not worried about a little discomfort when my son, and many others, have been through so much."

I smiled sadly, "Of course. Please come in. I'm actually on my way to the Presbyterian church now to help with the wounded there. Would you like to come along? Maybe we can find the whereabouts of your son."

"Oh, yes. Charlotte dear, leave your things here and let's follow Miss…oh I'm so sorry, we didn't even properly introduce ourselves. I am Anna Parker, and this is my daughter Charlotte. And your name is?"

"Elizabeth Tyler," I curtsied in return.

"Mrs. Tyler, it is a pleasure. Thank you so much for taking us in like this. I know it is inconvenient." The woman and her daughter laid their bags in the parlor and came back out. I wrapped the warm loaves of bread in towels and laid them carefully in my basket.

"No, no, think nothing of it. As you said, so many have suffered, we should not let anything so trivial inconvenience us." We moved onto the doorstep and the ladies waited as I secured the door.

The girl looked inquisitively at her mother and held a handkerchief to her nose. I glanced from one to the other, then stated sadly,

"The smell, yes, it's from the wounded…and the dead."

As we walked along the streets, I learned more about the ladies and where they came from and their family background. We spoke of the war and how we never expected it to last this long.

"So many of the townsfolk hid and slept in their cellars during the days of the battle. They emerged to find an alarming amount of death and damage to property. One of our own civilians was killed in her home." I spoke of Jennie Wade who had been shot through the walls of her own home by a stray bullet. I did not know Jennie well, but in my interactions with her she had always been kind.

The fighting had been real enough out West when I had witnessed it…but it was different here. In our own town…with people we had grown up with…dying so tragically where we had once played and laughed as children.

As we approached the Presbyterian church, the two women turned to ask a man if he knew the whereabouts of their loved one.

I touched the girl's arm, "I'll be inside. I'll look for you before I leave, but if we can't find each other, do you feel confident you can find the house?" The girl nodded with a grateful smile. "All right, I will see you soon." I squeezed her slender shoulder, and lifted my skirts, making my way up the stairs to the church doors. Stopping short, I almost ran into a very little child. The sight touched my heart. She was so young and innocent. With wide eyes she carried a basket of fruit up the stairs for the soldiers, her mother close behind. I caught the mother's eyes for a moment, and we smiled sadly at each other.

I made my way through the entrance and into the church. Rows upon rows of white pews filled with wounded soldiers greeted me as I entered. Over the last several weeks I had gotten to know some of the soldiers as I cared for them. At first, I had moved around, but lately I had been asked to stay at this location to care for the wounded here. It gave me a chance to develop friendships with the soldiers and to show them personalized care. I was eager to implement some of the things I had learned from all my research. Moving to the far corner of the church I stopped and set my basket down, unwrapping the freshly made loaves of bread. They were still warm as I tore off some pieces and began to pass them out.

"Good Morning, Derek," I handed a warm piece of bread to a kind faced soldier. "How are you feeling this morning?"

"Oh, you know, up and down," he shifted in his pew. His voice changed, "Honestly, Mrs. Tyler, I'm worried. I don't think I'm getting any better."

I sat down next to him, "Now Derek, we've talked about this. You have to think positively. You'll be all right, I just know you will. Think about the improvements you made in the last few weeks."

"Hey! Are you gonna share any of that bread over here or not?"

I rolled my eyes playfully, "And that would be Lenny." I leaned in and whispered, "Between you and me, he only likes to act like he's mean, but he's actually a very nice man." Laying my hand on Derek's shoulder, I gave it a squeeze, "It's going to be all right Derek. I'll bring you a book tomorrow, it'll help take your mind off things."

I moved over to where Lenny sat, sour look on his face and arm in a sling. "Good Morning, Lenny!" I said cheerfully, reaching into my basket.

"Hmmph," he grunted. "Thought I'd never get a piece of that rotten bread you make."

"Well, maybe I'll just give it to someone else who is more grateful for my *rotten bread.*"

"Oh, give it here, I'll take it." I watched as a subtle smile crept over the man's face as I handed him the bread. He said between bites, "You're gonna wear yourself out girl, taking care of all us wounded soldiers every day and not taking a moment for your own health." I smiled at his concern. *See, I knew he was a nice man.*

"Don't worry about me, Lenny. You just get better."

"Worried? Who said anything about worry? Go on and tend to the other soldiers," he waved his hand dismissively. As I got up to leave, I heard him still grumbling, "I'm not worried. Why would I worry about that girl?" I touched my hand to my lips to contain the small laugh that wanted to escape.

"Hello, Roger," I approached another of the soldiers.

"Hey there, how are you doing Mrs. Tyler? Seems it's been a little bit since we last talked. Oh! I see you've baked us some more bread. Thank you, thank you!" The stream of words continued as I nodded to his questions and handed him the food. He had such a good attitude amidst all this pain.

As I continued to move through the rows of soldiers, the minister stood up and asked if those who were able to would join him in singing a few hymns. I sang softly as I continued to pass the bread around to the more seriously wounded men and help them eat it.

Fairest Lord Jesus

Ruler of all nature

O Thou of God and man the Son

Thee will I cherish

Thee will I honor

Thou, my soul's glory, joy, and crown

All fairest beauty

Heavenly and earthly

Wondrously, Jesus, is found in Thee

None can be nearer

Fairer, or dearer

Than Thou my Savior art to me

Innocent Blood
Chapter 23

Amy

September 1863

AS WE TROTTED along a deserted foot trail that cut behind the Virginian farm fields, I found myself continually glancing back into the thick forest behind us. We were too far south to be separating from the main body of the regiment. And I knew better than anyone what lurked in the shadows of the seemingly abandoned forests. Though Anderson had awakened us in the dead of night, calling on his hand chosen soldiers for a "special operation", there seemed to be really no organization or strategy set in place for this mission. Anderson and the majority of the small squad had been continuously passing around liquor flasks since we had secretly left the encampment. Kicking my gelding to move in closer to the colonel, I pulled up beside him saluting.

"Sir," glancing nervously about, I stated, "Sir, we are in enemy territory."

The major snickered, turning back to me, "What's the matter? Are you scared, Corporal?"

Ignoring his comment, I continued, directing my attention only to Anderson,

"Is it safe for you to be moving around in enemy territory with only a small escort like this?"

Anderson took another swig from the flask and tossed it to the major at his side. Turning to me, he smiled and laughed,

"Indeed, it is, my good man. Though we are now in the territory of the treacherous 'phantom regiment.' His valley, as they call it. The farmers here are rumored to be helping, hiding and even giving arms to our worst enemy." Anderson leaned toward me, his breath smelling of whiskey, and in a low voice added, "That is precisely why we have a small company of men. This operation requires secrecy and a certain measure of hostility not many can stomach. Sometimes you must play the villain, to catch the villain." Anderson and the major exchanged a knowing glance. One of the clearly intoxicated soldiers sneered at me with a chilling grin.

I wondered what sort of "special" mission Anderson could be conducting with such a crew as this. Anderson turned the squad off the narrow path and onto a small trail, leading between two fields of corn. The moon was waning, causing hardly enough light for us to maneuver by, but Anderson seemed to know exactly where he was headed, as if he had traveled these paths many times.

Approaching a small white picketed farmhouse, Anderson held up a gloved hand, signaling the squad to halt. A single candle lit the tiny window in the home surrounded by tidy bushes. No doubt the farmers were already up, preparing for an early start to work their fields before the burning heat of summer was upon them. There was a large barn situated a few yards away from the cozy home from which a man rushed out, raising his hands in a defenseless position upon seeing us. Anxiously, he gazed around at the squad that quickly encompassed him.

"Colonel, I'm afraid there's not much here, but you're welcome to whatever supplies you need." He said in a rushed and fearful offer, "We're just peaceful farmers."

Anderson smiled cruelly, "Peaceful farmers indeed. This is the Harris farm if I'm not mistaken. My informants tell me you and your family have given a lot more 'help' than food to the Phantom Regiment." Anderson nodded his head to the major and suddenly a few soldiers galloped up to the house.

"Colonel, please! Take whatever you wish, just leave my family alone!" The man stammered with constant glances back to where the soldiers stood waiting. There was a pause and I almost believed Anderson would extend some sort of mercy to this poor terrified soul. But without another second of hesitation, he gave the signal to the men waiting on the farmhouse terrace. Busting down the frail wooden door they returned in only a few moments dragging a woman and two children outside. The girl, who looked no more than twelve, was whimpering as the corporal released his fierce grip on her hair, throwing her down into the dirt alongside her mother and younger brother. The man moved forward to Anderson, his eyes pleading after seeing his family so cruelly ripped from their home.

"Colonel, please, I don't know what rumors you've heard. We're just trying to live a quiet life here. I'm an abolitionist myself. I was called upon to join Virginia's cavalry and declined. I don't believe in violence." Anderson listened with an extremely smug, eerie smirk on his face, seeming to immensely enjoy the man's pleading.

"I'm sorry, Mr. Harris, but my informants tell me otherwise," he cooed condescendingly. "You've been seen supplying arms and ammunition to a Major…Seth Morgan and his company." Anderson paused as the man's countenance fell and his face went pale. "And on more than one occasion. Even giving them shelter here during a storm. Care to deny it?"

Then shaking his head hard, the farmer swallowed, sweat beading on his weather-beaten brow and he glanced back at his family, who now had rifles pointed at their backs. Hardly able to breathe, I felt like I had to do something to stop this situation from escalating. I spoke up, my voice quivering from the intensity of the moment.

"Colonel, perhaps they gave aid only to keep themselves alive?"

Anderson shot me a terrifyingly hostile look, "Silence, Corporal. I am fully capable of judging the situation for myself. You'll be punished for your insolent questioning!"

"Colonel, please take whatever you need." The man repeated, shaking his head, "Just leave my family in peace." Anderson glanced around at the beautifully kept farm and then to the family huddled together, still in their nightgowns. Eyes full of terror, as the mother held her two children close. Tears began to fall from her face onto the hair of her young son as she clutched his head to her chest.

"I'm afraid it's too late for that, Mr. Harris. Your family has aided those Rebels one time too many. But don't worry, you can make amends for the treachery of betraying your country." A look of relief began to show on the man's face, and he nodded, "You will aid the cause of the Union and help us capture the infamous Phantom Regiment," Anderson leaned causally back in his saddle, "with your deaths." Taking the butt of his rifle, a sergeant swung hard, knocking out the man's knees causing him to crumple to the ground. Suddenly four gunshots rang out consecutively.

"*No!*" I shouted in horror, blood draining from my face. Gasping for air, I felt as if my own heart had stopped as I stared at the lifeless forms, blood pooling under their heads. No sooner had I turned to confront Anderson, then I felt a harsh slap across my jaw, nearly knocking me off my horse, who screamed and jumped sideways skittishly. I grasped the reins to keep from falling off while clutching at my cheek. Blood dripped onto the white glove. Looking up into the cold, heartless eyes of the colonel, I sat stunned in the silence of disbelief. Anderson's anger toward my outburst was evident as he hissed in a demonic voice behind gritted teeth.

"You will control your childish outbursts, Corporal! *No one* questions my judgment! I will do *whatever* I deem necessary when setting the trap to obliterate those worthless Rebel guerrillas! No price is too high to pay!" Whipping his horse around, I heard him curse under his breath, "and finally destroy that idiot, Seth Morgan."

Then kicking his horse into a trot, he shouted back to the men, still standing over the fallen murdered bodies of the young family.

"Set the scene, Major!"

The squad pulled out several black knives, and other random blacked items and began their work of shaping the narrative…the lie that Anderson was continuing to invent. Turning my horse away from the gruesome scene, I began to follow Anderson back to the camp, my heart burning with disgust, rage and horror at this brutal killing as I viciously wiped the tears from my eyes. Gripping tight to the reins, I suddenly knew what I had to do.

* * *

The air was thick, the heavy tension that seemed to rest continually on this camp was stifling. Hands trembling, I quickly folded the stained piece of paper muttering to myself, trying to calm my nerves. Peering out of the tent flap, I quickly but carefully scanned the nearby canvases and wagons. Fires were extinguished, leaving only thin trails of smoke from a few burning embers. Thick clouds passed over the moon, causing the visibility to be inconsistent. Keeping low to the ground, I crept near the edge of camp, watching for the night sentry. Finally, I reached the cover of the forest, where I threw the small sack containing the note several times before it caught on a low hanging limb. There was a snap of a twig and I whipped around, breathing heavily. *Perhaps a deer or some forest animal.* Seeing no one, I turned my gaze back to the small package dangling in the branches. *He'll find it. They have to be trailing us now.* I tried to assure myself, before returning back to the camp. Crawling into my tent, I laid awake, staring through the slit in the canvas anxiously. Suddenly the chirping of the crickets ceased, as did all normal evening sounds. Something was moving through the forest in large numbers to cause such alarm to the animals. I held my breath, straining my eyes and ears. After a long pause, the singing of a night lark returned, and the crickets began their continual chorus. Laying back, I closed my eyes and breathed a sigh of relief.

These Honored Dead
Chapter 24

Elizabeth

October 1863

I HAD HEARD that President Lincoln was supposed to be visiting next month to dedicate our cemetery, which had expanded immensely. The last couple months I had avoided walking outside the town limits, not wishing to tread those now sacred grounds. However, today I decided to venture out of the town and into the fields and hills beyond. I moved through the streets on the outskirts of our old town. Stopping, I turned back to face the little village. The town seemed barely recognizable. I envisioned what it was like before the battle: people working in their shops, women scurrying about with children, dogs barking, the hurrying trod of horses' hooves, neighbors calling to one another in greeting. The quaint village surrounded by tall lush-green grass waving in the breeze, and the bright blue sky filled with the melody of birds.

I now walked toward Nathan's old shack on Seminary ridge. I tried not to gaze at the scene around me, there were places that still told of the blood of soldiers. Eventually the rain had washed the dirt off of the hastily dug trenches, which had been dug soon after the armies had gone southward, revealing the bloating corpses of soldiers. By this time, as far as we knew, most of the soldiers were finally laid to rest. Yet some rotting bodies of horses and mules still lay in the landscape. The hot summer sun had left us with a reeking stench that hung persistently in the air even now that the weather was turning. With the stench of death and decay came the vultures, swarms of flies and wild pigs. I tried to keep my gaze fixed on the path in front of me. *This beautiful town, our home, had become such a scene of desolation and death…* People demanded the government take care of the carnage and deal with burning the animals' bodies. Some farmers complained and demanded recompense for the bodies of soldiers that had lain covered in their vegetable gardens. As said before, some of our neighbors had even moved out completely, saying they could not bear to live here anymore. Eventually the soldiers would all be found…but it was a long and gruesome process.

I stood at the edge of the tree line on Seminary Ridge, looking out across the field. I could see our home in the distance on Emmitsburg Road. It was not the same. Nothing would ever be the same. Dare I cross this field? Dare I step on this ground where so many had bled and died? I picked my steps carefully as I started toward home. The ground was soft under my feet. The autumn breeze swept around me and added to the chill already crawling up my spine. The atmosphere was silent, almost too silent. Faintly though, in the distance the sound of the wounded still haunted the air…whether it was coming from the hospitals or from my mind, I did not know. Suddenly the quiet was flooded with the sounds of the battle that had taken place here. Cannon explosions, the rattle of musket fire, the screams of the dying, the shouts of the commanders as they had led their men across that deadly field…that field full of blood and fire.

My heart pounded at the vision, my throat tightened, and tears began trailing down my cheeks. Trying to block out the intensity of the noise in my mind, I ran the last few yards to the fence line on Emmitsburg Road. Grasping the rough wooden rails, I stared across the lane at my home. It seemed as though a shroud had been laid over it. Gaping holes in the brick walls, shutters hanging from the house, and shattered glass windows greeted me despondently. The white picket fence lay muddy and broken in the dirt road. I hadn't had time to come here, to clean and tend to our old house. I hadn't had the time…or I hadn't had the heart. I turned away as another tear slid down my cheek. *How would we heal this land…this country…after all this devastation to life and property?*

I climbed over the fence, being careful not to catch any splinters from its rough rails. Attempting to lift the white picket fence, I soon realized it was no use. There was too much damage for me to do any good. The fence landed at my feet with a clatter. I inhaled deeply and let out my breath slowly, still staring at the ruins of the old house. I had not been back to visit since that night…that night after the battle.

Walking up to the doorway, I grasped the handle and nudged on the panel slightly. It swung open on its hinges much faster than I expected. Though there were holes in the walls, I wanted to walk through the doorway. Standing on the threshold, I slowly took in the rooms around me. The smell of water damage and mold greeted me. The floor creaked as I walked slowly into the parlor. Stopping, I looked at the old hearth. Most of it was destroyed, laying in a heap on the floor. Approaching it, I knelt down and began piling up the hearth stones. My fingers brushed across grooves etched in one of the stones. Turning it over, my heart sank as I gently fingered the hearth stone with Father's initials carved into it. My eyebrows furrowed when I noticed the stone was very different than all the rest…it's shape and size… Suddenly I discovered a small box among the stones. It was very old and beaten. Laying it on my lap, my fingers fumbled with the cold metal as I slowly undid the latches. The hinges creaked open. What was that? A handkerchief? I lifted it out and fingered it in my palm. It was old…and delicate. It was beautifully made. A note accompanied it. It had been hastily written. The paper looked much older than most parchments I had seen.

Miss Rebecca,

I wish things could be different. I see in you such passion for the independence of the colonies. I admire and respect that.

I laid the paper down gently in my lap. Rebecca…Rebecca Matthews? Rebecca Matthews…Father's great aunt? This was very old parchment. I fingered the handkerchief once more. *Who…?* Suddenly, I was distracted by more papers in the small box. After all the shock of the last few months I had forgotten my purpose for coming back to Gettysburg. *Of course! Could they be? Marcus' papers?*

I pulled out a sealed envelope. Breaking the wax, I unfolded the old parchments and scanned over the words:

This is to certify that I, James William Matthews, do manumit and set free by inheritance of my father, William Daniel Matthews, my slave, Marcus, who was given to me as my slave on his day of birth, the 23rd day of July, in the year of our Lord 1834. I do manumit and set free Marcus Matthews on this day under my hand and seal, in front of the following witnesses.

Several signatures followed. I fingered the markings on the stone once more. Then, another paper, beneath the certification, unfolded. Slowly pulling it out from behind the first letter, I read over the hand-written note.

If you are reading this letter, then I presume you have found the place indicated to you in my letter and have done so while the family was away, as I requested of you. It would be improper for us to meet.

So, I thank you for taking what is yours and going on your way. Leave anything else in the box alone and replace the stone. I will take care of the rest.

I know your mother would have been proud to know her son is now a free man. But I am sure she knows, as she looks down from above. Go now…live well.

James William Matthews

A mixture of feelings came over me as I refolded the papers and stuffed them inside my dress. Something between anger at my father for never telling us about our brother, and a nervous anticipation for all that lay ahead, twisted inside me. *But why wait to give Marcus his freedom papers…why did he not free him as a baby? Perhaps Father changed his mind and didn't know how he wanted to handle the whole situation…that's why he ran away to the North to sort things out. Perhaps he felt the boy needed to wait until he was a man to gain his freedom for some reason. But instead of writing to his son when he was old enough, it seemed that Father had tried to forget he even had a son…until recently when he knew he was dying and then he wrote to Marcus about his manumission papers hidden in the hearth. He must have felt embarrassed and didn't want Mother to know about his past.* Frustration and confusion created a tangled web in my mind and heart.

I shoved the manumission papers into my pocket and hesitated for a moment before placing the handkerchief and old note inside my pocket as well. I would stash them among the collection of papers I had found at my grandfather's plantation…my only inheritance from my father.

Ugh! Amy! I didn't even mention Marcus and my purpose for coming to Gettysburg! What was I thinking? It must have been the shock from the battle and the surprise of seeing my sister again…I hadn't even mentioned our half-brother to her. *But perhaps, one day soon, she will meet him*, I consoled myself.

Sighing, I stood up and dusted off the soot and dirt from my skirt. Stepping carefully, I walked back out of the house and rounded the corner to the back. Feeling a sudden wave of emotions, I leaned my back against the bricks and took some deep breaths. I stared out across the fields…toward the small rounded hills where so much fighting had taken place.

I noticed a few horses in the distance. The Confederates had stolen many of our horses. They must have used them as needed and then left them…or lost them during the battle. Perhaps Shadow was among them. *Was he safe?* I had grown up riding him. He had been a gift from my father when I was a young girl. Picking up my skirts, I found my way back to Emmitsburg Road and began walking down the dusty path. The autumn leaves crunched underneath my boots as I continued down the lane. Finally reaching the distant fields, I searched the small herd of horses for a familiar friend.

"Shadow!" I called, whistling gently. Several horses perked their ears and turned their heads my way. They looked battle worn, and most seemed to be injured in some way…which attributed to why the Confederates left them. Just when I was about to give up hope, I heard a soft whinny. Ascending a small slope in the ground, I let out my breath as I saw a buckskin horse limping slowly toward me. I ran and flung my arms around his strong sleek neck.

"My dear friend, are you all right?" I asked running my hands along his hind legs to check for any more injuries. One of his legs did feel warmer than the others. "I'm sorry I didn't search for you sooner. Everything has just been such a blur. I hardly know what day it is." I continued to stroke his mane. "Come on, we will go home and get you all healed up." Shadow snorted and stuffed his muzzle into my hand, searching for a treat. Turning, I led him toward the road… and home.

* * *

November 19, 1863

Finally, today, the soldiers who fought and gave their lives here would be honored. A large cemetery, in our very own town, would forever hold the bodies of these soldiers in remembrance of those terrible three days when they gave their lives. A solemn reminder of true sacrifice and selflessness. Soon I was joining a large procession of townspeople. Not feeling in the mood for socializing, I shoved my bonnet closer over my face and kept my head down. The crowd slowly made its way out of the town and eventually came to the site of the cemetery. Waiting for the first speaker, I listened as a band played a triumphant song. The president himself would be here today and would say a few words. However, around me voices only spoke of the illustrious Mr. Edward Everett, who was to be the key speaker of the day. Soon the gentleman stood up on a platform and began his speech. Suddenly I felt a desperate longing to see Nathan again, I needed his courage. We had written many letters, but I needed to talk to him in person and tell him all that had transpired. Loneliness crept slowly through me; everyone I loved in this world was far away. I felt small and isolated, despite the myriads of people that surrounded me. Hours later, Mr. Everett said his final words.

"Down to the latest period of recorded time, in the glorious annals of our common country, there will be no brighter page than that which relates the battles of Gettysburg!"

After Mr. Everett descended the stage, a man stood up and introduced, "The President of the United States." People applauded as the tall, thin, gangly man moved toward the wooden stand. Wearing a black suit and tall hat, the man pulled out his sheets of parchment with a thin hand.

He began in a shrill, high voice, "Four score and seven years ago our fathers brought forth on this continent a new nation…" His remarks were not nearly as long or as eloquently spoken as Mr. Edward Everett's, and later I heard comments in the crowd about how disappointing the speech was. But something rang true in my heart as I listened to the solemnly spoken words. "The world will little note, nor long remember what we say here, but it can never forget what they did here." The tall man reached out a long arm, motioning toward the deathly fields that had once been our gardens, our pasture lands, our wheat fields. They had once held the laughter of children as they played and chased butterflies through the grass. They had seen the sweat of our farmers as they plowed and toiled in the soil. The president continued, "…that from these honored dead we take increased devotion to that cause for which they gave their last full measure of devotion–that we here highly resolve that these dead shall not have died in vain–that this nation, under God, shall have a new birth of freedom–and that government of the people, by the people, for the people, shall not perish from the earth." The crowd was still as Mr. Lincoln crumpled his papers back up and slipped them into his pocket.

We take increased devotion to that cause for which they gave their last full measure of devotion. The words rang in my mind. They instilled in me an even stronger desire to continue to help the soldiers who were fighting for what they believed in. My heart went out to both sides: Union and Confederate. Both so brave, so courageous, willing to go even to the point of death for a cause greater than themselves…something they believed in.

Deeds of Darkness
Chapter 25

Amy

November 1863

THE LONG, BLACK saber slid into its place at my side and I quickly clenched my hands into fists, trying to rid myself of their trembling caused by the plaguing sense of trepidation.

Anderson had summoned his "special tasks force" to prepare for another midnight assignment. The preparation details given me by the sergeant had only deepened the regret I had for ever believing Anderson to be the innocent party in this feud against the Phantom Regiment. I was handed a stack of black garments, black shoe polish and a tin of ground charcoal and told to get ready.

"Gentlemen," Anderson turned, looking each one of us directly in the eyes. "As many of you remember our informant has given us this location." He placed his finger on the map between us, "as a collection point for some of the Phantom Regiment's munitions. Obviously, there are Southern traitors amongst the townsfolk. Raid the homes, interrogate anyone in the buildings to find out where they've hidden the goods. Set fire to the buildings in which the supplies are stored…bring our informant to me. Our commanding general has given me direct orders to use whatever means necessary to free the Union army from the continual nuisance of this 'Phantom Regiment.' They are a constant threat to the Union, and the raids on supply trains, midnight attacks and brutal guerrilla warfare must be put to an end! Everything we do will have an impact in drawing them out, destroying their popularity even in the South, eventually leading to their demise. When they are weakened, we will strike such a blow no one will even dare speak their names. Remember your orders upon joining this elite unit. No mercy," he suddenly paused, his gaze intensifying before his final instructions. "Every scene we create that leads the public further into believing this façade of the cruel and immoral rogue Confederate regiment is a small victory…until they have no friends left in their capital. We will continue to paint a monstrous image, so atrocious that even their own mothers would call for their sons' executions in penance. They will die the death of cowards and criminals, in shame. And this victory will be worthy of every life that it demands."

There was another pause in which Anderson looked intently into the face of each man until he was satisfied with the hate in the eyes of the killers he had created. My heart shuddered inside me, so horrified at the ability of this man to devise and carry out such a scheme. Rolling up the map, all mounted their horses in silence and, taking their orders, the group quickly separated, galloping through the trees to the buildings just barely within view.

"Jones," Anderson stopped me, an uncertain look in his eyes. "You stay here. I won't have you making a fool of us again. Keep a lookout and alert us of any trouble. You will have one more chance to prove yourself…in time."

Holding my mount in check, I watched as the last of the dark riders followed him into the trees. Glancing around, I scanned the darkened forest, my heart quickening with every passing second.

"Where are you?" I whispered, searching for any hidden figures lurking nearby. My mind drifted back to the note hanging in the bag on a branch.

The vulture lures its prey
into the nest to stay.
Pretending it will save
then turning it to prey.

Now return to those today
who have helped you in small ways.
Or soon they will not say
a word down in their grave.

As the first in the long line of clues and hidden packages, I prayed Kelsey, or someone, in the regiment had found at least one of the many parcels I'd so carefully placed.

At great risk, I even enclosed some crudely drawn maps of our location, and the direction in which we seemed to be moving. Suddenly, a more dreadful thought crept into my mind. *Or perhaps they never found my note, perhaps those forms I had seen lurking near our camp had been only my own imagination or wishful thinking. Perhaps Kelsey had been called on another mission. But how could he turn a blind eye to the trail of destruction Anderson was leaving in his wake? No, they had to be near.*

"He'll come," I comforted myself. A sudden shriek filled the air and my heart stopped. Not much was visible from between the thick trees, but the unmistakable flickering of a flame caught my attention. More shrieks and screams filled the air, the gunshots, shouting, glass shattering.

Turning back for one last check into the forest, I gripped my reins tight, my knuckles whitening. There was no movement. Without thinking, I spurred my horse wildly forward, branches smacking at my face, until I came to the horrific sight. My horse reared up, terrified at the blazing inferno before us. Bloodied civilian corpses lay strewn on the ground, surrounding the tiny town of only a few houses and shops.

My eyes took in the horrific scene as the bloodied form of a shopkeeper, struggling, began to push himself off the ground in an attempt to rise. A hand raised defenselessly. Then a merciless shot rang out and the man fell lifeless, to the ground. Everything inside me was screaming in anguish and outrage. But I knew for the sake of many more victims, I must hold my tongue.

"Corporal!" A sudden shout came from my right and I whipped my head to the side, a hand on my saber. Anderson was approaching, the flames reflecting in his hollow, inhumane eyes. "How dare you leave your post!" He shouted, "You're leaving us blindsided you imbecile!"

"Colonel!" there was an interruption as a sergeant came forward, dragging a black man. His clothes were tattered and torn; his feet bare. A few others joined in the mob of soldiers now shoving, spitting on and mocking him, all the while laughing.

"Ah, our informant," Anderson's mood seemed to change instantly from anger to that of wicked delight. The sergeant kicked the backs of the man's knees, causing him to collapse to the ground before he roughly ripped the man's head back.

His eyes were wide, like that of a frightened animal, as he frantically glanced from one threatening soldier to the next, in the group that crowded tauntingly around him.

Finally, his eyes rested on Anderson. "Please, Massa, I done everythin' ya asked me. Please just le' me go to my fam'ly. Leave us in peace, Sir, please."

"I'm not your master, boy. You shouldn't worry, your family will be proud to know that by your death you helped to catch those Rebel cowards." The man folded his hands together, tears streaming down his cheeks, ready to beg for his life, which no doubt he had done before.

"How shall we take care of him, Colonel," a wiry looking lieutenant stepped forward, running a knife along the man's cheek that was glistening with sweat.

"Perhaps a rope would be the best option. So, he doesn't squeal and cause someone to hear," another soldier laughed, throwing over a rope they had retrieved from the ransacked buildings.

Anderson seemed to be concocting his own devious plan as he stared down, unblinking at the helpless form before him. A smile slowly spread across his face,

"I believe it would be in the best interest, and to aid in our deception, for the act to be done in such a way as would leave no doubt that the Phantom Regiment is responsible."

Tossing a black knife to the lieutenant, Anderson muttered words I couldn't believe I was hearing, and I felt my skin go cold. The man began to beg and plead, falling on his face in front of the colonel. But his pleas were silenced by a sharp kick in the side, followed by several others. The men started taunting and laughing. My stomach was turning, and I reached for the pistol at my side and unloaded a shot into the icy air.

"*Stop!*" I shouted my heart pounding. Suddenly, every eye was upon me as silence invaded the space.

"What did you say, Corporal?" Anderson spat in my face as he glared down at me.

Courage rising in my chest, I turned my eyes away from the cowering form, still kneeling in a heap of dust, and stared at that depraved leader whose motives I now understood all too well.

Trembling with anger, I gritted my teeth, "I said, *stop.*"

"Who do you think you are?" Anderson crowded into my space, but I stood my ground, never taking my eyes off of his.

"What? Are you not man enough to do your job?"

"No, I'm not demonic enough to partake in your monstrous, depraved actions. A real man would call out a coward like you. You and your disgusting followers are nothing but cowards and murderers, who slaughter unarmed and innocent civilians. Only a warped mind would come up with such a plan to make his enemy look like the monster that only he himself truly is."

To my surprise Anderson stepped back, a smile spreading on his face as he glanced around at his comrades.

"Did you hear that, men? Only Jones is a *real* man…," wicked laughter and jeers followed.

In unchecked emotion and rage, I spit back, "No, but apparently since there are none here, a woman must do the job." Without thinking I pulled off the cap and let the blonde hair fall to my shoulders. A shocked look came over Anderson's face.

"You're a spy." Gritting his teeth, he reached for his saber, but in one swift motion I had my pistol pointed directly in his face ready to fire again.

But before either of us could make another move, a chilling cry came from the woods, and suddenly the thundering of hooves came raining down upon us. My eyes darted to the first dark rider who became visible, bursting through the trees. Then without warning I felt Anderson knocking me to the ground and cold sharp steel against my throat.

"Traitor," he hissed and raised his arm, prepared to strike. But a black saber clashed with his, sending him rolling to the ground as a lone horse man engaged the colonel.

As I staggered to my feet, glancing around frantically, a hand reached down and grabbed my arm, pulling me up onto the back of a tall black horse in one swift motion.

"Ge' her out of here," I heard a shout from the rider who was now engaged in a saber battle with Anderson. The horse burst into a gallop, taking us deeper into the woods until the sound of fighting disappeared behind us. Finally, when we were surrounded by nothing but dense forest and darkness, the rider stopped and slid down from the horse before reaching into a small saddle bag. In stunned silence, I stared into the darkness, unable to comprehend what had just ensued, and the horrifying scene I had witnessed before my miraculous rescue. The sound of the dark rider digging in the saddle bag grew quiet and I felt a canteen gently pressed into my hand.

"Are you injured?" Major Morgan's familiar, and now welcomed, voice spoke up. Still shaking from the rush of energy, I took a deep breath and had to glance down at myself, unsure if perhaps I was injured, but just couldn't feel it through the numbness.

"I don't believe so," still holding the canteen, unable to raise it, I glanced down at Seth Morgan standing below me.

"You're exceedingly confusing to understand, Miss Amy. You escape, run back to your regiment, and then we find you holding a gun on Anderson... Whose *side* are you on?" The frustrated tone in his voice stirred me out of my shocked state.

"I...I wanted to find out the truth...and now I have....," my voice trailed off as a strange peace suddenly rested upon me.

"And what would you have done if we hadn't been there to step in?" He prodded, still agitated.

"I don't know what I would've done, but I think I would have rather died than stood by and watched that-," I choked, unable to finish my thought. Major Morgan stared at me in silence for a long moment.

He suddenly sighed heavily, "You're the luckiest, most courageous and craziest woman I've ever met, Amy Matthews." The tone in his voice caught me off guard as I had never heard it come from him before. I glanced down and, as we locked eyes, I found a look of admiration on his face. He quickly turned away and began leading the black stallion down what seemed to be a narrow deer trail. Coming upon a small clearing, still surrounded by woods, the major stopped and motioned me to dismount. Utterly exhausted, I slipped off the horse and plopped down with my back against an oak tree. Tilting my head back, I closed my eyes and listened to the quiet sound of the wind whispering through the treetops. Neither of us spoke a word and I drifted in and out of sleep, utterly exhausted. Suddenly a twig snapped, and my eyes popped open to see dark forms moving through the trees toward us. Whispers came from different directions. I jumped to my feet nervously before I caught sight of Seth Morgan's form standing in the middle of the small clearing.

"Colonel," there was a pause, "she's uninjured." Suddenly a dark figure approached me in the dim light. I made out the tall form of Kelsey.

"Amy?" The voice was almost a whisper and Kelsey stepped past the major. Taking a few steps forward, we stood a foot apart. His face was covered with black and flecks of blood from the battle. It carried a painful, solemn, yet confident expression. A million emotions rushed into my chest as I saw the weight of how my unforgiveness, and these past years at war, had affected him.

"Forgive me," the tears escaped, as I breathed the words I had been dying to speak for so long. "I judged you wrongly...I'm so ashamed of what I believed." For a long moment Kelsey stared deeply into my eyes, as tears spilled down my cheeks.

Stepping closer, he gently tilted my chin up. "Forgive ya?" His brow furrowed, "And here I meant to beg for your forgiveness. Lassie, I should have trusted ya. I should've told ya everythin' when this all began...but I let fear cloud my judgement...fear of losing ya, in more ways than one. And yet I still lost ya. I've watched your actions these past few months. I've seen the change in ya and the courage ya displayed. When it truly matters, ya judged correctly. Ya acted with wisdom and strength. Amy," his eyes conveyed a message stronger than any words that could be uttered next.

Feeling his strong arms wrap tightly around my waist, I hesitantly reached up and brushed the stray lock of sandy brown hair away from his brow. That moment my touch lit his face, it seemed as if a burden had fallen from his young shoulders and a deep sigh escaped from his soul. His face fell into my hand and, gently grasping it, he lightly kissed my palm.

"I needed to know the truth, the truth about everything Kelsey, to clear my mind of all those unanswered questions, fears and doubts. And I have…and now I know…I know where I belong."

Our eyes locked and I felt a strange emotion rise in my heart, "I belong here, with you…fighting for a cause I believe in. With a heart pledged to a new country, to an idea, that we, the people, can judge for ourselves best in what way to live our lives, raise our children and change the society we will live in. I would rather die fighting so that future Americans would have true freedom." Kelsey held me in a strong embrace and there was silence among the many soldiers who had now encompassed us.

Addition to the Mission
Chapter 26

Elizabeth

December 1863

THE JOURNEY BACK to Richmond from Gettysburg had given me time to think…and plan. I had talked to a lawyer about Marcus' manumission papers, to learn how exactly to go about this mission of freeing him from his slave master. I had visited a lawyer out of town to avoid the gossip and rumors that so easily flew around our small village, especially if and when Mrs. Denny moved back home. What a tale she would weave with such knowledge! After learning the details of what I was to do, I spent Christmas in Gettysburg. It was unlike any other Christmas I had spent. So quiet and dismal…the death around us still so fresh and always on the townspeople's minds. I used the opportunity to serve others, taking small baskets of food to neighbors and friends, trying to spread some cheer after such a hard year.

After the new year had come, I packed up my belongings, tucking Marcus' papers somewhere safe, and began the journey to the plantation in Virginia. I had started writing Nathan several times to explain my plan, but the letters would always end up crumpled on the floor. He would not approve of me going alone to try to free my brother. All I had was the knowledge from the lawyer on my side. Nathan would not let me go. And *I had* to go. Marcus *had* to be freed. I could not live with myself knowing my brother was being treated so harshly when there was something I could do to help him. I only hoped Marcus' master had not sold him and he was still in the same location I had left him. I quelled any nervousness that attempted to stop me from my mission to free my brother and set my mind hard and fast on what I had to do. Step by step. It may not be easy.

* * *

January 1864

We approached the blacksmith forge after dark. I knew Nathan would not be pleased with me for traveling through the streets of Richmond after dark, but it couldn't be helped. I walked beside the tall, quiet man, occasionally glancing up at him as my mind thought through all the details I now needed to figure out. The hardest part was past…Marcus was a free man. Now, however, I had to face Nathan. Perhaps I *had* done this in a rash manner…but Marcus had to be freed and where else was he to go? His "mother", who he had cared for, was no longer alive and the home he once knew had been sold to new owners.

I led him into the forge. "Stay here for now. I'll fix the place up for you…to make it more comfortable. I need to talk to my husband. He didn't know you were coming." I forced a smile, so as not to reveal my nervousness.

Marcus sat down on a rough bench in the forge. The hint of a smile crossed his face. "Don't worry Miss, this is much better than the slave quarters."

"Please, it's Elizabeth." I smiled, "I *am* your sister, Marcus." He nodded, awkwardly rubbing his hands together and looking at the ground. "Wait here." Backing away, I moved hesitantly toward the townhouse. If I was lucky, Nathan would be out on a mission and I would have more time to figure out how to explain myself. As I approached the door, I could see candles glowing from the windows. I heaved my bag up the stairs and knocked on the door. I didn't want to startle Nathan by walking in. Footsteps fell as he approached. The door slowly opened. He looked surprised to see me and then a gentle smile came over his face. Pulling me in, he wrapped me in a tight hug.

"It's good to have you back. I missed you, Elizabeth."

I smiled, it felt so good to be back in his arms. "I'm sorry I was gone for so long. I'm so glad you got my letters and understood why I had to stay in Gettysburg…after all that happened. Oh, Nathan it was terrible. I can't even explain what it was like. First the battle and then the wounded and death all around our town. It was like living in a nightmare."

He released me and held me back at arms' length. "And you saw Amy," his eyes searched mine.

"Yes. It was so good to see her. But in such a time and place… She returned to the South soon after though, we didn't have much time together."

He began closing the door behind me, "Come on, you'll have to tell me all about it. And Elizabeth," he turned toward me, "you should not have been traveling through the streets of Richmond in the dark."

I smiled softly: I knew that was coming. "Wait, Nathan." I stopped the door from closing. His eyebrows drew together inquisitively. "There's something important I need to tell you." He tilted his head, waiting for me to continue. "I…uh…I found the manumission papers and I was able to free Marcus."

"That's good," he said quietly, expecting more.

"But uh…Marcus…he uh, didn't have anywhere to go. I…brought him here." I finished quickly, wanting to be over with what I had to say.

Nathan's face changed into stone. My heartbeat quickened, and I nervously glanced toward the window. "I didn't know what else to do. He had nowhere to go, Nathan." Nathan pushed the door firmly shut, causing me to jump a little. He turned around and began pacing the dining room. I grimaced, not sure what to do. After a few moments he approached me.

"Where is he?" he said in a low tone.

"In the forge," I answered in almost a whisper, not daring to meet his penetrating gaze. Nathan disappeared out the door before I could add anything else. I went to the window and stared after his figure moving toward the forge. Putting my hand to my heart, I tried to calm myself. *What have I done?*

After a few minutes, I couldn't stand it any longer and followed Nathan toward the forge. Stopping just outside the entrance, I could hear the men speaking quietly within. After a few moments, Nathan appeared, his jaw set and his face showing signs of concern.

He stopped upon seeing me. "You should have told me your plans, Elizabeth." He paused, "He can stay a few days. If anyone asks, we will say we took on a negro to help me in the forge." Nathan brushed past me toward the house. I followed cautiously. He turned to me before we reached the door and whispered quietly, "Elizabeth. Did you even think about what this could mean? The danger you have brought upon us by bringing in another person?" Those cold steely eyes haunted me like they used to, as they flashed with a similar look of distrust and apprehension. I suddenly turned around and stayed outside as Nathan entered the house. *He's right. How could I be so thoughtless!* My heart wrenched at his reproach.

*　*　*

March 1864

It had been a couple months since I had brought Marcus to stay with us. He set up sleeping quarters in the spacious forge. He was very quiet the first couple of weeks. Surely, this was so strange and new to him…having a family again. It was still strange for me…to grasp that I had an older brother. I would take extra blankets, food and any other items to him that I thought might make him feel more at home. He would thank me politely, but not much more was said those first few days. I so wanted him to come inside and have meals with us at the dining table, but he refused. Nathan also reminded me where we were: Richmond…the capital of the Confederacy. Surely, it was not customary to have negros at the dinner table. We had to keep up appearances…for the sake of the mission. Once when talking with our neighbors they mentioned they had seen we had gotten ourselves a "slave". I recoiled at the term, but instantly remembered I needed to keep up the appearance and forced my voice to be calm as I agreed how nice it was to have a "man-servant" around to help Nathan in the forge.

Once he had cooled off, Nathan and I had discussed Marcus more thoroughly. With so much work pouring in, Nathan *could* use the help in the forge. But was it too dangerous? Surely Colonel Brandt would be opposed to the idea of Marcus staying here. I began to dread his next visit. I was glad he had been delayed for this long. Fortunately for me, circumstances had arisen recently that had not allowed him to come as often as he had been previously. However, I knew he would come…eventually.

* * *

Colonel Brandt rubbed his hand over the dark roughage on his chin. I felt the weight of his disapproval nearly crushing me. He would not look me in the eyes. *Oh, please just say something!* Finally, I couldn't bear it anymore.

"I'm sorry, Colonel Brandt. It's my fault. I just didn't know what else to do. And…he *is* my brother, Sir. Please don't be angry with me." He raised his hand to stop me. Feeling rebuked, I sunk quietly back into the sofa.

"Captain Tyler," the colonel suddenly stood and motioned for Nathan to follow him. They left the room and I heard their boots travel into the kitchen, where their voices became low mummers. I exhaled slowly and fiddled nervously with the lining of the sofa. *I have really done it now. Colonel Brandt will never forgive me. I put everyone in more danger. How he must despise me.* After a few short minutes, Nathan came back into the room. He reached out a hand to me. I arose and went toward the doorway. Colonel Brandt was at the entrance preparing to leave. My heart sank within me as I saw the seriousness of his expression. Nathan stayed behind as I approached the colonel hesitatingly.

"Colonel Brandt," my voice barely came out. He pulled on his gloves, but glanced up at me, his expression never changing. "Please forgive me," I whispered. He stopped what he was doing, then laid a hand on the doorknob. After a few horrible moments of silence, I heard him sigh, then turn to me.

"It's all right Mrs. Tyler, what's done is done." There was a gentle change to his tone. I swallowed hard as I felt my chin begin to quiver in relief. The colonel nodded to me and then stepped out into the night. After a moment, I felt Nathan's hands rest on my shoulders.

"He's not pleased with what you did, Elizabeth, but he said we will do what we can to resolve the issue. We may have no choice but to trust Marcus and make him part of the mission."

I turned and looked up at him, "Surely Marcus would never betray us."

Nathan stared out the window toward the forge, "I pray to God he won't."

I Had My Heart Again
Chapter 27

Amy

March 1864

THE MONTHS THAT had passed seemed like mere days, days that held the most precious memories of sweet reunions and cherished moments. A happier time in my life had not existed, except for the golden years of my childhood. After the bitter conflicts, losses and devastation of the past few years, this reprieve of peace felt more like a dream than reality. At last I had found peace from the troubled thoughts that had plagued my mind for so long concerning Kelsey. When we'd arrived back to that rose guarded entrance of the Morgan's mansion, there were only emotions of joy and gratitude. The acceptance of me from the regiment, their families and the Morgans was instant and without reservation. There was no strain of animosity, no feelings of resentment for any past conflicts. The news of my confrontation against Anderson had already traveled through the ranks of the regiment and their families. Bringing with it a gleeful delight to all that heard, as they thought of Anderson being opposed and humbled by a woman: a woman who had once lived among them as an enemy…but now I was one of them, with a new family and at last…a new home.

* * *

As the flames flickered and popped in the dark sky, laughter and boisterous conversation filled the air. The smell of Millie's delicious fruit cobbler, mixed with the comforting aroma from the burning wood, surfaced as the joyous crowd gathered on the outskirts of the encampment. Though the group consisted mostly of soldiers, a smaller portion were several wives and loved ones who had brought special food and needed items to uplift the morale of their men in arms. The regiment had been encamped just outside Richmond for nearly a week after having returned without their leader, whose special scouting often took him on much longer, and more dangerous, journeys.

Glancing over at Jane, who had her arm wrapped around her husband's, leaning her head against his shoulder, I felt an ache in my heart. Though Kelsey appeared occasionally it was never for very long and his duties put him at greater risk than anyone. Peter caught my eye and gave a comforting smile, seeming to read my thoughts.

Captain Hamilton was in the middle of a very animated story, entertaining all who gathered there, when the shriek of a horse and the pounding of hooves caused everyone to turn their attention to the pitch-black field from which the sound came. The thundering of hooves grew closer and, as several officers rose to their feet, the light from the fire revealed the sleek black coat of a handsome thoroughbred. Several staff officers accompanied the dark cloaked figure that halted abruptly outside the reach of the fire light.

"Colonel!" Peter shouted above the sudden welcoming cheers that arose from the group upon recognizing their leader.

I jumped to my feet, my heart racing at the sight of the young colonel now dismounting his steed, his closet officers surrounding him.

"Welcome, Sir," Peter gave a little bow, causing a smile to light the otherwise weary face of the colonel. Turning to the gathered crowd around the fire, his eyes searched the faces until his gaze fell upon me. Quickly passing by Peter, giving no attention to any of the watching eyes, I fell into his arms.

"Your back," I breathed in relief, then turning to stare up into his face still smudged with black soot, I felt his hand gently brush my cheek.

"Course I am, Lassie," the gentle melody of his voice soothing my anxiety.

"Come warm yourself by the fire, Colonel," Mrs. Morgan cheerfully spoke up from across the circle. Giving me his arm, we strolled back to rejoin the group as Jane added, "Have something warm to drink. Miss Amy has also baked a delicious cake. I'm sure she's eager for you to try."

Raising an eyebrow Kelsey glanced suspiciously over at me. "Now there's a challenge I shall certainly not forgo."

Pushing him lightly, I laughed and sat down beside him on the fallen log. Several officers crowded in near their leader, Seth, of course, taking his place at Kelsey's right.

"Colonel, how are things looking?" Captain Hamilton asked in a worried tone, his brow furrowed.

"We'll speak of it later, Mark," Kelsey stated calmly, glancing up from the steaming mug now handed to him. As he glanced around at the faces gathered there, a contented look came over him. Like that of a father finally resting his eyes on the welcoming scene of his family gathered around him at the end of a long day. "We are blessed with the presence of friends, mothers, sisters, children… family, let's not talk of war tonight." The boyish Captain sunk back into his seat, happily glancing around at the gathering.

Jane approached, carrying a small plate on which sat a piece of my masterpiece. Glancing over at me, Kelsey cautiously took the plate. Nevertheless, I felt confident, knowing I'd paid special attention to Millie's instructions. Offering a similar piece to her brother, Jane stepped away, smiling proudly at me.

Seth carefully set the plate beside himself on the log. "I think I'll wait…to see what happens first," he muttered under his breath.

Catching the humorous glint in his eye, I stared in shock at his jest and his, apparently, having been informed by his friend about the tales of my cooking.

"Appears our Major, who is so valiant on the battlefield, has his cowardly side," Kelsey laughed and, raising the small piece of cake in a toast to his friend, gingerly bit off a tiny corner. A look of shock came over his face and he nodded, "Now there's proof that miracles happen."

There was shared laughter and Jane caught my eye, smiling and shaking her head. "The pair of you are just awful," she scolded, "Miss Amy worked so hard."

The night moved on in stories and laughter, the joy and camaraderie shared was more of a family gathering around a holiday season.

Wives leaned tenderly on their husband's arms, children upon young fathers' laps or older brothers, sisters sitting side by side with their little brothers, now officers in an elite cavalry unit. Mothers lovingly offering food and drinks to all there, as if each one was their very own son. As I looked around at the familiar faces I'd come to cherish the past few months. I wondered how I had ever counted these people as my enemies. After a couple old hymns were shared and the last of the cakes and sweet breads were devoured, along with the coffee and tea, Peter rose up in the middle of the circle, holding his cup of tea.

Being instantly, though teasingly, met by a flurry of boos and shouts to sit down, he raised a hand to defend himself, "Calm yourselves chaps! I'm not going to torture you with a sonnet!" Peter winked, "Not tonight anyway."

"Boo!" came a cry from several of the younger officers.

As the soldiers quieted, Peter gazed around, a charming smile beneath his perfectly trimmed mustache. "Well, we have indeed been blessed with the presence of family which surrounds us tonight and honored with several songs and recitations." In a sarcastic tone he added, "A better group of artists I've yet to meet!" Laughter and jeers at Peter's jest caused him to chuckle, then he composed himself and, glancing over at Jane, a serene look came over his face. As he reached out a hand, his wife quickly rose and gave him something concealed in a light shawl.

In a softer, almost solemn tone, Peter added, "But…I think the evening will not be quite complete until we hear from a certain young colonel…and his lovely fiancée, who we are all proud to now call *our* family." Peter's eyes sparkled almost as if with tears as he turned toward us and slowly held up a delicate violin toward Kelsey. The men gave an encouraging cheer, all eager to hear from their beloved leader. Embarrassed by the show of admiration, Kelsey shook his head laughing, then seemed to be contemplating something for a moment, before he suddenly rose to his feet and turned toward me.

"Will you accompany me, Miss Amy?" he held out a hand. Caught off guard, I hesitated, but seeing the inviting look in the eyes of all watching, I glanced back up at Kelsey. The warm, gentle, loving look in his eyes melted away any apprehension. As we stepped near the fire, Peter handed off the violin to Kelsey with a gentle squeeze on his shoulder. All grew silent, aside from the light crackling in the fire pit as the wind gently blew through its embers. Then softly, tenderly, the solemn melody drifted from the strings of the instrument and, moved by the waiting, welcoming faces all around me, I felt drawn back into that place that seemed only a memory…that place that felt like home, once again.

I wish, I wish, I wish in vain
I wish I had my heart again
And vainly think I'd not complain
Is go dté tú mo mhúirnín slán

Siúil, siúil, siúil a rún
Siúil go sochair agus siúil go ciúin
Siúil go doras agus éalaigh liom
Is go dté tú mo mhúirnín slán

The camp had grown quiet, as the last of the family members had made their way back home, saying goodbye to loved ones, and the soldiers had climbed into their tents after extinguishing the fires. Leaning on Kelsey's arm, we strolled through the moonlit night back toward the town and the Morgan's mansion. Peter and Jane's voices drifted on in conversation behind us. Seth Morgan had accompanied his mother home earlier with Millie, who'd packed up the large basket of fixings she'd brought for "her boys." The stars seemed brighter in the night sky than I'd ever seen them after such a beautiful night. I felt perfectly content now with Kelsey safely back at my side.

"They adore you," I spoke, glancing over at Kelsey who, with head tilted up, was studying the dark canvas above. He dropped his gaze to look at me. "I've never seen such admiration for a leader."

"Haven't ya?" He stated nonchalantly, clearly uncomfortable with the praise, as always.

"You've earned their respect, their admiration…their love. They'd follow you into any battle."

"They're the best men we've got." He stated emphatically, while adjusting the bridle on the black thoroughbred walking calmly beside us. "Even if I wasn't here to lead them, I know they'd conduct themselves with honor…and with the greatest courage. I just wish the world could know them as I do. Anderson's done a wicked deed spinning lies about them. But the truth will come out…one day."

"Well, even if the world cannot see them the way you do…I'm glad I have," I breathed into the cool night air.

"Have ya now, Lassie?" Kelsey's eyes lighted up as he glanced hopefully down at me.

"They've truly opened their hearts to me. When I was their enemy, they showed me no spite…though I hated them." Dropping my gaze, I adjusted the thick shawl around my shoulders and muttered, "I feel so ashamed now."

"It's in the past now, Lassie," Kelsey took my hand. "Ya're here now. And believe it or not, ya've won their affection as well." He smiled, a look of pride on his face, "The tales of the lady captive have become regimental legends." I blushed, squeezing his arm. "I remember the night I first saw ya…still delirious from your wound. It was storming terribly. Seeing ya in such a panic and fever. It broke my heart, Lassie. I thank God ya're safe now. Safely away from the war."

"But you're not." I sighed; my heart heavy with worry.

Stopping, Kelsey took my face in his hands, "We are all safely in the palm of God, Amy. The days of our lives have been given to us since our birth. It's what we do with those days given to us that matters."

As we trod down the dirt path, nearly in view of the Morgan's mansion, I leaned my head against Kelsey's shoulder as he changed the subject to the lighter topic of a letter he'd received from his parents. He informed me they were living in Maine with a cousin. He had not told them many details, but he gave them a location to send letters to, so that he could keep in touch with them for the duration of the war. He laughed and continued on about something his mother had written, but the heavy weight in my heart made it difficult to concentrate. I knew that soon he'd be leaving on another operation. I had seen the signs of preparation in the regiment during my visits. They were getting ready to depart upon their leader's arrival. I'd caught sight of Seth prepping his gear in the quiet solitude of the stable, alone, preparing his mind for the coming battle.

"Amy," Kelsey's voice broke me out of my deep thoughts. "Are ya happy here, Lassie?"

The Morgan's mansion now rose within view, a comforting sight. Glancing up at him, I smiled thinking of the warmth I'd felt in my heart that night and the past few months.

"I'm more than happy…," I stated confidently, and in a whisper added, "I'm home."

* * *

"Goodnight, Miss Amy," Millie called from the kitchen, where Peter and Jane had paused for a last cup of warm tea.

"Goodnight," I answered, poking my head in to see the three gathered cozily around the small wooden table where Millie did her baking. Climbing the stairs with a full heart, I smiled to myself. *How many things I wish I could share with Elizabeth. One day I'll tell her every detail, every word from nights like these. When the war is over, and it's safe to speak,* I consoled myself. *If only she could be here with us all.* Coming to my room, I stopped short in the doorway at the sight of Seth Morgan, standing silently before the fireplace. His form silhouetted by the few candles that lightened the room. He stared up at the painting above the mantel as if captivated in a solemn trance.

Cautiously taking a step back, I tried to escape, but the floorboard creaked under my step and Seth turned. His face was filled with that deep sadness that seemed only fit for a man of many years, not one so young. It was quite a contrast from the more relaxed, even jesting, young man he'd been earlier that night when he'd arrived with Kelsey.

"I'm sorry, I just…I'll go," awkwardly I stuttered, turning away.

"No… please, excuse me," he motioned for me to enter. "I lost track of time. Come in. This is your room." The sadness in his voice caused me to pause, and for a moment neither of us moved. I studied him; his gaze fixed on the floor as if deep in thought.

"Major Morgan," I hesitated, "I don't believe I've ever thanked you, for taking me in as you did in the beginning. I know it was difficult for your family…having me here."

His head shot up, the expression on his face changing, as he shifted uncomfortably. "It was the only right thing to do," he crossed the room, ready to pass through the doorway.

"I'm greatly indebted to you. You took a risk for my, and Kelsey's, sake. I know that now. And I want to apologize for any trouble I caused you and your family while…" My voice drifted off.

Seth paused, watching me for a moment, and to my surprise he seemed to be suppressing a smile, "Not at all, Miss Amy."

"I know Kelsey values you as a brother. And I hope having put all the animosity behind us," I hesitated timidly, "I hope we can be friends."

Looking up with a soft expression in his eye, Seth nodded, "I would be honored." With a smile, he bowed his head, disappearing behind me. I breathed a sigh of relief I didn't know I had been holding and smiled.

Sitting down on my bed, opposite the fire hearth, I gazed up at the beautiful painting that hung there. As I curiously studied it, I wondered what dark secrets were hidden in the gentle smiling face that seemed to cast such a dark sorrow over the major. A light tapping at my door aroused me.

"Amy?" Jane's voice whispered through the cracked door.

"Come in," I called back.

Entering the room, Jane gave a warm smile and held out a steaming cup of tea. "Thought you might like some of Millie's special brew before you went to sleep tonight."

"Thank you," taking the cup, I nodded to Jane to sit down. "I wanted to thank you again for everything."

Jane cut me off, "Not at all. We're very honored to have you here with us, you and Kelsey. Both of you have brought new hope to us, and to the cause." Giving her a grateful look, I sipped the warm tea.

"Well, you are probably tired after this evening. Tomorrow, if you're up for it, I had planned for us to visit a few boutiques in town." Her eyes twinkled, "Perhaps start looking over some wedding décor? I know a few absolutely perfect shops in town where I had purchased most of my trimmings for my own wedding."

"Oh Jane, thank you. I would be delighted to go together." Nodding happily, Jane glanced around preparing to rise. Looking at the painting that hung above the mantel, I couldn't contain my curiosity any longer. I knew in my mind who this woman was, but something inside me just had to dig deeper into the past of the beautiful young girl I had stared at so many times.

"Jane," I called, before she could move, "Who was she?"

Jane followed my eyes, and a slight smile played on her face, "Mary…she was Seth's childhood sweetheart. They practically grew up together," her eyes twinkled. "She was like a breath of fresh air. Gentle, witty, so compassionate. There wasn't a soul on earth she wouldn't lend a hand to. They married a day before he left for the military academy. She moved so close that they were never really separated for long periods of time during his training. I've never seen my brother happier than in those days." Jane glanced down at her hands and a shadow passed over her face.

Unable to contain the nagging question, I asked in a whisper, almost afraid of the answer, "What happened to her?"

"She was…ummm," Jane swallowed hard and drew back the sudden tears clouding her eyes, "brutally murdered." A chill ran down my back in shock at the words I had not expected. "They said it was a small gang, looking for valuables, money," Jane struggled to continue, her voice now quivering, "but my brother had his own suspicions." I waited in anticipation. Leaning forward, I touched her hand lightly and she glanced up. "Revenge…unrequited love. A man just a few years older than my brother, rivals from a young age," Jane stared hard into my eyes and then revealed the shocking words, "Colonel Jason Anderson."

"*Anderson?*" I stated, shocked, the words barely making it out of my mouth.

"His family had a summer home near us. The boys were always getting in fights or competitions, mainly brought on by Anderson. He had such a hate for Seth, I couldn't understand it. They were always trying to outdo each other, always pitted against each other. It got out of hand. As they grew older Anderson had his eye on Mary. And when he found out Seth had married her…it drove him mad, so we believe. The constables never did a thorough investigation into him, but my brother did."

"I had no idea…," my voice trailed off.

"A part of Seth died that day, Amy. The light was stolen from his life. The only thing that keeps him going is his faith. But I still see it…a dark cloud that rests on him every moment. He's lost that joy, the joy he had before. He's never recovered from it. I'm not sure he ever will," Jane choked. "I never saw him smile, never saw him excited about anything, until he brought Kelsey home on one break from the military academy. Those two…they are like brothers." Her grip tightened around my hand, a grateful smile written on her face and in her eyes.

My face flushed, "Jane, I've been so wrong about so many things. I must admit your brother was one I judged too harshly. I regret that very much. I can see the great respect Kelsey has for him."

Jane's face brightened with a smile, "Don't rebuke yourself too harshly, Amy, we all are guilty of the sin of being too quick to judge our fellow man or woman." Finally rising from the bed, she released my hand, "Well, I'll see you tomorrow. We can busy ourselves at the shop while the men attend to their official business." With a final smile, she exited the room and I was left with my many thoughts.

Lost to History
Chapter 28

Amy

July 1864

"THERE'S NO QUESTION about it," Jane stated determinedly, turning to her mother while holding the beautiful cream-colored fabric up around my shoulders. "This is the perfect shade for Amy's complexion." Each of the ladies standing around me beamed with genuine excitement and joy as they anxiously nodded and agreed with Jane, who had become my main consultant and organizer in all wedding plans. Several wives and sisters of some of Kelsey's closest officers had formed a sort of bridal party to help Jane with the plans.

Millie, standing with hands clasped together, a giant smile glowing on her ebony face, stated in a proud voice, "Miss Amy, you'll be, no doubt, the most beautiful bride Richmond has seen since our Jane was married." Unable to contain myself, I grinned, blushing as I ran my hands gently down the silk fabrics.

As the other women gushed over the many lace and fabrics and other wedding garnishes that lay spread throughout the room, Jane whispered, her eyes twinkling, "What do you think?"

Turning to the mirror, I stared in disbelief. My heart raced as Jane rose and folded the cloth to fit around me. The pale glistening fabrics lay elegantly against my chest, creating an ethereal image against my long blonde curls cascading on either side.

"I never imagined such a wonderful gown…," turning toward her, I added, "or wedding. You've done more than I could ever ask for, Jane."

"Nonsense. You're one of us, Amy. A sister of the Confederacy. And I hope we'll always be close." As I stared at our reflection in the mirror, I was overwhelmed with gratitude. *Perhaps I could send another letter to Gettysburg for Elizabeth…perhaps she could be here for the wedding.* But I knew it could not be: Elizabeth could not know of all that went on here. I turned my attention back to Jane.

"But…are you sure? It seems so extravagant and costly during such a time." Suddenly feeling guilty, I dropped my gaze from the beautiful image. "The money could be used for better causes, Jane." I breathed, feeling a burden in my heart as I remembered the daunting and dark images painted in my mind by the foreboding headlines in the papers.

Jane's grip tightened. "Amy, I don't think you realize the great affect your wedding is bringing to people all over Richmond and the South. We need this; the Confederacy needs this to show our pride and spirit even during difficult times." She raised her head high, "And these are difficult times. We know what's happening even as we speak. We hear the rumors of General Grant moving up to Petersburg." Her voice became a whisper, "We know they're coming soon. We know what struggles we are to face. But that's why moments like these are so important and should be celebrated with all the splendor and glory of a Southern celebration, to give hope for a brighter future."

There was a faint galloping sound outside and Mrs. Morgan moved to the window, gently pushing back a lace curtain. Her brow furrowed confused. "Millie, please go and check who's arriving."

Millie nodded, "Yes'm."

Turning back to us, Mrs. Morgan smiled and raised a hand, "Well ladies! I think the finding of our silks and fabrics for the wedding gown calls for some sort of a celebration! Should we retire to the parlor for some refreshment?" The women all heartily agreed and began making their way downstairs and into the parlor, chatting excitedly about the future wedding preparations.

I exchanged a glance with Jane and could read the worry in her eyes over the unexpected messenger and what news they might bring, since we didn't expect to hear from Kelsey's men until next month. Trying to keep a positive and calm attitude, I forced a smile at Jane.

Mrs. Morgan gave us a reassuring look, "Let's not let idle worries ruin such a lovely day." Agreeing with her, we rejoined the others and were soon entangled in the joyous conversations over what should be served to the guests after the wedding ceremony.

"I would like to have something special prepared for our soldiers at the local hospitals as well," I added as Jane took note.

"Perhaps we can persuade the reverend's wife to prepare a batch of her homemade punch for the occasion!" Alison Webster animatedly put it.

The clinking of spurs on the wooden floor in the hall caught my attention and my hand instinctively flew to Jane's arm in excitement.

"Amy," turning with anticipation, I felt a wave of disappointment at the sight of Peter Kingston standing just inside the doorway with Millie behind him, her big black eyes filled with worry. A dark shadow loomed on Peter's dirt smudged face. The room was instantly silent, and I could hear the rushing blood in my ears from the quickening beat of my heart.

"Amy, come with me," Peter stated ever so gently, removing the hat from his head. He twisted it in his hands until his knuckles turned white, "It's Kelsey." With those dreadful words, all joy now turned to dread. Mrs. Morgan dropped down onto the couch with a slight gasp.

Swallowing hard, I managed in a quivering voice, "Is he injured?"

Staring hard, Peter seemed to be struggling, "Amy, come now, please. We got him as close to Richmond as... He asked me to come for you. We have little time."

As the horses galloped over the rolling hills and into the forest, I could only repeat over and over again, "Please don't take him, please don't take him." Soon darkness encompassed us, and we were forced to slow our pace. As I followed Peter through the thick trees, it seemed ages until the light flicker of a flame cut through the dense forest.

"Captain Hamilton," Peter shouted. The light moved and soon a hand took the bridle of my horse as I jumped down unsteadily, almost falling to the ground, my entire body shaking, weak, my mouth parched and dry.

"Take Miss Amy, Captain."

I felt the captain take me by the arm and barely heard half of his words, "He's this way ma'am…Major Morgan's been with him since the surgeon…lost a lot of blood…it was a deadly ambush as we were returning. A sharp-shooter…"

Suddenly, Seth Morgan was beside me, gripping my arm, almost holding me up on my feet while leading me to a small clearing, "Come, Miss Amy."

There on a rough dark blanket lay the young colonel, his side exposed, a white bandage wrapped tightly around his torso, blood still pooling on the ground beneath him. His face was pale, and pain twisted his expression.

Seth turned me sharply toward him, his grip suddenly tightening as he looked me fixedly in the eyes. "Make yourself strong, Amy. For him."

Unable to speak, I nodded, straightening before I turned once again to the harrowing sight. As I fell beside the form lying stiffly on the ground, I breathed. "Oh, Kelsey."

Turning, he opened his tortured eyes, a glint of hope in them.

"Amy…Lassie…I'm…"

"Save your strength, Kelsey, it's all right, I'm here with you." Falling beside him, I gently stroked his forehead, forcing a smile as tears suddenly began to spill down my face. Wiping them quickly, I inhaled deeply and confidently said, "You're going to be fine. I know you will." I touched his cheek and then hesitantly turned my attention to the wound.

"Saber?" I questioned the surgeon kneeling on the opposite side.

As he lifted his gaze to meet mine, a serious, daunting look rose in his eyes, "Bullet wounds…three…"

Overwhelmed, I turned in desperation to where Peter and Seth stood. Peter suddenly averted his gaze, overcome with emotion, but Seth stood unwavering, calmly staring into my eyes. My heart sank as he slowly nodded his head, the unmistakable answer written on his face. Unable to move, I felt Kelsey take my hand weakly in his.

"Amy, it's all right…I'm not afraid," he smiled weakly, as he touched my face.

"*No*…no," I shook my head adamantly in defiance, "You're going to be fine, Kelsey…you'll be fine." He began to cough, a thin stream of blood slowly running down from the corner of his mouth.

"Lassie, ya can't stop God's will," staring into those soft eyes I saw a peace I'd never witnessed before. "It's my time…and I go…," he choked, "with *no* regrets." He winced and a tear spilled from his eye, "My only sorrow, is for those I leave behind…for ya. For the struggle ya must now face."

"No, Kelsey," tears clouded my vision and I dropped my head onto his shoulder.

"I'm not afraid, Lassie." He repeated calmly.

"I am," I whispered fearfully. The gentle touch of his hand stroked the back of my head as I wept. "I can't lose you. I won't let you go."

"Ya have to Amy," he said gently. "Ya're strong, my high-spirited, Lassie." Tightening his grip on my hand, his gaze intensified, "Stronger than ya know. Remember Amy…we've all been given a set number of days. It's what we do with those days…that matters. Don't be afraid. I'll still be watching over ya. Proud of everything ya do."

Gasping, I muffled a sob in his shoulder.

"I love ya, Amy, always have, always will…never forget that."

"I love you, Kelsey," sobbing, I held his hand to my cheek. Taking his head in my hands, I pressed my forehead to his, the tears pouring from my eyes onto his face through agonizing sobs. With a tender squeeze on my hand, I felt him slowly relax. Then in a final deep, long breath, his gentle spirit escaped the suffering of this war.

All through the night, I stayed with his head in my lap, unable to move, think or feel. I felt the presence of Seth standing behind me all through the night, until the pale light of dawn broke.

Peter knelt down in front of me, "Amy…it's time. We need to take him now." The officers and several men stood respectfully behind him, waiting to lift the body of their leader.

"Take him? Where?"

"Back to Richmond now." Staring into my eyes Peter whispered, "It's time. You must let him go." The soldiers stepped up respectfully and took hold of the blanket on which lay Kelsey's lifeless body.

Still holding his head on my lap, I bent, kissing the cold forehead. Unable to let go, I felt frozen in time staring down at the serene and beautiful face, until I felt arms around me, gently removing my hands and I watched as he was carried away. My heart seemed to stop, and I turned, falling against Seth's chest sobbing.

"A great man has left this earth. A devoted soldier, lost to history."

The Unwanted Guest
Chapter 29

Elizabeth

August 1864

THE LAST FEW months had flown by quickly. I had started a small nursing clinic in the empty room of the house. Most people did not approve of a woman in the medical field, except as an assistant to a male doctor. However, soon I had at least one patient a week. Most cases were minor: a little boy who had scraped himself on the rough road, or an old lady whose arthritis was acting up. Our neighbor, Mr. Amerson even approached me asking if I had any ointments for his bad back. The work kept me busy and it felt good to be able to help people.

Nathan's blacksmith shop was busy nearly every day. He talked to many different kinds of people…and listened. There were Confederate soldiers that came and would talk of the war openly. Nathan gained valuable information from these conversations. My little practice was also a great coverup for any escaped prisoners we might be harboring. I would visit the market quite often in search of bandages or extra food for our secret guests. It might have caused suspicions had it not been known in town about my nurse's station.

The Northern soldiers didn't have an ample food supply as they were essentially out of their "country", but they had everything else to their advantage as far as any other supplies. Richmond itself was still suffering greatly from food shortages, so I had saved all the seeds I could and planted many vegetables and some herbs which I knew would be helpful for healing wounds and sickness. At the moment, we were keeping two escaped soldiers in the cellar. I had cleaned the cellar before they came, floor to ceiling, and arranged a fairly nice living area in the small, dark space for any future escaped prisoners we might need to hold. Nathan tried to keep the duration of their stay short. It was dangerous. The faster they were out the better. And so, we had our system: Nathan would go to the prison camps and help them escape. If he couldn't get them back to an army regiment that night, he would bring them home and I would tend their wounds and nourish them as best I could. Then Marcus, who had become instrumental in our system, would help them leave the house in the middle of the night and get them back to their units if Nathan couldn't. It was such a dangerous mission…for all three of us. If any of us were caught and found out, it could mean death…for all of us.

* * *

It was a busy late summer day. The soldiers in the cellar were getting restless and I had just come from checking on them. Marcus and Nathan were out in the forge working on horseshoes for some Confederate officers' mounts. The soldiers stood about smoking and laughing as they waited for the job to be done. In an effort to seem as supportive of the Southern cause as possible, I would always take any soldiers some water or some food, if there was any to spare. Peering out the window, I mentally took note of how many soldiers and reached into the cupboard for glasses and a pitcher of water. Marcus suddenly walked through the door. He had grown so comfortable with Nathan and me. It made me smile just to see him every day. He had changed from a solemn, fearful yet determined, slave…to a bright-eyed joyful soul. He was always finding ways to make Nathan and I laugh which was a great relief in such stressful times. He walked up quickly and nudged me as I arranged some bread in a tasteful manner on a tray.

"Don't mind if I do!" He reached over and swept up a piece of the loaf.

"Marcus! What am I to serve our…*guests*?" I nodded toward the window.

Marcus scoffed, "Some guests! Those fellows are so arrogant. Their leader is worst of all. Loves to talk about himself and his *heroic* deeds." Marcus rolled his eyes and munched on the bread, turning it over in his hand. "What? No butter and jam?"

It was my turn to roll my eyes, "Really Marcus?" That big smile broke over his face again as he backed away throwing a hand up in surrender.

"Best be getting back! Nathan's quite a task master. Sometimes I think I was better off at the plantation!" Winking, he slipped back out the door. He was such a blessing and a hard worker. I don't know how we had managed before without him. I wish Amy could know her half-brother. One day, one day.

Balancing everything on the tray, I strategically maneuvered the door handle and proceeded down the stone stairs toward the forge. The cigar smoke swirled around in the fresh spring air and the pounding of Nathan's hammer rang throughout the forge amidst the singing birds. Being careful to watch my step, I didn't pay any attention to how the laughter and talk of the men quieted and one of them approached.

"Here let me help you with that, Miss," a deep, warm voice called.

"Oh, thank you," I began handing it over smiling, "It is a little awkward. But I hope you enj-," Suddenly my breath caught in my throat and I would have dropped the entire tray if it was not for the young soldier holding it. In front of me was a person I thought I certainly would never see again…and one I never wished to see again. *Captain Luke Preston.* I started backward, trying to compose myself. My heart raced and my face paled. A look of shock came over his face as well. Then that conceited smile slowly spread across his lips. He raised his eyebrows.

"Well, well, well, Miss Matthews. I never expected to see you again." I opened my mouth to speak, but nothing came. "What's the matter? You don't seem happy to see an old friend," he chuckled in a most aggravating manner.

I finally began to regain my composure from the shock. "Captain Preston. How…*lovely* to see you again." I lied and curtsied formally. He reached for my hand and bowed taking it to his lips. Seeing him linger, I pulled away and quickly said, "Enjoy the bread. I must ask my *husband* something." I began to move past him. Again, he stepped in my way. This seemed to be a habit of his.

"Husband?" He raised his eyebrows, "How…," shaking his head gently he finished, "delightful." I felt a knot form in my stomach. He was dangerous, I could feel it. "And it's *Lieutenant Colonel* Preston by the way. I was promoted for bravery on the field of battle."

"How nice." I feigned a smile and moved past him again, this time making my way quickly into the forge. Nathan had just finished up and was beginning to nail the shoes onto the horses. Marcus helped him. I moved close to where Nathan worked.

He paused and looked up expectantly, "Did you need something, Elizabeth?"

I firmly shook my head, "No, I…I just wanted to see if everything was going well." I forced another smile. Nathan's perception was uncanny. He watched me for a moment then moved to another of the horses and said quietly.

"I'll be in shortly. You can wait for me in the house."

My insides shrunk. I didn't want to walk past Captain…or … *Lieutenant Colonel* Preston again! I twisted my hands and sat down on a nearby stool. "Oh, I'll just wait," I said, much too cheerfully. Nathan shot a strange look my direction, then continued his work. As he worked, I also worked…through my mind…as all the memories of Luke Preston circled around me. I had never told Nathan. *Oh, why didn't I tell him when we were in Gettysburg and I had the chance? Now it would be so strange, so awkward! What would he say? Perhaps I didn't need to tell him…*

Finally, he finished up. Wiping his hands on his leather apron, he walked out to talk to the soldiers. I sat, awkwardly waiting. Suddenly, Nathan called to me. I swallowed hard and moved to his side.

"This is my wife, Elizabeth." He turned to me, "They wanted to thank you for the refreshments." I nodded quietly, catching Preston watching us in disdainful amusement. That horrible smirk on his arrogant face made my skin crawl. I tried not to look his way, but I could feel him watching us the entire time as Nathan finished talking with the rest of the men. After what seemed like ages, the soldiers took their horses and rode off, the new shoes clinking on the cobblestone. I slipped my hand into Nathan's as they rode off.

He glanced down at me, "What is it?"

I twitched nervously. *The moment of truth…I can't.* "Nothing. I uh…it just makes me nervous. So many Confederate soldiers here lately." He turned to face me, his eyebrow raising skeptically. *He doesn't buy it, but he won't push the issue,* I thought.

Nathan moved back into the forge to help Marcus finish cleaning up and organizing everything for the night. I sighed, feeling heavy with a new fear…and a fresh guilt. Back inside, I stoked the fire and began preparations for dinner. That night Marcus and Nathan sat in the parlor planning out the next move to get the boys downstairs back to their units. After Marcus had retired to the forge for the night, I sat, still watching the flames licking at the logs in the hearth. I held a warm cup of tea, too distracted to drink it, but just letting the warmth move through my hands. I hardly realized Nathan was sitting in the room as well, watching me pensively…as I watched the flames. He never seemed to pry but waited patiently until I was ready to tell him something. Although, I always felt like it hurt him when I didn't open up to him about what I was thinking. But…I just couldn't. Not now. Not like this. He suddenly stood up and moved over to where I was sitting. I raised my eyes slowly to look up into his handsome face. Bending down, he kissed my forehead. I dropped my chin, ashamed of my concealment. Suddenly feeling his hand under my chin, he tilted my head back up, searching my face for a long moment. Then he gently brushed my cheek. My heart dropped and leapt all at once as I gazed into those eyes. Then the guilt spread through my veins again and I looked away.

After a pause, he whispered, "Goodnight," leaving me to sort out my troubling thoughts.

The Decoy
Chapter 30

Elizabeth

October 1864

A KNOCK ON the door startled me from dispersing the rest of the soup. The boys' heads shot up and searched my face for an answer. I forced a smile and set the ladle and pot of soup back on the counter.

I whispered, "Oh, no need to worry, I'm sure it's just the neighbors. Better get back to the cellar though, just in case." It was dark out, and deep inside I just knew it wasn't the neighbors...not at this hour. I stood at the door, my hand on the knob, but watched until the boys were safely out of sight and there was no longer any sound of footsteps to give them away. Another knock rapped against the door slab. I sucked in my breath. *Who could be calling at this hour of the evening?* Pulling the door open, I immediately regretted my decision to answer it. For there he stood, leaning casually against the frame, with that malicious smirk on his face...Luke Preston. Instinctively I pushed the door back to a smaller opening.

"Lieutenant Colonel," I curtsied, the irritation high in my tone. "How do you do?"

"Miss Matthews," he touched his hat with his finger then put a hand on his mouth. "Oh, do forgive me...I had forgotten it's Mrs. Tyler now, isn't it?" He stood upright and grinned. I could not help the glare that I knew was evident on my face as I waited for him to tell me why he was here. He suddenly motioned back to the forge. "Oh, I checked the forge…your slave said your husband wasn't here at the moment. I needed him to do some work for me."

"He is out," I caught myself, instantly regretting those words. "But he will be back…any minute now." I added, my eyes venturing toward the forge, hoping Marcus would come out.

Preston cocked an eyebrow, "Ah, I see. Well, I can wait for him here."

"No!" I said much too assertively. "Um, no, he's too busy to take any more work just now. I'm sorry." I began closing the door, suddenly Preston reached out and caught the door in his hand. My heart stopped a moment. *How dare he!*

"Don't be so cold to an old friend, Elizabeth." Holding the door open, he glanced around inside the house. "Entertaining company, are we?" A chill ran down my spine as I followed his gaze to the kitchen table where steaming bowls of soup sat, spoons still in them, right where the soldiers had left them.

"No, I…I set the table for Nathan and myself. As I said, he will be here any minute now."

Preston held my gaze for several agonizing moments before stepping back and releasing the door. "I see." I could see the suspicion in his every look. "I'll leave you to it then, *Mrs. Tyler*. Be sure and tell your husband I stopped by and will need him to work on something for me."

I watched him as he backed down the stairs, then turned and disappeared into the streets. Calming my breathing, I slowly latched the door. *He suspects something. Dear God, protect us from this danger.*

* * *

No matter how much I wished he would never return, he did, within a few weeks. The sun was heading toward the western sky when he arrived, filling the streets of Richmond with golden rays. Thankfully, Nathan did not have an escape planned for that night, or he would have found me alone once again. I cautiously watched out the window as Preston spoke with Nathan about the work he needed done. Then shocked, I watched as Nathan motioned him to the house.

What is he doing? Preston walked slowly toward the door as my heart sank into my stomach. I reluctantly pulled the door open after his tapping. That irritating smile greeted me again.

"I heard you're a nurse. I have a bad cut and some bruising. I fell off my horse."

Of course, you did. I doubted his every word. Motioning to the back room, I followed him in, leaving the door open and positioning myself to where I could still see the forge in the distance. Pulling up his sleeve he revealed a bloody gash. *It does need care.* I moved over to my shelves and selected what I needed. I began cleaning the wound silently.

"Your husband seems a good sort of fellow. Funny accent though…like yours. Seems like a Northern accent. Visiting more relatives' homes while you're here again?"

"As you well know my grandfather's plantation is near here," I replied shortly.

"Yes, but as I recall he died some time ago." He paused, "So how did you meet your husband?"

"If you don't mind, Sir, I don't feel like conversing with you about my private life. Let me just finish cleaning this up for you and you can be on your way."

"Oh no, I'm not finished, Elizabeth," I suddenly caught the scent of strong whiskey on his breath. "You see," he leaned in, "I believe you're keeping secrets."

I cringed inwardly, wrapping the wound even quicker, my heart beginning to pound. *I should have told Nathan about this man long ago and I would not be in this situation.*

He continued, "Why would a Northern man and woman be living in Richmond? And why would the man not be fighting in the Army of Virginia?"

I felt the uneasiness spreading and quickly answered, "There are many people who grew up in the North and then moved to the South, therefore they would have Northern accents. And as for my husband, he was injured in battle and for now he is serving the troops, such as yourself, as a blacksmith."

Preston snorted, "He seems in well enough condition to me."

I straightened up, "Your arm will heal soon, keep it dry and clean." I walked over to the doorway, waiting. The Lieutenant Colonel smirked and stood up as well, moving much too slowly to the entrance way. Before walking over the threshold, he stopped and looked over at the kitchen table.

"Any more *guests* tonight?" Then turning, he walked out the doorway and down the stairs.

Fear crept up inside my heart. *What does he know? What does he suspect?*

* * *

November 1864

The creaking of the house startled me from a restless sleep one particularly cold night. Nathan had gone out the night before on a mission and I had expected him home that following morning, but he never returned. All that day I had waited, paced and prayed. I had gone to bed that night, not able to sleep except for intervals of fitful tormented slumber. I sat up quickly in bed, heart pounding. *Did I actually hear that, or is it just in my nightmares?* Then it happened again, a clinking of a small rock pelting my window. My throat tightened. Hands shaking, I reached for a cloak and wrapped it around my nightgown. My knees threatened to give out from under me as I peered out. I couldn't see anyone. Then, hidden behind the bushes, a form moved.

Clutching the revolver in one hand, I descended the stairs and moved to the back door. Unlatching and cracking the door, I glanced around. Suddenly, Marcus appeared before me and quickly moved inside.

My legs almost gave way underneath me in relief. "Marcus, what on earth are you doing? In the dead of night?"

Marcus quickly bolted the door behind him and glanced out the window, holding the curtain mostly closed. "Something is not right. Nathan has been gone two nights now. And we are being watched."

I stared at him. "Maybe something needed to be taken care of and Nathan had to stay longer. We shouldn't act hastily," I told myself more than Marcus.

"Elizabeth, I'm telling you, we're being watched. It's only one person right now. I've been keeping an eye on him. He's stationed in the streets, watching the front of the house right now. I've seen him moving around. He'll watch the back for a bit, then move to the front."

A chill ran down my spine. "What are we going to do?"

Marcus' dark eyes darted about the room. "We have to get the escaped prisoners out of here. The sooner the better."

"But you just said we are being watched! We can't take them out now!"

"I know, but Elizabeth, if we wait who knows what'll happen tomorrow. And they might bring another spy in and then we won't be able to leave at all. At least right now there is only one. While he is watching the front of the house, I can get the soldiers out of the cellar and escape."

"No. No, it's too risky! Suppose he moves around and sees you at that moment. You can't do it, Marcus. I forbid it! Just wait for Nathan."

"Elizabeth, we've been found out…somehow. This is it. We can't hide anyone here anymore. The longer we wait the more danger we are in. We've got no choice. I'm getting them out tonight."

"How are we going to make sure he doesn't see you?"

Marcus thought a moment, "You're going to have to go out the front. Just walk around a little or even stay by the door and pretend to be doing something. He'll catch sight of you and watch."

I wiped a hand across my brow, "This is crazy." Then I paused, "But, maybe you're right. If we've been found out, we can't wait much longer." I sighed deeply, resigning myself to his decision. My throat constricted in the anticipation of what we were about to do. Thankfully, the boys in the cellar were doing much better and would be able to withstand the journey. I filled a knapsack and canteens for them and gave them to Marcus. Bracing himself by the back door, I moved to the front to give him the signal. Looking out the window, I stared as my eyes adjusted. Then noting the area Marcus had told me, I saw the form of a man. Shuddering, I looked back and nodded to my brother, then moved to the front door and outside into the chilly autumn night. Feeling I was on display and unsure of what to do, I cautiously moved down the stairs, being careful not to look the spy's way. My heart was racing and cold beads of sweat formed on my forehead. My whole body seemed to quiver. I began imagining Marcus, he must be in the cellar by now, getting the boys up, organizing them and their things. I clutched the revolver under my thick shawl, my knuckles whitening. Now he must be out in the back yard. They would be moving across the grass, past my ripened garden and into the fields beyond. Into the darkness…farther away…out of sight. I turned and began walking back up the stairs to the front door. Every fiber of my being screaming for me to run and slam the door shut behind me. I would not sleep the rest of this night.

The decoy had worked. Marcus and the soldiers had made it out of the city safely. The spy, and possibly the neighbors, if they were alerted by any noises, had watched a young woman wandering about the front of her house in the dead of night. Perhaps the spy thought she was sleep walking, perhaps he thought she was crazy…but whatever he thought…he did not see an escaping band of prisoners that night.

Haunted by the Past
Chapter 31

Elizabeth

MORNING DAWNED, AND with the brightness of the sun, it felt as if none of what had transpired the night before was even real. But Nathan was still not home. I sat up in bed. The anxiety of the night before crept back in. Taking a few deep breaths, I swung my legs out of bed, my feet hitting the cold wood. Running to the window, I looked out into the back yard for any sign of my husband…or Marcus. *Maybe he is in the forge.* Hurriedly, I slipped out of my nightgown and into a pale green, calico day dress. Pinning my brown waves into a neat bun, I stepped quickly down the stairs. They creaked and moaned their usual greeting. I reached for the handle of the door and swung it open. Jumping at the form in front of me, I quickly collapsed in relief into Nathan's arms, holding him tightly.

"Oh Nathan," I choked, "I was so scared."

Nathan stepped in, glancing behind him, then shut the door and bolted it quickly. "I know. I'm sorry. There were some complications with one of the escapes. The house was being watched when I finally came back. I couldn't risk it."

Nathan took my hand and led me to sit on the sofa. He sat down beside me, eyes watching mine. "Elizabeth, are you all right? Did anything happen?"

I swallowed, then recounted the events of the night. How Marcus had taken the soldiers out while I distracted the spy. I took a breath, *maybe now is the time to tell Nathan about Preston.* I had pushed it off for far too long. Before I could say another word, Nathan stood up.

"All right. We can talk more about this later. I need to get back out there. Some of the soldiers are back again with some jobs for me." He turned back around, "You're sure you're all right?"

I forced a smile, "Yes. Let's talk later." I sighed as he walked out the door. *Confederate soldiers…* I closed my eyes, wincing. *Preston is bound to be among them.*

I busied myself in the house and cleaned up what had remained of the garden. It felt good to be outside with the scent of dirt and grass close by as I knelt on a mat and pulled the remaining vines from the squashes, tossing them into a pile to burn later. Dusting off my gardening gloves, I rested my hands on my hips and peered up into the sunny sky from under my wide brimmed straw hat. Hopefully Marcus had come back to the forge by now after his escape with the prisoners last night.

Sure enough, the back door swung open and Marcus leaned in, "Nathan is asking for you to bring some water for the soldiers. He's finished their orders and was hoping you'd come out and show our *support* of the troops with some refreshments," he winked.

I stiffened, certain that Preston would be part of the group. "Of course," I said quietly, "I'm glad you're back safe, Marcus. Did the boys make it safely?" I whispered quietly, undoing my gardening apron as I moved into the house. He answered in the affirmative and took off back outside to help Nathan. Gathering the water pitcher and some cups onto a tray, I also gathered my courage and moved out the door. Quickly scanning the group as I stepped down the stone stairs, I nearly sighed out loud when I didn't see Preston among the soldiers. The men smiled politely and thanked me as they took the water.

Soon they prepared to leave when one of them called, "Johnson, where did Preston say he and Aaron were going?" At the mention of his name my insides flipped, and I felt instantly sick.

"Oh, there he is now!" One of the men shouted, "No doubt having a little drink as he waited for the work to be done." The men laughed and called to him. Luke Preston and the other officer approached the forge bantering back at the soldiers around them. By the looks of him, he had had more than "a little drink." I tried to melt into the shadow of the forge and prayed no one would see me slip away, but it didn't work.

"Mrs. Tyler," he smiled, "a pleasure to see you again."

I curtsied slightly, not looking him in the eyes and not saying a word.

Then he addressed Nathan, "Mr. Tyler, thank you for your work again." He shook his hand. "You have a lovely wife. We were friends long ago you know."

I felt the blood drain from my face. I was frozen and my feet became as lead weights. Nathan, who stood a few feet in front of me, glanced back to where I stood, still in the shadow of the forge. He raised an eyebrow inquisitively.

Preston smirked, "Or…oh…it appears she hasn't told you. I will allow her to do that then," he looked over at me, waving a hand. "Elizabeth, dear, perhaps you would like to tell your husband about our past history." He began moving in my direction.

"That's enough," Nathan cut him off, moving directly in front of him and laying a hand on his shoulder. Stepping in closer, Nathan threatened in a low voice, "Don't ever address my wife like that again."

Preston pulled his shoulder away from under Nathan's firm grip. "And what will you do about it if I do?" he growled under his breath.

The soldiers around Preston straightened up. One of them moved over and pulled at his arm, "Come on, Sir. Leave it alone."

Preston slapped his hand away and took a step forward at Nathan. Nathan stood his ground, staring him in the eyes calmly but resolutely. Suddenly, Preston's glare turned into a wicked grin. Scoffing, he kept an eye on Nathan but backed away toward the group of soldiers.

"I don't have time for this now. But believe me, I know what's going on here and you won't get away with it." He swung up onto his horse, then spun it back around and looked at me again. "Elizbeth, do tell your husband about us. Ease his mind, will you?" Nathan started toward Preston's horse, but Preston just laughed and kicked his mount into a trot as the group moved away. My insides quivered, and I could hardly believe what had just happened.

Nathan stood watching the disappearing horsemen for a long while. I shrank within myself, wanting more than ever to disappear into the wall of the forge. When he turned around his brow was pensive, and a dark cloud had passed over his face. Running his hand over the roughage on his chin, he brushed past me into the forge. I stood, still frozen in place. Without saying a word, he began hammering a red-hot iron. The clang was so loud as he beat it harder than I had heard him beat an iron before. I could see his jaw clenched, and after about five strokes he shoved the metal and threw the hammer and iron onto the floor. They all landed on the ground with a loud clattering. He turned quickly away and walked toward the back of the forge, running his hand through his hair. My body jumped and shook as I watched all this from my position.

After a couple minutes, he came back and said quietly. "We can't take in anymore prisoners. They've found us out." His eyes shot up and stared solemnly into mine. That cold blue stare that I had fought against so long ago. I felt myself wanting to hide from it again and again lately. His voice dropped into a deeper, even more intense tone. "Elizabeth, is there anything else that has happened here…or in the past…that you need to tell me about?" The guilt hit me with vehement force in the chest, nearly knocking the wind out of me. His eyes pinned me to the wall. It was my fault. I hadn't told Nathan about Preston, or his more recent unwanted visits. I felt my face flushing in the anguish of it all. If I had only told him, back in Gettysburg, this might have been avoided. My heart began pounding so loudly, I was sure he could hear it. Without thinking, I rushed back into the house and into the kitchen. I quickly grabbed some teacups from the cupboard and pulled a skillet out. Soon I heard Nathan's footsteps stop in the entryway behind me. Hands shaking, I hurriedly moved around the kitchen, all the while my mind racing with the thoughts of what I had done by not letting my husband know about this dangerous man.

Suddenly, I felt Nathan close behind me. "Elizabeth."

"I'll just be a minute, I have to make us some food," even my voice faltered.

Suddenly Nathan's hand covered mine on the handle of the tea kettle, stopping me from what I was doing. He took both my trembling hands in his. Tilting his head down to look directly into my eyes, he asked sternly and slowly, "*What happened?*"

I couldn't meet that gaze…those eyes that searched mine so deeply. I suddenly took a deep breath, pulling my hands out of his I covered my mouth. Shaking my head, I whispered, "Nathan, I…should have told you long ago. I didn't think I needed to, and I didn't want you to be upset. Now it's come back to haunt me. We could be in so much trouble because of it-,"

"Elizabeth," Nathan cut me off, then repeated slowly. "What happened?"

I took a deep breath again and moved to the kitchen table. We sat down, and I began telling him…*everything*. How I had met Preston after we had escaped the prison camp. How I had allowed myself to be swept away in a frivolous lifestyle for some time. How he had come to the forge a few times. I told him everything, just as I should have done long ago.

Nathan had sat quietly the entire time, never once interrupting me. Yet, I watched his expressions darken and change throughout the story. At the end of my tale, he still said nothing. I sighed deeply, feeling like a great weight had been lifted from my shoulders, but still a deep-seated fear rested in the pit of my stomach.

Reaching for Nathan's hand I said, "Please forgive me."

Nathan allowed me to take his hand, but only nodded. The dark cloud still hanging low over his countenance. Then he stood up, slowly pulling his hand out of mine and walked to the door.

"Nathan, please-," I followed him reaching out, but he stopped me, holding up his hand.

"Just…give me some time," as he looked up, I could see the hurt in his eyes. Then he moved out the door, closing it softly behind him. The rest of that day into the evening all I heard was the pounding of the hammer on the anvil and the occasional sizzling of the red-hot iron in water.

The Broken Hearted
Chapter 32

Amy

November 1864

THE DARKNESS THAT followed over the months after Kelsey's death was like nothing I had ever experienced in this horrible war. It invaded every aspect of my life, my waking and sleeping hours. In the midst of my dreams I would see him, memories from the past and images of the future we'd lost together. Several times I tried to write another letter home, to Elizabeth, to tell her of Kelsey, but I could never bring myself to write the words. *I can't, not right now…I will write her another day.* Then, when I'd learned Anderson was responsible for Kelsey's death…my heart turned cold and dark, like stone once more, full of hate and anger, and I knew I would never rest until that murderer had finally met his end.

* * *

Only a dim light glimmered on the horizon of the deep blue mountains as the weary men made preparations for a well-deserved rest. Horses were picketed and given what feed the soldiers could muster and then left to graze. A few of the men dropped onto soft patches of forest floor with rolled up blankets or pillows, but most took a few moments to gently curry their mounts. It had been days since we'd abandoned the Morgan's mansion in Richmond, gathering up only what belongings were necessary for the journey and closing up the house. With the growing threat of a siege against Richmond and the news of Sherman's destruction in Georgia, Seth Morgan had decided to finally put into motion the plan he and Kelsey had devised if such a situation were to arise. That plan to take their families deeper into the foothills of the Appalachian Mountains, to an obscure location for safety. A secluded farm had been chosen, hidden away from Anderson and any possible threat on the capitol from Grant's army through the long siege of Petersburg. Rumors had reached us of disappearances and sudden deaths of family members of some officers in our own regiment, creating a silent but evident panic in the ranks. Many soldiers were sent home to attend to the safety of their families and find new temporary homes for them, away from danger. Only a small unit now accompanied us on our journey. In my sleepless nights, I had caught sight of Seth pacing the border of the camp, deep in thought, tense, worry written on his face. With the loss of my greatest friend and fiancé, he had also lost his only true confidant and support…and now the weight of responsibility rested on his shoulders alone.

"Here," Captain Hamilton appeared beside me, holding up a brush, startling me out of my daydream.

Managing a small smile, I glanced up and gratefully took the brush. "Thank you, Captain."

He nodded, pulling his black mare up beside my gelding and began grooming.

They had tried to keep it discreet, but it was obvious the remaining officers had made it their duty to keep constant vigil over me after my loss. In the depths of my sorrow, I welcomed the constant companionship from whomever assumed the assignment next. It gave me something to occupy my mind, even though I sometimes craved the solitude in which I could release my true emotions.

I was deeply touched by their concern and the respect they showed me, though I felt I had done little to deserve it. Though Peter was often away on missions now, he was my greatest source of comfort, yet I'd been almost surprised that in my grief I'd found myself drawing the most strength from Seth Morgan.

His ever-constant, quiet presence created a peace and security. The knowledge of his brotherly friendship with Kelsey sealed a surprisingly stronger bond than I expected I could ever have with someone so reserved. Yet, in such a difficult time as this was, I wouldn't question it. I would simply be grateful for his continual support since Kelsey's passing. Feeling suddenly anxious, I glanced around and couldn't help but observe the missing face amongst officers' present.

"I don't see Major Morgan."

Mark Hamilton wistfully glanced amongst the faces. "The major often goes off on his own. Don't worry, Miss Amy. We're far from enemy lines. We are not at risk. We'll have you and Mrs. Morgan and Mrs. Kingston delivered safely to your destination soon."

Nodding disinterestedly, I finished grooming, gave the gelding a gentle face rub, pulled a shawl around my shoulders and sat down under an oak tree. A sergeant came by with two tin mugs full of a hot stew for me and the captain. After holding it a moment, I placed the nearly full cup aside, my stomach too twisted to eat. Captain Hamilton glanced down at my unfinished stew.

"Miss Amy, please, try to eat something. I know it's not much, but you need to keep your strength up." Resting the back of my head on the tree, I turned to the young worried captain. Our eyes met and, seeing the resignation in mine, he looked away and forcefully took the last few gulps of his own food.

"I promised Peter when we departed from Richmond that I would watch out for you. All of the men are anxious about you. They feel a special fondness for you especially since…," his voice broke and he glanced about agitatedly. "You need to take care of yourself, Miss Amy." Placing a hand on his sleeve, I quieted the anxious boy.

"I know Mark, I know. I'm fine." Still looking unconvinced, he nodded. "Please, tell me about something else…tell me about yourself, your life. How did you come to know the Morgans and join this regiment?" I asked, wearily closing my eyes and leaning back again. After a long pause, in which I could feel the young officer studying me, I heard him shift about and then begin.

"Well…my family didn't grow up with much. My father died when I was too young to remember it. I suppose it was just a stroke of luck that I happened to be in a group of older boys, playing in a field just outside Richmond, when I met Seth Morgan. When Mr. Morgan heard of my family's situation, he reached out to offer my mother help, but she was a proud woman. She wouldn't take charity. So, he offered her a position as a seamstress. She worked in the mansion for Mrs. Morgan, and when townsfolk saw her skill, why she had more work than she knew what to do with. My sister and I grew up in that mansion, you could say…spent more time there when school was out than in our own house. Mr. Morgan helped me get into the school where his son had graduated from and, when I showed an interest in the military, he set up a small trust so that when I was old enough, I could enter West Point. But then the war started." Hamilton paused and I could hear a smile in his voice, "Those were the days, Miss Matthews. A poor boy growing up in a rich house, suddenly having security…a family. The Morgans were our family. Are our family."

Mark's stories rolled around in my mind as I tried to drift off to another restless "sleep", but even after the entire camp had gone silent, I could not quiet my mind. Listlessly rising to my feet, I glanced over at the forms of Jane and her mother covered in a thick woolen blanket. Slowly leaving the group, I paced outside the camp limits through a small grove of trees on the edge of a steep hill. My heart heavy and my mind spent, I trod through the last line of trees where I spotted Seth Morgan, standing on the precipice of a sort of cliff, one hand on his sword hilt, scanning the darkening hills. Somehow sensing my approach, his head shot up and he threw the last of the cigar to the ground, stepping on it with his black boot to demolish the smoke.

"Miss Amy."

"Major," stepping beside him, I viewed the rolling forest hills, shrouded in a heavy evening fog. Wrapping the light shawl around my shoulders tightly, more for comfort than warmth, I sighed deeply.

"How are you?" The gentle tone in Seth's voice caused a painful ache to sweep over my body again.

Swallowing hard, I turned, "I'm well enough."

That piercing gaze seemed to reach down into my soul and the unconvinced look was evident on his face. Looking away, I shook my head defeatedly. *There was no deceiving him. Far too perceptive.*

He waited expectantly in silence, while I composed myself. Finally, in hardly more than a whisper, I released the truth, "I'm afraid, afraid that this darkness," I choked, "this weight I feel, will never be lifted…that I'll never truly feel-,"

"Alive again," Seth finished my thought.

Allowing the heavy tears to roll down my cheeks, with a strangling emotion in my throat I whispered, "Yes." Turning away considerately, he allowed me my privacy. I joined him in studying the vast starry expanse, feeling some relief in knowing I had a companion in my struggle.

"Years ago, I lost my wife," Seth spoke up, in a voice rigid and filled with sorrow. "I know that pain, that emptiness. Every day making the choice to keep moving forward, to keep going even when you feel you've lost the *reason* to keep breathing." Sighing, he lifted his face to the darkening sky, "I've lived through some of the darkest days of my life alone. No words can comfort, no one can understand. And there are days still…," he paused for a long moment and I dared not turn to face him. Sighing heavily, he continued, "Days where the pain feels too difficult to bear, the memory too overwhelming. But you make it through, even when you want to give up." Wiping roughly at the tears that clouded my vision, I pushed back the stray hair in my face.

"Don't let the anger and bitterness overtake you."

My head shot up. "What do you mean?" I hesitated anxiously.

"When you first came to us, it was eating away at you." He paused, "With the pain of loss, in any respect, it can invade your mind and heart. You build up hard walls to protect your most vulnerable emotions. It's how you cope. I've been where you've been, felt what you felt. That's how I recognized it in you." Keeping his gaze on the rolling hills he continued in a reverent voice, "When you lose someone, you're never the same again, you never will be, nor would you want to be. The change in you is inevitable…but who you become is up to you. As this war has changed you, so can you change the war within you."

Struck by the profoundness of his words, I turned to study him and found his calm, confident gaze already locked on me.

"But never alone, Amy. You'll never be free from the heartache, nightmares, the anger…alone. You need help, and I believe you know where to find it." Seth's voice was but a gentle whisper as he added reverently, "He's still there."

Nodding softly, I swallowed back tears, the heavy weight on my heart beginning to break free. *Perhaps it's time, time to let go. Let go of all the anger, the questioning…to trust Him again.* Seeing the resolve in my distant gaze, the young major turned to leave me in the peace of the evening.

"Thank you, Seth," instinctively I reached out and touched his arm. He paused, looking down at me, locking eyes for a brief moment before he disappeared into the line of trees.

Through Fire and Water
Chapter 33

Elizabeth

December 1864

THE LAST FEW weeks had been hard. Nathan seemed distant ever since the incident with Luke Preston and my confession of all that I had kept hidden from him since we had been married. I wished there was some way I could change the past. I wished I could go back to that night in Gettysburg when John Barnes had visited, and Nathan had asked me what Mr. Barnes had been talking about. But I had been too prideful…too fearful. And now, look at the trouble it had caused us: a dangerous man haunting us, our mission to help prisoners escape threatened…ruined, and my husband who felt as though our trust had been broken. I knew that was what bothered him the most. Those first couple years of knowing Nathan…trust was so important to him. And I had broken that. How would I ever win him back after this? The guilt hung over me constantly…like a heavy rain cloud threatening to burst. Our conversations were short, to the point, and quiet. I could feel the tension in the room, the words that needed to be spoken but were forever trapped in the thick air.

One snowy night Colonel Brandt came. He had not been to our home for some time. I was glad to see him, even if just to break the tension that had gone on for so long between Nathan and me. I took the colonel's coat and hat, hanging them on the wooden pegs by the door. He greeted me, then took a second glance at my face. I knew he could see the tension. He looked perplexed but he did not ask for an explanation. We moved into the kitchen area and he shook hands with Nathan before they both sat down. I poured coffee into both their cups as they talked of what was going on in the war: Abraham Lincoln's re-election, Sherman's march to the sea and Grant's plan of executing his "total war" strategy. I thought back to the days when Grant was only a brigade general and I had been a nurse helping in his unit. It seemed he had risen quickly through the ranks to be the top general of the Union Army.

Much too soon, the conversation shifted to our mission here and the escapes Nathan had led from the prison camps.

"You have done well, Nathan," Colonel Brandt spoke softly, but honestly. "So many officers and men have you to thank, most likely for their lives, if not just for their freedom." I busied myself cleaning the dishes in the wash basin, trying to be quiet and invisible. "You should be very proud." Nathan nodded his thanks but dropped his eyes humbly. Colonel Brandt watched him carefully, "General Grant himself has spoken highly of you, and I wouldn't be surprised if he asks to meet you in person one day."

"Thank you, Sir. I'm only trying my best to serve my country," Nathan stated.

"Well, you have done that, Captain," Colonel Brandt smiled softly.

"Sir," Nathan hesitated, "I believe we are in danger of discovery."

Colonel Brandt straightened, "What's happened?" he asked in a low tone. I could feel my body tense and breathed in a slow breath as Nathan continued.

"Some of the Confederate soldiers come here often for me to do certain projects for them in the forge," Colonel Brandt nodded for Nathan to continue. "Their Lieutenant Colonel… a Luke Preston…has said some things that have led me to believe he has found us out. Elizabeth and Marcus have seen someone watching the house as well. I wasn't sure what to do yet, and you have been so busy I didn't know how to notify you except in person, for fear of letting the secret out if written on paper and delivered. So, I haven't gone out on a mission for several weeks now. It's been quiet here, and I haven't seen anyone watching us anymore. I don't know how to proceed until we know exactly where we stand."

Colonel Brandt rubbed his chin. His brown eyes pensive and darkening. I felt the knot in my stomach tightening as I slowly dried a dish with a towel. After a few moments, the colonel asked Nathan some more questions, digging deeper into the situation. I almost breathed a sigh of relief as Nathan never once added my name into the very problem that I felt I had caused. He would have been correct if he had told Colonel Brandt that I knew the leader of this Confederate group and that I had been careless enough to not mention the warning signs to my husband. But Nathan was bigger than that…and even though I felt his distance and his distrust of me now, I knew he was a good man. And though I didn't deserve his love, he would still protect me and care for my well-being and my honor.

After a moment of silence, Colonel Brandt stated, "We need to move you to a new location. Start packing your things…we should try to get you out tomorrow or the day after. We must not delay any longer." Nathan and Colonel Brandt wrapped up the last details and they moved to the door. I followed quietly. Colonel Brandt glanced at me, I could tell he sensed something was off, but he said nothing, only nodded to me and touched his hat as he exited the door.

Nathan turned back to me after the colonel left. His steely blue eyes watched me for a moment. Then he said softly, "Get your things together, Elizabeth. Be ready to leave at any moment."

My heart clenched, not only because of the danger we were in, but more so because of the distance in Nathan's demeanor toward me. I dropped my eyes and nodded, moving slowly up the stairs to begin packing our belongings. As I folded the few dresses I had, I smoothed my hand over a deep blue calico. The emotions of all that had happened lately seemed to well up inside me. Suddenly I just wanted to go back to Gettysburg again. But even there the landscape had been changed and altered by so much death and devastation. And now I felt tension and unrest even in my own home.

I whispered, "Why can't there just be peace…somewhere…a place to rest from all this?" I wiped at the tears spilling onto the folded dresses in front of me. As I gazed out the small window, I remembered someone once saying that sometimes in this world we have no physical place of refuge to run to. The place of refuge is not on this earth, yet our mind and soul can still be at peace no matter our physical location. I whispered a verse that I remembered mother reciting long ago, "And the peace of God, which surpasses all understanding, shall guard your hearts and minds in Christ Jesus." A peace that surpasses all understanding…that was what I needed. I dropped to my knees and prayed to the only One who could give me such peace.

* * *

The next day I stood looking at the few bags filled with the little we owned. I had carried them down the stairs and laid them all next to the back door. I re-tucked the stray hairs into a bun at the nape of my neck and smoothed down the skirt of my dress. Nathan had been in the forge all day, finishing what jobs he could and packing up the tools we might be able to carry in the wagon. Marcus had gone off to the market to see if he could find any extra food for the journey.

Suddenly I heard strange noises coming from the forge. I quickly stepped out the door and ran to the entrance of the forge. The breath caught in my throat as I tried to scream, "Nathan!" I couldn't believe what I was seeing. Nathan and another man were throwing punches and flinging each other to the ground, and I was fairly certain who the other man was. As the other man's head came up before another punch, my fear was confirmed – Luke Preston! Soon enough Nathan landed Preston on the ground and straddled him and began throwing punch after punch.

Before I knew what was happening, Marcus came flying in, dropping the contents of what he had bought at the market in the snowy street. He grabbed Nathan around the waist, struggling to drag him off of Preston.

"No! No! Nathan, stop! Stop it!" Marcus yelled in his ear as he struggled with Nathan, pulling him off of the Lieutenant Colonel. When Marcus finally got Nathan to his feet, Nathan lunged at Preston yelling, "Get out!"

My insides shook. I could only imagine what had caused this fight. Preston leaned on his elbow, wiping at his battered and bleeding lips. His face hot with rage, he struggled to his feet.

Spitting out blood he shouted, "I know what you've been doing here. Hiding escaped prisoners. We caught one of your boys, and he told us…he told us everything. Now, on top of it all – you've made a terrible mistake! Attacking an officer! I swear you will pay. You will pay dearly for this! All of you…I swear it," he hissed the last words.

"*Get out.*" Nathan's voice was a tone I had never heard before, and it struck a deep sense of fear within me. Preston backed away, finally getting on his horse and cantering off. I slowly approached where Marcus still stood holding Nathan's upper arms loosely, as they watched the disappearing rider. Marcus, on seeing me approach, released Nathan and quietly picked up the food that lay strewn in the road. Nathan's eyes never left the disappearing figure, even as I approached.

I reached to touch his shoulder, "Nathan…"

He pulled away, shaking his head.

I felt my chin quiver, "Nathan, please, I just-,"

"No, Elizabeth. Not now," his voice was so stern, I bit my lip to hold back the emotions. After all this, would he ever trust me again? I felt as if I had lost him…even living in the same house I had lost him. It was like we were back to the beginning of when we first met…but worse.

* * *

I laid in bed still tossing and turning. How could one sleep on such a night? Nathan had not come to bed. I finally gave up and slipped on a comfortable calico and crept down the stairs. I was only halfway down when I saw Nathan sitting in one of the chairs, rifle in hand, watching out the windows. I stopped, not wanting him to know I was there. Slowly, I tried to turn around and go back up the stairs without him noticing. Just then I saw him stiffen and clench the rifle. I stopped and listened intently, I could barely hear it, but it sounded like hoofbeats, many hoofbeats, approaching. Then I heard shouting and saw the flickering of light coming through the windows. Nathan cocked his rifle and stood. Watching the window, he backed toward the stairs, then turned and saw me. His eyes were alert, yet they held something else…trepidation? Dread?

"Nathan? What is it?" I swallowed, clenching the stair rail.

He motioned me to come down. Once I was close to him, he whispered, "We have to leave now. Go out the back door, run to the woods beyond the back yard. Wait for me there." His eyes flashed as he looked from me to the window. Now I could see it, reflections of fire…torches? Suddenly the hoofbeats stopped in front of our house. Horses neighed, stomped, and snorted amidst the talking of men.

Then a man yelled, "We know you're there. Come out!"

My heart pounded. *Preston.* Nathan pulled me down the stairs and pushed me toward the back door. My feet felt heavy. As I moved past the window I looked out and saw…several horsemen, all carrying torches. Some shouts and laughter rang in the air. Preston had brought his friends, angry and drunk. I saw the bags I had packed by the back door.

"No, Elizabeth, leave them…take the one bag and go out the back. Hurry!"

Suddenly Marcus appeared in the kitchen. "Nathan, you take Elizabeth and get out of here fast. I will slow them down."

"No, Marcus," Nathan argued. "You can't-,"

"Listen to me!" Marcus pulled me to the back door and shoved the bag into my hands. "You both have to go now! Nathan, you mean too much to the Union cause to die like this. You can't fight them. Leave me here. I can at least give you some time to get away. They are going to kill you…*and Elizabeth.* Whatever happens…you keep running. Do you understand me? You *do not* come back for me! Promise me, Nathan! Promise me you will keep going, and make sure Elizabeth gets to safety." He stared Nathan hard in the eyes, "*Do not come back for me.*"

Nathan swallowed hard, his jaw tensing. After a look in my direction, he grabbed Marcus' hand and placed the rifle in it. "Then take this," Nathan clasped his shoulder, "brother."

Suddenly a pounding on the front door rang through the house, it felt as though it shook the walls to its very foundations. "Come out now, Yank! Or we will burn your house to the ground with you and your pretty wife in it!" I felt the blood drain from my face. Hands shaking, I reached for the doorknob and pushed the door open. Glass shattered through the kitchen. The sound of it pierced my ears as it clattered all over the kitchen floor, the butt of a rifle sticking through the window.

Marcus shoved us both. Nathan wrapped his hand around my wrist and pulled me through our garden. I stumbled, hardly seeing where I was going, the night was so dark and my mind so filled with fear. The sound of breaking glass and the flashing of the fire grew less as we moved farther away from the terrible scene.

As we made it to the tree line, I suddenly heard gunshots. They stopped me in my tracks. Turning, I saw forms in the yard, silhouetted by the backdrop of our house in flames. The gunshots were still echoing in my ears when my eyes distinguished Marcus' form dropping to his knees. Someone moved slowly over to him, jerking him up by his shirt collar, shouting, their face close to his. Then roughly they released his collar and kicked him in the stomach, Marcus falling flat on his face. Then another gunshot.

The whole world went silent. I screamed, but I could not even hear my own scream. Then something welled up within me and I moved quickly to rush back toward the aggressor. But strong hands held my arms and pulled me back farther into the woods. My whole body trembled, and I felt as if none of this was real. Surely, I was only having a nightmare. Another nightmare. But no, it *was* real. Flames flew up the sides of the house from the broken windows and began licking the roof. We were about one hundred yards away, but I could clearly see the silhouettes of the invaders moving around the house still and tossing more torches into it. I struggled with Nathan, trying to pull my arms out of his strong hands to rush to Marcus' side. The world was so still, so silent, so strange. I couldn't hear anything, even my own screams…at least I thought they were coming from me. Or perhaps there was no sound I could make that would describe the anguish I felt in my soul. The invaders began moving toward us. They were searching for us. Nathan dragged me away from the scene…at least he must have…I did not know. My mind was dark and still. I could not see the woods we fled through, the freezing streams we crossed, the miles we traversed in the dark night and even into the next night. I could not see it, nor did I want to. I did not want to see anything anymore.

Hidden Foothills
Chapter 34

Amy

December 1864

THE QUIET COUNTRY house seemed to be in its own world, as if there were no war, no threat of an invader. Thick, snow laden clouds hung low above the hills and forests that were almost completely silent, except for the chirping of a few sparrows on their afternoon search for food. The little house sat against the bottom of one of the many foothills to the Appalachian Mountains. An old, weathered barn accompanying it only a few yards away in the small valley. The previously tilled farm fields lay unoccupied with only a few straggling bramble bushes sprouting randomly. The house gave the appearance of an abandoned building; dormant vines clinging to the walls, windows caked with dust so thick, nothing but a shadow could be seen within. A narrow trail of smoke rising from the musty looking chimney was the only sign of life. Sighing with relief, Jane glanced over at me, her eyes tired and full of sadness. At last we had reached safety, or so we hoped.

We were ushered inside by our gracious hosts, a tall willowy farmer and his equally frail looking wife. Standing in the dim yet cozy little parlor, where a small fire was lit with a kettle hanging over it, I tried to convince myself this was the best option for our safety, but the feeling of uneasiness at separating from the regiment still plagued me. Voices murmured in the hall as the farmer's wife showed Jane and Mrs. Morgan to the room we would share. The air smelled of dust and freshly chopped wood, and the inside of the house was as dim as a dungeon. Dropping my bags to the floor, I walked over to the window watching the small group of soldiers still mounted outside, waiting for their leader.

"Miss Amy," turning swiftly, I spotted Seth standing in the wide opening that began, what I assumed was, the parlor. He glanced back toward where the others had disappeared to before stepping in closely and lowering his voice. "The Wilsons will take good care of you. This is a very secluded area, very unsuspecting…that's why of course Kelsey and I felt it would be best…" He stopped, unable to finish and I nodded knowingly.

"I trust your judgment, Major." There was a long pause as I turned around, taking in the dreary scene of the room.

"I hope you can find some peace here," Seth spoke up again, his tone softer, "away from all the memories…and begin to heal."

I froze, my back still to him, the heaviness in my heart swelling.

"Perhaps," I agreed, my voice a meek whisper. Finally, sighing, I gathered my courage, "You should be going, Major, your men are waiting."

He hesitated a moment, and in his usual way when feeling uneasy, laid a hand on the saber at his side, seeming to draw some confidence from its presence.

"I want you to know," he hesitated awkwardly, "I don't consider myself worthy to take his-,"

"Kelsey would want it this way," I forced myself to swallow rigidly, knowing my approval was essential to his confidence as Kelsey's successor. "You know them better than anyone. You knew Kelsey's desires and plans better than *anyone*. There is no one more suited to lead them."

A look of peace came over his face and a silent acknowledgment of respect passed between us. Seth slowly stepped in closer to me and held something out between us. Confused, I glanced down at the black pistol revealed in a small cloth.

"This was his…," he said reverently, with as much unconcealed emotion as I had ever seen the reserved young man allow. "Don't underestimate them." He looked me directly in the eyes, his warning stern yet tender, "Use your instincts.

Your abilities. You've proven yourself a soldier. I would trust you with my family's lives. I *do* trust you."

Unable to speak, I took the pistol and carefully concealed it. My heart dropped in a sickening sadness, knowing this could be the last time I saw any of these soldiers, these comrades that had become brothers of Kelsey…and also of mine. The South was suffering, the future seemed foreboding and bleak now. As if Kelsey's death had begun a chain reaction, and now we found ourselves in the direst of circumstances within only a few short months. *Will any of us make it out of this nightmare alive?*

Before long, the farmer followed Seth Morgan back outside, receiving the last few instructions and warnings from the major. Unable to hold back, I ran after them and stopped just a few feet away from the entrance to the rickety shack.

"Seth!" I blurted out fearfully. "When should we expect your return?"

There was a look of pity in his eyes, but unable to answer, he turned, saying nothing, and mounted the stallion that was now brought up beside him. With one final glance back at me, I felt my stomach drop as I watched the small group disappear into the hills.

A Colonel's Insignia
Chapter 35

Elizabeth

December 1864

THE SIGHT OF those white canvas tents and Union flags were such a comfort as we finally arrived to where we knew Colonel Brandt was stationed. Nathan took my hand and helped me up the small incline toward the encampment. I stared blankly ahead, my mind still trying to grasp what had just happened…and all I had lost. A cold winter breeze blew around us. Some snow still on the ground caused my feet to slip occasionally. I pulled Nathan's jacket closer around me, wondering at how he could keep going with just his long sleeve shirt in this cold breeze. As we entered the encampment, a guard called to us. Nathan identified himself and the guard motioned for us to follow him. We approached a large tent and the guard went ahead of us and informed the colonel that we were here. Colonel Brandt appeared quickly, concern written in all of his features. He locked eyes with Nathan.

"What happened?"

"He found us out, Sir," Nathan's jaw tensed. "Lieutenant Colonel Preston, he came with a group, burned down the house…," Nathan glanced quickly in my direction, then said in a lower tone, "killed Marcus." I looked away and stared off at the distant tree line. The barren trees reached their dead hands up to the sky as if grasping for hope. A tear slipped down my cheek. My eyes burned from the sleepless nights, the many tears…it seemed I had cried all the tears I could possibly have. Colonel Brandt looked my way, but he did not address the topic.

"Come with me," the colonel's deep voice was filled with compassion. "You both look in need of rest and some clean clothes."

Once inside a tent of our own, I sat down on the blanket, the hard, cold ground beneath me.

Nathan moved to the entrance, but looked back at me, "I'll go get some food. Try to get some rest."

I nodded and looked down at my dress. I hadn't noticed how sorely I was in need of a good cleaning and a change of clothes. The hem of my dress was covered in frozen mud, and streaks of dirt showed throughout the dress. It was torn in places and had burrs and thorns in others. My hair disheveled, mud and grime on my hands and face. I dipped my hands into the water bucket they had provided and began wiping myself with a rag. Once I was clean enough, I changed into the one dress I had put in the only bag we had brought with us. Doing my best, I ran my fingers through my hair to brush it, then tied it back up in a bun. My body ached all over as I laid back on the blankets. It was uncomfortable to be sure, but here I felt safe, at least for the time being. Here I could rest. The cleaning and new dress helped me to feel somewhat refreshed, on the outside at least. But my heart ached every time I thought of Marcus and how he had been killed, and more tears moved slowly down my cheeks. I felt so angry at the men who had killed him…a feeling of deep hatred filled my heart. I tried to direct my mind to home…to the past…what it had been like living in Gettysburg as a young girl. And there…my mind was finally able to rest, and I fell into a deep sleep.

* * *

I woke up, stiff, but feeling rested…and very hungry. I sat up slowly, taking in my whereabouts, remembering why we were here in a tent…in the army again. I straightened the dress I had slept in…how long? Smoothing out the wrinkles, I moved into the outdoors and sunshine. The sun felt so good on my face as I squinted into the blue sky. It was good to see the sun, especially in this winter weather.

Suddenly I felt someone next to me, "You slept most of the day away." Nathan handed me a tin cup full of black coffee. I wrinkled my nose at its bitterness but appreciated the warmth that ran through my body as I drank it. We moved over to a campfire and sat down on a log.

Nathan watched me, "Are you all right?"

I nodded, feeling the numbness return as I thought through our narrow escape.

I looked up cautiously at Nathan, "I will be…thanks to you," I offered. I felt some of the tension that had been between us lessen…at least a little. Even if he didn't feel like he could trust me, I knew he cared. He had proved it again and again as we had escaped and made our journey through rough terrain back to the army.

"Nathan I…I know you feel like I've broken our trust. I should have told you about Preston and everything that had happened long ago. I was afraid…I didn't want to hurt you by bringing it up and it was embarrassing and awkward. I'm so sorry that I did hurt you and put us in so much danger. And now Marcus is gone, and I feel like it's all my fa-,"

Nathan cut me off, "No, Elizabeth." He set his coffee cup down and turned to face me. "Marcus' death is not your fault."

I covered my face with my hands. "He never even got to meet Amy. And I wanted to take him to Gettysburg, I just wish…," I shook my head.

Just then Colonel Brandt approached us, we stood, and he motioned for us to sit back down. He then sat down on the other side of Nathan.

"Take some time to rest, as long as you need. But I do have another location we can station you, for the same mission. There is a prison camp…Camp Sorghum, is what the prisoners call it. It is outside of Columbia, South Carolina. There have been successful escapes from this camp. It contained about fifteen hundred Union officers. These were prisoners at a camp in Charleston, South Carolina which they moved inland in October. They had an outbreak of yellow fever and didn't want them infecting the civilians in town, so they transferred them there. They were also afraid of Sherman coming and freeing them in

Charleston. It is a five-acre open prison. However, they just recently moved the prisoners to a walled enclosure that shares ground with the State Lunatic Asylum, thus calling it Camp Asylum. I want you, Nathan, to go and break out as many prisoners as possible. We have reason to believe there are over one thousand officers held captive there. I don't know how much longer this war will last…perhaps it will soon be finished…but there are no guarantees." Colonel Brandt paused. "However, everyone will understand if you need to take a break from this kind of work. There's a place for you here in the army if you'd rather just do that."

Nathan looked off into the distance for a moment, then answered, "No, sir. They need my help. This is what I'm supposed to do."

Colonel Brandt nodded, then was quiet for a moment. Finally, he stood up and shook Nathan's hand. "General Grant has requested to meet you. I've arranged for you to go with me tomorrow night…and you as well, Mrs. Tyler." He smiled softly at me. "For now, get some rest."

We watched as he left, then Nathan turned to me, "You don't have to go with me this time, you know that, don't you?"

How much longer will this war last? How long will we be living in this kind of danger…for this "mission" of helping prisoners of war escape? I took a deep breath. Then I looked into Nathan's eyes, "If this is your mission…then it's my mission too." A sad smile fell on his lips, then he bent his head and kissed me on the forehead. Perhaps I could rebuild his trust.

* * *

Christmas Day, 1864

I walked through the rows of tents, reminiscent of the times I had been a nurse under General Grant's brigade in the West. And now, here I was…about to meet the general once again, yet this time he was the commander of the whole Union Army. He had certainly risen through the ranks. And he wanted to meet Nathan. Nathan had told me some of the stories of the escapes he had led, but I wondered how much he did not tell me. He must have done so much for the cause to have the top general's interest. I smiled softly with pride and lifted my eyes, thanking God that He had protected him during those dangerous escapades. It was already growing dark, as evening settled over the encampment. I wrapped the thick, dark blue shawl around me to keep the winter chill off as I moved in the direction of Colonel Brandt's tent. Just then, the colonel and Nathan appeared from behind the tent flap. I stopped in my tracks when I saw Nathan. He was in his officer's uniform. I hadn't seen him in it for so long. Of course, he was always in civilian clothes because of the secret mission. I couldn't help the smile that spread over my face as they approached.

Nathan's blue eyes met mine and I could tell he also was trying to suppress a smile, "Elizabeth, are you ready?" I nodded taking in the impressive image in his Captain's uniform. Colonel Brandt cleared his throat. I jumped a little, remembering his presence.

"Shall we…?" he chuckled, motioning toward some horses. We rode for several miles, until we finally approached the general's headquarters. Flags flew above the little cabins that had been built in place of the tents for the winter months. Fires were blazing all around. Colonel Brandt called out to the sentry, we all dismounted and one of the young soldiers took our horses. I subconsciously began smoothing out my dress and hair from the ride. A chill breeze swirled the snow that was on the ground encircling our feet. The night sky was crystal clear, and the stars twinkled like diamonds against a black velvet cushion. The door of the cabin swung open and General Ulysses S. Grant appeared. His uniform was muddy as were his long riding boots, his hat crumpled and worn. His eyes looked as though they were carrying the weight of the world. He pulled the stub of a cigar out of his mouth and tossed it into the snow, stepping lightly on it. His eyes brightened as he surveyed our faces, then rested on Nathan.

Colonel Brandt stepped forward, he was so much taller than General Grant, I smiled softly as I watched.

"General Grant, Sir, it's my privilege to introduce you to Captain Nathan Tyler. You requested to see him due to his successful career in the special operations of leading so many prison escapes."

General Grant smiled lightly as he approached Nathan and took his hand. "Captain Tyler, it is an honor to finally meet you. Colonel Brandt informs me that you served in my brigade when I was stationed out West. I've heard much about you from Colonel Brandt, as well as other sources. You have done a great work and saved many lives, at the risk of your own. The army needs more men like you…as does this country." He glanced over at me, "Ma'am, I understand you are to be thanked as well. You serve your country well by your husband's side." His eyes narrowed, "Have we not met before as well? You look vaguely familiar…"

I smiled and curtsied, "Thank you, General, for your kind words. Yes, I was also under your brigade in the West, helping as a nurse for the army. It is a pleasure to see you again."

He nodded and smiled, "What a coincidence…and I assume that is where the two of you met then?"

I looked to Nathan who answered, "No, Sir, we came from the same town…but it is a long story."

The general smiled, "Then I look forward to hearing it over dinner tonight, if you are willing. But first, there is a matter of business I want to attend to before moving on. Step forward, young man," General Grant motioned to Nathan. He then turned back to his staff officers who stood on the outskirts. "Rawlins," he waited as the officer approached and handed something to the general. General Grant looked down at the items in his hand, then back up to face Nathan. "Captain Tyler, because of your bravery in the face of such danger, the many successful rescue missions you performed, and your willingness to risk your own life and freedom, it is my great honor to promote you to *Colonel* Nathan Tyler." He handed Nathan the bars with eagles on them…the insignia of a colonel. "Congratulations, Colonel."

"Thank you, Sir, I was only doing my duty," Nathan's face was serious, but I could see the appreciation in it as well. The two saluted each other. After some talk, the general invited us into his cabin for dinner. It was a night to be remembered: having dinner with the general of the whole Union army…and seeing Nathan promoted to colonel.

Kidnapped
Chapter 36

Amy

December 1864

THE NIGHT WAS dark with clouds obscuring the frail sliver of a moon that struggled to peer out from between them. A thick fog lay over the hills and I could hardly make out the tree line as I squinted from my position in the old barn. Not a sound could be heard in the cold winter air that seemed still and frozen, like everything else in this land.

"Amy?" Jumping, I turned around, my hand instantly on the pistol beside me. Jane raised a hand, realizing she had startled me and held up a steaming cup of soup.

"Thank you," relieved, I set aside the weapon and reached for the soup.

With a sad sort of smile, she sat down opposite me on a bale of musty smelling hay.

"I thought you'd appreciate it after Mrs. Wilson's…um…dinner." We both exchanged a knowing glance and I chuckled.

"We shouldn't complain. It's far better than what those poor souls in Petersburg are eating tonight."

"Indeed," Jane breathed, casting a small cloud of vapor in the air. After a long pause, she spoke up, her voice but a soft whisper, "Amy, what are you doing out here? It's so dark you can't even see the first line of trees."

I shrugged and drank the warm soup Millie prepared as an evening snack, so religiously, every night.

"I don't," I hesitated, weighing the effect of my words, "I just can't shake this anxious feeling."

After a long silence, Jane said gently, "I know, after so many rumors of the enemy's movements, spies infiltrating the capital and even our ranks, it's hard not to be a little shaken. The thought of the enemy sweeping up from behind us, and Anderson moving deeper south, doing God knows what is unnerving." Seeing the worry on her face, I regretted having opened my mouth.

"I'm sorry. I shouldn't have-,"

"No, Amy," Jane turned toward me, her beautiful face wrinkled with worry of the foreboding future, and reality, we now faced.

"I think we all know the final days of this war will be, without a doubt, some of the darkest any of us have ever faced…no matter the outcome. The South has slowly been declining. We can no longer deny it. We struggle to keep our fighting men equipped for this war." A heavy sorrowfulness seemed to rest upon us. Shaking myself out of the mood, I tried to think of something light-hearted to say to break this wretched spell.

"You know, Peter was right. You're getting far too gloomy these days." I teased, and Jane burst into a smile and chuckled at the reminder of her husband's gentle teasing.

"Oh…I suppose I am." Burying her head in her hands still smiling, she breathed in deeply, "How I miss him."

"Mmm," I nodded, feeling a twinge at the remembrance of the company's departure. *Another difficult goodbye.* I had become almost inexplicably attached to them. It was as if Kelsey's spirit lived on eternally through those men. *They have kept his memory alive, honoring their leader's death with the valiant way they fight, live and conduct themselves as soldiers.* Feeling both pain and pride, I rose, picking up the gun and placing it in its hidden place at my side.

"Come on, let's go back inside."

Glancing up, Jane also rose to her feet collecting our mugs. "Perhaps a cup of tea before bed?" Jane asked invitingly and I began following her back toward the small farmhouse, when a strange sound caught my attention. Turning slowly to glance back toward the haunting woods obscured by the fog, the shriek of a horse rang out and I felt Jane touch my arm.

"Amy, what is–," I motioned for her to keep quiet while I waited. A rumbling sound grew louder until I saw shadows moving through the forest coming directly toward us.

"Dark riders," I whispered.

"Do you think it's Seth?" Jane whimpered, fear in her voice. The small entourage drew closer and I felt my grip tighten around the cold handle of the pistol. Unable to make out the faces of the riders, who were half masked in thick black scarves, we had no choice but to wait. Grabbing Jane's arm, I pulled her closer to me and felt the cold sweat on her trembling hand. The leader pulled up, his mount snorting and chomping at the bit, while his small squad encircled us, kicking up the icy snow as they came to a halt. Planting my feet, I held the pistol down out of view waiting for the first threatening move.

"Well, well," the menacing voice that broke the silence caused my heart to instantly drop from my chest. *Anderson.* "Miss Amy Matthews, we meet again. Or perhaps shall I say, for the last time." Nudging the horse closer to us, I could make out the familiar face as his eyes lighted on my companion. His voice suddenly changed, and in a softer tone of surprise, he added, "And Miss Jane Morgan! It's been some years. What a *pleasure.*" Jane's voice came back with a strength I hadn't expected from such a meek young woman.

"Pleasure, Colonel? As I recall there have never been any sentiments of pleasure or anything good at your arrival." Anderson's laugh was joined by his depraved comrades.

"How true for so many, how true indeed." He laughed, while dismounting the big horse. Approaching daringly close to us, he stopped, his face just inches away from Jane's. Slowly I began to raise the pistol at my side so as not to be noticed, when suddenly an arm encircled my waist and the gun was kicked out of my hand while the ice-cold blade of a knife pressed up against my throat. Unable to hardly swallow, I met Jane's terrified gaze out of the corner of my eye.

Anderson stood, still studying her, an ugly grin spreading on his lips. He raised his hands, motioning to his men.

"What a delightful opportunity this is, gentleman. Fate has *indeed* smiled on us tonight! It seems we have just the right bait to finally draw Major Morgan in."

"You'll never defeat him. Just as you've never been able to defeat him before," Jane shot back proudly. Anderson raised a hand harshly, gripping her chin, his eyes flashing as he hissed through gritted teeth.

"There's one thing you must learn about me, *Jane*. I always get everything I want! And no matter how long I must wait, the death of your brother *will* be one of those fulfilled wishes...*Mrs. Kingston*." Anderson smiled proudly, seeing the shocked look on Jane's face. "Oh yes...I know everything. My informants have done, well, let's say, a very thorough job. Now, if I'm not mistaken, I've been informed that you worked as a spy for the Phantom Regiment, even before the war began, as did your husband. We simply cannot let that deception go unrewarded."

Jane's eyes flashed as she held her ground, "If you dare to harm any of us, you can believe me, Seth will make you regret the day you were born."

Anderson looked amused at this threat, "Oh, really? The way he made me regret what I did to Mary?" He paused, keeping his eyes locked on hers and shouted to his men. "Raid the house, kill everyone inside, except Mrs. Kingston here. I think we have other plans for her." Slowly, he scanned her up and down, then added, "Miss Amy will be coming with us." With a blade pressed hard against my throat, I was dragged toward a lone horse as I tried to fight back.

"Get your filthy hands off me!" I heard Jane angrily shouting. The rider forced me up in front of him, and the mount was spurred into a gallop toward the trees. Struggling against my captor, I strained to catch one final glance back. Only dark silhouettes of forms could be seen against the white snow. Shrieks and screams of pain and terror pierced through the icy night, surrounding the horrific scene and sending a chill through my body.

"*No!*" I screamed, my heart bursting inside me, unable to bear the knowledge of the attack now being carried out on my friends. In one final effort, I tried to fight against my enemy. Then a terrible unearthly shriek pierced my ears.

"Peter!" came the final scream of desperation and agony from Jane's voice.

Long Awaited Revenge
Chapter 37

Amy

December 1864

FOLDING UP THE note he had just received, a look of triumph lit Anderson's face. "At last. You'll never escape this time." He muttered to himself with malicious delight. A foul, deathly odor filled the small cold shack that rested in the middle of the desolate valley. A single candle sat on the table, struggling to illuminate the tiny room. Adjusting myself against my constraints, I kept my eye on Anderson, who paced the floor a moment, deep in thought before a deranged smile spread across his face. Before I could look away, he suddenly turned, his eyes locking on mine.

"Well, girl. I hope you're satisfied with the end to which your path of treachery has brought you. Was it too much to ask you to be loyal to the country and people that have given you everything?" Pacing across the floor, he slowly lowered himself down in front of me. Forcing out painful stifling breaths, I lifted my chin defiantly.

"I will never regret defying you, you murderer. As for my country… I am ashamed of the views and path it has taken; that the people of the Union cannot see their own grave faults but prefer to paint their neighbors as inhumane monsters."

Anderson scoffed, "Shame. It seems you've been infiltrated with their radical way of thinking...lies, demented ideas. Seth Morgan indoctrinated your mind as much as he did that Irish dog." Gritting my teeth, I kept my eyes on the floor, my heart burning. He continued in the slow, somewhat tranquil, voice as if in some strange trance. "You know...I quite enjoyed watching those bullets finally meet their mark. Much like watching a good hunt. The witless creature shriveling in pain as the deadly wound is inflicted. Oh, but perhaps I shouldn't talk like that in front of you. I forgot...you once had feelings for that...animal."

Twisting my wrist, I strained against the ropes that bound me. Staring him squarely in the eyes, I choked in anger, hardly able to utter the words, "My only wish before death is to be able to see you writhing in anguish as you breathe your last wretched breath. Your end is coming soon, Anderson. And on that day, you won't show half the strength and honor those you murdered did in their final moments."

"Is that so?" he almost laughed, though his face grew red.

"You can mock and slander, murder and destroy, to spread the lie that paints your enemy as the monster. But we both know the truth...that you'll never be half the man that Kelsey McCarthy was. And though you pretend to be so fearless, you're more terrified of Seth Morgan than anyone, because he holds the truth about the abhorrent murderer you really are. The fact is, your neck has long been avoiding the noose it deserves. But you can't hide forever." Eyes blazing with unrestrained anger, he whipped out a small dagger, turning the knife over in his hand menacingly.

"Colonel," an officer suddenly burst into the shack, nearly ripping the feeble door from its hinges. "A lone horse man is approaching!" *He's here.* I swallowed in relief, my heart still beating rapidly. Anderson pulled me to my feet, roughly dragging me from the dilapidated building. Passing through the crowd of soldiers that was forming, the colonel shouted some orders before fixing his gaze on the approaching horseman. Through the falling snow, the dark form of horse and rider emerged from the tree line serenely. The tall black stallion elegantly picked up his legs, as he waded through the deep snow. Anderson's guard moved anxiously forward, clearly nervous that this lone rider could be more of a threat than he appeared.

"It's him." Anderson hissed delightedly and roughly grabbed me by the arm, yanking me forward.

"Careful, Sir, it could be a trick," a lieutenant raised a hand.

"Not a chance, the spies in the woods would have alerted us if there was a threat."

Breathing heavily, I looked longingly at the only chance of my rescue now coming to surrender himself to the enemy…and certain death. As our eyes met, I could see a sorrowful resignation in his ever-composed countenance.

The Colonel raised a hand and Seth halted, dismounting from his horse. Anderson pulled me forward with his staff around him, guns drawn to meet the lone soldier. Drawing his knife up against my bare throat, he held me in front of him. Major Flint gave a nervous command, and Seth slowly dropped the pistol from his holster into the snow and drawing the black saber, held it out in both hands. Anderson motioned to one of his men and the soldier ran forward, taking the surrendered weapon nervously, while keeping his eyes on Seth, who held his gaze in a long unwavering stare that seemed to terrify the man. Inching back, the soldier presented the surrendered sword to Anderson, who nodded, smiling wickedly.

"At last," he breathed. "Well, Seth…I wish I could say I'm surprised by your surrender. But you are nothing if not predictable. I knew you couldn't resist a damsel in distress," the men around Anderson laughed mockingly. "And she does indeed look distressed, now doesn't she?" he stated, as the knife slowly began to break through my skin, creating a burning sensation causing my vision to cloud. I opened my mouth, but nothing came out but a wretched gasp for air.

"You have me, Anderson. Let her go," the controlled voice quickly demanded.

Anderson beamed, "Such weakness is unbecoming to a leader of your reputation. Haven't you learned what it takes to be a real man yet, Seth? A hardened heart my friend…but I suppose you were always lacking in that strength."

"You mean the kind of strength it takes to order the murder of hundreds of unprotected innocent old men, women and children?" Seth shot back, disgust in his voice, "That's the act of a true coward, not a man. And that's all you are and ever have been."

"Careful, old friend," Anderson growled menacingly, "I hold both your lives in my hands now. And though *you* may be unafraid to meet your end, I don't believe you'd be too interested in watching Miss Matthews here suffer a slow and agonizing death." Tossing me roughly to another soldier, Anderson approached, locking his gaze on Seth's, "Or perhaps you'd like to know just how your sweet Mary died."

At the mention of his wife, Seth froze. "I came here…," his voice wavered now as if someone had plunged a knife into his heart. Straightening, he continued, "I came here to surrender myself…at your request. With the promise you'd set Miss Matthew's free."

"What's the matter, Seth?" Anderson taunted, "You don't want to know?"

Turning his gaze downward, I saw Seth take a deep slow breath in. His hands clenched as he did everything possible to control himself. Anderson looked him up and down, a smug expression on his face, delighting in the emotional mental torture he knew he was inflicting upon his enemy.

"Do it, Seth," Anderson whispered into his ear, "give me a reason to end both your lives right now."

"As a soldier of the glorious state of Virginia and the regiment I serve, I am prepared to die with honor." Seth responded methodically, "I will not disgrace the uniform I wear."

"Oh, the ever-honorable Seth Morgan…always the saint!" Anderson proclaimed loudly, before lowering his voice to a demonic whisper, "But you can't fool me. I know you're burning with vengeance. I know you hate me the same way I've always hated you. You always thought you were better than me." Anderson stood back, his face bright with sudden unchecked anger, "You always took everything that was mine…the recognition, the position, the glory…Mary. And she *was* mine. I made sure she knew it with her dying breath. And now…the secret of her death will go to the grave with you." Anderson stepped in closer, "You see Seth, I always win."

"It's a shame really…all those innocent lives…all those people who had to die…simply to get to you. Now their blood is on your hands. And with so much evidence mounted against you, the world will fully believe the perpetrator of those crimes has finally met justice. And it was Colonel Jason Anderson who wielded that sword of justice against such a *monster*....and with you out of the way the Phantom Regiment will soon be obliterated in one final bloody attack."

Seeing the burning look of anger in Seth's eyes, Anderson smiled satisfied, then, stepping over to me, he tilted my head up with the tip of the black saber. His eyes burning, as he glared down at me.

"As for Miss Amy." He said slowly, thoughtfully, "you can't really blame me that she was stupid enough to get involved with you…I believe her penance for her betrayal will cost her… her life." The guard held the knife tight against my throat, waiting for Anderson's signal. Delightedly he turned around to face Seth once more.

"You coward," Seth breathed in disbelief.

"Don't worry, Seth. I'll make it quick and painless for her since you gave yourself up to me. But you should've known better than to trust me. In trying to be the hero, you've lost…everything."

Anderson paced around Seth, circling him like a vulture, dragging just the tip of the black saber on the white snow. Pausing before him, he motioned to two of the soldiers, who grabbed Seth harshly by the arms and forced him down to his knees before stepping back. Anderson slowly raised the saber, studying it while menacingly turning it over at eye level to his captive, "Your life has been nothing but a complete and utter failure…and now you shall both die." Fearlessly, Seth stayed silent, staring defiantly into Anderson's eyes. Raising the black blade high in the air, Anderson beamed, "I've been waiting for this moment for a long time, Seth."

As he brought down the heavy blade, Seth pulled a knife from his boot in one swift motion, thrusting it into Anderson's heart.

"Justice for the lives you stole." The rigid form hung over him for a moment, eyes bulging, until Seth threw him to the ground. Withdrawing the blade from the now lifeless body. All time seemed to stand still in silence, as the young Major, blood dripping from his weapon, rose in the crimson stained snow. Suddenly, the thundering of hooves came from all around us and with it, the eerie shouts of the Rebel cry from the surrounding woods.

"Impossible!" Major Flint turned white, as he anxiously drew his saber and shouted the command, "Kill the prisoners!" Seth locked his gaze on me as the soldier nearest raised the knife to plunge it into my chest. Feeling the air abandon my lungs, I watched as the bloody knife left Seth's hand, flying past my ear and plunged, just an inch away from my head, into my captor's eye. The man screamed in pain and dropped to his knees. With a rush of fear, I quickly snatched up the fallen pistol beside me and took aim at the closest attacker, pulling the trigger. All around, dark riders swooped in, mercilessly cutting down the now fleeing enemies. Just as I fired the last round in the pistol, I heard a shout.

"Amy!" I hardly had time to react as Seth reached down from his tall black horse to pull me up behind him. Wrapping my arms tightly around his waist, I choked as the rush of cold air filled my lungs. I winced in pain at the several lacerations I had sustained.

"Hold on!" Then giving the stallion his head, we flew into the misty darkened forest.

* * *

Standing at a respectful distance so as not to intrude on the privacy of this moment, I found myself unable to tear my eyes away from the painful scene. It had been several days since our narrow escape. Captain Hamilton had solemnly related to me how they had received the ominous note left by Anderson's men, threatening to end my life if Seth did not surrender himself at once. Instantly they rode the three days journey without stopping but, making it back to the farmhouse, were met with the devastating scene. Hardly able to continue, the young captain had tears in his eyes as he recounted the discovery and burial of the four bodies inside the house, including Mrs. Morgan and Millie. I'd placed my hand on the young soldier's shoulder, knowing the strong bond and affection he had for those killed. Jane however they had found hiding in the dilapidated barn. She was delirious, bloody, and half froze with only a wool blanket for warmth. But worse yet, she seemed to have lost any will to find help…or to live.

Only when Peter had finally arrived in the camp, had Jane opened her mouth to speak, though she still wouldn't eat a bite of food, and she recoiled at every attempt of a comforting touch.

Numb to the cold wind blowing at my skirt, I watched as Jane, now hardly able to stand, gripped Peter's sleeves, her hands white, tears pouring uncontrollably down her face. Her horrific encounter now revealed to her husband. My chest constricted as I watched the scene until Jane collapsed into Peter's arms sobbing. Turning away, I clutched a hand over my heart, breathing heavily.

"Are you all right?" A gentle voice spoke, and I glanced up quickly to see Seth standing before me. His face was void of any expression, smudged with black soot and dirt. Nodding, I wiped away the loose strands of hair with stained hands. Seth turned to watch the husband and wife now comforting each other in their pain and grief. We had hardly spoken since my rescue. Ashamed, I felt unable to offer the same comfort to him for the loss of his mother and his loyal servant Millie, as he had offered me during my time of grief. *It is a strange thing to lose someone during times of war…you hardly have a moment to reflect and grieve before it forces you to keep going.*

Seth suddenly shifted, but still keeping his eye on his sister stated in a most indifferent tone, "Go home, Amy." The words caught me so off guard, I whipped around for a moment, unable to speak in disbelief.

"What?" I asked breathlessly. Seth's back was to me, his hands hung at his sides, a heavy weight resting on his young shoulders.

"Keeping you here was a mistake. I was a fool to think I could keep you safe, though I promised I would. Kelsey would have never wanted you in such a dangerous position."

"We agreed going further south into the foothills was the best option," I stated, my heart beating anxiously.

"Yes, and look where it brought you!" He snapped, turning around sharply, his face full of pain. "Anderson was right. I'm a danger to anyone near me. Too many have died…because of me."

"Anderson is dead," I reminded him quickly. "He can't do us any harm now."

Seth scoffed, pacing, agitated, "He's left a string of lies in his wake. We're being hunted still. The Union papers are full of false accusations and horrific stories about us. The news of the 22nd Cavalry being completely destroyed will only fuel the fire against us as ruthless murderers. Each man here has a bounty on his head as does anyone near them. I'm as much a danger to you now as I was before. You cannot be safe in the presence of an outlaw, Miss Amy. It's because of me that so many paid with their lives."

Stepping forward, I slowly shook my head, unable to believe what I was hearing. "You can't believe that. You did nothing to deserve such blame. You're not responsible for his wicked acts!"

With a look of defeat, Seth hoarsely stated, "My wife was murdered, Kelsey is dead, hundreds of innocent civilians slaughtered…Millie…my mother…" Holding out his hands he whispered, "Their blood is on my hands."

"It's not your fault." I asserted, trying to convince him. Seth met my gaze, his face twisted in anger and pain. "You are *not* guilty for the crimes of a murderer. He wanted you to live with *his* guilt. But he has paid for his actions…*you* brought justice. *You* avenged their deaths." Insisting, I tried to search my mind for the right words to convince him. Collecting himself, he swallowed hard, gripping tightly onto the black saber hilt. His gaze, distant and transfixed, "I cannot allow you to stay here. I will not let you die like-,"

"I am not afraid of death." I stiffened, clenching my jaw, "I'm afraid of living a lesser life than the one that was destined for me. I'm afraid of losing the family I gained through Kelsey. You all are his family…and now mine." Swallowing back the emotion, I asserted stubbornly, "You can't force me to leave, Seth. I will not give up on the cause Kelsey died for! I will not abandon the country I have come to believe in, nor the friends I have come to love. Though it may demand my own life."

When I looked up again, the expression on his face was that of admiration. "You do not disappoint, Miss Amy. You are exactly who I thought you were."

A voice called out and a sergeant galloped up leaping off his horse. I stepped away, pondering Seth's words. The shouts of several officers met my ears and soon the whole camp was quickly preparing to depart. As Seth was mounting his black stallion, I approached gripping tightly to the horse's reins. He glanced down at me standing there. My face smudged with dirt, my dress fringed with wet cold mud, a white scarf bandaged around my throat where the blade had done its damage.

"A wise man once told me," I breathed, an unexpected peace washing over me, "The days of our lives have been given to us since our birth. But it's what we do with those days given to us that matters." Seth's expression softened with remembrance as he recognized the words.

"I choose to spend my last days, if necessary, in the service of this regiment…with my brothers." As he studied my face, the look of resolve in my eyes, a proud smile seemed to play on his lips before he nodded, a gentle salute, and whipped the stallion around. Before any other words could be spoken between us, the small company galloped off through the valley.

A Precarious Passage
Chapter 38

Elizabeth

January 1865

SOONER THAN MY heart was ready, we were headed out in another
wagon to Columbia, South Carolina. It took us a couple days, but eventually we
arrived in the Southern city. I gazed over the large fields that grew cotton and
corn in their seasons. That much cotton could surely be mistaken for a strange
snow flying through the air on a windy summer day.

I glanced behind me in the wagon bed. Colonel Brandt had seen to it that
we were furnished with enough items to make it seem like we really were just a
young couple moving into the city. *Could we really keep up this masquerade?*
Again, Colonel Brandt made sure that Nathan was fitted with supplies for a
blacksmith shop. Though he warned us that this time it would not be as spacious
as the one in Richmond. Nathan would have to begin over again and build
himself a little area for his forge. Colonel Brandt mentioned sending someone to
help Nathan eventually…as Marcus once had. I suppose he had finally realized
how much Marcus had benefited the mission.

The colonel tried, but he could not find a townhouse on the outskirts of the
town. However, this one did have some back alleys that would help with privacy.

There was a cellar on the side of the house in the alleyway. I noted it, thinking of the soldiers we had hidden in our cellar in Richmond. Yet, Colonel Brandt's warning rang in my head, "You can't harbor anymore soldiers in your home. It's too dangerous." I would just have to content myself with keeping house. However, I instantly began thinking of ways I could help. I needed to keep busy…so many memories and thoughts of Marcus constantly appeared in my mind throughout the days. I missed him. I missed Amy. I missed our home. *When will this war end?*

* * *

Nathan entered the back door one morning, after a week of nightly missions. He looked exhausted. I took his coat from him and hung it on the peg by the door, following him into the parlor area. I waited quietly as he sat, drinking the coffee I had prepared for him. His countenance looked dark and weary, as though he was carrying the weight of the world. Finally, he set the cup down and leaned back in the chair, rubbing a hand over his face as he let out a sigh.

"Nathan…what is it?" I ventured.

He looked at me a moment, then answered. "I have seen so many prisoners over these last couple of years, Elizabeth. So much miserable death. I always think, maybe eventually it won't bother me anymore…but I can't seem to get away from the horrors of these prison camps. But after living in one myself…I can't bear the thought of just walking away from them either…," his voice trailed off and he stared out the window at the rising sun.

I leaned forward, taking his hand, "You're doing what you can."

He slowly shook his head, "It's not enough. Not for all of them. Elizabeth, in Camp Asylum, there are men living in holes in the ground. There are some barracks, but not enough." He stood up, walked away and set a hand on the hearth. "Some of the men I helped escape last night told me that at Camp Sorghum most of the prisoners dug holes and covered themselves with branches to protect themselves from the weather. They had no latrines…so the guards would take them out to look for food and better sanitation. Which enabled them to make some successful escapes. Camp Asylum is a bit harder. It is surrounded by a twelve-foot brick wall."

"It never stopped you before," I offered, thinking of the camps in Virginia that Nathan had rescued many men from.

"I need something…an opportunity. I have to get them out." He stared hard into the flickering flames in the hearth.

* * *

One early morning, I awoke to the sound of Nathan's pounding in the small forge. He had been out on a mission all night again, and now he was working on something in the forge too. I shook my head, throwing off the blankets and hurrying to dress myself before making my way through the little rooms of the town house and out the side door into the alleyway. The winter air greeted me, causing me to tug the shawl closer around my shoulders. I shivered as I looked up into the clear crisp sky. Walking down the narrow alleyway toward the forge, I noticed Nathan talking to someone and approached hesitantly. A young man stood next to Nathan watching him work and asking questions. Curly, sandy hair topped a face full of curiosity. On seeing me, Nathan set his tools down and reached out a hand for me to approach. Next to the younger man, Nathan suddenly seemed so much more mature to me. The years and the experiences in this war had made him older and wiser. The young man turned on seeing me, removed his hat and smiled, nodding in my direction.

"Elizabeth, this is Titus Sutton." Nathan's voice lowered, "I helped him escape from the prison camp a couple weeks ago."

I smiled and curtsied but wondered why this young man was here now.

Titus saw the question in my face and played with the hat in his hands, as he explained, "Mrs. Tyler, it's a pleasure. I guess you're wondering why I'm here. Once I was back in the army, I asked around about the man who had led our rescue until I found Colonel Brandt. He was very hesitant at first, but I convinced him that I wanted to help Nathan…however I could. I was not in the prison camp for long, but it was so terrible, I have to do something to help the men I left behind. And I can help in the forge too!"

The young man seemed so eager to please, that I couldn't help but smile, "Well, Titus…if Colonel Brandt thinks you will do well here, then so do I."

Nathan nodded his agreement and clasped a hand on Titus' shoulder.

"Now let's see how fast you can learn this." Nathan held out the hammer to the young man, who took it eagerly.

$$* * *$$

February 1865

I descended the creaking stairs of the old townhouse. Pale light softly made its way through the windows, casting a solemn wintery glow into the corners of the dark house. I was grateful for the woolen socks that protected my feet from the cold wooden floor as I lit a small lantern on the corner table. My hand froze above the lantern, as I heard a noise coming from the little dining room. Moving to the entry way, my eyes were drawn to another lantern lit in the other room. There sat Nathan, maps and papers scattered around the table. He moved a pen across the map, studying it intently, the light flickering on his handsome face. I approached quietly, laying a hand on his shoulder.

He startled a bit, then smiled, whispering a soft, "Good morning."

"I hope you haven't been up all night working on this…," I waved a hand at the scattered notes and maps. Raising my eyebrows, I added, "You do need to sleep sometimes." Too often Nathan was out on a mission, and during the day he continued working in the forge, taking long naps here and there, whenever he could.

Taking my hand from his shoulder, he kissed it, then led me to sit down in the chair next to him. Dropping the pen, he took a deep sigh. "Sherman's army is coming very close. If the next escape is successful, then all those soldiers could find refuge within the army. I feel it's the perfect opportunity to help as many men as possible out of that hell hole, Camp Asylum. The trouble is," Nathan moved his fingers over the map, "once free from the prison camp, they'd have to cross the Congaree River to get to Sherman's army. At present, it's most likely frozen solid and safe to walk across. But we don't know what might await us on the other side…"

"What about the bridge?" I asked studying the map in front of him.

"No, it's too risky, there is bound to be someone watching it." He moved his fingers along the river, stopping suddenly at a point and tapped the paper. "We'd have to cross here. Lots of trees to cover our movements…far enough from the bridge and secluded." I nodded, feeling a cold chill run down my spine. "If we could station someone on the other side of the river, so that they could signal us when it was safe to cross…," Nathan mused, then shook his head, "but I need Titus with me for this one, I need his help getting them out."

I felt a sudden impulse, a tugging desire to help in this. *I could do it.* I took a deep breath, part of me screaming no, the other part speaking the words out loud, almost involuntarily, "I could do it."

Nathan's head snapped up to look me in the eye. The look of surprise on his face was quickly overcome by resolution.

"No," he said firmly and turned back to the map.

"Nathan, I have been involved in this mission from the beginning. I'm already in as deep as you and in as much danger as you. I've had all the danger, without the reward of being able to do my part in seeing these men freed."

"You did your part, Elizabeth. In Richmond you cared for several of the escaped prisoners." He wouldn't look me in the eyes anymore but kept studying the map as he spoke.

"But it's like you told me the other day, 'it's not enough.' I want to do it for them, Nathan. I *can* do it." I leaned in, trying to see the reaction on his face.

He let out a sigh, jaw clenched, then shook his head. "No."

"I'm not afraid. You have to let me do this – for them! It's not about me anymore, it's not even about us…we have to help them!" I reached toward him, "Nathan-,"

"No, Elizabeth." He cut me off, shoving his chair out and leaving the room.

I stood up, following him, but he walked out the door, shutting it firmly behind him. I stood staring at the door panel. *I have to do this.* Letting out a breath, I turned back to the dining room. Tilting my head, I watched the sunrise paint beautiful streaks of vibrant gold and blushing rose all over the glass window, melting away the frost. *Surely what God has called us to do, He equips us to do.*

* * *

I don't know how Nathan's mind was changed. Perhaps it was God. Perhaps he had no other choice. But here I was standing on the edge of the Congaree River, staring across into the dark night, lit only by a partial moon in the clear night sky. My objective was to cross the river, make sure all was clear on the other side, then signal back to the escaped prisoners that it was safe for them to cross as well. Then I would have to cross back over to get home.

The snow on the ground reflected the moon's light, making it a little easier to see in some places. Thick dark trees surrounded me on every side and reached their long fingers to touch the blackness above. The night was bitter cold, I shivered from the wintery air, but also from the anticipation of what I was about to do. My breath came out in clouds, I felt sure someone would see it…someone who may be watching from across the river at this very moment. What was I to say if I came upon someone in that darkness beyond the river? I sucked in the cold air; it filled and hurt my lungs simultaneously. Reaching into the woolen coat pocket, I fingered the small mirror that had been tucked away in the folds, beside it the delicate pocket watch. My eyes adjusting to the dim light, I was able to read the time. *Fifteen more minutes.* I shivered again. Standing here, alone in the dark, time seemed to drag on.

I moved closer to the water's edge. The river was indeed frozen, but how solid was it? I knew it was not a very deep river, but still…if it should break…the wet, the frigid temperatures, the current…it could be very dangerous. Laying a foot cautiously on the snow-covered ice, I tested the strength. Soon I was standing, both feet planted on the frozen river. Reaching for the pocket watch once more, I noted it was finally time. Bracing myself, I stared across the wide-open space between me and the opposite shoreline. Breathing up a prayer into the starry sky, I began walking cautiously across the river. The wind that had been blocked by the trees on the shore now rushed against my face, causing my eyes to water and my cheeks to sting. Nathan had not told me how they planned to get the prisoners out. I only knew they had been working on this escape for some time. He never told me the details of the escapes, and I knew it was for my own safety.

As I moved across the ice-covered river, I tried to envision the soldiers escaping the prison camp…to focus on them and not on my fears. *Halfway there…* I took another deep breath and set my sights on a tall tree on the opposite shore, focusing on its long branches, counting each one. Just then I heard a crack under my feet. My foot slipped on the glassy ice, and I landed with a thud on the frozen river. Being too afraid to move for a moment, I lay there on the cold surface, seeing the cracks in the ice reaching out underneath by body. Shaking, I pulled myself to my feet. I stepped quicker into a light jog, heart pounding as I listened for any more cracking noises under my feet. There were some, but I prayed with each one – *God give my feet wings to fly over this river.* After what seemed like an eternity, I landed on the opposite shore, hands to the snowy earth, gasping in the cold air. *Thank you, God.* Knowing I did not have time to rest, I scrambled to my feet and began pacing the new shoreline. Walking in one direction, I moved as close to the bridge as I could comfortably get. Scanning the shoreline around through the trees, I then walked as far back down river as I felt necessary. Thankfully there weren't many homes in this section. One lone farmhouse and barn loomed on the slope nearby. But all was quiet, as though the family were asleep. *All clear.* I fingered the little mirror, pulling it out of my coat pocket and aligning it with the moon beams. Being careful not to throw the reflection elsewhere, I directed the beams back across the river to where I had just come from. Faintly, I detected men lining up on the banks across the river from me and I continued to target the moon beams in their direction. They had made it out of the prison camp. I smiled with relief. Now for the river crossing and then into Sherman's army.

I breathed out a silent prayer, watching my breath float away as a cloud in the still night air. Minutes passed by, suddenly I heard the snap of a twig behind me. Freezing in place, I dared not move.

"Who goes there?" A strange voice called, "Speak up now, ya hear! Or I'll shoot!" Turning slowly around, I faced a scraggly old farmer. "Speak up!"

"I, uh…I…," I stammered, trying to catch my breath. "I'm sorry to disturb you, Sir, I got lost…and can't seem to find my way back home."

The man drew closer and peered into my face suspiciously, "'Tis a bit late for a stroll by the river, Missy!"

"Yes, Sir," I tried to calm my voice, all the while thinking about the prisoners who were at this very moment moving across the frozen river in our direction. Suddenly the crackling of ice echoed across the river.

"What in blue blazes…," the man moved past me to the shoreline. I could now faintly see the escaped prisoners nearing the riverbank. The ice was weakening, but it had not cracked through completely yet. The man's back was to me as he tried to distinguish what was going on. Reaching once again into my coat pocket, I gripped the barrel of a revolver. *We can't take any chances.* Raising it up, I then swung it down, crashing the handle of the gun on the back of the man's head. He crumpled to the ground. Before I knew it, I was surrounded by many soldiers, or what was left of them after life in a prison camp. Nathan was at my side in a moment.

"Elizabeth, are you all right? What happened?"

"It's all right. He's just a farmer, but I didn't want to take any chances."

Titus knelt down beside the man, examining him.

"You really gave him a wallop, Mrs. Tyler!" Some of the men in the group chuckled.

I could feel my cheeks redden despite the cold.

"I hope I didn't hurt him too badly."

Nathan smiled over at me, "He'll be all right. Titus, help me carry him. We'll put him inside the barn to keep him from the cold. He'll be right as rain once that big bump goes down." Nathan winked at me. The men laughed quietly again, ready to be on their way. "You men split up, take different directions, we don't want to draw attention. Remember the location I gave you for Sherman's Army. Titus and I will meet you there and talk to the general." Nathan approached me as the men dispersed. "Elizabeth, walk down the river for a while, in case the guards have started following. Once you're on the other side, signal to us that you made it safely, then circle back to town. Titus, you stay here and wait for her signal, I have to go ahead with the men." Titus nodded as he moved back over to the farmer, ready to carry him to the barn.

Nathan pulled me in close, "Be safe," he whispered, breathing a soft kiss on my cheek.

"You too," I felt my voice quiver. Moving down the riverbank, I turned back to watch Nathan and Titus carry the farmer to the barn. My stomach turned as I thought about crossing that treacherous river once more. But the men had made it, they were free now. We had done our duty.

Unyielding Hearts
Chapter 39

Amy

February 1865

A PALE PINK sky greeted us amid a light flurry of snowflakes against the mountainous hills.

"We're nearly there," Peter whispered, keeping his eyes on the narrow deer trail we followed as best we could. Glancing over my shoulder, I counted again the number of wounded still mounting. The stronger ones leading the horses of those more seriously injured, who could only focus on staying in the saddle. Not a complaint came from their lips, though their faces were pale, twisted in painful grimaces, and many with a delirious look in their eyes. I shifted to check one of the youngest boys, who I had loaded onto the back of my horse. His skin was covered in sweat and white as the snow we trod through in this dense forest.

"Stay strong, Sam. We're almost home." I whispered back to him, doing my best to support the weight leaning heavily against my back. With nowhere safe left to go that had even an ounce of medical supplies, we were forced to return to Richmond. Peter, with his extensive knowledge and journeys as a spy, guided us along paths that kept us clear of enemy lines.

"Head straight for the Morgan's house when we arrive. Not a word about anything that's transpired," Peter warned sharply, and I nodded.

Finally, the hollow shell of the once magnificent mansion rose within view, a sorrowful symbol of what the South had become. As we entered the safety of that familiar abode, I couldn't help but hold back tears at the now painful memories of what had transpired here so many months ago. The news of Kelsey's mortal wounds, and the memories of quickly packing as we left, with Mrs. Morgan and Millie still beside us, seemed to haunt the halls of this once glorious estate. I caught a sob and then forced myself into a working attitude as I helped the wounded soldiers into the parlor.

"I'll start the fire and get something edible prepared." I stated, passing Peter who was nearly carrying a young private in. Hours later, after all souls had been fed, wounds bandaged and placed into makeshift beds in the one warm room of the house, I sat alone by the window. Amid the darkness outside, I watched flickers of light passing to and fro. Shouts and screams of wild, brawling, drunken civilians and soldiers were accompanied by the vile cackling of women with no morals. The city had changed for the worst and become a place of dissipation and waste since all families and working folks had fled in light of the inevitable oncoming siege. It seemed now certain that in the very near future Petersburg would fall and the way to Richmond would be opened to the Union troops. Fear grew in the hearts of even the most valiant soldiers now facing the possible downfall of the capital. *How could this happen? The South, a rich and vibrant culture of its own, now left in total ruin and waste.* Wearily, I rested my chin in my hand staring blankly outside. *Sherman is coming, sweeping up from the South, following Grant, burning and plundering the glory of the Confederacy.*

"It's a terrible shame," Peter Kingston spoke up, stepping beside me, "How such beautiful things can be transformed into hollow shells during war."

I raised my eyes to study him. The tall proud form of the English gentleman now disheveled; face unshaved, clothing in tatters and the obvious look of malnutrition, that was haunting so many in the South, was apparent on his young face. Glancing over at the small sofa pushed near to the waning fire, I saw Jane's face relaxed in a deep sleep. A peaceful picture at last.

"How is she?"

Peter turned to gaze on the sleeping form of his wife. "She's recovering."

"I'm sorry Peter…," I choked overwhelmed, "I should have protected them better."

Staring in shock, he scoffed lightly, "And how I ask you, do you place the responsibility of what happened on yourself? You're a good fighter, Amy. I'll admit that. You've honestly surprised me. But in no world could you stop such a large group of soldiers as descended upon you that night. No one can blame you. It's a ridiculous notion all together."

Shaking my head, I continued gazing out the window. The solemn silhouettes of the willow trees seemed to droop lower than usual in the desolate garden, now deprived of its former beauty.

A moaning sound caught my attention, and springing to my feet, I scanned over the still forms wrapped in blankets, laying almost lifelessly all around the rooms. A slight movement caught my eye and I carefully maneuvered my way through the wounded.

"Captain Hamilton?" I whispered to the young man covered in a gray wool blanket. He was tossing, his eyes open, unfocused, as they searched the room.

Catching sight of me, he paused and slowly a look of recognition came over his face. "Miss Amy, are we home yet?"

Trying to smile, I grabbed his hand. "You're home, Mark. Back at the Morgan's house." Turning confused, he tried to search the room again.

"Morgan's…home…Where's Mrs. Morgan? Why isn't Millie here?"

Chest constricting at those words, I forced back the tears, "It's ok. I'm here with you. Peter's here."

Taking a cold cloth, I held it against his head, trying to smooth back the blood matted hair. Watching me closely he seemed to relax, his eyes focusing for a moment.

"Where's Seth?"

"They're away. Trying to deprive the enemy of some reinforcements if possible."

The captain watched me for a moment, then, suddenly looking confused, he stated slowly, "I saw him…Colonel McCarthy." My heart stopped. "He was… he was riding a white horse." Mark smiled as if recalling a precious memory, "he told me I'd follow him again, soon."

The young man eased back onto his makeshift bed, looking comforted. "I think, Miss Amy. I think I wouldn't mind that." Reaching out, I took the thin blood-stained hand. After holding it a moment, I rose to my feet.

"I will see you tomorrow," I whispered, unable to meet his gaze.

Hamilton shook his head feebly, "Who are we kidding, Miss Amy. I won't be here tomorrow."

My heart breaking, I stared down at the young face, more a boy's face than a man's.

"You must. Who will keep me company? Make me smile even in the midst of all this?" As I tried to give some relief to this young man, I suddenly choked, my throat constricting as I whispered, "You've always been so kind to me." A tear spilled down his cheek as he forced another brave smile. "I *want* to see you tomorrow," I stated determinedly, and the captain nodded gently as I turned to my temporary bed near the fire.

"Goodbye, Amy…" I heard a faint whisper behind me.

* * *

The solemn, ominous words of the reverend echoed in my mind, "Like so many he was taken too early, his life snapped up in the midst of his youth. May his soul find peace, and may we never forget the sacrifices of so many of these…boys, so many as young as Captain Mark Hamilton."

The dim flicker of a flame caused me to stir out of my deep exhausted sleep. *Where am I?* I turned and, recognizing the room, felt a wave of sadness. *I must've fallen asleep without realizing it.* Exhausted, I stared up at the dark ceiling and felt the tears spill down my cheeks. *The funeral last week was too much to bear.* With a sinking feeling I turned, then froze, spotting a dark form in the corner of the room near the window. For a moment he didn't stir, but I could feel his eyes on me. Then as if he'd noticed me looking back, turned his head ever so slightly to stare out the foggy window. Focusing in the darkness at the black outline, I caught a glimpse of light reflecting off the dark patch that covered one eye. *Seth.* Feeling relieved but exhausted, I lay still, only watching him for a moment. As I kept my gaze fixed on the unmoving dark outline, a strange remembrance came over me. In the dark trees he'd always lurked, a dark rider unmoving…watching. I'd never quite known who it was and now I began to wonder. *Had he always been there, silently watching?*

Moving as if in a trance, I rose carefully, gliding over the wooden floorboards so as not to disturb the sleeping wounded soldiers. Wrapping the wool shawl around as I felt a sudden chill, I kept my eyes locked on him as I lowered myself onto the bench opposite. The stillness of his form caused me to wonder if I was dreaming.

"Miss Amy," the voice that spoke seemed hollow, "You should rest."

"What's happened?" I asked bluntly, feeling the exhaustion in my bones.

"Complications. Peter has left. Hopefully he can bring us some information." Tilting his head down, he rubbed the back of his neck. The blackness of the night, accompanied by the strange wild noises of the city, created a frightening ambiance. Shrinking into the padded bench and leaning my head against the frame of the window, I watched Seth for a moment longer, while pondering the question now nagging at me.

"It was you, wasn't it?" I lowered my voice, not wishing to be overheard. He continued, unstirred, to stare out the window. "You were always there, watching in the shadows." Suddenly Seth turned, a confused look apparent on his handsome face. "I would catch a glimpse of a dark rider in the woods…silent, still, just watching, before disappearing." Puzzling, I added, "And then I caught Peter leaving in the middle of the night. He was meeting you?"

Seth turned away again, before softly answering, "Yes." I waited expectantly. "As we stalked the 22nd Cavalry, I would keep watch overnight. An added precaution, in case they had caught wind of us trailing them and would attempt to turn and attack us during the night. And…I was meeting Peter for intelligence."

"When did he tell you about me?" I asked curiously, "I know…I overheard that you were informed…before Kelsey."

Looking a little surprised, Seth nodded thoughtfully, "Yes, he," he cleared his throat, "Peter did tell me of a woman in the ranks…he didn't know who you were of course. Not, that is, until I saw you at the edge of the camp one evening… I recognized who you were."

I stared, perplexed at him, "That easily?"

Seth shifted uncomfortably, "I have a good memory." Pausing a moment, he began thoughtfully, "I wasn't quite sure what you were planning. Your involvement with Anderson was rather concerning. Peter was convinced you knew nothing of Anderson's 'plans', but I wasn't so sure…that is until I observed your actions last spring."

In a gentler voice, he added, "In all honesty, your courage to go into battle when you had no obligation, no duty…it deeply intrigued me. Even when you were still our enemy." Turning to me, I saw a glimmer in his eye, "Not many would do what you did. And still you stay."

Feeling unworthy of any praise, I glanced down at my hands, my heart still full of sorrows.

"This war has been fought by every American, Northern and Southern. Each of us in our own unique way, Major. Some fight it in the government, some on the home front, some in the hospitals, and some on the front lines. But we are all part of this war. Whether we choose it or not. And war seems to bring out the worst…or the best in a person." Looking up, I could almost see the scenes of my life those few days after the war had begun. "I suppose…when I lost Kelsey, when he left Gettysburg…and my sister departed for the West, I suppose I had come to a fork in the road. To stay in Gettysburg, watching neighbors return home in wooden boxes, while I pined over my own losses or to join such a defining conflict and possibly sacrifice my own life…to find out who I truly was."

"And did you?"

"No, I think the experiences changed me into who I am today. And be that for better or worse, I wouldn't change my decision. Yes, I've seen things, wicked acts of hatred, jealousy, immorality, corruption, experienced horrors, losses…but I've also experienced forgiveness, friendship, love and seen acts of courage and kindness I never imagined could exist in a human soul. And that has made the scars of this war worthy of bearing."

Consumed in Fire
Chapter 40

Elizabeth

February 15, 1865

DUST ROSE IN a cloud as I walked through the dirt streets of Columbia, South Carolina. Wagons and people on horseback maneuvered around me. Stepping onto the porch of our little house, I sat down on a bench outside the door.

Staring into the busy streets, I thought, *the South seems to be losing manpower and supplies…It can't last forever. Enduring these times will only make us stronger in the end.* The sound of gun shots echoed in the distance. The busyness of the streets suddenly quieted as everyone stopped what they were doing to listen. More firing continued.

"Oh no," I whispered, fear gripping my heart.

Just then, someone rode into town and began shouting, "Sherman is attacking our defenses five miles south of here!" Just the name was enough to strike fear into the hearts of the Southern people as they had learned about the burning of Atlanta and all the desolation left in Sherman's path wherever he marched. Chaos ensued as the sounds of the battle grew more intense. The townspeople began running in different directions, most heading for the railroad depot. I hurried into the house, knowing I could not leave without knowing where Nathan was.

He and Titus still had not yet returned from the night of the river escape. I went up to our room and remained there, praying for courage and their safe arrival. At about midnight, I heard the beginning of cannons being fired. *I can't stay here.* Stepping out quickly into the night, the sky lit up before me with each cannon roar. I moved to the entrance of the cellar on the side wall of the house. Pulling the door shut behind me, I climbed down inside. Hunkering down in a corner of the small room, I spent a long night and the entire next day praying and listening to the roar of cannon.

* * *

February 17, 1865

I lifted the door of the hide out. What townspeople were left were in great alarm. I had stayed in the cellar all of yesterday as I listened and waited. I escaped a couple of times, long enough to retrieve some food and water from the house and to survey the area for any sign of Nathan. Stepping out into the alleyway, suddenly I heard screams ringing through the city. Down the alleyway horses flashed past with Union riders on their backs. My breath caught in my throat. *Sherman is here.*

"Elizabeth!" Titus' voice reached my ears and relief flooded through my veins. The young man grabbed my shoulders, "Are you all right? We couldn't make it back into the town sooner. After that escape, we made sure everyone got back to Sherman. Then we got tied up with some other matters. I lost track of Nathan in the chaos coming back."

I felt limp, "I hid in the cellar," I answered weakly. Titus looked down the alleyway into the main street.

"Those Yankee soldiers are getting drunk with whiskey and vengeance. They're looting the town now, breaking into stores and banks. When they first came in, everything was orderly, but now…I don't know if even Sherman is aware of what some of his men are getting into." He shook his head, "I have to get you out of here."

"Not yet, please. Nathan is bound to come back here looking for me. Let's just wait for him a little longer." I pleaded, nodding toward the cellar. After some persuading, he agreed. We waited until no one was around and slipped back into the hole.

It was quite dark when we opened the latch again. Titus had finally convinced me that we had to get out...*now*. He assured me that Nathan would find us eventually. As we moved into the streets, I noticed the night sky gradually lighting up in a red glow. It appeared to be almost daylight, but I quickly realized it was the glow of fire that lit the sky, not the sun.

I gasped as we walked into the main street. Shrieks pierced the air as houses and stores shot up in the flames. Titus pulled me back into the shadows of the alleyway. Union soldiers ran mad in the streets, dipping balls of cotton in turpentine and kerosene, lighting them, and throwing them into and under the buildings. My stomach turned as I hid my face from the sight of drunken men, dancing and cursing in the streets. *Is this the way we are to represent our country?* The flames flew high into the night. Black billows of smoke ran across the red sky. I could hear the sounds of buildings cracking, some crashing to the ground with a roar. From the screams, I knew that townspeople were being murdered and unmentionable atrocities done to others. Tears streamed down my face and anger burned inside me. My heart screamed within me and I suddenly tore out into the streets, stunned by the barbarism before my eyes and ears.

My vision blurring, I screamed at some men in the street who were tormenting a civilian, "Stop! Stop it! This isn't the way! Can't you see that?" My voice was hoarse with emotion. Every muscle tensed within me, I felt Titus tearing me away from the danger. Two men turned as they caught my words. Numbness overcame me from what I had just seen, and I felt indifferent to what might happen to me. Vaguely, as if in a dream, I saw the men coming toward me, the sounds echoing, as if in the distance, in my ears. Titus' figure appeared between me and the soldiers. Hazily, I perceived him trying to stop the men from coming any closer. A gun shot fired through my muffled hearing. Titus crumpled to the ground in front of me. I stared at the form as the men came closer, all feeling seemed to have left me. I felt numb and frozen in space. *Kill me too. I am finished seeing all those I care about die.* Then one man roughly grabbed me by the wrist, and the other pulled me away by the waist into the blazing streets. Anger suddenly awakened me from my trance and took over. I struggled with all my might to free myself from the man's iron grip. My eyes burned with resentment and my vision clouded as the man dragged me farther up the street amidst the smoke and chaos. Buildings continued to crumble around us. The smell of burning wood and furniture was over-powering and I could almost taste the thick black smoke that billowed upward. Just when I had nearly exhausted my strength struggling with his tight grasp, the man was violently knocked to the ground by a solid punch landing squarely on his face. Suddenly free, I scrambled to my feet out of the dusty street. Turning to see who my liberator was, my eyes stung as I saw Nathan's form standing between me and my aggressor. The vile man had recovered and staggered to his feet. He cursed and growled something at Nathan, whipping a knife out of his belt. Nathan yelled to me, this time I could hear the words.

"Go! Now!"

I watched as the man flew at Nathan, knife glinting in the firelight. *Titus.* I ran, blindly stumbling back through the burning streets toward our home. Sliding to the ground, next to Titus, I felt for a pulse. *He's still alive!* Glancing around quickly, I wrapped my hands around the boy's wrists and dragged him into the dark alleyway. I brushed the sweaty hair back from his forehead, the flames reflecting off the boy's pale face. When I finally stood, my vision blurred once again. I tried to catch my breath, leaning with my back against the building. After a few minutes, a silhouetted figure came walking toward me in the darkness of the alley. I took a deep breath as I recognized Nathan. He bent down next to Titus, then, almost effortlessly, lifted the boy over his shoulders.

"Elizabeth," he stared into my eyes as he approached.

I nodded, "I'm all right." His eyes searched mine, filled with concern. I took in another deep breath, trying to reassure him.

"Let's go," he said in a low voice. My legs felt weak beneath me as we walked quickly into the darkened surroundings, our forms silhouetted by the great fire behind us…the screams and sounds of the destruction still following us closely.

After a few miles, we stopped near an abandoned barn and rested under a tall pine tree. Nathan laid Titus down on the pine covered ground and tended to his gunshot wound. I stood near the edge of the branches, gazing blankly at the burning city in the distance. I knew I needed to help Titus…but for some reason I felt numb, like I could not even move myself to walk toward him. *How much longer will this suffering and death continue?* Feeling a touch on my elbow, I looked up into Nathan's face.

"How could they do this, Nathan?" I asked. "They say their fighting to save the Union. Patriotism and unity…but this is *not* patriotism…this isn't unity. It's immoral, and complete evil. It's just like what those Confederates did to our house in Richmond…to Marcus. It's the same thing." Nathan stared into the night, I watched his eyes, searching for answers.

"These men are not in their right minds. You cannot judge all the Union soldiers for what these men did here tonight, Elizabeth. Just like you can't judge all the Confederate soldiers for what those men did to Marcus." There was a pause, "Just as these Union soldiers should not have judged and punished these Southern civilians for imagined crimes or the wrongs of someone else."

I turned and stared up at him. "And…like I judged you in Gettysburg that first day?"

Nathan smiled sadly down at me, "Yes. Like that." Cupping my face in his rough hands, he gently wiped the tears away from my eyes.

After a long moment, he looked toward the place where Titus lay, "Now, there's someone who needs your help."

* * *

I slowly raised my head from Nathan's shoulder. Lighter shades of gray peaked through the cracks in the old barn. I stood from my sitting position against the straw bales and carefully stepped over to where Titus lay. Pressing my fingers against the young man's neck, I anxiously felt for his pulse. Relieved, I felt the steady beating and watched as his chest rose and fell in deep slumber. Fingering the cloth around the wound, I tried to examine the wound without disturbing him. A groan escaped his lips as I did so. Pulling back my hand, I sat motionless, waiting for him to fall back asleep.

"Thank God the bullet was lodged in the muscle. Not in an organ," a low voice said softly.

Turning, I realized Nathan was still awake…had never gone to sleep.

"Do you think…," my voice choked, "do you think he'll live?"

Nathan nodded. Just then a noise caught my attention. Nathan started and gripped his musket. Sure enough, voices echoed in the distance. Nathan moved to a crack in the barn wall. Quickly, he turned around and gathered up the two bags of supplies I had taken from the cellar; all we had left of our possessions from the house.

"We've got to move out."

"What is it, Nathan?" I asked, tensing up.

"Sherman's soldiers. They're probably out looking for livestock. But we can't take a chance. After last night, who knows what they might be up to."

I glanced over at the young man lying wounded on the ground and shuddered thinking of what might happen. I took the bags and rifles Nathan handed to me and slung them over my back. Nathan shoved a pistol into his own belt and lifted Titus over his shoulders. He made the task seem easy, but it must have been the simple strength from years of being a blacksmith. Soon he had the wounded man draped over his broad shoulders.

"Let's go," Nathan whispered forcefully.

I stepped out quietly into the gray dawn. The black outline of trees around us became visible as my eyes adjusted to the new surroundings. In the east, the faintest streak of pink lay despondently on the horizon. Nathan moved out behind me and we silently walked in the opposite direction of the soldiers' voices.

* * *

The wagon rattled and shook underneath me as I sat beside Titus, tending his wound as best I could in the circumstances. Nathan occasionally looked back at us to see how we were doing. After we had left the barn that night, escaping Columbia, Nathan had stopped in a town nearby and was directed to a place where he could rent a wagon and team for our journey. Along the road I stopped to gather any herbs I could think of that might help Titus until we reached the army doctors. He seemed to be holding up well, but I knew he needed more help to fully recover…and soon.

After a couple of days, we finally arrived back at Grant's headquarters. Once again, we had been chased from our "home" with fire and death hot on our heels. Nathan left immediately to meet with Colonel Brandt. I stayed with Titus in the wagon, breathing a sigh of relief when some medical people finally came and took him away on a stretcher.

It was hard…building friendships when at a moment's notice…they could be gone. I had seen too many taken from me over these past years. I was so grateful to always have Nathan, but then the fear of losing him…I could not even think of that. I thought I had lost him once…I did not want to feel that pain again. Yet, I knew I needed to hold those I loved with an open hand… surrendered to God's protection and providence.

The Burning of Richmond
Chapter 41

Amy

April 2, 1865

THE SIGHT OF the pristine white pillared Episcopal church rose before us in the cold morning air, a beautiful yet solemn reminder of the once glorious city. Holding tightly to Jane's arm, I led her to a vacant pew in the back of the church, trying not to attract attention, though the wooden floorboards creaked under our boots.

The whole city seemed to be holding its breath in anticipation of some impending disaster. Gazing about the small congregation, my eyes rested on the tall slender man in a black suit. The gray hairs of his head wove through the long, thick brown hair. His eyes were dim, his cheeks sunken above his strong jaw. Yet the determination written on that countenance was that of a steadfast and fierce leader, a leader who had endured years upon years of painful decisions, long nights of planning and strategizing to gain victory over his oppressors. As President Davis glanced distractedly down at the Bible in his hand, the sermon began, the music fading. Though the pastor spoke in a commanding voice, it felt as if no one was truly paying attention. The atmosphere was tense and unsettled. People shifted anxiously in their seats, many peering out windows every few seconds.

"We must find the scout and get the message back to Peter soon." I whispered to Jane, searching the faces of all present. With the stability of the Confederacy hanging by a thread, the news from Seth was imperative. *We have to get the wounded out soon. Time is short.*

Suddenly, a door burst open. The man, not even trying to muffle his footsteps, rushed in whispering loudly to the church attendant who confronted him at the entrance. The attendant took a small piece of paper in his hands before hurrying up the aisle, without trying to hide the look of blatant distress written on his face. Every head turned. Every eye rested upon the Confederate President, who was now looking up to the telegram being held out to him.

Even the reverend seemed to hesitate as the president took the paper in his hands and calmly glanced down at its contents. Without taking my eyes off him, I reached out, grasping Jane's frail hand in mine. The middle-aged man's brow furrowed. Silently he rose from his chair, his staff hastily following his lead out of the church. There was a deathly silent pause as each attendee weighed in their hearts the meaning of this foreboding interruption.

"I think our scout did not make it," I breathed heavily.

After the sermon had finished, without a word between us, we quickly found our way to where the president must now be having a meeting with his cabinet over the mysterious telegram. With Petersburg, the supplier of the capital, on the breaking point, and Richmond itself in great distress, this telegram undoubtedly held the fate of all the Confederacy.

Peering up at the shrouded windows for any hint of movement, I now paced anxiously on the busy walkway. At this very moment, a monumental decision was taking place behind those closed doors. Officers came and went quietly, and a few occupied the steps outside the building, whispering amongst themselves.

Then a lieutenant burst from the doors, clamoring down the stairs in a rush. His uniform gave him away as an aide to a high ranking general.

"Lieutenant!" I shouted, causing the officer to pause momentarily. Running up, I raised a hand. Upon seeing a woman, the man looked annoyed at the seemingly unimportant interruption and began to turn away.

"Lieutenant," I panted, reaching him, my voice cracking from stress, "What's happened?"

He stared at me almost scoffing, "Miss, I have orders, civilians will hear the news soon enough."

"Wait!" I lowered my voice, "I'm with Major Seth Morgan's regiment. I'm staying at the Morgan's mansion. We have a few wounded. Colonel McCarthy was my fiancé." My voice wavered at the last words.

The lieutenant suddenly straightened up, a look of respect and realization in his eyes.

"Ma'am, excuse me. I didn't know." Despair washed over his demeanor, "Grant's soldiers have broken through Confederate lines at Petersburg. Lee is in retreat...Union soldiers will soon overtake the capital."

"I was waiting for a scout, a message from the major at the church...with our orders." I insisted.

The lieutenant shook his head, "I doubt your contact made it. Take your wounded and leave the city as soon as possible." In shock I stood frozen, processing the lieutenant's words. Staring after the fading form of the officer, who soon disappeared into the crowd, I felt my knees weaken under me.

"It's happened," wrapping my arm around Jane's frail waist, I tried to usher her through the chaos erupting in the streets as the word spread like wildfire. Bells began clanging in haste, proclaiming the inevitable approach of the enemy.

I heard a loud, frantic voice reaching above the screams and shouts around us.

"Prepare for a full evacuation! Petersburg is overtaken! Richmond shall fall! Richmond shall fall!" Forcing my way through the treacherous crowds of now rushing and panicked men, women and soldiers, it was all I could do to hold myself and Jane from being thrown to the ground in the street and trampled amidst the frenzied mob. Upon reaching the Morgan's mansion, I threw open the heavy doors, Jane trailing, phantom-like, behind me.

"Peter!" I shouted, searching the rooms desperately. The few wounded soldiers that had remained in the Morgan's mansion laboriously rose, trying to find out what all the commotion was about. Gasping, I halted at the bottom of the stairs, seeing the thin Englishman trotting down, his eyes dimmed and weary.

"There you are!" Clutching my stomach, breathing heavily I burst, "The Union broke through our lines at Petersburg. Lee is in retreat. They're evacuating the city."

Peter stared with a look of confusion and astonishment on his face. "Amy, are you sure?"

Nodding hard, I tried to catch my breath as he searched my face.

"Did you meet our contact?"

"He didn't make it," I choked.

After a moment, Peter suddenly jumped into action, "Pack what you can."

As I turned to run up the staircase, I stopped short, seeing Jane slowly sinking onto a hard, wooden chair in a vacant corner of the room. Her eyes scanned the room: every rug, every shelf, every inch of the elaborate molding around the ceiling. Staring intently at one random corner, then moving to a chair or some other part of the room, as if she was seeing in that moment a conversation, or a memory trapped in her mind. There was a haunting look in her eyes, as if in that moment all the memories in that house were returning to her. The deepest pity overwhelmed me as I realized she was now losing everything…just as I had once done.

Bells began to clang; shouts and screams filled the air as the clatter of wagon wheels could be heard rushing here and there in the city streets. Stuffing what I could into the last bag, I slung it over my shoulder and stumbled out into the hallway and down the stairs. The few wounded soldiers were gathering what belongings they had, as Peter handed them each a sack filled with what food he could gather from the kitchen. As I turned to help Jane, I ran into an officer who'd just burst into the house.

"Ugh!" Gasping, I tried to catch the bag that fell from my shoulder, but the officer had caught it ahead of me. As soon as I glanced up, a wave of relief surged through me and tears sprang into my eyes.

"Seth," I breathed, nearly sobbing.

"It's all right. We're here to get you out." His calm, confident voice gave assurance to this confusing and terrifying moment. Peter came rushing in, throwing his arms around his brother-in-law.

"You're safe. Thank God."

"I came straight from Petersburg, the minute we realized they would break through the lines. We can't hold them off from Richmond now. We have to get out as soon as possible. The streets will be packed soon."

As the two had been speaking, several officers entered behind their leader, all of them I recognized. Our wounded followed behind Peter, carrying bags and anything he had given them. Peter anxiously searched Seth's face.

"What have you heard? What are the orders?" The room grew painfully silent as Seth struggled to find the words. I could read the painful resolve on his face as he finally replied.

"She must burn… We will not leave a single useful weapon for our enemies to wield, or a chance for them to use the wealth of Richmond against us. Even if it means the destruction of our own homes."

"Surely not the entire city!" Lieutenant Harves, one of the wounded, spoke up in a panic-stricken voice.

Seth turned to the horrified lieutenant, "No, not all of the city…but how can we be sure that the fire will be kept within the limits." A heavy sigh escaped his lips. "The order has been given. General Ewell's men will carry out the torching of the warehouses. We've been asked to keep watch from a distance, report on any enemy movements nearing the city." He paused, continuing with difficulty, "and help cover the retreat. The time has come for our glorious city to see her end."

As the sun began to set, we made our way slowly down the dirt path leading out of the city. Not a word was uttered. Deep in the hearts of us all lurked the dark shadow of defeat. The city was falling, and it seemed the end of all that was the South, was slowly dying.

"I can't! I won't leave! I won't leave our home to those Yankees!" The shrill shrieks of Jane came from the back of the column as we crested the hill.

I rushed back, handing my bag to Lieutenant Rogers as I passed him, a worried, yet solemn, look on his thin face.

The scene that I met was distressing. Jane was struggling, her eyes flashing as she pushed away at her husband, as if she didn't even recognize him.

"Get off me! Don't touch me!"

The soldiers at the end of the column were turning now to investigate the disruption. Seth suddenly cantered up beside me on his tall black stallion, quickly jumping off.

"Move along men," he ordered in a collected tone, not revealing his concern. As the disheartened soldiers turned away to obey their leader, Seth looked at me. "What's going on?"

"She's confused, it's just an episode. She's been having them regularly since-," I hesitated, unable to finish. "She forgets where she is…who we are." My hands trembled as I took the reins Seth handed to me before approaching his sister. Peter had backed off in hopes that giving her space would help his wife regain her senses. The pain in his eyes as he turned to me for help tore at my heart.

"Jane," Seth gently put his arms around his sister, and she fell into his chest sobbing.

"I won't go…we can't go…I won't." She muttered exhaustedly into his shoulder, like a child on the verge of an exhausted sleep.

"We will return…I promise." Seth whispered, "I need you to trust me, sister."

As she finally fell limp, Seth carefully gathered the delirious young woman, and lifting her like a baby, gently placed her in her husband's arms.

"She's too delicate for the trauma these months have brought her." He wearily patted Peter on the shoulder, "Don't lose heart brother. She'll return to us with time and rest."

Peter, looking small and frail himself, solemnly turned and carefully cradling his wife, tracking several paces behind the column.

Turning to follow them, still gripping the stallion's reins, a hand took my elbow, stopping me. Behind me Seth stood with his back to the erupting city, yet his attention was fixed on me; a desperate look in his eyes. He was alone…the supporters disappearing, fleeing the city, comrades dying one by one. As I looked at him standing there, a wave of pity flooded my heart.

"I need your help, Amy," his voice was full of defeat and desperation. A young man, thrust into a position of terrible responsibility, trying to hold the remnants of his regiment, and his family, together in the darkest of days.

Nodding solemnly, I saw a look of relief in his eyes. "I'm here, Seth."

* * *

As the first flickers of orange flames sparked down in the city, a silence came over our company on the overlooking hill. Rapidly, the flames grew higher reaching into the black sky, creating an orange glow over the horrific scene. A strong Southern wind began to pull the flames further and further from the warehouses, rolling into the river, causing a great steam and hissing as a giant cloud rose from its banks. All chaos broke loose as men began to loot the houses that were about to become engulfed in the flames. Glass shattered and burst from the overwhelmed buildings.

Filled with rage at such actions, a few soldiers began to take the law into their own hands, and I watched as a looter was dragged toward the bank. A shot rang out and the lifeless body was tossed into the river. As several others, within our view, broke into homes and stores to snatch left behind supplies, I felt a rage building inside me. Kegs of whiskey were being poured into the streets, possibly a planned move to cut back on the chaos by taking away the chance for drunkenness. Yet many were stooping to catch the whiskey in their hats which was now running freely through the streets. The looting and drunkenness by stragglers, both soldiers and civilians, became so chaotic it was difficult to control the wild anarchy.

One of our officers tightened his reins, his mount reacting to the tension by stomping his hoof, while anxiously chomping on his bit.

"Major…Major, we must do something." He started out respectfully but now almost shouted in anger. "Have they no restraint? No dignity? No sense of patriotism or love for their city?"

No reaction came from the major, sitting on his black warhorse as he overlooked the burning city of his home. In an ominous defeated voice, he answered, "Nothing can be done now. We must leave her to her fate." Shrouded in the darkness of the forest, what was left of our company stood, in a solemn silence, at the fateful spectacle before us. The once glorious and magnificent city…finally crumbling to its knees.

Beauty from these Ashes
Chapter 42

Elizabeth

April 1865

OVER THE LAST couple of weeks, battles had taken place; sometimes bringing success to the Confederates, but in the long run the Union seemed to be gaining a stronghold over their enemy. Nathan was asked to stay with General Grant and his officers. I, however, asked if I would be able to go along as a nurse in a medical unit. Nathan needed a little convincing, but he knew how much it meant for me to be of service and, after some time, he gave his consent.

Soon after being assigned to a medical unit in the Fifth Corps, I saw him again, the young colonel who had led the charge down the little rocky hill at Gettysburg: Joshua Chamberlain. He was now a Brigadier General, and at the most recent battle at the Five Forks his horse had been shot. The bullet had passed through his own coat as well, badly bruising his arm, moved through some small items he carried close to his heart…and then traveled back out of his coat! As I was caring for the wounded after this battle, many of the men I tended told me the story of their brave general. And at Petersburg, they said, he had been shot through the hips while leading an attack and was left for dead, but returned… fully recovering, to lead more charges such as this one. He was just a college professor, they told me. Even though he was in pain and very weak, his superior general asked him to lead one more charge to finish off this battle. He had pulled himself onto his wounded horse, led the charge successfully and even captured a whole regiment of Virginians.

I heard so many amazing tales of bravery like these over the years…of men fighting for what they believed in. I felt honored to do what little I could do to help them.

* * *

April 9, 1865

I woke up to the chill of the spring morning. Moving out of my tent, I was greeted by a fog that had settled over the land. *Maybe today.* I had heard rumors that General Grant had sent General Lee terms of surrender. Just then, in the distance I heard the gun shots, the beginning of another day's battle. Sighing, I moved back into the tent to gather my things to prepare for more wounded soldiers. My heart felt heavy and weary, as if it too were covered in a thick fog. The battle raged on for a couple hours, when suddenly…it stopped. Silence flooded over the valley. I had been helping in the medical tents, rolling bandages and cleaning knives, preparing for the wounded. All our heads shot up with the sudden silence. We looked long and hard toward where the noise had come from, but it was still…and quiet. We glanced around at each other, unsure what to say, afraid to even hope. After several moments, we resumed our preparations, still wondering at the silence beyond. After a while, I heard hoofbeats moving toward the medical tents. Lifting the flap, I walked out into the fresh air.

Some men called out, "General Lee has agreed to meet with General Grant this afternoon!"

My heart lifted. *Could it be…could this be the end?*

Soon after, I heard someone calling for me. "Mrs. Elizabeth Tyler! You're wanted outside!" Cleaning my hands in a wash basin, I rubbed them on my apron and moved out of the tent. Nathan stood, holding his horse's reins in hand. The eagles on the shoulder bars of his Colonel's uniform glittered in the sunlight. A small, knowing smile came over his face when he saw me, and he nodded his head. I sighed with relief. *So, it is true…Lee will surrender to Grant.*

"General Grant wants me to be part of the group he takes with him to meet General Lee. We are meeting in the McClean house, in the village of Appomattox Court House. Come with me?" Nathan asked, extending a hand. "I don't want to lose track of where you're at when the armies start convening and everyone is moving around." I felt as if I was in a dream…but this time…a good dream. *Is this really happening? Truly? What would it be like…life without a war?* I went to gather my things, then met Nathan and he lifted me onto his horse. We rode toward the small village.

I stood outside of the McClean house. The two-story brick structure rose up, with several stairs leading up to the door and porch. A white picket fence surrounded the yard. Many officers stood around outside the house. I watched from a distance, noticing the stark differences between the two generals as they entered the building. General Lee was formally dressed, he looked very regal, head to toe a gallant soldier. General Grant came in, after a whole day of riding, coat and hat rumpled, boots spattered with mud. The only way to tell his high rank was from the four tarnished stars on his shoulders. Several of the Union officers entered in with Grant, but only one Confederate officer entered with Lee. Nathan, with a few other men, entered for a short time, but came back out and waited around the McClean property for the outcome.

Sitting on a log, I picked at the grass around my boots and fidgeted with a piece in my hand. I could see Nathan a short distance away, talking with another officer. After a long time of waiting, General Robert E. Lee appeared on the porch. There was a heaviness in his eyes. I automatically stood up upon seeing him, dropping the pieces of grass I had been weaving. He looked about the landscape, then pounded his gloves together three times and moved down the stairs to his beautiful horse waiting below. General Grant and his men followed him, and they all removed their hats. Lee turned to them and did the same. It was a silent and respectful moment. All the men around the yard were quiet as the elegant General turned his horse down the lane. Once the Confederate General was in the distance, the officers turned their eyes back to General Grant.

Nathan and the other officers moved over to where Grant stood, and he talked with them a while before mounting his horse and riding off with his staff officers.

Nathan spoke quietly to some of the other men before coming back to where I stood waiting. He took my hands in his, "It's done. Lee has accepted the terms of surrender." I exhaled a heavy breath I felt I had been holding for many years now. The death and pain, the wounds and cries of the dying...it was all over. I reached up and wrapped my arms around Nathan's neck, letting the tears of joy and relief flow freely.

As we rode back to where the medical unit had been encamped, Nathan told me about the terms of surrender. The Confederates would be allowed to keep their side arms, their horses and other private belongings. It seemed General Grant wanted to show honor and grace to the valiant soldiers of the South. There were still more surrenders that would need to take place in different parts of the country with other army units for the war to officially be over, but this was the start, this was the example.

* * *

April 12, 1865

I stood next to Colonel Brandt. Today the official surrender ceremony would take place. I was reminded that this also marked the four-year anniversary of when the first shot was fired at Fort Sumter near Charleston, South Carolina. Soldiers from both sides had gathered around Appomattox Court House for the surrender event, the stacking of arms...the folding and surrendering of their Confederate flags. My heart felt free, but with a sadness for all that had been lost during this war, and especially as I watched the faces of the Confederate soldiers. The sky was a bright blue and birds sang in the trees above us. Colonel Brandt was not a man of many words, but when he spoke, I always appreciated his insight.

"This war has been more than mere men fighting amongst themselves over ideas and rights. It has reached into our very lives, between us and our loved ones: separating brother from brother, sister from sister, lover from lover." He paused and looked down at me, "Nevertheless, in some cases, bringing two very different people together." I looked into his dark eyes and he smiled down at me, then I followed his gaze as he lifted his head. Yards away, Nathan stood leaning against a low tree branch, gazing out into the wide-open fields surrounding the town of Appomattox Court House. I felt a gentle, fatherly nudge from the man beside me, and I walked quietly over the grassy space separating Nathan and me.

Approaching, I leaned against the branch beside him. Nathan looked over at me and then laid his arm around my shoulders, kissing my forehead. I rested my head on his strong shoulder. A verse from the Psalms rang through my head. *We went through fire and through water: But thou broughtest us out into a wealthy place.* It certainly seemed as if we had been through fire and water, yet now the sun shone brightly and seemed to flood the land with a sense of peace and reconciliation. It was as if a great dark cloud had been lifted from the country.

Cannon fire suddenly shook the town. The very sound that had haunted this country for four long years, now resounded through the air in celebration. But it was soon quieted, for General Grant was not a man to display pleasure in the sight of others' defeat. As we walked to where the stacking of arms would take place, I looked up at Nathan. I could see the joy in his face, even in his quiet way of showing it. The soldiers had lined up in blue columns along both sides of the dirt road. Then the column of gray moved up the sloping road, led by Confederate General Gordan: lines of blue and gray, as they had appeared so many times throughout the years. But this time, no guns were fired, no cries from the wounded were heard. We stopped in the grassy fields and looked on. Again, I recognized the officer who received the surrender of the arms: Brigadier General Joshua Lawrence Chamberlain. He had always led the men with such courage and inspiration. I knew General Grant must esteem him as well since he had chosen him to receive the surrender.

Chamberlain watched as the column of gray approached. He suddenly ordered, "Carry Arms!" A salute of honor, given to the Confederate soldiers who had honorably pledged their lives to fight for their beliefs. I had learned so much from this war…but most of all, not to judge people by the group…but to take people…one at a time. At the sound of a clattering salute, General Gordan's downcast demeanor changed, his head snapped up. Recognizing this honor, he turned his horse to face Chamberlain. Making his horse rear slightly, in graceful gesture, both man and horse bowed, General Gordon lifting his sword and then lowering it to the toe of his boot. I felt a chill come over me at the significance of this moment in history. Honor to honor…

After the ceremony, I watched with unexplainable feelings as the boys in blue and gray approached each other and began talking and sharing food, souvenirs and even money with each other. A beautiful picture of reconciliation. This was a war ending in unification of the two groups. Whereas, not too long ago, our War for Independence from England, was a war ending in separation. That was the difference. We were welcoming our adversaries back as our brothers. We would not triumph over them and see them humiliated. We wanted reconciliation and the unification of our country.

* * *

May 1865

As the wagon rolled up the old familiar dusty lane, my heart skipped in anticipation. At last we were home…for good. I reached for Nathan's strong hand and smiled up at him. He glanced down at me, giving me a warm, reassuring look. As my mind flew back through all the memories I had with this man, I wondered at how far we had come together. I thanked God for teaching me all he had through my relationship with Nathan and for bringing us together. They say the Lord works in mysterious ways. He certainly had in my story with Nathan. My heart swelled with joy and peace as we neared our hometown.

Once we were back in the army, I had sent a letter to Sarah in Gettysburg, who in turn began forwarding letters to me from Amy along with her own. Amy did not give me many details, but it was good to read her words, to know that she was safe. But, my heart broke, once again, as I read of our dear friend Kelsey. I felt as though I could not bear another wound such as this one. He had always been like a brother to me ever since we were children. *Peace, Kelsey. We will see you again, my dear brother…I know.* Tears stained the words on the paper that my sister had written. I had hoped…that Nathan and Kelsey would know each other, that we would all live close and be reunited. But it was not to be, not in this life. I sighed heavily, looking down once again at the satchel at my feet that contained the letters. I still wondered at her most recent letter after the war had ended. That she planned to stay in Richmond with the people who had originally taken her captive. But her words sounded so assured and decided, I felt that she must have found a purpose there. We would visit her…someday soon. But for now, we were headed home.

I looked back up at the road in front of us. Suddenly I squinted, not believing my eyes. *Our house? Wait, there is our house!* Standing and complete, it was more beautiful than ever. My eyes locked on it, confused, then I looked to Nathan.

I stuttered, "It was destroyed…I saw it…the battle here…how…who?" As we pulled up, I leapt down from the wagon and ran to the painted picket fence. Stopping, I stood gazing at the beautifully restored home. Nathan climbed down from the wagon and moved up beside me, resting his hands on the fence. There it stood, all the colors around me more vibrant than ever. The navy-blue shutters and roof, lace curtains in the windows, the brick path lined with flowers of various hues, and the old oak tree that had survived the battle and stood now inviting us to the swing hanging from its branch. The spring air swept the scent of the flowers around us and the sun smiled down on the fresh spring soil. I felt as though perhaps I had only dreamt it all…the battle here had only been a nightmare. But the full graveyard in the far distance told otherwise. I stood in utter shock and confusion, until the big door opened unexpectedly and out marched John Barnes.

"Mr. Barnes?" I asked almost in disbelief. A grin spread over the old, worn face when he saw us.

"Well, it's about time you got here!" He approached and wrapped me in a fatherly hug.

I laughed, "How? Why?"

Releasing me, he clasped Nathan on the back and gave him a firm handshake. "I heard the news; the war is finally over. Well, what do you think of the place? Several of your friends and neighbors rebuilt it…to wait for your return. They've been going around trying to set things right again. A new start for all of us."

Nathan shook his head and patted John Barnes' shoulder, "I don't know what to say. Thank you. It's good to see you again, John. It's good to be home."

An overwhelming feeling came over me. The goodness of God. At last, we were where we belonged. Amy seemed content and safe, and we planned to visit when we could. The memories of those who had given their lives for our freedom and peace would never die. We would honor them with our lives.

Mr. Barnes moved away, "I'll unhitch the team, you two go in and take a look around," he smiled.

Nathan took my hand and we ran to the doorway. I stopped before going in, gazing out over the fields and farmlands with the dark mountains in the distance. Wrapping my arms around Nathan's waist, I laid my head on his chest as I watched the grass sway in the breeze across the fields. Warmth flooded through my heart. We were home, once again in the safety of a peaceful quiet town, though forever remembering the blood-stained fields beneath our feet. It was not perfect; it still held the signs of death that had occurred on these now hallowed grounds. We would remember them…all of them…the many lives that were lost on these sacred fields. We would carry their memory in our hearts and in our land and tell our children what had happened in our town. Yet, it was still our home and the war was over. We had finally moved beyond the war cries, beyond the war-torn lands and prison camps, beyond the sound of cannon, musket and destruction…beyond the fields of fire. After all the pain and suffering, God had brought us back home and blessed us…beyond measure.

Resurrection
Chapter 43

Amy

Two Years Later…

TINY DROPLETS OF water formed on the freshly budding tulips. Though the steady mist continued, the air had gradually grown warmer. An early Virginian Spring had begun to bloom all around us. New life was awakening in the mountains, the fields and the slowly resurrecting city. My eyes took in the sight from the hill overlooking that infamous city full of life again, full of hope. I lowered my gaze slowly and knelt beside the mound now covered with grass, buds of wildflowers and the lilies I had planted myself years ago.

Placing a hand on the name carved into the beautiful stone, I smiled before letting a healing tear fall from my cheek to the grave.

"Things are finally mending. The scars are still there, but people seem to be ready to move forward," whispering softly, I gently sat back on my heels, "You'd be proud of your men. They've been leaders in this healing process. I've tried to aid in whatever way I can. Elizabeth wants me to come home soon. Home…I don't seem to know where home is anymore…not after all this. Don't worry about your mother and father. Elizabeth and her husband are always looking out for them, and I keep in touch. I suppose I'll see them again soon." With a heavy sigh, I choked out the words, looking up to try and hold back the tears, "They miss you…we all do. Seth talks about you often. I think he feels unworthy of having to had stepped into your shoes. I know you'd be proud of all that he did after you left us. He's held us all together." Taking my hand off the cold damp stone, I brushed back the wet hair now clinging to my forehead. Then slowly, I removed the tiny silver band from my finger, placed it in the small hole I made near the head stone, and reverently smoothed the dirt over top of it. "I'll never forget you Kelsey…never." Rising from the soft dewy grass, I finally turned away, ready to begin a new life. My heart swelled with sadness and yet, the realization that I knew, I must let go.

Turning for one last look back, I smiled feeling a warmth in my heart. *It's time…* "Goodbye, Kelsey."

* * *

A warm summer breeze filled the mansion, lace curtains dancing at the windows, the smell of freshly baked bread and cinnamon cakes filling the air, mingled with joyful laughter in the kitchen. The playful giggling of the child, now toddling in the parlor amongst her toys, lifted my heart. All that had been broken and lost to the glorious heritage of this mansion had finally been restored. The memories of the war had slowly been scrubbed clean from the surface of her floors, the blood that had dripped from wounded soldiers, the black soot of gunpowder and fire, the busted windows and walls had been made new…though the memory never faded from each of us who had lived through such times. The absence of Kelsey, Mrs. Morgan, Millie and Captain Hamilton created an empty void that could never be filled. Yet, their lives, their presence and their happy voices seemed to live on in this home.

Hearing the heavy footsteps enter the parlor, I glanced up from my knitting of the small pink blanket in my lap to where Seth was now stooping down to lift the one year old, who excitedly hurried toward him. He spoke gently to the child, his face always lighting whenever he saw her.

Glancing over at me, he nodded, "Miss Amy. What's this?" My eyes followed his gaze to the blanket in my lap.

"Oh, something for little Katherine…to remember me by," my voice faded at the sudden realization of what I was saying. When I looked up at Seth again, he had not taken his eye off me and I instantly noted the sadness written on his face. Nodding softly, he directed his attention back to the little girl.

"Well, there you are!" Peter strolled into the room, wiping his hands on a dish cloth, "So you were able to finally pull yourself away from the governor's cabinet for tonight I see."

Placing the child on the thick rug after kissing her cheek, Seth glanced over at his brother-in-law.

"I thought it appropriate," turning his head toward me he added, "since it was important to Miss Amy."

"Well, you'd better go change. I believe we should be hearing the knocking of our guests at the door any minute now. Isn't that right, Miss Amy," Peter flashed me an enthusiastic smile.

"Oh, yes I should be heading up as well." Excitedly, I stood, wrapping the unfinished blanket into a bundle, before placing it back in the basket. But before I could take one step in the direction of the stairs, I heard the clattering of wagon wheels on the cobblestone and my heart skipped a beat. Anxiously, I turned to see Peter motion for me to go.

Bursting from the big doors, I was met with the eagerly anticipated sight of the small family now strolling up the cobblestone path, surrounded by the blooming white roses.

"Elizabeth!" I screamed, giving no heed to who heard or saw me now. Tears filled my eyes as I fell into my sister's waiting arms.

"Amy," her gentle voice breathed in my ear as she held me tightly. Stepping back after the strong embrace, I gasped delightedly when glancing down at her slightly pregnant belly.

"You didn't say!" Excitedly I covered my mouth as she smiled, placing a hand on her stomach. Shaking her head, she flushed, and Nathan stepped up, carrying the little boy in his arms.

"Little Marcus, do you remember your Aunt Amy?" I asked, kissing his cheek as he shyly sank into his father's shoulder to hide.

"Amy, it's good to see you again," Nathan said, a handsome smile on his tan face, "You look very well."

Emotion rising in my chest, I stated confidently, "I am."

Seth suddenly stepped up beside me. "Mr. Tyler, Mrs. Tyler, it's a pleasure to see you again. You're welcome in my home."

After the reintroductions and general formal inquiries, Jane bid us all sit down to dinner, as our guests must be hungry from their journey. As we sat around the long elegant table, the room filled with lively conversation, smiles and laughter. Peter seemed to carry the conversation for the men, as neither Nathan nor Seth were much for small talk, though I was surprised when they did seem to strike up a rather enthusiastic discussion. Peter shot me a look, making a face, relieved he had been able to successfully draw the two out of their stoic natures. Stifling a laugh, I smiled to myself. Jane peppered Elizbeth with questions of her pregnancy, and they shared common scenarios and stories about being mothers with small children.

With emotions of pure joy, I marveled at the irony of this scene. So beautiful…and so surreal. I almost felt as if it was all just a wonderful dream…or it *was* reality and I had awakened from a nightmare.

"Major Morgan," Elizabeth addressed Seth, laying aside her silverware on the delicate napkin. "I understand you have great influence in the government here and an interest in shaping the minds of your fellow Virginians to, shall we say, a rather unconventional way of thinking."

Seth rested an arm on his chair leaning back, "Yes, Ma'am, it is my earnest desire to mend the differences in our societies. As only through reconciliation can we move on from the dark history we have experienced so recently. And the sooner the better, for there can be no real progression in our communities, economy, no building of any industrial trade, until we at least attempt to compromise with our Northern neighbors and understand their way of life."

Nodding, Elizabeth smiled, a look of surprise on her face, "It's a shame more people were not as broad minded as you, Major. You speak with such eloquence, I believe if both Northern and Southerners had opened their minds and ears to such balanced and sensible speech, there never would have been a war."

"I thank you, Ma'am, but I don't believe the hearts of my fellow Virginians were ready to lay aside their stubbornness for a compromise at that time. My father and I had campaigned in the government for years before the war to prevent such an atrocity, but alas both sides were unwavering in their refusal to compromise. And in my heart, though I prayed it would not come to war, I knew without a doubt I would stand with my brothers. As my own personal beliefs on the subject of state sovereignty could not lead me to any other conclusion at that point." There was a heavy silence in the room at the mention of the war.

Seth stirred, turning his attention to me, "Your sister has proven herself invaluable to the resurrection of this community as well. Her ideas and advice have been vital to me in my own endeavors. She has as great an influence on our community here as any hero of the South."

"Indeed, she has," Peter agreed proudly, while scooping up a bite of his wife's pie.

Embarrassed, I shook my head slightly, fiddling with the fork in my hand. "I don't believe I've been as essential as you claim. What I've done, I've done from my heart, out of the love and respect I have for these people. I hope in some small way I have helped to improve their communities for the better. Though I would hardly call myself a *great influence*."

"I must respectfully disagree, Miss Amy." Seth stated, his tone more serious as he stared at me for a long moment. Elizabeth turned, a soft smile on her lips, though her eyes seemed to study me with a curious expression.

Finally, the men moved into the parlor, deeply engrossed in their own conversation about the industries now rising in the South. I trailed behind, as Jane led Elizabeth up to the rooms that had been prepared for them and their child. Both the toddlers, who had been playing excitedly on the floor together, were now complaining and rubbing their sleepy eyes as their mothers carried them up the stairs. Watching my sister softly placing her little boy in his bed, I marveled at the change in her. She possessed a quiet confidence and contentment as a devoted wife and mother.

"You've changed so much, Elizabeth." I commented in a hushed tone, so as not to disturb my sleeping nephew. "You remind me of our mother."

A grateful look in her eyes, she smiled at me as she brushed the boy's hair off his forehead. For a moment I thought she would speak, but staying silent she studied me, her perceptive eyes seemed to reach into my soul.

"You've changed too, Amy." The words, though simple, seemed to hold a hidden implication that I had not understood. She turned away and began preparing herself for bed, removing the pins from her hair, letting it fall freely past her shoulders.

Watching her for a moment, I sighed heavily.

"Good night, Elizabeth," I said, turning distractedly to leave.

"Amy," Elizabeth's voice stopped me in the doorway. As I turned, she approached and taking me by the shoulders, looked deep into my eyes. There was a hint of a tear in her eye, though she seemed to force a soft smile. "You're young, Amy," she whispered, "your life doesn't have to end because Kelsey's did."

Staring confused at her, I nodded, unsure how to answer, or even what exactly she meant. Walking slowly down the long hallway, I pondered her words while heading to my own room.

With each passing hour, the night grew longer, and the time of our departure drew gradually nearer. I found myself growing more anxious by the minute and, close to midnight, I sat up frustrated, yanking off the heavy quilt. *Why am I so restless?* A twisted feeling in my stomach, I wrapped myself in a shawl and, seeking some reprieve, followed my path to the solitude of the back gardens. Here I had always found solace on so many difficult nights. As I breathed in the fresh night air, I froze, hearing the sound of a boot scraping on the stone walkway. Cautiously following the bend in the path, I peered curiously around. There on the stone path stood Seth, still fully dressed in the clothes he'd worn to dinner, as if he'd not even attempted to sleep tonight. Somehow sensing my presence, he turned, clearly surprised when he caught sight of me.

"I um," I hesitated awkwardly, "I couldn't sleep. I had no idea anyone else was still awake. I was just going to take a turn around the gardens for some air."

"I'm sorry if I startled you," Seth shifted, and glanced down the path. "Would you like some company?"

I smiled, relieved, "I would."

As we started down the path, I realized how many times we'd walked this way, deeply engrossed in conversations. Even in the silence that enveloped us now, I found comfort in the calming presence of my companion. Though I cherished my relationships with each member of the former regiment and their families, especially Peter and Jane, Seth had become my closest friend here. He was not a man overflowing with things to say, but when he did speak it was always honest, always meaningful and well thought out. Whenever I was struggling with something, he was always the one to notice. His acute ability to read my emotions better than myself was almost irrational. *He knows me better than anyone.* I acknowledged in amazement. Then, suddenly turning to him, I realized that despite his quiet nature, I could also almost always tell exactly what he was feeling. Seth's brow was furrowed in deep thought and he seemed to be struggling with something.

"Seems like a lifetime ago I first wandered onto this path." I breathed in the sweet smell of the rose garden. "I shall miss it."

As Seth glanced quickly over at me, I could feel his gaze upon me, before he said in a gentle tone, "I hope you know you'll always have a place here." With a voice full of gratitude and yet pain, he added, "You've helped me…more than you know."

Unable to meet his eye, I forced a quick smile, "I supposed we both have." Feeling a deepening grief, I asserted, "Your friendship has become invaluable to me." Glancing around at the solemn peaceful garden, a strange emotion came over me as I whispered, "I'll miss our long conversations out here."

"I'm surprised I didn't bore you with my extensive ideas for reformation." Seth smiled, glancing down at his feet.

"Not at all," I insisted, "You're a man of intelligence…and honor."

Seth shifted his attention to the surrounding gardens, clearly embarrassed at the praise, "What will you do, when you return to Gettysburg?"

Never having considered the question, I stated blandly, "I'm not sure."

As we strolled the remainder of the garden in silence, I could feel an odd tension between us, though I couldn't put my finger exactly on what it was.

"You should try to get your rest tonight," Seth stated as he slowed his pace. "Tomorrow will be a long journey as you return home."

"Yes…home," I repeated, though the words felt hollow now when I thought of returning to a life in Gettysburg. "I suppose it's time I returned…to where I belong." There was a slight pause as I pondered the change in my life that would take place the next day.

"Do you?" Seth spoke up gently, "belong there?" Raising my eyes to meet his, I could see by the expression on his face there was something nagging at him. He seemed to be hurting, almost confused. Lowering his gaze, he paused, catching sight of my hand as I stopped beside him. "Have you lost something?"

Glancing down where the thin silver ring had formerly sat, I breathed. A weight entered my heart as I recalled the courage it had taken to finally remove it.

"We all must learn to finally let go…" Sighing heavily I whispered, "even of those things most precious to us." The resignation in my heart echoed in my voice.

"Yes, I suppose we must," Seth muttered as he contemplated my words. The garden faded away as the vacant stone path led up to the mansion. Saying a final goodbye to the enchanting gardens, I trod, disheartened, toward the house.

"Amy, I-," Seth's voice came from further behind me. Turning, I was surprised by the troubled look on his face. He seemed to be hesitating, rethinking the words. Suddenly his countenance changed, and he added softly, "We will… we will never forget you."

* * *

The heaviness in my heart had grown almost to an unbearable weight as I lifted my bags, at last prepared for the final goodbyes. With a final glance back into the mansion, I turned away, holding back the tears. The wagon was at the gate, the team hitched, and bags loaded.

"Write to us when you return home," Jane choked, forcing a smile before squeezing me tight.

"Of course."

Peter put on a brave smile, "Miss Amy, may you find the peace and contentment in life you so deserve." Staring deep into those familiar, friendly eyes, I felt unable to contain my sorrow. As Peter gently hugged me, he whispered in an emotion-stricken voice, "We're going to miss you terribly." Releasing me, he smiled bravely, and as I turned to follow Elizabeth to the wagon, I felt a deep pain welling in my heart. Seth stood beside the team, fastening the last few buckles on their harnesses.

While Nathan loaded his little family into the wagon, I walked over to where Seth stood. For the first time since I met him, he did not even attempt to hide the pain on his face.

Holding out a small wrapped package, he explained. "I hope you'll accept this gift…it's from the regiment." Unwrapping the small wooden box, I carefully touched the inscription so elegantly engraved on the lid.

With our deepest respect and admiration.

Unable to speak, I put a hand to my lips, struggling to hold back the growing emotions. Looking up at Seth, I could see that the familiar shadow of sorrow had returned onto his young face. The darkness that had seemed to lift from him after the war, now settled over him like a plague once more.

"Goodbye, Amy."

The tender words lingered in my mind as the rickety creaking of the wagon continued up the road. The voices of my sister and her husband echoed, as if far off, behind me. Nathan kept his steady hands on the reins, guiding the team of draft horses. Elizabeth held tightly to the child wrapped in a shawl on her lap, while smiling and chatting, her eyes sparkling as she stared at her husband in the seat beside her. All the noisy sounds of the city faded as I stared at the small family. *They have each other. They are complete, happy with their life and their destiny… What's mine…?* Still clutching the little wooden box in my hands, I opened the lid. A flurry of trinkets lay inside: a random dried flower, small notes of well wishes, a confederate button, random decorative gold trimmings of uniforms… *The highest honors they could bestow.* Taking one tiny paper that was tied with a red string, I opened it and stared down at the few words written there.

My dear Amy, I hope you will never forget us…as I know I will never forget you.

Something in me seemed to rise out of the depths of my heart, where the answer had been hiding all along. My throat tightened and I quickly turned back to see the distant, motionless form of a lone horseman seated on a tall, black stallion. Silently he kept watch, as he always had. With a sudden revelation, I sat up, my eyes fixed on him.

"Nathan, stop!" I shouted over my shoulder, "Please!" Turning, I locked eyes with Elizabeth, her brow furrowed in surprise and confusion. Time stood still as I stared deep into my sister's eyes, anxiously wishing to speak, but unable to find the words to share the longing, the realization that had now come to light in my heart. But as sisters always can…she read the look on my face. Then, without a word, her worry disappeared, a gentle peaceful look covered her face as tears of joy…and sadness…danced in her eyes. With a soft smile, she nodded, and I knew…*she understands*.

Jumping off the wagon, I grabbed my one small bag and ran until I was mere feet from Seth. Breathlessly, I stopped as he stared down at me perplexed.

"I didn't know where I belonged before…" I breathed, still panting, "I've been drifting, searching for a home, a family." Seth stared, unmoving still, his expression softening. "I know now." Tears spilled down my face, "I know where I belong, where my home is." I lifted my arms, my eyes taking in the beautiful Virginian countryside. "*This* is my home, *these* are my people…you…are my family and everyone who I have shared this incredible journey, sorrow and joy with. My heart is here…with you. And after all we've gone through together, I cannot bear the thought of losing you." As the young man dismounted the tall war horse, I felt my heart suddenly beat with new life once more.

* * *

I never left that place, and as the years passed the memory of my sweet Kelsey lived on through Seth and me. We would never forget his courage, his friendship and honor. And as the time of his passing grew gradually more distant, so did the pain, which was replaced only with fond memories and the deepest respect. I now know in my heart that he never belonged to me. His life and the lives of so many like him were sacred. Devoted to a cause. And looking back now at those years during the war, the choices we all made, the life altering choices, I feel at total peace with my own decisions. Perhaps people back home would never understand my resolution to join the Southern cause. But all I know is, I have experienced and grown to respect and love these people. I have seen the way they fought, lived and died, and I never once doubted my decision. Even now, weighing all the consequences, I know I will never regret my choice to follow them beyond the fields of fire.

THE END

"In great deeds something abides. On great fields something stays. Forms change and pass; bodies disappear, but spirits linger, to consecrate ground for the vision-place of souls. And reverent men and women from afar, and generations that know us not and that we know not of, heart-drawn to see where and by whom great things were suffered and done for them, shall come to this deathless field to ponder and dream; And lo! the shadow of a mighty presence shall wrap them in its bosom, and the power of the vision pass into their souls."

—Joshua Chamberlain, speaking at the dedication of the Monument to the 20th Maine October 3, 1889, Gettysburg, PA.

About the Authors

Jessica Elam

Jessica Elam is a young Christian woman living in the rolling hills of Indiana. Studying early American history is one of her greatest passions and she visits National Park Battlefields and historic sites as often as she can. Jessica loves her job as the office manager at a local hardware store and enjoys interacting with the community and her coworkers. Besides writing, Jessica enjoys being outdoors, traveling, hiking and spending time with her friends, family and her two dogs. Jessica wants to dream big, impact others and live every day to its fullest potential.

Alexandra Haliti

Alexandra Haliti met and married her husband, Lirim, on a mission trip overseas, and they now have two beautiful little girls. At this stage in her life, Alexandra is embracing her God-given role as a wife and mother. She recently began a small group for young Christian wives, desiring to revive the beauty of true biblical femininity. Alexandra deeply cherishes the moments of laughter that she shares with friends and family. She is passionate about history and inspiring others through the communication of writing and music.

Thank you for reading! If you enjoyed this story, we'd love for you to **leave a review**—your feedback not only helps other readers discover the series, but it also means the world to us.

Stay connected! Follow us on Facebook at **"The Beyond Series"** for updates and exclusive behind-the-scenes content.

Dive into the story that started it all! "Beyond the Bleeding Heart" is the first book in **The Beyond Series,** where love, danger and the unexpected collide. If you haven't started your journey yet, now's the perfect time to begin.

* 9 7 8 1 9 6 5 1 2 1 2 3 8 *